"WE HAVE GREAT CHEMISTRY, MAC."
HE KISSED HER WITH EACH WORD.

McCall cupped his face in her hands, kissing him long and hard, trying somehow to make the mark permanent. "I didn't lie when I said I didn't love you for your mind." She pressed her hand to his chest. "I love your heart."

"Well, that's good, Mac. Because I think I've just wrapped it up and put a ribbon on it for you."

It was the perfect thing to say. It made her feel safe. As if he was telling her he was hers to keep.

Mac turned on her side, cuddling up against him. Jake knew the exact moment she fell asleep. He could feel the gentle rise and fall of her chest, a perfect rhythm.

The things he'd learned about the investigation rose up like ugly unanswered questions. All the pieces were coming together. The only thing that didn't fit was the woman in his bed.

"Please, Mac," he whispered softly, so he wouldn't wake her. "Don't be one of the bad guys."

Also by Olga Bicos:

WRAPPED IN WISHES

SWEETER THAN DREAMS

MORE THAN MAGIC

SANTANA ROSE

WHITE TIGER

BY MY HEART BETRAYED

RISKY GAMES

Olga Bicos

Zebra Books
Kensington Publishing Corp.
http://www.zebrabooks.com

ZEBRA BOOKS are published by

Kensington Publishing Corp.
850 Third Avenue
New York, NY 10022

First Printing: July, 1997
10 9 8 7 6 5 4 3 2 1

Printed in the United States of America

For my sister, Leila, who never missed a recital, a performance, or a tryout.

And for my husband, Andrew, who looked across a crowded room. . . .

Part One

Transformation

"Looking-glass upon the wall,
who is fairest of us all?"
—*Snow-White and the Seven Dwarfs,*
Brothers Grimm Fairy Tale, 1814

Prologue

If I have ever done anything wrong in my life, it must be now. I feel close to evil, and yet, I do see the genius in what he is doing. He is absolutely the most exciting man I have ever been with. God forgive me, I think I'm in love with Dr. Frankenstein.

—Excerpt from Dr. Alicia Goodman's lab book

McCall Sayer tried to focus on who she would become tonight.

In the room next door, she could hear the water running for the twins' bath, could hear them laughing as they tried to escape Stan, their father. McCall smiled, realizing she was happy, staying here as Barb and Stan's house guest, a part of their family. She sorted through the makeup on the vanity, choosing a tube of lipstick labeled *Le Baiser,* the kiss. Rimming her mouth with a cerise red, she hummed along with Stan's tenor belting out a chorus of "Baby Beluga."

Tonight, Dr. McCall Sayer was wearing black fishnet stockings. She thought it was a nice touch.

Lifting the wig off the stand, she brought the blond page boy over her red hair. She was instantly transformed, her eyes taking on a deeper blue. Another woman altogether.

"I do believe I look Southern," she said in a soft drawl. "Why, yes. A true Southern magnolia."

"Hey, McCall," she heard Barb call up the stairs. "Taxi's here."

"Be right down," she shouted back, dropping the accent.

She turned on the stool and stepped into T-strap heels, buckling them at her ankles. She'd decided on an ice blue slip dress, one provocative enough to draw notice. Over the years, she'd discovered people needed something to classify you. A hook. Tonight she would give them "sexy blonde"; it wouldn't be confused with next week's fare, a brunette wearing glasses and a drab suit.

Grabbing her evening bag off the vanity, she caught sight of the lab book reflected in the vanity mirror, DEPARTMENT OF BIOLOGY spelled backward in the glass. The lab book was overlarge, twelve by nine inches. The kind she'd always preferred.

McCall picked up the book, staring at it a moment . . . then quickly knelt down to shove the book in the bottom drawer of the dresser, covering it with sweaters. She stood and kicked the drawer shut. She squeezed her hands into fists, then opened them. *Open, close. Open, close.* She raised her hands up, spreading her fingers. They were shaking.

"Almost there, McCall," she whispered. "Almost there."

One

Tonight her hair was red.

Jake Donovan stared across the floor of the New Orleans *River Palace,* his eyes on the woman. He'd been watching her on the surveillance cameras earlier, taking her in from different angles. Now he stood in the pit just a few feet away, wondering what he was going to do about her.

She was dressed all in black. Black suit, sheer black stockings, black stiletto heels. The suit was sexy as hell, hiking halfway up her thigh as she sat perched on the stool at the blackjack table, V-necked, so if she leaned forward the dealer would see the lacy cup of her bra. Jake watched as she crossed her legs, swinging her foot provocatively. She'd twisted her hair up in a fancy knot and the highlights sparked Fourth of July fireworks as she turned her head, catching the light from the chandeliers overhead.

She looked like one of those divas in the classic films, a Greta Garbo or a Rita Hayworth. But she was drinking champagne like it was medicine, almost grimacing before she put down the glass. He noticed she bit her nails. It was the only thing she hadn't bothered to change or hide.

Last week, she'd been a studious brunette with glasses. The week before that, a blonde wearing fishnet stockings.

"So. You going to nail her, or what?"

The ever-eloquent Costandinos Tropedis, Dino for short, slumped boneless against the pit stand. The redhead was just a couple of tables down from them, concentrating on her cards and her champagne.

Dino brushed off a piece of lint from the sleeve of his suit and slid his fingers through hair that hadn't seen a day without gel. "She's a honey, though," he said with a wink. "Wouldn't mind giving her the tap on the shoulder myself. But hey, you're the boss, Irishman."

Jake made a noncommittal sound. He was thinking about the Donovan Curse, trying to convince himself that the red-head didn't have the curse written all over her.

As a shift manager for the *River Palace,* it was one of Jake's duties to oust the professionals. Casinos hated card systems, didn't allow them. This was an adult Disneyland. You come in, sit down, play the games. A skimpily clad cocktail waitress gives you free drinks, the staff is friendly and courteous—the dealers dole out advice in a pinch, the change girl points out the machine that's hot. If all goes well, you lose your money slowly so when you go home you think, "Gee, I lost two grand, but I had a hell of a good time."

That wasn't the case with professionals, blackjack players who had systems. Most often, they would count cards, figuring out the odds to beat the house. The true professionals wore disguises to keep from getting tossed out on their asses. Once a casino spotted you, a friendly call around town made sure you were blackballed from every place within a two-state radius.

"Will you look at that," Dino said. He gave a soft whistle. "Swear to God, Jake. She's giving the guy next to her the nudge."

The shoe with the killer heel broke its rhythm to tap the leg of the man seated on the stool next to her. The guy—couldn't be older than nineteen—shot her a look. She glanced at the dealer, waited for that nearly imperceptible instant when the dealer's eyes shifted elsewhere. She gave a tiny shake of her head.

"There!" Dino said. "You see? You watch—he won't take a card even though the idiot was busting all night."

Watching from the pit, Jake could see the cards face up on the table. The man stood on sixteen. Showing ten, the dealer drew a six and then busted with the queen of hearts.

The kid next to her looked like he was going to start crying as the dealer pushed a pile of chips toward him. Rita Hayworth just stared into the distance. There was easily over three grand stacked in front of her.

"Looks like someone just did her good deed for the day," Jake said.

"Yeah, it's fucking Christmas out here," Dino answered.

Jake watched the cocktail waitress bring the redhead another drink. She'd been steadily anesthetizing herself all night, something she hadn't done on previous visits. She came to the *River Palace* an average of three nights a week. Dino had spotted her a couple of weeks back—the blonde wearing fishnet stockings. Until tonight, she had always drunk ginger ale, plain—Jake had checked with the waitress. And she always left the table before she won too big, trying not to draw attention to herself. That's why Jake had let it go this long, keeping an eye on her on the video monitors in the surveillance room.

"She's got a system," Dino said. "A damn good one."

Jake hesitated. The words "Donovan Curse" flashed like a neon sign inside his head. *Donovan Curse. Donovan Curse.*

"Why don't you go over and have a look?" Jake asked.

Dino stood a good half foot shorter than Jake's six feet, three inches. He had to crank his head back to look Jake straight in the eye. Jiggling change in his pocket, Dino did a little assessing, trying to figure out the angle—why a red-blooded male would give up this chance for small talk as he escorted an inebriated Rita Hayworth out the door.

Jake knew the exact moment the lightbulb came on over Dino's head.

Dino's grin grew bigger by the second. "Come on, Irishman. She won't bite. You're going to be old before your time if you don't loosen up a little. In fact, you know what you need?"

"For you to shut up?"

Dino did his best to look injured. "I'm just saying it ain't healthy. A guy like yourself, always alone. You know, use it or lose it."

Good ol' Dino, always full of advice.

On a roll, Dino gave Jake's plain white shirt and chinos with suspenders a critical once-over. He shook his head. "And would it kill you to wear a suit once? You're the manager here, for Christ's sake."

Jake thought about the closet full of clothes he'd given away to the Salvation Army. The day he'd walked out of the Attorney General's office, he'd sworn never to wear another monkey suit. The only thing he'd kept from his old life was his Breitling watch. Big, black, and displaying three time zones, Jake figured it could probably get him out of the Amazon jungle in a pinch.

Not getting the rise he was after, Dino gave Jake his what-am-I-going-to-do-with-you shrug and straightened his Hugo Boss tie. "Mr. Donovan, Cinderella awaits. And I do believe she needs her ass escorted off our riverboat."

Jake nodded, leaning back on the pit stand as he stared at the woman. Normally, he would have stepped in by now, wouldn't have waited for Dino, the floor person, to point her out a second time. Normally, he wouldn't have tried to pass off the job of dealing with her to his friend.

But the truth was, Jake Donovan—ex-attorney, ex-husband, and ex-believer in lost causes—had instincts about this sort of thing. He knew the signs. He'd lived through them enough to be cautious now.

She always came alone . . . and she had that look about her, like someone accustomed to glancing over her shoulder. Tonight she was drinking as if she had something to forget. And she was gambling ferociously, not trying to hide that she was winning, flaunting it in their faces, begging to get caught.

Oh, yes. Bells and whistles were going off in his head with this one.

"Yeah," Jake said, bowing to the inevitable. "Hold down the fort for me."

The *River Palace* was one of the few remaining riverboat casinos to stay financially afloat on the waters of the Mississippi in the downtown district, a life that would be tested in the upcoming parish vote on gambling . . . not to mention the competition of the biggest land-based casino ever conceived, just a few blocks away, if Harrah's ever got off the ground.

Like the Hilton's *Flamingo,* its fellow survivor, the *River Palace* also had a posh hotel towering over the Riverwalk. A cozy five hundred accommodations small—half of those luxury suites—the River Palace Hotel was built in a style reminiscent of the stately plantation homes, only with the wattage of the Las Vegas Strip. The riverboat casino of the same name featured three decks of gambling. The ship was currently moored off the Riverwalk owing to choppy waters, a boon for the *River Palace,* which was otherwise required by law to sail every three hours.

Jake walked across the dizzy-patterned carpet, the design calculated to bring the eye up from the floor to the brightly lit slot machines. Out of habit, he tuned out the aria of arcade noise and the percussion of coins falling through slots and into metal trays. On this deck, the *River Palace*'s motif was Mardi Gras. Gold, purple, and green splashed across every surface; enormous feathered masks sprang from each corner. At the *River Palace,* life was one big party.

When he reached the blackjack table, he sat down on the empty stool next to Rita Hayworth. He put down a bet. Out of the corner of his eye, he watched the redhead take another sip of her drink. Again, the grimace.

"So," he said casually, glancing at the cards Cynthia, the dealer, tossed at him. "If it's Sunday, you must be a redhead?"

She glanced at him. Her eyes were an unusual blue with a rim of green. It was a little startling to watch her, she was that good-looking. Straight nose. Full mouth. Not much makeup—didn't need it. His eyes unconsciously dropped to her breasts to where her suit had puckered a bit. Just as he'd thought; not a bad view.

She put down the glass. "Boy, you don't look the type."

"The type for what?" he asked. He winked at the dealer. All under control now.

"I wouldn't have pegged you for the bouncer." Rita Hayworth turned on the stool and gave him the kind of deliberate once-over that let him know she'd caught him sizing her up. She narrowed her eyes, thinking. "You look like a . . . a Boy Scout."

"Eagle Scout," he said. "Third rank." He shook his head. "Them were the days. So," he said quietly enough that only she could hear. "What's with helping the kid?"

She picked up the glass and finished her drink in one swallow. She shrugged, not bothering to deny anything. "If you sit here long enough, you hear their stories. His wife is six months pregnant. He lost his job. The landlord is threatening to evict them. He came here looking for a miracle."

"Let me guess. You're his fairy godmother?"

She smiled, putting down her glass. "Is this where you tell me to exit, stage left?"

There was this bullhorn going off inside him . . . *do not proceed beyond this point* . . . but he shook his head anyway, jumping in feet first like the idiot he was. Thirty-six years and a lifetime of mistakes and damn if he still hadn't learned his lesson.

"No," he said, watching Cynthia take his cards. He told himself maybe Dino was right and he'd been cautious for too long. Looking at Rita, he didn't feel like being careful anymore. "This is where I ask you out for coffee. You interested?"

Her eyes widened just a bit. They were this incredible color, like maybe she wore contacts to make them so intense. He could see he'd caught her off guard. But she answered, "All right, Boy Scout. Lead the way."

She stood, a bit unsteady. The booze, Jake figured. Perched behind her on the stool was a pile of papers. She reached for it . . . missed. The pages fluttered to the carpet. For an instant, he thought he might have to fight the kid from the table over them, but one look sent the man scrambling back to his stool and his winnings. Jake smiled. Still hadn't lost his touch.

He glanced over the papers. It was a photocopy of an article published in *American Science* magazine. The title was "The Search for Human Pheromones," the author, one Dr. McCall Elizabeth Sayer.

Jake took a minute to skim the bio at the end. McCall, the article rhapsodized, had done postdoctoral work in molecular biology at the California Institute of Technology. McCall had earned a doctoral degree in developmental genetics from Harvard.

The redhead had her back to Jake when he stood. She was saying something to the kid. There were tears in the guy's eyes when she left the table.

"I'm all yours, Boy Scout."

He glanced at her winnings on the table behind her—chips the younger man now scooped into a plastic cup with the *River Palace* logo, a riverboat with gold coins spouting from its smokestack.

"You're kidding," Jake said.

She watched her protégé wind his way past the tables toward the cashier. "I made him promise he wouldn't gamble it. I told him he's not very good." She sighed a little, showing she felt the loss. "It's only money."

"McCall?" he asked on a hunch.

"Yes?" She looked up at him, her eyes a bit unfocused. Then she seemed to realize he knew her name. Her gaze fell to the papers he held out to her. "Oh. Thanks."

She tucked the article and a purse that couldn't hold a wadded-up handkerchief under her arm. She hesitated, then looped her arm through his. The gesture came off a bit awkward. She was looking everywhere but at him.

"So what do your friends call you?" he asked as she walked alongside him.

"McCall," she said. The look she gave him, a little prim, a bit arrogant—it had Harvard written all over it.

"Really? Just McCall, huh?" When they reached the casino doors, he held them open for her. "Well, you look like a Mac to me. Yeah, you have Mac written all over you. Come on, Mac. Something tells me you could use a good hot cup of coffee."

Jake watched Mac seated across the table from him. He'd brought her ashore to his favorite place at the River Palace Hotel, the Cascade Lounge, a glass-roofed atrium where you could hear water falling from ten feet into a dramatic rock formation. They kept turtles in the pool below.

Finishing off another glass of champagne, Mac ignored the steaming cup of coffee he'd ordered for her. He was pretty sure she was smashed, but he had to give her credit. She could hold her own.

"You haven't touched your coffee." He pushed the cup closer to her hand, as if distance might make the difference. It was his absolute sacred rule never to sleep with a woman who was drunk. But God help him, sleeping with Mac was looking like a pretty great idea right now.

Mac pushed aside the coffee, reaching instead for the champagne bottle she'd ordered. "So how in the world did a Boy Scout like you end up working in a casino?"

He steadied the bottle before she poured the champagne on the tablecloth. "How does a Ph.D. in genetics end up playing blackjack professionally?"

She shook her finger at him, smiling. "I asked first."

He shrugged, watching her take another sip, wondering if his visions of wild sex wouldn't dwindle to an evening of baby-sitting after all. He didn't think she could drink much more. Though she was tall for a woman, maybe five foot, seven inches without the heels, there wasn't much meat on her bones.

"It wasn't my first career choice," he said, "but it seems to have worked out. What about you? You always bring a science article along when you leave the house?"

That faraway look came back to her eyes. She glanced at the pages stacked next to her foot on the floor, the sheets uncurling from the tube she'd made of them. "Someone gave it to me just before I came here." She shook her head. "I should have thrown it away. I don't know why I. didn't."

She looked in her mid-twenties, young to have earned all those degrees then blithely turned her back on them. "So tell me what it says." He nodded toward the pages.

She glanced back at him, then took another drink of the champagne. "That's ancient history. I'm onto my second career choice."

"Gambling?"

"I'm good with numbers."

"I bet," he said, taking in the view offered by the gap in the linen suit. If he were smart, he'd get her outside and in a taxi right now, before he forgot the sacred rule about drunk women and invited her up to his room.

"Are you going to turn me in?" she asked.

"You mean to the other casinos? Definitely."

She leaned forward, looking him in the eyes. "Maybe I don't care anymore." She took his hand and started drawing circles on his palm with her index finger. "Maybe it never mattered."

For a come-on, it seemed a little naive, but he had to admit, it was damn effective. Already, a little voice inside his head urged him to take what she might offer. Jake stared across the bar at the lights shimmering off the black mirror of the

Mississippi beyond the floor-to-ceiling windows, getting this really bad feeling.

When she laced their fingers together, he told himself Murphy's Law couldn't strike twice. So what if she was a little drunk? He hadn't slept with a woman in so long, he was actually beginning to worry about Dino's accusations of celibacy, and he was so hard just sitting across from her that he could taste their night together. Could almost hear the music of it in his head.

But Jake Donovan had a legacy of sorts. Just watching her, the jungle-drum beat of it sounded in his head: *Donovan Curse, Donovan Curse.* Try as he might, he couldn't shut off the warning. He shook his head, realizing he must be taking the curse more seriously these days.

He slipped his hand from hers and sat back in his chair. He curled his fingers around the coffee mug.

"You know what, Mac?" he said. "I think you're plastered." This was what the situation called for, he told himself. A little damage control before he made a big mistake. Locking it in place, he added, "I think any minute now, you're going to fall out of that chair and I'm not going to be fast enough to catch you." He shrugged, thinking this wasn't bad for sabotage. "Then there's that whole passing-out thing to worry about."

She sobered instantly, the words scoring hard, as he'd known they would. You didn't bother with postdoctoral work at a major university without acquiring your share of pride along the way.

She put down her champagne glass very carefully. "Well, I suppose that puts the evening to a charming end." She shook her head. "And I was going to sleep with you and everything."

He nodded, as if she'd just asked him about his coffee. Still, there were some very real regrets going through his head. "Why don't I get you a cab?"

She was staring at her champagne flute. He thought she wasn't going to answer—or maybe she would just pick up the glass and toss the champagne in his face.

It shocked the shit out of him when he saw tears pooling in her eyes instead.

He could see she was blistering mad. But there was pain there, too, clearly visible in the white lines around her mouth and eyes.

"I buried my mother this morning." She enunciated carefully, as if suddenly, she wanted to be sober. "I am entitled to get drunk. I am entitled to a one-night stand, if that's what I want to help me get through it." She glanced up, her eyes looking more green than blue with the tears. "I believe people do it all the time." She smiled. "But no, I had to pick the Boy Scout out of the crowd."

She pushed back her chair and stood. Acting as if there weren't tears slipping down her cheeks, she said, "Thanks for showing me what a lousy idea this was."

Before he could respond, she dropped some bills on the table and turned. She ran for the door.

Jake cursed under his breath, taking off after her. God, he'd known she was trouble from that first time he'd seen her at the table. The way she moved, her intensity while she bet . . . every delicious curve, every graceful move, had smelled of trouble. And like an idiot, he was running after her anyway.

He found her leaning up against the wall at the bank of elevators. She was turned away from him, but he could see by the way her shoulders trembled that she was crying. Watching her, he forgot about the Donovan Curse; he forgot about everything.

He touched her arm and turned her around.

"Why couldn't you have let it be simple?" she asked, her eyes fierce. "Why couldn't you just let me have my champagne and help me forget?" She wiped the tears from her face and laughed. "My first attempt at a one-night stand and it's over before it even starts. Boy, I sure can pick them."

She was staring up at him, wearing all her emotions for him to see—the hurt, the loneliness, the fear. At that instant, something connected between them. He could feel it sizzle and pop in the air around them. A click sounded in his ears, almost like a door slamming shut or a lock snapping in place—or his sacred rule about drunk women being flushed down the toilet.

He'd seen it coming when he'd watched her as a brunette with glasses. He'd been wary of it when he walked past the blonde with the fishnet stockings biting her nails and drinking ginger ale.

The interest. The intrigue. The inevitable for Jake Donovan, a two-time loser who knew the signs enough to see he was hopping back on the merry-go-round for another ride. There she was, the damsel in distress. And once again, he was playing the knight in shining armor . . .

A real personality flaw. That explained it in a sentence. How he always made his life more complicated than it needed to be.

He sighed, not fighting it anymore, channeling his energies in a completely different direction. He should have known all along. He thought maybe he had.

"Actually, Mac. I believe I picked you. And you're right. I tend to make things more complicated than they need to be. It's a problem. I have to work on it. Really, I do."

She looked at him suspiciously. "Are you after another merit badge?"

"Nah." He reached up and brushed his thumb over her mouth, something he'd been wanting to do all night. She had these really soft lips and he liked the curve to them. A cupid's bow.

He gave her his best smile, the kind that used to knock out juries. "I was thinking I have a room upstairs." He reached and took her hand. He locked their fingers together, just as she'd done at the table, and gave her hand a squeeze.

That stunned her into silence. And then she laughed. "Now you're coming on to me?"

"How about we start with a nightcap? See where it leads?"

She looked at him as if she were seeing him for the first

ime. He realized that's where he'd been going with it the
whole night, making sure she really knew what she was doing,
hat there wouldn't be all those regrets to deal with come
norning.

"What's your name?" she said, caring enough to ask for
he first time.

"Jake. Jake Donovan." The elevator doors opened. He
guided her inside and pushed the button for his floor. "I hope
you like music. I have a pretty decent collection of CDs. Ever
heard of Druha Trava? No? Well, let me be the first to introduce you to the pleasures of Czechoslovakian bluegrass."

Two

McCall Sayer thought she might have gone temporarily insane.

Taking a deep breath, she stepped inside the hotel suite. She tried not to walk into anything or stumble, already embarrassed to her soul that she was this drunk. The enormous suite had a unique design, but it was its elegance that surprised her. It didn't seem to fit her image of the Boy Scout.

Rounding the granite counter with built-ins that separated the kitchen area from the living room, McCall stepped toward the floor-to-ceiling windows showcasing a sweeping view of the river. She dropped her gaze to the Berber carpet, fighting vertigo as she made her way to one of two pristine kidney-shaped sofas. She felt a little ill—and she was having serious reservations about her one-night stand.

The last time she'd slept with a man she'd been nineteen and a virgin.

Maybe ten years was too long to spring into this sort of thing, she thought, sitting down, holding her purse and the rolled-up pages of the *American Science* article Roger had given her earlier. And then there were those memorable moments with her thesis advisor, her first and last experience with sex. Quick and painful, with a lot of grunting on his part on the floor of the lab, the earth hadn't exactly moved.

"So what would you like?" Jake stood behind the granite counter of the kitchen. "I even have champagne." He pulled out a half bottle from the sub-zero refrigerator behind him.

She grimaced. "Coffee. You made me ashamed of myself back there."

"Been there . . . done that. I just thought I should let you know, you wake up in the morning and feel lousy, and the problems are still there, big as life."

She gave him a tired smile. "You really are a Boy Scout."

"Hmm," he said noncommittally. "Do you mind instant? I think I have some of those flavored coffees." He disappeared behind the counter. She could hear him rummaging around. He stood, holding up a tin. "International Irish Mocha something."

"That sounds great."

The teapot he set on the glass burner was painted to look like a cow, its head, a spout for pouring. It seemed out of place in the ultramodern setting where framed prints vied for attention with waist-high ceramic vases topped with willow sticks and silk flowers. Everything in the hotel room was polished, designer perfect, and varying shades of cream.

"Did you decorate this place yourself?" she asked, thinking it couldn't be possible. The furnishings reeked of a feminine influence.

"It's a long story," he said, pouring water from the sink into the cow tea kettle.

McCall settled back into the kidney-shaped couch, watching him spoon coffee into two mugs. For lack of anything better to do, she fidgeted with the article, then set the pages and her purse on the oblong glass coffee table before her.

When she'd ordered the champagne, she hadn't intended to get drunk. But drink after drink, she found herself trying to wash away the images of the funeral: the suspicion she'd seen on her sister's face, the disapproval on her father's, the sight of her mother inside that lacquered white casket laden with lilies and carnations. McCall had been back in New Orleans only three weeks. She had thought her mother would have more time. She had prayed for more time.

And then the edges had started getting blurry with the

champagne, hurting a little less. She'd ordered another glass. Then another.

She'd gone to the *River Palace* by cab directly from the funeral—her first mistake. She'd been like a pressure cooker ready to blow, looking for a place to let out a little steam before she exploded. Too vulnerable.

McCall glanced down at the curled pages of the article Roger had shoved in her hand with that knowing smirk, the paper a poignant reminder of the years he and his father had stolen from her. She wondered if that's what this night was all about. Her meeting with Curtis Clarke. Revving up for one last risky game.

But then the Boy Scout came toward her holding two cups of steaming coffee. He was tall and built like an athlete, with strawberry blond hair he'd buzzed short, George Clooney style. He had these beautiful brown eyes. Dimples. And there was this intensity about him. At the blackjack table, he'd made her feel as if she were the only person in the room. Watching him cross the room, she knew she was kidding herself if she thought tonight was only about distractions.

McCall took the coffee mug, her gaze following Jake as he walked over to the entertainment center that lined one wall. Before tonight, whatever sexual feelings she'd experienced had been nurtured along, carefully seeded and cultivated until she readied herself for some nebulous next step that never came. She had never just looked into a man's eyes and felt desire.

But when the Boy Scout lowered his gaze to her cleavage at the blackjack table, she'd felt it then. Down to her toes. He'd watched her with that hungry look of his. And she'd liked it, the warming seduction of that look. Very much. It was something she couldn't walk away from. Something she wanted to explore, to see where it might lead.

She heard the soft crooning of a saxophone piped into the room from some hidden speaker. She realized he'd put on a jazz CD. "That doesn't sound Czechoslovakian," she said.

He sat down on the couch next to her and clicked their

mugs together before taking a drink. "I thought I would ease you into my collection. Start out with a little jazz. Work you up to the bluegrass. So. What's your story, Mac. Bad day?"

"Not one of my best. And my name is McCall. I don't really care for nicknames."

"Yeah?" He touched her mouth again, rubbing the pad of his thumb over her bottom lip in a way that made strange things happen in the pit of her stomach. "Well, you'll get used to it," he said, putting his coffee down as he leaned toward her.

Immediately, she knew his kiss would be different—she just hadn't been prepared for how much. The men she knew weren't physical types. They spent a lot of time hunched over computers and test tubes, just like McCall. They were clumsy and a little desperate in their sexual advances, always racing to the finish.

The Boy Scout was kissing her as if he had all the time in the world.

She would give a merit badge for this kiss, she thought as his lips played over hers. This was nothing like Paul, a man who—after their one and only consummation—had profusely apologized as he wiped the sweat from his face with his handkerchief. A man who, a year after taking her virginity, published all her research under his name without giving her credit, forcing her to change universities. It had been a painful reminder that men weren't after her body.

But the Boy Scout, he wasn't the least interested in her mind. He made her lips wet with his tongue, and then he eased his tongue inside her mouth. She couldn't believe she was actually moaning, but the sound seemed a natural response.

He pulled back, smiling. He had the nicest smile. She felt a little dizzy just looking at it.

"Careful," he said gently, taking the coffee cup she'd almost dumped in his lap.

Suddenly, she felt all fired up inside, while he calmly set

her coffee mug next to his on the glass table. Perhaps he was familiar with the routine. But then she remembered how hard he'd tried to keep her sober . . . and there was this focus to him. She'd seen men use less concentration while waiting for Nobel Prize caliber results from their data.

He was taking the pins out of her hair and letting the heavy strands tumble down to her shoulders. She felt out of her element. She knew she shouldn't have drunk so much. The champagne was beginning to sour in her stomach as her anxiety hiked up a notch. She prayed she wouldn't get ill or pass out.

She needed to catch her breath. She stood, slipping out from under his caress, overwhelmed by the desire coursing through her. She walked over to the entertainment center, ignoring the expensive knickknacks that lined the shelves to examine a set of framed photographs. She had this horrible sensation that the room was spinning. She leaned against the shelves and focused on the photographs. She didn't know if she should stay or go.

She wanted to stay. Very much.

She realized through her champagne haze that the photographs were all of a little boy at different stages of life, beginning with those newborn "baby's first photos" that made children look like aliens, and working up to home snapshots of a preschooler around the same age as Barb's four-year-old twins. Smiling, she picked up a frame made from different shapes of pasta pasted on cardboard and spray-painted gold. It looked like something a child might make in preschool. Like the cow teakettle, it didn't fit. She guessed it was one of the few personal items in the room.

The little boy in the photograph was sitting in a swing on a woman's lap, mugging for the camera. He had a full head of strawberry blond hair and there was a cluster of freckles across his nose. He had chocolate brown eyes that could melt the heart of any mama within striking distance. The resemblance was uncanny.

Jake walked up behind her. His arms came around her waist as he pulled her back against him. He felt so firm, all muscle. She thought this was how a man should feel leaning against you. She'd never felt it before, this delicious friction he set off inside her. She was a little out of breath as she turned around, holding the photo up to him.

"Any relation?" she asked.

"My son." She could hear the pride in his voice, could see it in his smile. He was digging his fingers in her hair, watching it slip through his hands.

She licked her lips, starting to feel queasy again. "He looks like you."

"Yeah, I know. He's just a whole hell of a lot cuter."

She put down the photograph. "Are you married?" she asked.

"Not at the moment."

"That sounds a little suspicious. Do you have a harem of ex-wives lurking around or something?"

"Or something," he said, his mouth once more covering hers.

She didn't fight it this time; she just let herself drown right into his bone-melting kiss. He was good at this. Women would probably pay money for this kiss.

"So what the hell is a pheromone, Doctor?" he whispered against her mouth.

"I'm not sure I should tell you," she said, kissing him back, getting into the rhythm of it. "I think I'm trying to seduce you . . . I don't want to scare you away."

"Don't strain yourself, Mac. I'm not playing hard to get."

Taking her by the waist, he drew her toward him, letting her set the pace. She edged closer, stopping when her hips pressed against his. Suddenly, it all caught up with her. The champagne, the tenderness of his mouth, the way his hands caressed her. She felt dizzy with it. He leaned forward, moving their bodies to the sound of the saxophone, his hand cupping her buttocks through her skirt.

"You smell so good," he whispered, rubbing his mouth against her neck. His hand crept up her hip to her breast, slowly, as if he were memorizing every curve along the way. "I lied about being a Boy Scout," he whispered, biting her lower lip gently.

"I know," she said, her arms reaching around his neck. "There's no such thing as an Eagle Scout, third rank."

"Imagine that."

He tasted like chocolate. That International Mocha Irish something, she thought vaguely. It was slightly sweet, intoxicating, like champagne.

"Your perfume's driving me crazy, Mac."

Crazy, she thought. Yes. That's what this night was all about. Going wonderfully, incredibly insane.

They were still swaying to the music. Jake unbuttoned her jacket and drew it over her shoulders as he pulled her toward the bedroom. It was a short trip, smooth, like his dancing. Before she knew it, he was kissing her hair, turning her toward a king-size, antique iron bed, making her even dizzier.

"I think I should warn you," he said. "The last time I had a one-night stand, I ended up married."

"Then I better not leave you my number," she answered, her mouth covering his, wanting more.

He tossed her jacket to the floor as the back of her knees hit the bed. She kicked off her heels and scooted back over the covers, pulling him with her, helping him shrug out of his suspenders and shirt. She hadn't been wrong about the muscles. They were all there, hard and defined. *He works out,* she thought. She put her hands on his chest, feeling the hair curling beneath her fingers. It was a shade darker than the hair on his head, almost a rusty brown. He had freckles on his shoulders.

They ended up kneeling on the bed, facing each other, sharing hot wicked kisses. She was having trouble catching her breath, but she didn't care. He'd unsnapped her bra. He was palming

her breasts, brushing the tips with his thumbs as he kissed her.
She felt dizzy with his kisses, so dizzy. Incredibly dizzy.

Sick dizzy.

"Ohmigod."

Jake looked down at the woman in his arms. For some
reason his lust-laden brain couldn't fathom, she had suddenly
tensed. Now, she was perfectly still, kneeling in front of him
on the bed as he held her breasts cupped in his hands like
two apples outstretched to Adam. Her eyes grew large and
luminous in the light coming from the front room. One hand
covered her mouth. Then the other.

She lost every speck of color.

She scrambled off the bed, barely making it to the bathroom
before he heard the sounds of her tossing her cookies.

"I don't believe this." He fell back onto the bed. He tried
to catch his breath, letting his body catch up with the message
his head was getting loud and clear with the noise coming
from the bathroom. "I don't fucking believe this."

He told himself to take a couple of gulps of air, come back
to earth slowly. He probably deserved this, he thought, breaking the sacred rule and all.

And then he grinned. But God, it had been worth it.

By the time he got himself together and brought her a clean
towel, she was sitting on the bathroom floor leaning against
the wall. She was dressed in only her skirt and stockings, her
color still pretty green around the gills.

He handed her a towel. She used it to cover herself, looking
absolutely miserable.

"You okay?" he asked, leaning against the doorjamb.

She closed her eyes. It looked like she was still battling
the nausea. "I've never drunk more than two glasses of wine
in my life."

"Something tells me seduction isn't part of the repertoire
either."

A shadow of a smile crossed her face. "And here I thought
I was faking it pretty well."

"You were doing just fine, Mac." He dug his hands into the pockets of his trousers. "You want a shower?"

She nodded. "Please."

He brought her a couple more towels and his terrycloth robe. Listening to the water running, he went back to the kitchen bar and poured himself three fingers of Stoli on the rocks. Then, thinking better of it, he grabbed the bottle. He only got drunk on special occasions and this was nothing but special.

Sinking back into the couch, he sipped the vodka. He glanced up at the photograph of Michael she'd been looking over earlier. The joy in his son's eyes could always make Jake smile. But this time, he stared at the woman behind Michael on the swing.

She was a brunette, very pretty, thirty-nine years young when they'd met—an accountant who'd quit her job to go the mommy track once they'd been married. He took another drink of the Stoli.

"What a night."

At least history wouldn't repeat itself, he thought, remembering the pain of the custody battle, of having Michael only on weekends. "Thank God for small favors."

Jake finished off the Stoli and started crunching on the ice cubes. The water had turned off and he stood, figuring he should check on her, make sure she hadn't fallen in or something.

He knocked on the door. "Mac?" He knocked again. "Hey, Mac. You okay in there?"

He opened the door a crack, peeking inside. She was curled up on the black oval rug, wrapped in the terrycloth robe he'd given her. She was snoring gently.

He swung the door wide open, shaking his head as he stared down at her. She looked very peaceful, lying there. "We could have been something, Mac."

He carried her to bed and tucked her in. He headed for the spare room, Michael's room. He stripped down to his Jockey shorts by the light of the aquarium and the computer's screen saver and slipped under the killer whale sheets. His feet hung over the edge of the twin. He had a hell of an erection.

"A sad state of affairs, Jake Donovan."

It took a long time before he fell asleep.

A bank of clouds hung a great platter of a moon against the midnight sky. Far from the lights and noise of the French Quarter, the homes in Slidell were silent on the warm summer night, their occupants asleep in their beds, the streets empty. Quiet.

At 12:30 A.M., Sierra made her escape.

It had taken the golden retriever most of the night, but Sierra managed to dig a hole big enough to squirrel under the fence. The dog had a distinctive look, the ears a little too long and floppy for a purebred, the tail, curling up to form a complete circle. She'd been after a possum, giving chase, only to see her quarry escape through a gap in the moldering boards. The hole had been too small for the dog, forcing the retriever to dig her way out.

By the time she got through, the possum was gone. Sierra followed the scent, then glanced back at the darkened house, anxious. The dog's owner was a little girl named Megan. Her father had given Sierra to Megan only last year when she started having trouble in school. Megan hadn't adjusted well to the move from California; she missed her friends. A puppy had gone a long way to healing those hurts, and Sierra and Megan spent a lot of time together.

The golden retriever took a few steps back toward the house, but then Sierra caught sight of another dog, a black German shepherd. The retriever turned, racing ahead after the shepherd, her tongue lolling, barking her heart out.

She'd spent a good long time with the German shepherd before the retriever tried to find her way home. But the streets didn't appear familiar anymore. Pawing it down the sidewalk, the dog became hopelessly lost.

A soft whistle pricked her ears. Not Megan, the little girl who took care of Sierra, but certainly someone who might take the dog home. In Sierra's experience, people were good. They petted her; they gave her treats.

The golden retriever ran toward the tall man still whistling to her. But when the dog reached the dark figure, he yanked a rope around her neck, choking her.

"Gotcha," he said.

He dragged the retriever toward a big white truck. There were dogs inside; the retriever could smell them. Could smell their fear.

The dog fought hard not to go inside the truck, but the man pulled her up by the rope, giving her no choice. Sierra had never bitten anyone; she'd been trained not to bite. Instead, she whined softly.

The dogs inside weren't barking; they smelled of urine and feces. The man tied a muzzle around the retriever's mouth so she couldn't bark either. And then he took the rope away from her neck and unbuckled her collar. He peered at the tags in the semidarkness, then tossed the collar out onto the road. He could say he found the dog without its collar. Collars did that sometimes, slipped off. He shoved Sierra inside a cage with another dog, the black German shepherd the retriever had been chasing earlier.

He had no intention of taking Sierra home to Megan.

The telephone was ringing.

Jake palmed the side of the bed for the phone before he realized where he was. He groaned, then forced himself out of Michael's bed. He walked barefoot into the kitchen and picked up on the sixth ring, catching it just before the machine answered.

"You didn't sleep with her, did you?" It was Dino.

Jake tried to clear the cobwebs from his brain. Coffee. He needed coffee. He tucked the cordless phone between his ear and his shoulder and reached for the coffeemaker. The kitchen clock said it was just shy of eight. "Not that it's any of your business, but no. Happens that I didn't."

"Look, Irishman, just tell me you're not in love. I sat up half the night thinking I made this terrible mistake sending you into the trenches like that. I mean, what was I thinking? With your track record? Sweet Suzy and that bitch, what's-her-name."

A man of many opinions, Dino. "Her name is Hope."

"Whatever. I mean, how could I forget about the Donovan Curse?"

"You know, Dino, you're a real pain sometimes."

"Just humor me here, Irishman. I just need to hear you say it."

Jake filled the coffeemaker with water and coffee grounds, then switched it on. "I'm not in love."

"Oh, for the love of God, say it like you mean it. No. Forget it. There's no hope for you. You are meant for this kind of thing. You're going to marry her. You're going to have a kid. You're going to pay alimony."

"I don't pay either Hope or Susan alimony."

"That's because you got lucky. You mark my words. You're not going to be so lucky this time. She'll take you, Jake. This one looks real smart. Sly even."

"All that from watching her gamble? What? You reading coffee grounds like your Greek grandmother?"

"She's a pro-fes-sio-nal!" Dino strung out the syllables, as if maybe Jake needed the word spelled out. "Do you know what kind of balls that takes, to play blackjack like that?"

He stared at the rolled-up article from *American Science* she'd left on the coffee table. *Doctorate from Harvard. Post-doctoral work at Caltech.* "Maybe she's real good with numbers."

"Not to mention the greed factor," Dino continued, on a roll now. "Oh, yeah. This one will take you for all you're worth."

He glanced toward the bedroom. He could just see the door. It was closed. "Which isn't much."

"It doesn't matter; she as good as has her hands on your bank account. I know these things."

Jake padded back into Michael's room, finding his trousers. "You know shit, Tropedis." He stepped into his pants and buttoned them before he headed for the master bedroom.

"I'm going to have to do penance for this one."

But Jake wasn't listening. He opened the door slowly, staring into the room.

The bed was empty.

"Jake? Jake, you still there?"

She'd made the bed. There wasn't a single sign that she'd slept there—except for a long-stemmed red rose and a folded sheet of paper on the pillow.

"Jake?"

"Hold on."

He opened the note. It read:

It was beautiful, Boy Scout.

"She must have had better dreams than I did," he said.

"What the hell are you talking about?"

"Hey, Dino." Jake crumbled the note into a ball and tossed it at the trash can in the bathroom, making the bank shot. "You know anything about pheromones?"

"Sure. Where have you been? Don't you watch the talk shows?"

"Must have missed that one."

"Pheromones, you know, it's a kind of chemical. As in that special scent that makes a woman attractive to a man and vice versa. They put them in perfumes and crap."

He remembered her perfume, how it had driven him crazy. Something exotic, like jasmine mixed with a sort of spice.

"Why, Jake?" Dino asked. "You looking for a love potion or something?"

Three

We lost half the experimental group today, ten rats in all. The autopsies were inconclusive as to cause of death. He wants to ignore the results, forge ahead. What we're doing is vital, he says, significant enough to merit the risk. I only protested a little. I feel as if I'm falling under some sort of spell. Will I do anything he asks?
—Excerpt from Dr. Alicia Goodman's lab book

"The Love Doctor." The lilting cadence of Curtis Clarke's drawl didn't hide his sarcasm. "How things do change."

McCall managed a smile despite a sledgehammer headache threatening to pound her into mental meltdown. After her vanishing act from Jake's hotel room, she'd hustled back to Barb's house and downed enough aspirin to anesthetize an elephant. She'd spent most of the morning pacing Barb's spare room, preparing for this meeting, trying to exorcise the mixed-up images from last night.

Now, sipping her iced tea while Curtis waited, she told herself this is what those years at the blackjack tables had trained her for. To be someone else for this single instant, the kind of woman who could offer Curtis Clarke a billion-dollar product and use that leverage to beat him at his own game.

"Gloating, Curtis?" she asked. "How unlike you."

"You bet I'm gloating. You turned me down flat four years ago, girl. I could have made something of you at Clarke Labs.

But you thought you were too good for me back then, don't say you didn't. Now . . . now you're peddling a love potion."

They were seated at a secluded table in the courtyard at the Court of Two Sisters restaurant. Looking like fairy dust, white Christmas lights festooned the restaurant's jungle growth of vines. A three-piece jazz band played in front of the courtyard's fountain while smiling German tourists took turns posing next to the snare drum. A waiter stood at the ready, snapping their photographs.

McCall leaned across the table toward Curtis, the kind of man who would demand a meeting the day after she'd buried her mother. "Yes, Curtis. I am quaintly referred to as the Love Doctor and it's taken me too many appearances as a hired gun on infomercials and talk shows to earn that crown. And just as you predicted four years ago, I have come back to you, begging on hands and knees." She shifted aside the slit of her ankle-length skirt and bared her kneecaps. "Look. I even have calluses."

Curtis took a drink of his iced tea. His gaze remained on her legs, then slowly rose to her breasts. She was wearing a sheer teal blouse with a slightly metallic shimmer that revealed a matching bra beneath—the fabric all too thin under Curtis's stare.

Nearing sixty, Curtis Clarke wore his sandy brown locks frosted and permed; a man vain enough to use makeup. But despite the tanning booth complexion and the girdle he surely wore beneath his oh-so-sharp Prada jacket and trousers, he'd only managed to camouflage his age. Curtis, the cosmetics king, was looking old these days. But he was still powerful, and capable of vengeance.

For a moment, McCall allowed herself to think about the past. It pulsed between them, the day she'd laughed in his face at his suggestion that she leave her post at the prestigious Louisiana Institute of Technology and replace her father as head of Research and Development at Clarke Labs. She'd been a highly respected scientist then, devoted to cutting edge research . . . experiments that held the potential of finding a cure for the ravages of brain damage suffered by millions of victims of disease and strokes. She would never have stooped to something as insignificant as working for a cosmetics company in those days. She even thought she'd used the words "cheap" and "trivial" when she'd turned down his offer.

Two weeks later, her career flatlined. But she'd never been able to prove Curtis was the man behind the accusations that ruined her.

Curtis took an inordinately long time before his eyes left the vicinity of her breasts to meet her gaze. "I never knew you could be beautiful," he said.

"Lordy, Curtis. Is this a come-on?"

"Just an observation. You used to be so plain, girl, with your big glasses and your hair pulled back so tight I thought it must give you migraines. Daddy's little scientist. Why, all you lacked was a sense of style."

"It's true that I've had a little time on my hands to work on my look, since the professor thing didn't work out."

He put down his glass. He leaned close, so she could smell his aftershave, a pleasant citrus scent. "It's a shame, I admit, the way they ousted you from that university of yours on so little evidence. And now, you've come begging me for the job you once threw in my face. If I weren't a generous man, McCall, I might be tempted to tell you to go to hell. But since you beg so pretty . . . and the thought of you on your knees right there before me is so tempting."

"I'm going to eat crow, Curtis. I've had the taste of it in my mouth for the last four years." She looked him up and down, taking in the excessive polish, the slight paunch over his Gucci belt. "But I'm not that desperate."

Curtis laughed. "You still have spirit. I would have hated to kill that in you."

McCall thought of all the things Curtis had killed. Her career, her father's love—and if her suspicions were correct, he was capable of much worse. Even murder.

"And I'm greedy, Curtis," she said, taking their meeting to the next level. "I want money. Lots of it. And my own lab, with state-of-the-art equipment and no one looking over my shoulder for results. That's what it's going to cost you to get your hands on my research."

His slate gray eyes lost any hint of amusement. "That's asking a lot."

She slid a black notebook across the table. "A genetically engineered compound that mimics human pheromones, producing ten to a hundred times the response of the real thing? The Omega Principle isn't a gimmick. It stands to make a woman irresistible." With the sweetest of smiles, she echoed his drawl. "Why Curtis, I do believe you're licking your chops."

McCall stood, picking up her black leather case. "Show my father my data. My card is inside; you can give my service a call. I'm certain I'll hear from you soon, but I'll give you a week before I open myself up to the highest bidder. *Ciao*, Curtis. As always, it's been grand."

He grabbed her hand, not letting her leave. "Why me, McCall? It's hard to believe you would do me any favors."

She let the silence draw out between them, knowing this would be the turning point, the final ruse she'd rehearsed since the day she'd discovered the lab book and its awful warning. "A favor? Hardly. I just don't want you to ruin me a second time. And I know if I didn't come to you first, you just might." She winked. "For old times' sake."

"You still blame me for everything. Even for that woman's death."

"No, Curtis," she lied. She followed it up with the wholehearted truth. "But sometimes, I still blame myself."

He seemed to think that over. "It's true that I tend to take it personally when a woman turns me down. Sit, girl. I've invited a few people I thought you might want to see."

His smile warned her first. Smug and wide. And his eyes narrowed, becoming flat, like a snake's, but the color of gun-metal. She turned around, not prepared. She should have been prepared.

Her father was walking toward her, a tall man with graying hair and the odd-colored blue-green eyes she'd inherited. Unlike Curtis's excessive veneer, her father's polish was unforced, the classic look of patched-elbow jackets and wire-rimmed glasses. Walking past the wrought iron chairs and tables, he appeared self-assured, as he'd always been. And he was looking everywhere but at McCall.

Right behind him was Belinda, McCall's baby sister. Her willowy frame swayed with a rhythm earned by years of ballet lessons, making her dress and its pattern of daisies slip across her thighs as she walked. Wearing her straight blond hair back in a simple knot, she clutched Roger Clarke's arm like a lover. Roger Clarke, Curtis Clarke's son, the man who—along with his father—McCall suspected of murder.

McCall sat down, not because she wanted to, but because she had to. She'd seen them both at the funeral yesterday, Belinda and her father. But she hadn't spoken to either. Not since the day Dr. Donald Sayer, her father and mentor, had demanded she leave his home four years ago had they exchanged more than a few words. Even when she'd visited her mother the past weeks, Belinda and her father had been carefully absent. And at the funeral, the minute she'd taken two steps in their direction, Daddy had hustled Belinda away.

All because of Curtis. Because of what he'd made her father believe about McCall, his own daughter.

She told herself to cool down. In the past, her greatest weakness had been arrogance, but now it was anger. The emotion rose up inside McCall, waiting to blast the men she felt responsible for the death of her partner and the desertion of her family. But her anger was futile here, and she knew it, as debilitating as her arrogance in a game she felt ill-equipped to play, but must.

"Well, now," she said almost under her breath. "Does this mean you've dictated a family reconciliation?"

"As you know, I have a great deal of say in what your father does or doesn't do." The soothing cadence of Curtis's drawl seemed almost like a background whisper, a voice-over to a reunion she'd conjured in her head too many times. "For me, he's agreed to at least hear you out. I told him he was a little hard on you, throwing you out when we didn't have real proof that you committed those awful things. I think he just might give you a second chance."

Not because she was his daughter. But because Curtis Clarke, his boss, had decreed it.

McCall rose. "Daddy," she said. For her, the years slipped away. She wanted to throw her arms around him. She wanted to cry about her mother with him, to let him hold her as he had in the past, when she was little and he still believed in her. But he didn't come close enough to touch her.

"Hello, McCall," he said softly, his voice devoid of the condemnation she'd expected.

"Have you heard the happy news?" Curtis asked, not bothering to rise from the table as the others approached. "Roger and Belinda are engaged."

McCall refused to react, knowing he was testing her, pushing and prodding her like some experiment. But despite her resolve to give nothing away, Curtis's words ricocheted inside of her head like gunfire. *Her sister engaged to a murderer.* For thirty years, Curtis Clarke had held a death grip on her father. Now he was sinking his tentacles into her baby sister.

Her eyes turned to Belinda. She looked beautiful. Pale and slender. So fragile. Even the dress she wore was too delicate, short and diaphanous with big print daisies, the spaghetti straps clinging to her slim shoulders.

Roger pulled up a chair for Belinda, then took the seat between her and his father. Roger Clarke was his father's greatest creation. Everything Curtis had tried to manufacture in himself with cosmetics and personal trainers had come naturally to Curtis's only child. In Roger, Curtis's beefy features had turned almost delicate, extremely fine. A good six inches taller than his father, Roger had the build of a triathlete. His brown curls were sun-blessed with blond highlights and the planes of his face could give a male supermodel a run for his money. Only the eyes were the same—gray, sly, and hinting of evil.

"You are one sick son-of-a-bitch, Daddy," Roger told Curtis, his voice holding the same musical cadence of a Southern native. "I told you this meeting was stupid." He glanced over at McCall, grinning with that incredible bad-seed charm of his. "Sorry, darling."

McCall ignored Roger. "Belinda. It's good to see you."

"Is it?" her sister asked. There was a dull sheen to her blue eyes.

"Sit up, Belinda," her father whispered. Whether he'd intended it or not, the censure in his voice came across loud and clear to everyone at the table.

Belinda rose from her slouch to lean indolently into Roger's arm. Her eyes never leaving her father's, she said to her fiancé, "Order me something, sweetie."

There was a slight slur to her words and an unidentifiable languor to her posture. McCall realized she was drunk. Straight up noon and her barely twenty-one-year-old sister was drunk. Just yesterday, they had buried their mother, a woman who had died from the effects of alcoholism.

McCall stared across the table. Curtis waited with a knowing smile, his orchestrated move scoring big to unnerve McCall. Roger played with the fingers of Belinda's hand, shifting the enormous marquis diamond she wore so that it would catch the light. Her father, too, waited expectantly, as if she might suddenly be able to explain away years of his doubts.

McCall rose from her chair. Emotions shot through her with the frenzy of a casino arcade. She wanted dearly to speak to her father, but not like this, with the two of them performing for the great Curtis Clarke. Outflanked, she glanced at her watch, searching her mind for an excuse. She couldn't bare to stand there any longer, her heart exposed, waiting for Curtis to take aim and do his worst.

"I'm sorry," she said, finding her exit line, giving the first round to Curtis. "If I'd known this was going to be a family reunion, I wouldn't have scheduled my next appointment."

Curtis flipped out his cell phone. "Cancel."

"I'm late as it is," McCall said, backing away, because the words were just a ruse and everyone at the table knew it. "I'll expect to hear from you soon," she said to Curtis. "Daddy, Belinda. It was wonderful to see you both."

She walked away as fast as she could without running. Outside, she hailed a cab, lucky enough to find one turning into the street. She leaned over the driver's window, giving directions as she caught her breath.

Inside the car, McCall dropped her case to the cab floor and collapsed against the seat. She rubbed her temples with her fingertips in small circular motions. It would always be this way, she warned herself. Curtis would always have some trick up his sleeve to unnerve her, to trip her up and force her hand.

She had to be better than this. She must be better.

She searched her purse for aspirin, then gulped down two without water. Her headache felt like hatchet blows to her skull, fueled by the vision of her father watching her, waiting for her to come up with the magic explanation that would wipe away his years of misgivings. Belinda drunk. Engaged to Roger Clarke.

"Belinda," she whispered. "How can you be this messed up?"

But after a four-year absence, she knew very little about her baby sister. The woman clutching Roger's hand could be anyone. It was possibly McCall's greatest regret, that Belinda, too, should be a casualty. That McCall hadn't been there for her little sister.

McCall stared out the window, watching the tourist-clogged streets and colorful store fronts of the French Quarter inch past in the traffic. She thought of her mother so pale and gaunt, finally finding her courage on her deathbed to ask her black sheep daughter back to say her goodbyes. But they'd waited too long to let her know Mama was sick. She'd had only the three weeks.

McCall pressed her cheek against the window, taking a breath, caught in the memories of those last days. She'd wanted so dearly for them to be a family again. But in the end, she'd come back only to watch her mother die.

"I should have stood up to him," her mother had whispered in the cultured tones that had been as much her birthright as the silver spoon she'd been born with. "I should have told him he was wrong to send you away like that, no matter what you might have done."

McCall smiled as she remembered those words. How clearly they showed that her mother believed the accusations against her daughter. But that didn't matter, not anymore. McCall wouldn't stoop to protesting her innocence at her mother's sickbed, trying to ignore the oxygen tubes in her mother's nose and the IV drip. Lucinda Sayer barely had the strength to hold McCall's hand, much less accept convoluted explanations about the past. McCall was just happy to see her, to have this chance to speak to her and hold her again.

She remembered how her mother had looked away, her expression one of great pain. "I abandoned my girls. I let him send you away, and then I handed him Belinda," she said, choking on the words, "letting him steal her from me to take your place because he missed you so—"

"Mama, please. Try not to upset yourself."

"I'm not smart like you and your father, McCall. But I know how to love. My crime is that I loved him more than my children." The tears had come then, pitiful and painful to watch. "I shouldn't have done that. It wasn't natural. And now God has punished me for it."

"Hush, Mama." McCall had stroked the parchment paper

skin of her mother's hand, unable to hear any more. "I'm here now. I'm here."

"But you do understand, don't you, darling? How wonderful he can be, how blinding the light of his love when he gives it?"

She'd nodded, because she did understand. For so many years, McCall had been the focus of that intoxicating attention. "Yes, I know."

"He loves us; he does. It's just that, he's such a hard man. He doesn't allow weakness. With time, he can hate you for it." Her mother shook her head. "And now, here I've gone and killed myself with my weakness. And I'm leaving you and Belinda alone. Forgive me. Forgive me."

She had held her mother as she'd cried, being careful not to bruise the translucent skin or dislodge the IV, telling her mother she didn't need forgiveness. McCall didn't blame her. In her heart, she held too many of her own recriminations. There wasn't room for her mother's sins.

Staring out the window of the cab, McCall pushed away the painful memories. She told herself this was the worst it would get . . . that it couldn't hurt more than this. She would be strong. She would fight Curtis and his son to get her family back. But her mother's words kept echoing in her head. *I'm leaving you alone.*

Alone. She felt so very much alone.

Out of nowhere came the image of the Boy Scout. She remembered how he'd kissed her, so beautifully—how he'd touched her, intimately, as if she were some special gift to be cherished. No man had ever touched her like that. The past years parading through casinos, men had come to sit beside her, to coax her from her perch at the tables. She knew the disguises she chose sometimes brought them out, an unwanted nuisance.

But the Boy Scout had been different. It was almost as if he'd been acting out of duress, struggling not to give in to some great desire to touch her. To talk to her. To stay near her. She remembered all the kindness she'd seen in his face, the pains he'd taken to try and get her in a cab sober before she did something she might regret. And the charming mysteries he'd placed in her mind, unanswered questions about ex-wives and elegant furnishings . . . none of which fit the label she'd given him. Boy Scout.

"I've changed my mind," she told the cab driver. "The River Palace Hotel, please."

Dino flipped through the pages of a magazine sporting a scantily clad supermodel on the cover.

"Hey, Jake. Why do you think they make the articles in women's magazines so much more interesting than the men's? I mean, listen to this. 'Erotic Sex Secrets from the Orient,' " he read out loud. " 'Multiorgasmic Women Talk Technique.' "

"Looking for pointers?" Jake frowned. He'd been going over last night's take, Dino having brought over the receipts from the tables. Bart was seriously down. Again.

"Hey, I'm Greek. I don't need pointers." Dino pressed a hand to his gelled hair, a wasted effort. Not a strand had broken rank. Today, Dino wore black jeans and a black bomber jacket over a black T-shirt. Jake figured all he needed was the cape and the mask and he'd be making the mark of the Z on the door. "I'm just saying it's interesting reading, you know?"

Jake glanced at the address label that showed the magazine Dino was reading belonged to one Susan Donovan. "You and Susan are seeing a lot of each other lately."

"That bother you?"

Catching Dino's guarded look, Jake put down the receipts. "What? You want my blessings to date my ex?" He made an exaggerated sign of the cross. "Go with God, my son."

Dino flipped the page, looking disgusted. "It's not like that with me and Suzy. I'm after a cut in her business. And trust me, that's going to be a hell of a lot harder to get into than her pants. You know she's a barracuda when it comes to that

PI firm of hers." He shook his head, holding out the magazine, looking over a perfume ad featuring a naked woman with strategically placed hands as if it were a centerfold. "God save me from independent women."

"Plan A not going well?"

Over the past year, Dino had been helping Susan with her private investigation business. To hear Dino tell it, he was intrigued by Susan's success and he'd saved some money . . . enough that, lately, he'd been thinking of asking her to let him in on the action. A partnership. After all, he wasn't planning on being a floor person all his life. And he liked the gadgets. But Jake had seen the two of them together. There was more than business on both their minds.

"Are you kidding?" Dino said. "I've got Suzy all figured out. I make myself indispensable, me being so mechanically inclined and good with electrical shit. Before she knows it, she won't be able to run the place without me. Exhibit A—to use vocabulary you lawyer guys understand—last night, she comes by the casino looking for me. She wants me to help her with a new security system. Bingo. This morning, I am impressing the shit out of her. Plan A is as good as executed, my man. By the way, she saw you leaving the casino with Madame X."

Suddenly, the receipts on the table held an inordinate amount of Jake's attention. He concentrated on the take, making notes, filing away some numbers.

Not one to give up easily, Dino said, "So you got Madame X all the way up here and you expect me to believe you didn't sleep with her?"

Jake glanced up. He hadn't said anything about bringing Mac here.

Dino grinned, then jogged his head toward the kitchen counter. Two coffee mugs waited to be loaded into the dishwasher, one with lipstick on the rim.

"Go fish, Dino," Jake said. But he was impressed. Maybe

Dino was cut out for this spy stuff. He tapped the receipts from Bart's table. "What are we going to do about this?"

Dino shrugged. "A dealer has to entertain the clients. You and I both know it. Otherwise, you might as well be dealing cards in the middle of the Sahara for all the action you'll see. And Bart, well, since he's been doing AA . . . let's face it. The guy's fucking boring. Sometimes I feel like checking to see if he's still breathing."

Jake nodded. "I'll have a talk with him."

"You had a talk with him last week."

"Then you talk to him."

"I had a talk with him last week."

Jake met Dino's gaze. Tropedis popped a toothpick in his mouth. He maneuvered the thing from one side of his mouth to the other.

"You don't let someone go because they're trying to put their life together," Jake said. "He has a family, for God's sake. He's better off not drinking."

"So tell Garrett he's a charity case and see how far that will get you."

Garrett Renault owned the *River Palace,* along with a group of investors, a key one of which was his grandfather. Needless to say, Garrett ran the show. He was young, only thirty years old, and self-indulgent. Definitely not into charity work.

"I have a better solution. Maybe you could spend a little time over at his table. You're a hell of a guy, Dino. Very entertaining."

"I'm a floor person, not a trained seal."

Jake winked. "I'll put in a good word for you with Susan."

"You're barking up the wrong tree. I have it on good authority the woman's heart is already spoken for."

"I meant for the business," Jake said blandly, catching Dino's slip. Following up, he asked, "Susan seeing someone? First I've heard."

"Yeah? Well, maybe she thinks you wouldn't approve."

Before Jake could comment on that cryptic statement, the

doorbell rang. Jake got up, walking to the door. He pointed to Dino. "That's one you're going to have to explain."

He told himself he would know if Susan were involved with anyone. He and Susan had gone through a lot together, eight years of marriage, divorce while she ran through her inheritance trying to get over her mother's suicide, and even a failed reconciliation a few years back. Now, they were good friends. Susan had been there for him, helping him get through the hell of Hope, his second wife.

He grabbed the doorknob, still wondering if he could possibly be wrong about the fusion reaction he'd seen warming up between Dino and Susan. When he opened the door, he wasn't paying attention, thinking about Susan . . . Bart and the receipts. That changed the minute he saw her.

Mac was standing there, big as life, waiting for him.

He should have been surprised. Dr. McCall Elizabeth Sayer, mystery package behind door number three. But he wasn't. Nor did it surprise him that his pulse was racing and he couldn't help the stupid grin on his face. He'd been thinking about her all morning. A sweet obsession. Somehow, he'd known last night wasn't the end of the story.

"I have two questions," she said. "Who decorated the hotel suite, and how many ex-wives do you have?"

He opened the door wider and leaned back against it, crossing his arms. She was really a looker, even more gorgeous in a flowing skirt and the peek-a-boo top that showed God had taken a little extra trouble with this one. She'd done her hair in corkscrew curls that just brushed past her ears. She looked natural with the hairstyle. Earthy. But it made him wonder, how she could completely change her look like that overnight.

"Come inside, Dr. Sayer," he said, gesturing her in. "Dino here was just leaving."

"Like the Flash. Doctor, huh?" he asked, standing, smiling for all he was worth, getting ready to unleash the Tropedis charm. "You know, Doc, I've been getting this weird pain right about—"

"If you really hoof it, Dino," Jake said, pointing to his watch. "You'll just make that meeting."

"The meeting? Oh, yeah. *That* meeting." Dino snapped his fingers, as if he'd just remembered. He stepped into the hall, but stopped to wave the magazine over the back of McCall's head. "Should I leave you the report?" he asked with a grin.

"I'll catch you next time," Jake said, pulling Mac inside and shutting the door in Dino's face.

He turned back to Mac. He told himself to be on his guard. Dino was right. He was a sucker when it came to women like Mac, and a real bad judge of character for those life-long commitments. And God help him, this woman had "lifetime" written all over her.

Just to her right on the coffee table, he could still see the papers she'd left last night, the article about pheromones she'd written. He breathed in cautiously, getting a whiff of the same exotic perfume that had driven him crazy last night.

"Have a seat, Mac. Turns out, I have a few questions myself."

Four

"I didn't mean to scare off your company," she said.

"You didn't." Later, Dino, private investigator wannabe, would rake him over the coals, but Jake didn't care. A little interrogation was worth having her here again, knowing that she'd felt it too, that something special they hadn't nearly finished last night. "Dino and I work together at the casino. He doubles as floor person and assistant manager. We finished our business."

He watched her stroll around the room, looking skittish as she slipped her sunglasses into a purse that could pass for a lunch pail. She had this really great walk, not a bump-and-grind exactly but with enough swing to get the imagination going. He could bet she hadn't developed that walk in graduate school, studying genetics. No, he figured it would be the last couple of years of McCall Sayer's life—the ones that had her wearing disguises at blackjack tables—that would tell the tale. But he appreciated the view.

Mac settled on the couch and crossed her showgirl legs. He could smell her perfume lingering in the air, that special scent that made him think of jasmine and some exotic spice. He remembered what Dino had said about pheromones. *They put them in perfumes and crap.* Jake shook his head, telling himself he was losing it if he believed she was using a love potion on him.

He nodded toward the lunch box purse. "Is that a fashion

statement or do you want a drink to go with the lunch you packed?"

She glanced at the purse, smiled. "Funny man."

"I've been accused of a sense of humor. The offer for a drink stands."

"I'm not thirsty." She pushed her bangs out of her face as he sat down on the sofa facing her. She had all this hair. He wondered how the hell she'd managed to get it up inside those wigs. "I should probably apologize for last night. You were real sweet."

"Sure." That was him, Mr. Fucking-knight-in-shining-armor. "Thanks for the rose."

He watched the way her lips curled into a smile of pure mischief. "I stole it off a breakfast tray outside your neighbor's door."

"Resourceful lady." He leaned back, hooking his elbows over the low couch. He marveled at the difference in her appearance, the hairstyle, the clothes. It brought a couple of questions to mind, but he was good at reading body language, a skill he'd developed during years of jury selection. Mac looked antsy. He thought she might be getting ready to cut and run, regretting the impulse that had brought her here.

"So, you want to play truth or dare?" he said, bringing them back to her questions when he'd first opened the door. Like Dino, he knew the number one rule: To keep customers at the table, a dealer had to entertain. "I have two ex-wives," he said, getting to it. "Not exactly a harem, but not a good track record either."

"And one of them was an interior decorator?"

He shook his head. "This place used to be Garrett Renault's love nest. Garrett owns the hotel as well as the casino. The lucky lady of the moment always got the go-ahead to redecorate. Only, the current holder of that status has a little more class. She didn't take him up on the offer to stay here. Keeps her own place." He shrugged. "Garrett offered me the suite as a sort of perk. I thought it was just temporary at the time, but it's been almost four years."

"You haven't made much of a mark," she said, referring to the pristine surroundings. "Except for the cow teakettle, of course."

"Actually, it's a Tea Cattle." He grinned. "The box said it's 'udderly adorable.' " He waited as Mac groaned. "A gift," he said. "Dino, too, has a sense of humor."

He knew better than to ask her anything probing right now. He thought she was trying really hard to appear casual about being here, but she was sitting on the edge of the couch, ready to bolt. Not wanting to scare her off, he tossed her a lob. "Your turn. Now that you're going to be blackballed from every casino in a two-state radius, what do you plan to do with yourself?"

His teasing question didn't have its intended effect. She frowned, as if he'd reminded her of something not so pleasant. "As it happens, I had a job interview this morning."

"It didn't go well?"

"On the contrary. They'll hire me."

She looked away. Apparently, she was leaving it at that. He couldn't figure out if she was trying to be mysterious or if she had something to hide.

"Maybe this wasn't such a good idea." She stood, grabbing her purse, catching him off guard. "Thanks for putting up with me last night."

He jumped to his feet and blocked her way. "It wasn't exactly a strain. Sit down. I'll get you a ginger ale."

"I told you—I'm not thirsty."

He grabbed her wrist when she tried to step around him. "So maybe you should take the damn drink to be sociable. Look, you didn't come here to tell me thanks then blow me off, so have a seat."

Her eyes were this incredible green as she stared at him, the center ring of blue almost entirely gone now. Last night, he could have sworn her eyes were more blue than green.

"Careful," she whispered, glancing down at his hand around her wrist. "I have a lunch box. And I know how to use it."

He held his hands out in capitulation and stepped aside. But Mac stayed where she was, appearing to think about it. She shook her head, as if she couldn't believe what she was doing. This time, she sat back on the couch, looking less tense. "Could you put ice in the ginger ale, please? I have a bad habit; I love to chew ice."

"I can think of worse things, Mac."

"McCall," she said, correcting him. "You could at least do me the favor of using my real name."

"Now would that be any fun?" he asked rhetorically, making it clear the nickname would stick.

When he came back carrying a Corona for himself and a glass of ginger ale for Mac, he found her holding the same photograph of Michael on the swing.

She took the glass as he sat down across from her. "Is this one of the harem of ex-wives?" she asked, putting down the photograph of Michael and his mother.

"Ex-wife number two. My last foray into the state of wedded bliss."

"Tell me about it."

"More truth or dare? A woman who likes games."

"It depends on what I'm playing."

"Very provocative. I like that. Maybe I'll take the dare."

"The truth, Boy Scout. I could use a little of it today."

It was the closest she'd come to saying anything personal about herself. And there was a tension to Mac, a focus. She appeared too uptight for a woman looking for a little distraction. He knew she was good at pretending, could put on her costumes and be someone else for awhile . . . but it was only an act. Eventually, the real Mac would emerge. He thought he was seeing a bit of her now, a woman who wanted the truth from someone, even if he was a stranger.

"I'd just signed the divorce papers Susan had sent," he said. "That's ex-wife number one, just to keep it straight."

"Sounds like pretty fast work."

"Actually, we'd been separated for two years. I think she was doing a stint in Alaska when the papers arrived. Finding herself in the beauty of the glaciers. I went to the local bar to get stinking drunk. You know, celebrate that my life was totally screwed. Pretty soon, I wasn't alone."

"Somehow, that doesn't surprise me."

"Yeah, I guess I was looking for trouble." He sipped from the beer bottle. "And she found me," he said, nodding at the photograph. "This lovely lady sits on the stool next to me and we're doing tequila shooters, talking about our mutual broken hearts. She, as it turns out, had been seeing a married man for seven years. Unfortunately, she's feeling her biological clock humming like a time bomb. She asks him to choose— her or his wife."

"And he picked the wife?"

"Hence, the night of tequila shooters at the local watering hole." He smiled, a little surprised that he would reveal so much. But perhaps it was calculated. *I show you mine; you show me yours.* "That's about the time I finally asked for her name. She looks at me and says, 'Hope.' " He shook his head. "Can you imagine? Hope."

"You believe in omens?"

"Under the influence of José Cuervo it was the green light from on high. One broken condom later, I'm going to be a daddy on a one-night stand. Now, I ask you. Can you beat those odds?"

"Maybe some things are meant to be," she said, perfectly serious.

"Well, you know, Mac. That's what I was thinking. So I married her and we had Michael."

She drank a sip of ginger ale. He tried not to watch her lips as she took an ice cube in her mouth, sucking on it, tried real hard not to get ideas.

She put down her glass. "Another damsel in distress," she

said, coming surprisingly close to voicing the Donovan Curse. "No wonder you're gun-shy around drunk women."

"Shy, yes. But I can be had."

She smiled at that. "I bet you're the kind of dad who changed diapers."

"And not those Nancy boy disposables, either. Hope insisted on the real thing: cloth diapers with Bio Bottoms, so his little tush could breathe." He took another drink. "I used to come home pretty late from work those days. Michael would be in his crib, waiting for his bottle. I did the night feedings so Hope could sleep a little. He would chug down that expressed breast milk as if there were nothing sweeter in the world. I even tried it once. See what the excitement was all about."

"And?"

He shrugged. "There wasn't a repeat performance." He turned the Corona in his hands, watching the condensation perspire down the bottle, remembering. "Them were the days."

"What happened?" Her voice was almost gentle. She sounded like someone who might be familiar with losing something you loved.

"Turns out, I'm just the motivation old Dickey Harper needs to leave his wife. He comes back, begging Hope to give him another chance, divorce papers in hand. Now I have Michael only on weekends."

"Didn't she love you?"

"Hope and I got together because of Michael. She was thirty-nine. She was pregnant, and she wanted to have the baby. So did I. And we loved him. As for me and Hope, we probably would have left it to the one night."

"His name isn't really Dickey, is it?" This, with a small smile.

"Oh, it's Dickey, all right. She calls him Dickey; he answers to Dickey. Even Michael calls him Dickey. Me, I was calling him something else for a few years there, until Michael became the human tape recorder."

She shook her head, then stared down at her glass. "I shouldn't have come back."

He hadn't expected that. Here he was, spilling his guts . . . thinking they were connecting . . . and the customer wants to leave the table. "Now what makes you say that?"

When she looked up, her eyes appeared blue again, making him wonder if they had ever been green at all. "Because you're sweet," she said, surprising him yet again. "The kind of man who would marry a one-night stand when she found out she was pregnant and believe they could make it work. Because I like that in a person. And because this isn't the time for me to like anyone."

"Not that I'm saying we should be an item, but you want to clear up that timing part?"

He could see it then, the concentration she'd used at the blackjack tables, an incredible focus that might belong to someone calculating odds.

"What am I doing?" She said it softly, speaking to herself.

He didn't say anything, waiting for her next move. He hated these kinds of puzzles, primarily because they intrigued him so much. *Solve the mystery, build the case.* With that elusive quality, Mac was taking them deeper down the very path she was trying to avoid. Ever since last night, she'd been sending her message loud and clear—she was alone . . . she was in trouble—making him want to know the story behind it.

"I have to leave," she said, standing.

She was almost to the door when he saw the article. He snatched it up, intercepting her. "You left this last night." As she took it from him, he said, "You know, I read it," he improvised. "I didn't understand everything," he said to cover for himself, since he hadn't really gotten around to reading a single word, "but it sounded interesting. Do you really believe all that stuff? About love potions, I mean?"

"You can say it's been my life's calling."

When she didn't clarify, he pushed it. "I don't think you're playing fair here, Mac. Truth or dare, remember? It's your turn."

She seemed to think it over. And then, "I'm hoping to develop a new product for a cosmetics firm. That was my interview today."

"Like a love potion?" He whistled. "Do you have the kinks worked out? I mean, does this stuff really work?" He leaned casually up against the doorjamb. "Kinda spooky for us guys. That somebody could spritz something on themselves and we'd be helpless not to respond." He kept thinking about all those degrees she had. Harvard. Caltech. "By the way, I like your perfume. Same stuff you wore last night, right?"

Her eyes lit up. That slow sweet smile eased across her mouth. "You're wondering if I'm wearing pheromones."

"Yeah," he said, crossing his arms, surprised that he might actually entertain the idea. But the chemistry between them was almost too good to be true. It made a guy wonder. "It's crossed my mind."

He could tell she was trying hard not to laugh. "Some scientists claim there are no such things as human pheromones."

"But not you."

"There's some very sophisticated research that shows adult humans have a full-functioning vomeronasal organ."

"No? Really? A vomeronasal organ," he repeated, nodding as if he knew what the hell that was. "And that would be located . . . ?"

She grinned. "In the nose, Boy Scout. The VNO is inside the nose. One in each nostril."

"Up the nose. I like it. It has that romantic ring to it."

He could tell she was enjoying herself. "In animals, the VNO receptors react to pheromones. A female gypsy moth can give off just a few molecules and attract a potential mate miles away. Some products on the market today have synthesized compounds that stimulate VNO receptors in humans. Pheromones."

"And what about you, Mac? What does your research show?"

"Oh, I'm going for something much more ambitious. I'm developing a product that mimics pheromones, but concentrates their effects."

"A super love potion?"

"Worried, Boy Scout?" she whispered, biting her bottom lip as she smiled. "Wondering if I have a secret weapon?" She eased closer, not quite touching him but making the idea almost palpable. "What if I told you that I was wearing it now?" She put her arms around his neck, this time leaning into him, making memories of the night before come zinging back into his brain. "That with my perfume, you don't have a chance of resisting me? You're completely under my control, you poor thing."

She eased his head down to hers and brushed her mouth across his, then licked his bottom lip provocatively. "That's right, Jake. It's futile to resist." Her mouth pressed against his as she whispered, "You're mine."

The kiss lasted a few seconds, or an eternity, he couldn't decide which. He just knew he was totally and completely screwed.

But just as he reached for her, she slipped past his arms and grabbed the doorknob. "You should know something about cosmetics, Jake," she said. "It's all about illusion."

Their eyes met. He stood there, completely speechless, not even making a move to stop her as she opened the door.

"I can't for the life of me figure out who's more dangerous to whom," she whispered.

"You're just going to walk away from this?" he asked, challenging her. "Exit, stage left?"

She lifted her chin in that way of hers, letting him know he couldn't take her lightly. And then, she told him, "Friday night, I'll be waiting in the hotel lobby. Eight o'clock. And I want to gamble. At the *River Palace*. Someone told me it's the best. I'm sure a man with your connections can work it out, despite my banishment." She stepped into the hall, giving him a sexy half smile. "Remember. You're under my complete control."

Jake stared at the door as it shut behind her, then glanced back at the article he still held in his hands. "Holy shit."

And then he grinned. A super love potion? Did he really believe all that crap?

"Jake Donovan," he said to himself. "You just made a royal ass of yourself."

And then he sat down and started reading.

Curtis Clarke dropped the black notebook onto his stainless steel and black teak desk, the cover spotlighted by the office's recessed lighting. To the right stood a twenty-inch linga balanced on a circular yoni base. The polished oblong rock came from the Narmada River in India, a symbolic phallus representing the god Siva the Destroyer. It was one of the few items the overpaid interior decorator had purchased that Curtis liked.

"What do you think our little girl is up to?" Curtis asked. He lit the Romeo y Julieta, a Cuban cigar he had smuggled in special from Canada.

Roger lounged in a crimson leather wing chair whose modern design practically encapsulated his head in the smooth curve of an eggshell. "Hell if I know." He grinned, showing perfect white teeth that had never needed braces or caps. "But it's going to be fun to find out."

"Just make sure you don't have as much fun as you did with that dead girl," Curtis warned.

Roger made a face. "I do miss Alicia. I loved her, you know. In my own way."

"You hush," Curtis told him. Sometimes, the boy gave him pause. Curtis was willing to do what was needed, but he had his suspicions that Roger enjoyed himself a little too much at the task.

Curtis pulled out a slip of paper from his pocket and tossed it to Roger. "Here's the number for the dog dealer. Make sure they're healthy this time. At five hundred dollars a pop, I can't afford to lose any."

"I'll call today."

"And for God's sake, be careful. All I need is those PETA bastards on my back."

Most of the products sold by Clarke Cosmetics were labeled HUMANITY FIRST—NO ANIMAL TESTING. Any work with animals was done in the high-security laboratory, away from prying eyes. Curtis didn't want to alert the activists at PETA, People for the Ethical Treatment of Animals; didn't need them picketing the lab and bringing the press.

Curtis nodded toward the notebook. "Why don't you use those fancy degrees of yours and have a look at that for me?"

Along with an MBA, Roger had earned a doctorate in developmental genetics. "I'll run a couple of programs. Hell, even if she came up with something half convincing, with a good campaign behind it . . . who knows?"

"No promises. No guarantees," Curtis said, grinning around the Cuban cigar. "Just a product made to enhance, help the wearer feel sexy. More confident."

"And no FDA approval required," Roger finished, echoing his father's smile. As long as the product wasn't marketed as a true aphrodisiac, a drug, it wouldn't be regulated by the government. "The Omega Principle," he said, trying out the name. "You know, that's not half bad."

"Donald won't touch it," Curtis said, referring to McCall's father, the head of Research and Development at Clarke Labs.

"No surprise there."

Both men laughed, knowing what was behind Donald Sayer's reluctance. But Sayer belonged to the Clarkes. He'd do what he was told.

"You give it a look-see, Roger."

"And McCall?"

"Hell, if she's going to cause trouble, isn't it better to keep her here? Under our nose, where we can watch her?"

"Maybe I should work with her on this," Roger said, glancing through the folder.

"Don't you be getting ideas, boy. McCall hates your guts. You're going to have to hang on to that skinny ballerina of yours, the one with the big tits and no brains." Seeing Roger's petulant frown, he added, "Never you mind. I'll put someone on it."

"And what if it's all smoke? What if she's here about Alicia?"

"Well." Curtis took the cigar out of his mouth. "It's not as if we haven't dealt with meddlesome women before, now, is it?"

McCall laughed until tears filled her eyes. "So I told him he shouldn't even try to resist. That he was under my complete control."

She was in the back room of Barb's shop, Do Your Own Thing. Situated in the heart of the French Quarter on Royal, the ceramic painting studio allowed patrons to pick out mugs, plates, and figurines and paint them. Barb would then fire the end product in her kiln. After hours, the back room served as Barb's studio.

Barbara Rojas sat behind a potter's wheel, digging her fingers into her newest creation as it spun before her, her black, gray-streaked hair dabbed with clay. The elegant vase appeared to grow upward, out from her fingertips.

"This is the one," Barb said, pushing back her long braid. "Finally, you're going to fall in love." When McCall stuck her tongue out at her, she added, "Look at you." Barb slowly brought the wheel to a halt. "You're glowing. This man has you glowing."

McCall sighed. "Maybe," she said, giving in that much.

She smiled, remembering. "You should see him, Barb. He's huge. Tall, with lean muscles. And he has these hands," she said, holding out her own. "They're twice the size of mine. But you just know he wouldn't hurt a fly, not with those dimples. Those eyes. And he's funny."

She started laughing again, picturing his face when she'd given him that kiss and told him he was under her control. She'd never done anything like that before. "He actually thought I was using pheromones on him."

"Maybe you were. You just didn't know it. Natural pheromones. Not the synthesized, genetically engineered kind. Ever thought of that, Dr. Sayer? In Spanish we say, *'Encontrastes la otra mita de la naranja.'* You found the other half of the orange."

"You're a hopeless romantic."

"And maybe that's part of your problem. You try so hard to crush that inside yourself. You have passion, McCall. *Pasión.* Don't try to deny it so much."

McCall glanced away, pretending to examine the ceramics lining the shelf. Barb, the Latin artist, had passion. But sometimes McCall believed she'd spent too many years concentrating on strands of DNA to claim that emotion now.

She dropped down into a stool and turned a small vase glazed in blues with her fingertips. Passion. Was that what this was about? The sense she had every time she was near Jake that she wanted to lose control? Break the rules and see where it would lead? "I didn't even sleep with him."

"And when you see him Friday?"

"I don't know," she said honestly, knowing it would be difficult not to. That first night, he'd broken through years of reserve. She'd thought it had been the champagne . . . her loneliness after her mother's funeral. But now she wondered if it would have been any different if he'd approached her the week before, when she'd been stone-cold sober and concentrating on the cards.

She shook her head. "I've done so many crazy things these

last couple of years, worn so many disguises. What if I'm beginning to believe I can be that woman, the one at the black-jack tables and on the infomercials." She frowned. "I'm not really that woman."

Barb stood up and wiped her hands on a towel. She put her hands on McCall's shoulders. "I'm worried about you."

They were talking about something else now, no longer teasing about the possibility of love.

"I know what I'm doing with Curtis," McCall told her.

"A man you believe ruined your reputation, turned your father against you, and possibly killed your partner?"

"It was ruled an accident."

"But you never believed that!"

McCall stood, walking past Barb. "I've put the past behind me, Barb. I told you that when you offered me the spare room. I'm here only to make a connection with my family. Why is that so difficult to believe?"

They'd had the same argument many times. McCall had known Barbara Rojas since their university days at Harvard, where Barb had been the teaching assistant in a contemporary art class McCall had taken. They were both from New Orleans; it was natural they'd become friends. But McCall had always wondered if it hadn't been Barb's maternal feelings that had brought them together, motivating her to take pity on McCall, a socially awkward girl five years younger than her other classmates.

Over the years, McCall had been the maid of honor at Barb's wedding, the godmother to her children, the twins, Dylan and Maria. Barb and her husband, Stan, had been there for McCall when the bottom had fallen out of her career and her father had disowned her.

"I should move out," McCall said.

"Don't you dare. I would be worried sick about you."

Barb, always with her feelings. She claimed she was in touch with the spirit of her ancestors. The artist, Barb. The astrologer, Barb.

"Please, Barb. Don't push me." *Don't make me tell you the truth.*

Barb held up her hands. "I'll believe whatever you want. I always do, don't I? But let me worry just a little."

"Then worry about whether I'm going to make an idiot of myself with the only man I've found interesting in too many years."

"You'll do fine," she said, hugging McCall.

McCall sighed, holding her dearest friend, a woman whose plain face might be considered unattractive if it weren't for her lovely brown eyes and giving nature. A woman who didn't bother to camouflage the twenty extra pounds she'd gained with the twins, but favored clothes because of their colors and texture. Barbara was the most honest person she knew, as well as a generous spirit.

"Remember how Stan and I met?"

"Across a crowded room," McCall said, knowing the story by heart.

"Let yourself feel that, McCall," Barb said, stepping back to look at her. "It's something very special."

"You make it sound so simple. Just the natural course of things. It must be wonderful to believe that love is inevitable."

"What a cynic you've become. Listen. Just because you're a late bloomer doesn't mean you missed your time to blossom."

But McCall wasn't so sure. She thought about her baby sister, how she'd looked, sitting there drunk next to Roger Clarke. Perhaps those magical emotions Barb hinted at could never belong to the Sayer women.

"I'm not here to blossom with love, Barb," McCall said, feeling cynical. Love was a luxury she couldn't afford right now. She had four days until she was to meet Jake at the *River Palace.* By then, Curtis could have accepted her offer, forcing her to begin their game of cat and mouse.

Five

He believes the problem is with the rats. It's not a system close enough to our own; that we will get better results with the monkeys. But I wonder. Will the outcome be a breakthrough or a death sentence for these animals?
                    —Excerpt from Dr. Alicia Goodman's lab book

"Heads up. This one's going long."

Jake watched Michael jog backward for the Nerf football, then trip. He waited as his son clambered to his feet, then ran back a couple of steps, his little denim-clad legs pumping beneath him.

Releasing a gentle throw high up into the air, Jake shouted, "Atta boy," encouraging Michael. His heart filled with pride as his son waited, arms outstretched, concentrating on the spiraling ball as it arced toward him. The sun made his hair look more blond than red. He was big for a four-year-old. Tall, like Jake.

The ball bounced into Michael's arms, teetered. Almost too late, he curled his arms around the ball, cradling it against his chest, bringing it home. Michael stared down at the ball as if he couldn't quite believe it was just sitting there. His mouth dropped open. He looked up at his dad.

"Yes," Jake whispered under his breath.

"I got it. I got it!" His first catch.

"Give that boy the Heisman!" Jake shouted, his fist shooting into the air.

Both son and father let out a war whoop and did a victory dance á la Deion Sanders. Jake scooped up his son, throwing him over his shoulder, giving him rib ticklers until Michael begged for mercy. Jake pretended to stumble, then wrestled with Michael in the grass. Later, they both lay on their backs, watching the clouds as they floated over Jackson Square, giving names to their shapes.

These were the moments Jake lived for. Hope had an appointment and had asked him to baby-sit, knowing he wouldn't need to be at work until later that night. It couldn't have been better timing. An afternoon with his son—just what the doctor ordered. It was already Thursday, and he hadn't decided what to do about tomorrow night and Mac.

He'd given Dino the rundown. The Greek had summed it up just about as Jake had expected.

"I don't like it." Dino had shaken his head, looking at Jake as if he were already pheromone roadkill. "She's using you, Irishman. If you bring her here, to the *River Palace*—a card counter—and Garrett gets wind of it, he'll have your ass. I know the guy thinks he owes you, but hell. The way she plays, she could really do some damage."

Damn straight, Jake thought.

"Mom's late."

Jake looked over at Michael lying on the grass beside him. In the background, he could hear a pipe organ playing, most likely from the *Natchez* paddle wheeler. The sound was an odd counterpoint to a trumpet soloist playing for coins across the street at Café du Monde, an outdoor café great for beignets and people watching. He smiled, ruffling his son's strawberry curls. "You hungry? We could get a Lucky Dog or something?"

"Nah. If she comes back and we're not here, she'll worry."

It was the kind of thing Michael would say. Sometimes, it worried Jake that his son was so mature for his age. Too adult-like. Hope thought it was because he was an only child. She was desperate to get pregnant again. Hence, today's appointment.

"Dad. I don't want to play the violin anymore."

Jake bit down on a blade of grass, thinking his answer over carefully. He'd heard it before. Hope had enrolled Michael in a Suzuki violin class the day he'd turned three. She'd read somewhere that children exposed to music before the age of four were significantly better at math. Michael wasn't exactly enthusiastic.

The problem was, he was good at the violin. A star student. But then, Michael was good at a lot of things.

"Is there something else you'd rather play?" Jake asked.

Michael's brow furrowed. He jammed a piece of grass in his mouth and stacked his hands behind his head, imitating Jake. "Banjo."

And wouldn't Hope just love that, Jake thought, knowing she would nix the idea. "How about if I buy you one? You can play it when you stay with me on weekends, or take it with you to your mom's, if you want. No lessons or anything," he added, believing that Michael already had too much of that crap cluttering his life. "Just mess around with it? Hey, remember the fiddler at the bluegrass concert? How would you like to play like him someday?"

Michael's eyes lit up. "Yeah!"

"I bet he started with the Suzuki method."

Michael rolled on his side, trying to figure out if Jake was serious. "You think so?"

"Well, something like it. You always learn the classical stuff first. It makes you a better artist, teaches you technique."

"Okay," Michael said, nodding, suddenly seeing a better angle to the violin lessons. "Hey, there's Mom!"

Jake recognized her right away. The other mere mortals that crowded the grounds appeared to step aside for her, a parting sea to her haute-couture Moses. Hope stood out. And not only because she wore a suit in the humid June heat without breaking into a sweat. She had this way of walking, a sort of march, as if she were always in a hurry to get somewhere. With her brown hair styled short and her blue power suit, she reminded Jake of her days as an accountant at a top-notch firm in town. Hope had specialized in audits.

He stood and grabbed the football. He dumped it in his duffel bag and squinted across the square at Hope. She looked pretty upset, even at this distance.

He dug a bunch of quarters out of his pocket. Crouching down in front of Michael, he put himself at eye level to his son and placed the money in Michael's palm.

"Why don't you get an ice cream?" He nodded toward the stand in front of the St. Louis Cathedral. Just outside the wrought iron gates, the ice cream vendor was only a few feet away. There was a line of kids waiting. "I want to talk to your mom about something." Hope looked like she needed some time to calm down before she took Michael home to the house-that-Dickey's-money-built, a renovated Creole town house on St. Ann. "And don't run with the ice cream stick in your mouth," Jake shouted when Michael took off, "or your mom will kill me."

Jake stood, waiting for Hope, keeping his eye on Michael as he took his place in line. Hope could be overprotective, but she was usually right about keeping Michael out of harm's way. But the way she looked now, he wondered if she would even notice Michael with his ice cream.

She came to a halt in front of Jake and ripped off her sunglasses. She was barely five feet, and peered up at him, looking for all the world as if she might burst into tears at any moment. He could see she'd been crying.

"Sorry I'm late," she said, turning to wave to Michael. "I was walking around a bit . . . thinking."

"I told him he could get an ice cream." They started walking toward the lamp-topped gates and the cathedral beyond, catching up with Michael. "We could sit down for a bit. Let him enjoy his ice cream."

"Thanks," she said, surprising him. No you'll-spoil-his-dinner or rot-his-teeth remarks? He figured whatever was wrong, it was serious.

Outside the gates that enclosed the square, Jake showed Michael where he and Hope were going to sit a few feet away. Walking past the gauntlet of tarot card readers and palmists who, along with street artists and mimes, lined the pedestrian walkways here, Jake picked a bench across from the Presbytère not far from Michael's ice cream cart. Just ahead, he could see enormous white trailers jamming the narrow street. Another movie filming.

"You want to talk about it?" Jake asked.

It took her a while to get composed, as if she were trying really hard to keep it together. "I am not pregnant. And in the good doctor's estimation, I will never be pregnant. Not again."

"I'm sorry to hear that, Hope." The last two years, Hope and Dickey had done everything humanly possible to conceive. Dickey, already the father of five girls, had undergone surgery to reverse his vasectomy. Hope, too, had gone through a few procedures. "I'm really sorry."

"Are you?" She was watching Michael reach up to get his ice cream from the vendor. She smiled. "Are you certain there's not a little part of you that's secretly happy. That bitch," she said, as if she were voicing his opinion of her. "She deserves this."

Jake had never made any bones about the fact that he thought Hope had used him to get old Dickey back. It wasn't so much that she'd left Jake that had set the sour note in their relationship. It was all those nights Jake had come home early from work at her request, thinking of how his first marriage had fallen apart because of his job, vowing he would struggle to make a go of this unconventional marriage. For Michael's sake. Things had been different for him and Susan; there hadn't been children to think about in their decision to dissolve their marriage vows.

And all those evenings he'd watched Michael, giving Hope the opportunity to get out and supposedly see a movie or go shopping, to make up for a day cooped inside with a baby, she'd been secretly meeting Dickey, seeing her attorney, plotting on how to get custody—in case Jake should fight her over Michael.

"Forgive me. That was a stupid thing to say," she said, touching his arm lightly. "I really can be a bitch."

She lay her head on his shoulder, which made Jake nervous. Hope wasn't exactly the cuddly type.

"No babies," she whispered, sounding incredibly vulnerable.

He did feel sorry for her. He remembered how much she'd loved getting round with Michael, never regretting a pound or carping about swollen ankles. Even though she could ease up a little on all the rules and the classes, she was a good mother, reading the baby books . . . concentrating on giving Michael the self-esteem she claimed her parents had stolen from her.

She looked up at Jake, her eyes brimming with tears. "I keep thinking how easy it was for us," she said almost tenderly. "Just a bottle of tequila and a broken condom."

That's when he figured what she wanted. She'd already asked him once. "Forget it, Hope."

She sat up straight and grabbed her sunglasses. She shoved them back on her face, switching off the charm as suddenly as she had turned it on. Hope, the great impersonator of human emotion.

She sniffed. "Is it really so much to ask?"

He banged his fist on the bench. "You know, you are a piece of work. How do you think I felt when you took Michael out of my life? I went to every fucking ultrasound; I cut the cord when he was born, for Christ's sake. And every night I watched him, you and Dickhead were plotting on how to take him away from me."

"How was I to trust you? I hardly knew you when we

married. I thought you would be angry, that you might use Michael against me."

"Because that's what you would do?"

Her mouth snapped shut. "Look, you did the right thing insisting that we see that child psychologist. Joint custody was best for Michael. Things are different now. As it is, I wish you would spend more time with him. You have so much more energy than Dickey," she said, referring to the fact that Jake was a good decade and a half younger than Dickhead. "Though he does try to keep up with Michael. It was your choice to have him only on weekends. He could spend a few holidays with you, if you wanted. The summer even."

"Long days in a hotel room with a baby-sitter." He shook his head, the argument old ground. "As long as you're not working, he's better off with you."

That was the one thing he had to give Hope. She was a dedicated mother, as if—by waiting this long to have a child— she had worked out any ambitions or needs she had for herself. She was completely focused on Michael.

"You're denying him a sibling," she argued. "And why shouldn't we have another child together? Michael has three doting parents. The best of all worlds."

"God, Hope." He stood, signaling Michael to hurry over. "You can fucking adopt, if you think it's so important that he have a brother or a sister. Personally, I think he's doing just fine."

She grabbed his hand. "All right, all right. I'm despicable. But I'm desperate. Can't you think about it, at least?"

"Hope," he said, speaking slowly, carefully, so she wouldn't miss a word or a nuance. "You made my life a living hell for an entire year. You made me believe you would take my son away from me," he said, reminding her of the threats she'd made to cut him off completely if he challenged her for custody. "As long as there is breath in my body I will never fuck you again."

"Forget it," she said. "I was just deluding myself anyway.

Dr. Stella assures me it won't work." She wiped away the last of her tears impatiently. "Don't tell Dickey I asked you. He was dead against it."

"Imagine that." Dickey Harper was a tax attorney, a rich and powerful man in New Orleans, which Jake had always suspected had been a big part of the draw for Hope.

"Let's go, Michael, honey," she called out, standing. "Don't let him see you're mad at me. He's very sensitive."

He refrained from making any comment.

"He really should have brothers and sisters," Hope said doggedly. "You might think of getting married yourself and giving him one. You're a damn good father."

With that said, Hope walked away, taking Michael's hand when he raced up to her. Once she had him in tow, they both waved goodbye. They lived just a few blocks away, well within walking distance. Michael glanced over his shoulder at Jake and mouthed the word "banjo." Jake gave him a thumbs-up.

He told himself to forget it, that Hope and her little digs weren't worth the aggravation. But the damage was done. *Damn you, Hope.* She always made things more painful with her hidden agendas and manipulating personality. And she always knew how to get to him.

Standing in the middle of Chartres Street, watching his exwife hustle his son down the sidewalk, Jake felt empty and incredibly alone.

He thought it was damn well time he did something about that.

"Stupid mutt."

Sierra didn't even bother to look up as the woman tossed down a bowl full of dog food. From the woman's tone, the golden retriever recognized the woman didn't like her.

"You're a fancy dog, aren't you, dear." The woman stepped closer to Sierra. Very early that morning, a man had brought the retriever to this house. The yard was full of long skinny cages. It was nothing like the place where Sierra lived, a big yard where she could chase balls and bury bones. The cage where they put Sierra was dirty and smelled of animal feces.

The woman was smoking a cigarette. She was fat and stank of sweat. Megan, the little girl who took care of Sierra, always smelled like milk and dog biscuits, and the scraps she sneaked Sierra under the dinner table. Dropping the cigarette on the concrete directly in front of the dog's nose, the woman stomped it out. She was wearing sandals and nudged Sierra with her toe. The dog wasn't used to such ill treatment. She whined softly.

"Don't you worry, sugar. Fancy dogs don't last long here," the woman said. "They're the first to go." She walked toward the door, kicking the food bowl so that it clattered across the concrete, spilling food. "Stupid mutt, you better eat. Goddamn dog. Can't afford to lose another one."

She left the cage, shutting the door behind her. Sierra glanced at the food, but the dog didn't get up to eat.

In the cage next to hers, the black German shepherd lay on the concrete, panting from the heat. The retriever crept toward the wire fencing that separated the two animals. She put her nose to the mesh, whining softly.

For a little while, the German shepherd stayed where he was. The dogs sensed they were in a very bad place. A place that smelled of death.

Slowly, the shepherd crawled to the side of the cage where Sierra waited. The dog pressed his nose through the wire mesh. Sierra began to lick his muzzle gently.

Jake stepped into the office to find Stacie Winn nestled on Garrett Renault's lap, the top two buttons of her dealer's shirt opened and Garrett working on the third.

"Sorry," Jake said, doing an about-face to walk out of the office.

"You haul your sweet bottom in here, Jake," he heard Stacie's Georgia Peach voice call to him. "I was just leaving."

Jake turned slowly, giving them time to wrap it up. At the moment, the two were still lip-locked. "It's no problem to come back later."

Stacie wiggled off Garrett's lap, only to have her employer and lover of four years corral her back with his arm around her waist. She slapped his hands away, flashing her talon-length nails, her trademark as a blackjack dealer. Today, she'd painted them gold.

"Shame on you, Garrett. You'll embarrass Jake. Besides. You know I need to get to the tables."

"I have it on good authority you can talk your boss into giving you the day off," Garrett said, nuzzling her neck as he winked at Jake.

She laughed. At thirty years of age, Garrett Renault was the *River Palace*'s maverick owner. Along with his grandfather, a silent partner, he had a controlling interest in the casino and hotel, both run by a privately held corporation. He was incredibly young for his accomplishments, and a good seven years Stacie's junior, though you wouldn't know it by looking at them. With long sexy black hair and green eyes, Stacie was pretty much Playmate of the Year material—which Jake figured was the initial draw for Garrett, a guy who didn't over think these things. Still, over the years, Jake could see it had gotten serious between them.

"Leave work on such short notice?" Stacie asked. "Not a chance. And Dino will kill me if I'm late again. You think you're the only man in my life, Garrett Renault?"

"I sure as hell better be."

Stacie kissed Garrett full on the mouth. "I have to go." She sashayed past Jake, giving him her Miss America smile and wiggling her fingers goodbye at Garrett from the door.

Before she walked out, Garrett glanced down. "Stacie." He picked up a slick folder off his desk. All Jake saw was the logo: A highly stylized depiction, it used only a few lines to suggest a woman kneeling naked, her hair covered with flowers. The vining roses appeared to flow down to pool into her cupped hands.

Stacie hesitated before coming back to take the folder. "Garrett, sugar. I'm not sure about this."

"Just look it over," Garrett said, sounding impatient. He shook his head as if Stacie had said something stupid. "I'll see you tonight."

Stacie stared at the folder as if she were going to argue with him, but Garrett was already concentrating on the papers littering his desk, dismissing her. She glanced at Jake, who did his damnedest to keep his mouth shut. Sometimes, Garrett could be a real asshole to Stacie. But as long as she was willing to take it, it wasn't going to help anybody for Jake to butt in.

"Have a seat," Garrett said to Jake, pointing to the chair in front of his desk without looking up from his papers. While Jake's office was in the hold of the riverboat casino, Garrett's was located at the Casino Executive Offices on the first floor of the hotel. When the door shut behind Stacie, Garrett pushed aside the paperwork and dropped his Mont Blanc pen. "She's going to blow a great opportunity."

Again, Jake refrained from comment. Though generally a good person, Garrett could be a hothead. Sometimes it was better to let him talk it out.

Garrett leaned back in his chair, giving Jake his crooked Eric Roberts's grin. He even looked a little like the actor, with his curly brown hair worn long in the back. Blue eyes—broken nose. "I have an old school friend whose father owns a top-notch cosmetic firm," Garrett said. "He's letting us in on a clinic they're setting up for a cutting edge beauty product. Says it will make alpha-hydroxy and DHEA seem like the Stone Age. I thought Stacie might want to sign up, but she's dragging her feet." He shook his head, looking at Jake as if to say, *What can you do?*

Jake took a moment to think about the message Garrett

was sending Stacie—a woman seven years his senior—by pushing her to use some sort of wrinkle cream or youth serum.

"Why don't you have a talk with Broomhilda outside?" Jake asked, dropping into the chair in front of Garrett's desk, coming to the dealer's defense from a different angle. "That's the second time she's waved me in when Stacie was here."

"My protector?" That's what Garrett called the blue-haired lady who served as his secretary. "She thinks I shouldn't be fooling around with the hired help."

"And here I thought Stacie was too good for you." But Jake was careful to say it with a smile.

"Tell me something I don't know," Garrett answered, for once seeing something clearly about his personal life. He nodded. "I'll talk to her." He picked up his pen and started tapping it against the desk. "So what can I do for you?"

Jake had never before asked anything from his employer. He had no idea how Garrett, a man who suspected people wanted to use him for his money, would handle his request. But he figured he'd built up a little goodwill. Years ago, Garrett had gotten into trouble with the law for drug possession. His family's influence had earned him a berth in a program for troubled youths instead of jail. Jake had been a volunteer counselor at the time.

During the weeks it took Garrett to sober up to what a waste he was making of his life, Jake had worked with him, letting him know he could turn things around. He'd even called in Garrett's grandfather when his parents had washed their hands of their son. Luckily for Garrett, his grandfather had been willing to step in, really caring about his grandson.

And to give Garrett credit, he had gotten his act together, though Jake had always suspected teaming up with his grandfather to buy the casino and hotel was his way of telling his society parents "Up yours." After he'd opened the *River Palace*, he made it a habit to call Jake at the Office of the Attorney General in Baton Rouge every six months to offer him a job. It must have shocked the shit out of him when Jake finally took him up on it.

"There's this woman," Jake said. "She has a system. A sure-fire one. She's a counter," he said, referring to the fact that she counted cards to beat the odds. "I want you to let her play tomorrow. Anything she wins, you can take out of my salary. But I want Stacie to deal."

"Holy Lord," Garrett said smiling, enjoying it. "Dino's right. Hey now, when you fall for a woman," he said slipping into a more pronounced accent, "you fall badly, man. How much are you going to let her take you for?"

"I guess I have more faith in Stacie than you do."

Garrett's smile tensed, getting Jake's double meaning. Not one to let a person get the best of him, he asked, "What about Bart?" Bart was the dealer whose table had been doing so poorly the last month. Jake had made a pitch to allow the recovering alcoholic time to make good. "Am I going to take his losses out of your paycheck, too?"

Jake did some quick calculations. It didn't look good. "If that's what it takes."

Garrett kept tapping the Mont Blanc on the table, watching Jake. "What the hell," he said, breaking first. "It's only my money. I'll give Bart until the end of the month, but the lady's playing with your dime tomorrow night. Stacie will deal. She's crazy about you."

"Thanks," Jake said, standing. "I owe you."

"No, Jake," Garrett said, perfectly serious. "You don't."

Jake nodded, reading between the lines. Garrett would always remember those days when Jake had been the only one who believed in him.

Outside, Jake whistled softly to himself. He figured this is what he'd needed all along, to make a decision about Mac, a woman who liked games. Well, hell. He was pretty good at a few himself.

He gave Garrett's secretary a salute as he passed her desk. "Have a nice day, Attila."

He was already planning tomorrow night.

Six

When McCall was five years old, her father taught her magic.

"This is what we are made of, McCall." Standing behind her in his laboratory, he'd guided her latex-gloved hand holding the glass rod, turning, turning. There was always an incredible excitement to those experiments with her father, making the moments special. To her mind, she'd been holding a fairy wand, stirring the glass rod in a clear liquid—a magical potion that made her nose smart with the odor of alcohol. Like cotton candy wrapping itself around a paper cone, a nearly invisible presence had curled around the rod, thickening it to the size of her finger, reminding McCall of liquid spiderwebs as she continued spooling the DNA.

"This is what gives us life," he'd told her, stepping back, leaving her to stir the rod in the ethanol-spiked liquid. "Without this, we couldn't exist. If we could only learn its secrets, McCall," he said in a Pied Piper voice. "Imagine. We could banish all illness, cure any deformity . . . perhaps live forever."

In those days, Donald Sayer welcomed his daughter into his lab, setting up step stools so she could reach the lab's bench-top tables, granting her entry into a world normally not open to a child. He was never too distracted, never too tired to teach her. She felt, in fact, that she was his whole focus. Because she was smart. She was so very smart. Her father treated her as an equal, as if nothing were beyond her intellect. And every lesson gave her a sense of power . . . a purpose.

Sometimes, she thought he'd done his job too well, grooming her arrogance, nurturing an ability to cut off emotions and focus on only results. But there was no denying he had taught her wonderful things. Donald Sayer had shown his daughter the essence of life.

McCall rubbed her eyes and stared down at the lab book cradled in her lap. DEPARTMENT OF BIOLOGY was printed across the top. Sitting cross-legged on the bed in Barb's spare room, McCall hugged the old terrycloth robe around herself. She opened the book.

Page after page, she watched Alicia's scribblings grow smaller, more slanted. She could almost visualize the frenetic energy Alicia must have felt as she wrote the words. She'd been thinking about her father because of the book. Donald Sayer never liked Alicia, a woman who'd taught McCall disdain for his work as a biochemist at Clarke Labs, encouraging her to break away, rebel, and follow that spark he'd ignited the first time he'd let McCall spool DNA, only in a direction different than he'd intended.

Dr. Alicia Goodman, her partner. Now dead.

McCall turned to the next page, realizing she still missed her. Alicia had been her friend, a woman who, like Barb, had changed McCall . . . for the better, she thought. McCall often read the lab book Alicia had used as a diary, believing that one day she would scan these passages, go over the shorthand only Alicia could decipher, and finally understand.

To that end, she read the book over and over, never tiring, even swiveling the book on its side to make out the scribblings in the margins she'd already memorized. Alicia had written more and more of these toward the end, the words always circling the perimeter of the page like predators, as if these little notes to herself were unconnected to the main body of the text and must be written apart from the rest. There was a theme to these scribbles. *Beauty is vain . . . All beauty comes from beautiful blood . . . Be beautiful and be sad . . .*

Beauty. Cosmetics. Clarke Labs. It was an easy connection to make.

The questions would start then. Was Roger Clarke the man Alicia refused to name? Her Dr. Frankenstein? Were the strange experiments Alicia wrote about still taking place? And if so, had they continued at Clarke Labs, maybe even now putting McCall's father and her sister at risk?

"You miss it, don't you?"

McCall turned around, startled from her thoughts. Barb stood at the door.

"I knocked. You were in La-La Land." Barb nodded toward the lab book. "Do you think you'll ever go back to it?"

Barb had seen McCall poring over enough lab books that she wouldn't know this book was special. Just the same, McCall closed it and set it aside. "I don't know. If I could even get a job in genetics, which is doubtful, I'm not sure I have the confidence I had in those days."

"It seems such a crime. You had so much to give."

"Does that mean you don't believe the Omega Principle is worthy of me?" she asked with a small smile.

Barbara Rojas had brown eyes that could look straight through to your soul, reading it like the headlines of Sunday's paper. "I don't know what you're up to, McCall, but I sincerely doubt you're peddling just a love potion." In her no-nonsense style, Barb pushed back her braid, the gesture conveying impatience. She held out a set of keys. "Stan says to use the car tonight. If things go well, we won't expect you back until morning." She cocked her head to one side. "Why don't you ask the Boy Scout his birth date? I could do a star chart on the two of you."

Before McCall could think up a suitable remark, the sounds of the twins going AWOL downstairs blasted into the room with the force of an air raid siren. Barb threw up her hands, exasperated. She dropped the keys on the vanity and made for the door. "I'm too old for this. Coming!"

McCall put the book back in its hiding place, then sat at the vanity, her stomach doing flips worthy of an Olympic medal as she stared at the car keys. She could see the Boy Scout clearly in her mind. Over the past days, she'd made a study of him, analyzing the color of his hair to decide if the strawberry waves were more blond than red, trying to remember if he had freckles on his nose like his son. She'd memorized the angles of his face, the special resonance of his voice, recalled the lingering presence of his touch . . . and she realized that a very important part of her was happy not to have heard from Curtis about the Omega Principle. It left her one more night to pretend her life could be normal. That she could meet a stranger across a crowded room and fall in love, just as Barb and Stan had.

She stared in the mirror, seeing herself devoid of makeup. Her eyes were her father's, curiously changeable with mood and light. Her hair was her mother's, a dark auburn that defied easy description. She picked up the eye shadow she would wear, leaning closer to the mirror.

Be beautiful and be sad. The words echoed singsong in her head. It was Baudelaire; she'd looked it up. Three years after first reading it, McCall still didn't know what it meant for Alicia.

Jake tapped his fingers against the edge of the table, mentally counting the chips stacked in front of Mac. She'd started with two hundred, betting hundred-dollar chips two or three at a time. Now, she was almost at three thousand.

He remembered his promise to Garrett. It was going to be an expensive date.

He watched Stacie deal each player their cards, the jewelry she wore flashing under the lights. She had a ring on every finger, even her thumb . . . two on some fingers. He glanced at Mac beside him as Stacie dealt her an ace. He had this really bad feeling when the next card came up with a face. It was her third snapper this shoe.

"Twenty-one," Stacie announced.

When the hand finished, Stacie deftly counted out Mac's winnings and popped the cards into the discard rack. He thought of asking Stacie to burn the deck, something he'd normally do if he were on shift. A shift manager couldn't let a table dump money. When a table was dumping, the dealer would burn the deck, taking the top card from the shoe and ditching it in the discard rack. Maybe it was superstition, but sometimes a dealer could change the table that way.

"Why, thank you, sugar," Stacie said when Mac slipped her two twenty-five-dollar chips as a tip. Stacie winked at Jake, knowing full well the money was his.

"Criminey," a woman at the far end of the table whispered, looking at Mac with awe. She peered at the shoe holding the remaining cards with longing.

Jake took a drink of his vodka on the rocks, glancing up as Stacie dealt him a meager hand of twelve. Stacie was show-ing an eight as her "up" card, and he was casually wondering what she had in the hole. Again, Stacie winked. She mouthed, "Thanks," and glanced at her shirt pocket, now bulging with chips. Mac had been generous.

"Better watch it, Stacie," he said, giving her a look. "She's making you look bad. You're going to have Tony looking over your shoulder if she keeps this up," he said, referring to the floor person. On a ship like the *River Palace*, the pit boss was called the floor person.

"You just keep on winning, precious," Stacie drawled, giv-ing Mac a wink as she jingled the chips in her shirt pocket. "That mean old Tony doesn't scare me one bit. And neither do you, Jake, honey."

Jake took another drink of his vodka. He repeated to him-self what he'd been saying all night. *It's only money.*

But it was eerie to see Mac play. She wasn't like any other

professional he'd known. She hadn't asked to play at the two-deck table, but allowed him to steer her to one running four decks. Most "counters" liked to keep the number of players down to three. Jake had purposefully set her up with a table where all five stools had butts plastered to the vinyl. Two of the players were drunk, tourists playing casually, not even following the basics. The other guy was a flea, a regular known for small bets and no tipping.

Bad players could be deadly to a professional. They changed everything, breaking your concentration. But even that hadn't fazed Mac. She'd been winning steadily.

Jake busted, his card count going over twenty-one, and waited for the others to play out the hand. The way Mac was working it, her game went way beyond counting or any system she might devise.

The woman was hot.

He glanced down at her legs, bare of hose and exposed to midthigh by a little black number she could have purchased at Dupont. Jake, too, had dressed up for the evening, wearing his good jeans. But Mac, she'd outdone herself with the dress. And she had on these patent leather, high-heeled sandals, with straps that crisscrossed over her foot in a sexy pattern. She'd painted her toenails a sort of black-red.

"Vixen," she said, extending her hand so he could see she wore the same color on her nails. Unlike Stacie, Mac had really short fingernails, the polish, he suspected, hiding the fact that she bit them.

"It matches my lipstick color," she said, puckering her lips as if to blow a kiss.

He stared at her mouth, her lips, looking so soft and lush, then raised his eyes to take in the rest of her. Tonight, her eyes appeared a luminous blue-green under the casino lights, with large dark pupils.

He thought it was crazy that he could just sit here, happy to watch her win his money, actually contemplating that the gig might be worth the couple of thousand it was going to cost him.

"Vixen," he said, still staring at her mouth, forgetting caution and wishing they could go somewhere more private. "Who comes up with that shit?"

"Some very highly paid marketeer." She took out the lime she'd requested in her ginger ale and sucked on the slice, then popped it back into the plastic cup. She jammed it down beneath the ice with her stir stick. "It's all in the packaging, you know."

And didn't she have some dynamite packaging tonight, he thought. The clingy black dress left little to the imagination; the bare legs and sexy sandals completed the picture of sophisticated vamp. She wore her hair long and straight, curled slightly at the bottom so that it framed her face, showing off simple diamond stud earrings.

"What are you going to call your love potion, Mac?" he asked, tossing a twenty-five-dollar chip to replace the bet he'd just lost, letting Stacie know to deal him in despite the fact that he wasn't giving the game his full attention.

"I was thinking 'the Omega Principle.' I want to make it appealing to both sexes."

He made a rude noise. "Men aren't going to fall for that stuff."

She doubled down on her hand, an eight and a three, adding another two hundred to her bet. "Stone, Rock Hard, LoveStone," she said, mentioning one of many fads in aphrodisiacs. "FDA banned, some even deadly. There's been several deaths associated with men using dried toad secretions, and it still sells."

She leaned closer to him, picking up her glass of ginger ale to take a slow, languorous sip. "You think men aren't interested in sex, Jake?" She licked her lips. Making a show of it.

He wondered why she did that, changed her identity with her clothes. Tonight, she was the man-trap, flirting outrageously. "You asking for trouble?"

She smiled, putting down the glass. "I thought you and I decided we liked games."

Incredibly, she slid most of her winnings into the betting circle. There was almost two thousand dollars piled there.

All eyes on the table riveted on Mac. She had this strange smile as she kept her gaze steady on Jake. He knew she didn't have eyes in the back of her head. She couldn't possibly see her cards staring at him like that.

"Hit me," she told Stacie when her turn came, scratching the table lightly to let the dealer know she wanted another card.

Mac was showing fifteen. Stacie's up card was an eight. The dealer turned over the two of diamonds to give Mac seventeen.

Jake could feel his heart pumping hard in his chest. What she was doing, it was crazy, betting like that. And still, it was exhilarating. A roller coaster. And he was riding it right along with her.

"Again," she said.

Everyone at the table held their breath. Stacie turned over another two. There was an audible gasp from the woman down the table.

"I'll stand," Mac said, making a sharp slicing motion with her hand to show she didn't want any more cards. "I believe it's your turn," she told Jake.

"If I didn't know better," he said, liking the game they were playing, the adrenaline rush of it. "I'd swear there was something stronger than ginger ale in that glass."

But damn if he wasn't enjoying it as much as Mac. He'd never gambled more than fifty bucks on a hand. He just figured it wasn't his thing. But now, his heart was galloping in his chest as he thought about getting back his two thousand . . . or having twice that come out of his pocket if she won.

Stacie played out the hand, dealing everyone at the table something better than seventeen. She flipped over her card, showing thirteen. She dealt herself the next card, an eight. Twenty-one.

"Sorry," Stacie said over the groans of the players. "House wins."

Mac only shrugged, going back to jabbing the stir stick in the ice. "Easy come. Easy go."

He couldn't help thinking this was just part of the persona she'd taken on for the night. The siren. The risk taker. He thought he was crazy to sit here, lusting after her, falling for the act.

"Don't look so worried," she said, smiling as if she could actually read his mind. She leaned back in her chair and crossed her legs, swinging one sandaled foot back and forth. "I'm still up a thousand."

"Maybe it's not the money that worries me."

Her eyes lit up blue with a rim of green. "Are you worried about my pheromones?"

"Nah. Because you know what? I think all that love potion stuff is crap. I believe you're using good old-fashioned charm on me."

"Is it working?"

"Like dynamite."

She laughed. "That's the first time a man ever accused me of being charming."

He thought about that a minute, wondering what she could mean. Mac wasn't exactly wallflower material. But then he saw her stiffen in her chair. She sat up, pulling away from the table, looking real alert. He thought maybe she saw someone in the crowd, but then she looked back at him, as if she realized he was watching her and she'd given herself away.

He forced himself not to turn around and search the crowd, knowing it wouldn't do any good. He hadn't a clue what to look for. Beside him, Mac picked up her glass and poked at the ice cubes and the lime slice with her stir stick, the motion more agitated, as if she thought the lime might come to life and she wanted to put it down for the night. She focused on the cards, avoiding his eyes. But he could feel it, Mac slipping away.

He tipped her head up to his, forcing her to look at him. "Hey? What just happened here?"

She shook her head, giving up the pretense. "I'm sorry." She put down her glass. "I think I should cash in." Then, looking back at Jake. "I'm sorry."

He grabbed her hand before she could pull away. *I'm sorry.* It struck him that he'd heard those words before. Susan, when she'd left him for the frozen North. Hope, when she'd taken Michael, letting Dickey's lawyer try to tell him what was in the best interest of his son. *I'm sorry.*

He could feel her hand trembling under his grasp. Almost as if she couldn't help herself, she glanced back through the crowd. When she faced him again there was this strange distance to her. He had the idea that if he let her walk out now, he wouldn't see her again.

"Maybe you should let her go." It was Stacie speaking, that sweet circumspect Georgia Peach he'd begged to deal for him. "You're only down a thousand. A few minutes ago, she would have cost you three times that."

Mac's gaze turned sharp, focusing on him. He could almost see the wheels turning in her head. "What does she mean?"

But he could see she'd figured it out. "You didn't think I was going to let you play with the casino's money, did you? That would have meant my job."

She looked dumbfounded, then uncomfortable, like a kid caught doing something not so nice. "Of course. How stupid of me. I never meant . . ." She pushed all her chips at him, even the two hundred she'd brought to the table. Grabbing a twenty from her purse, she handed the bill to Stacie. Her hands were visibly shaking now.

"Thanks," she whispered to the dealer. "Please, don't follow me," she told Jake when he stood as well.

He watched her wind her way around the tables, forcing

himself not to run after her. He tried to tell himself maybe
this was for the best. *Let her go. Don't try to figure it out.*

"I'm sorry, Jake. Hey, don't kill me, okay?" Stacie said as
another dealer tapped in, ready to take her place.

"It's all right," he said automatically, still fighting the urge
to follow Mac.

Right then, Dino stepped up beside him, whistling softly
as he watched Mac walk away. He was dressed as casual as
it gets for the Greek, a snazzy patterned black and white shirt
he said his mother bought him on vacation in Paris. Dino's
mother was a widow. She loved to travel; Dino loved to in-
dulge her.

"What gives?" Dino asked. "I told Suzy to meet me here
to witness 'The Date.' I thought the doctor was going to wipe
you out, that maybe Suzy and I should stick around, be here
to pick up the pieces and start you on a twelve-step program
against meeting women in bars and casinos." He held his hand
out toward Mac. "Now I'm watching her walk away with
nothing? What did I miss?"

Dino considered himself a man not often wrong.

"It was me," Stacie said, slipping out from behind the table
now that the game she'd been asked to deal had ended. "She
seemed so sweet. I didn't think she'd want Jake's money. I
kinda let it slip out."

Dino looked down at the pile of chips, quickly making out
it was over a thousand. He shook his head. "Lucky break for
you, Irishman."

"I don't know," Stacie said, looking worried. "She was so
upset. Did I do wrong, Jake?"

"It's okay," he said, as he watched Mac disappear into an
alley of video poker and slot machines.

"She really is sweet, you know," Stacie said. "A nice girl."

She was talking about Mac. A woman wearing a black dress
that hugged her ass and who wore some color called Vixen
on her nails. A "counter" who had stacked up a good sum

of his money—then handed it back when she knew what was
what.

The thing was, he knew Stacie was right. And he just
couldn't figure it.

Pheromones. Blackjack. A nice girl.

It just didn't make sense.

McCall waited until she was sure Jake hadn't followed her
before she even dared look for Belinda.

She found her sister seated at a dollar machine, laughing
and flirting with a guy wearing a bad rug and glasses. McCall
remembered the banner at the gangplank: WELCOME ABOARD,
AMERICAN SOCIETY OF NEPHROLOGISTS. This man looked like
a prime candidate for the convention.

Belinda had on a pumpkin-colored rubber outfit that bared
her midriff, her blond hair pinned up so that soft curls tumbled
around her face. At the moment, she was giving the conventioneer the thrill of his life.

McCall walked past the crowded machines, turning in her
sister's direction. She didn't know what Belinda was doing
here, but she had a secret hope that her little sister had sought
her out, calling Barb to discover her whereabouts. The minute
she'd seen Belinda, she'd wanted to run after her. Only she
hadn't wanted Jake to be part of this meeting. Things were
complicated enough between McCall and her sister.

She picked up the conventioneer's bucket of coins and
pushed it several machines down to where an empty machine
waited.

"Do you mind?" She winked. "Just a little girl talk."

"Hey," he said, standing. "I've been working that machine
all night."

"Really?" she said.

She didn't know exactly what made her do it. A feeling. A
mood. Or perhaps Barb and her star charts was wearing off
on McCall. Whatever the reason—despite the fact that it was

completely outrageous—she lifted three coins out of his bucket and put them in the machine.

She pulled the lever and watched the blurred images in the three windows until they stopped. Three sevens dropped into place: red, white, and blue. *Plunk, plunk, plunk.*

The machine lit up like Fourth of July fireworks. Bells and whistles screamed for attention as coin after coin dropped into the metal pan beneath.

She could feel the breath catch in her chest. The adrenaline high of the moment almost took over, but she forced herself to face the conventioneer and say mildly, "I guess now you can go somewhere else. This machine appears to be empty."

She turned to her sister as the man dove both hands into his winnings, hooting and hollering as the coins kept dropping. Belinda was staring at McCall with something akin to awe. That look from her baby sister set off more bells and whistles inside McCall than any jackpot ever could. She sent up a little prayer of thanks, knowing this bit of luck was exactly the kind of introduction she'd needed after four years.

Taking her sister's hand in hers, she smiled. "Come on. Or is your machine too hot to leave?"

Belinda didn't say a word. She grabbed her roll of coins and dropped it in her purse. She stood, following McCall.

Trying to avoid running into Jake, McCall took them down a deck to the bar at the far end of the ship. This one had a safari theme, complete with bamboo awning and fake zebra skin stools. Finding two empty spots, she sat down, ignoring the video poker machines that were built in beneath the glass, encouraging people to play as they sat at the bar. Apparently, no space was wasted on the floating casino.

"How did you know that machine would hit?" Belinda asked, a little of the wonder that McCall had seen on her face slipping into her voice.

McCall thought of how best to answer her sister's question. She settled for the truth. "Actually, I would have bet it wouldn't hit. I was going to say something cute like, 'Looks

Olga Bicos

like it's not your lucky day.' Ginger ale," she said to the bartender. "Lots of ice and a twist of lime, please."

She turned to her sister, waiting to see what she wanted to drink. Belinda took one look at the bartender, a bald man in his late fifties, and leaned low across the bar, giving the bartender a beautiful view of her breasts cupped in the skin-tight rubber bustier.

"I'll have a slow comfortable screw," she said in a deep, sultry voice that seemed entirely genuine, "up against the wall."

The man didn't even blink, just reached for the Galliano and the sloe gin and began pouring the fancy screwdriver. But there'd been something unsettling about the way Belinda had just acted. McCall remembered the conventioneer at the machines, how her baby sister had been with him.

She thought of her own games with the Boy Scout. Tonight, she'd flirted outrageously, something very unlike her. But it didn't compare to the little touches and smiles Belinda had given the conventioneer, a man she would bet was a complete stranger. The game playing out between McCall and Jake seemed special . . . and very personal. Their particular dance was private. Belinda, a woman engaged to be married—a girl just barely out of her teens—was flaunting it to anyone bothering to look.

The bartender set their drinks on the bar. McCall watched her sister reach for hers. Her fingers trembled.

She's shaking.

Without even thinking, McCall placed her hand on her sister's. Belinda peered up from beneath her lashes looking terribly young and a little lost, bringing to mind what their mother had told McCall just before she died. *I gave him Belinda, because he missed you so much.*

McCall squeezed her sister's fingers, thinking she understood what her mother had meant. She felt suddenly as if she had a lot to make up for, but she didn't know where to start.

"Barb told me where you were," Belinda said. She shrugged.

"But then I saw you over at the table. I guess I got cold feet." She took her hand away and picked up the screwdriver, taking a drink. "It didn't seem like such a great idea anymore, following you here."

McCall thought about the last four years; how she'd dreamt of this moment. A second chance. "No, you were right to come. It's been too long, Belinda. You can't know how happy I am that you're here."

It was an awkward moment. The two of them had never been close. By the time Belinda was born, McCall had been almost nine, enrolled in so many special programs, she had little or no time to spend with her family. She knew breaking through those years of silence would be difficult, but she thought it was important. McCall had allowed her father to be the focus of her life. He'd built a wall around her, so that in the end, he was the only person who'd mattered. When he'd condemned her, believing the worst, there'd been nothing left for McCall. She didn't want the same thing to happen to her sister.

Belinda shook her head. "I still can't get over how that machine hit. You were always so lucky."

Lucky to have Daddy's attention. Lucky to be so smart. It was easy to read between the lines.

"Belinda. I know Daddy would have said things . . . about me and what happened four years ago." Suddenly, she wanted to make a connection with her baby sister. "I know what he believes, but it's not true. None of it," she said.

But she knew her words were inadequate—a case of too little, too late. Even to her own ears, she sounded too defensive.

"You're saying you didn't doctor that data? That it was all a mistake?"

"Why don't we just start at the beginning?" McCall said, backing up a bit, telling herself to be careful. Belinda was engaged to Roger. Like her father, she had a connection to the Clarkes. She wouldn't want to hear McCall's suspicions without proof.

"How are you, Lindy?" she asked instead, using Belinda's nickname as a child. Then, reaching for the one thing she knew would always matter to her sister, she asked, "How is your dancing?"

Incredibly, it was the wrong thing to say. She saw it immediately. Belinda's face hardened in a way that no twenty-one-year-old's should.

"I don't dance anymore." She reached for her drink. The glass slipped through her fingers, spilling onto the bar, dumping ice cubes on Belinda's lap. She jumped to her feet, brushing the cubes and orange juice off her dress with a napkin. She wadded up the napkin and dropped it on the bar. "This was a really dumb idea. You're just going to lie about everything and ruin things," she said. And then, as if she regretted her words, "Look, I gotta go."

Caught unaware, McCall stared at her sister's retreating figure. Almost too late, she surged to her feet. Belinda was already making her way through the crowd when McCall caught up with her just a few feet from the double doors. The ship had already docked.

"I'm sorry, Belinda. I just thought—"

"I know what you thought," she said, brushing McCall's hand aside.

"Belinda, listen to me. I know we were never close. But I've had a lot of time to think about the way I've lived my life. I've changed so many things. Please, let me change this."

Belinda's eyes softened through their haze of alcohol. For an instant, McCall thought she might have gotten off on the right step at last. She could see again the worship-filled face of her young sibling, a girl who had always looked up to her, settling for the tiny moments McCall had granted.

But then her sister's features changed subtly, becoming a little sly.

"We'll see," Belinda said. She turned sharply on her heels, teetering for a split second before she staggered forward. Waving her hand over her shoulder, she said, "See ya, sis."

Seven

Belinda Sayer was hiding in the women's bathroom.

She sat in one of the stalls, on the toilet, the seat down. She was very familiar with the rest rooms here at the River Palace Hotel. The restaurant on the top floor, the River's Way, was a favorite of Roger's, a place where he could lord over the staff his friendship with the hotel's owner, basking in the special treatment. Belinda, she liked the bathroom.

She considered it a pink marble refuge, the kind of bathroom her Southern Lady mother would have approved. Palatial in a town where space was at a premium, and elegantly supplied. Perfume, hair spray, even mouthwash with little paper cups lined the sink like good soldiers. Hand towels lay rolled and stacked in a basket with tiny orchids resting interspersed among the towels. The doors to the stalls were real doors, reaching to the floor, enclosing you in your own private chamber, a place where you could cry miserably and no one would notice.

Belinda stared down at the hand towel she'd taken, now stained black in a Rorschach pattern from her mascara. The comforting fog of the alcohol she'd drank had faded. It never lasted long enough, not nearly long enough . . . but she was too scared to keep drinking. She didn't want to become an alcoholic, like her mother. She didn't want to lie in a bed with tubes in her nose and needles in her veins, dying the same ignominious death.

Closing her eyes, she listened to the music they piped into

the rest room, Tchaikovsky's *Swan Lake*. She imagined herself dancing as Odile, the black swan. It was almost as effective as the alcohol, the music in her head, the picture of her body turning and leaping. She'd danced all her life.

It's not as if you're a soloist in an established dance company.

Not famous, like McCall.

McCall, the apple of her father's eye.

She tried to shut out the words. She didn't want to hear that constant wave of criticism telling her she wasn't good enough, a weakling. Her mother had been weak, a woman who couldn't take care of her children, couldn't keep her father's interest. A useless woman.

Belinda, you're just like me, her mother whispered.

I'm very disappointed in you, Belinda, her father countered in her head.

"No!" Belinda clamped her hands over her ears.

Disappointed, disappointed, disappointed. It was a familiar litany. A criticism her father had come to associate with his younger daughter.

Better than being ignored. Better than being invisible. Better than being weak. That's what she told herself anyway.

She thought about her father, waiting up for her. That's what he'd done last night, sipping tea at the kitchen table of their Garden District home, a regal gem her mother had inherited, a home Lucinda Sayer had given all the love and care she'd never shown her daughters, restoring its murals, selecting its period furnishings. Belinda sniffed back her tears. Certainly, Daddy would be waiting up for her, worried that she'd come home drunk. Again.

She pictured her father pacing around the kitchen table, using a gait that she always experienced as menacing. It was just a habit of his, pacing like that. A way of gathering his thoughts. But the motion intimidated her as she waited, bringing to mind those movies where the prisoner sits under hot lights.

The light buzz she'd built up from the alcohol came crashing down then, leaving only a dull headache as she sat in the restaurant bathroom thinking about her father. She'd started drinking the previous year, coming home drunk from the party scene with Roger. She knew it irritated her father. She thought maybe that's why she did it. *Better than being ignored.*

"I am going to ask you something very important, Belinda." Even his words appeared to circle menacingly inside the stall as she remembered them. "God forgive me, I wasn't able to help your mother. But you're my daughter. I have to help you. Belinda, do you think you have a drinking problem? Do you need help? Something discreet, a clinic somewhere. You could say you need a vacation."

She remembered how he'd knelt down beside her, surprising her because he'd taken her hand. Her father, the consummate scientist, rarely displayed affection.

She realized it was times like those that she knew he really cared. When she was bad, it always brought out the father in him, almost as if she were reminding him of his duties.

"Everyone I love is gone," he'd told her, rubbing her hand between his two as if he might somehow rub off the tarnish that had gathered the last months. "Don't you understand? You're all I have left."

She could feel something going soft inside her even with the memory. She wanted to be the one he loved. She wanted very much for him to need her. For someone to need her. She didn't want to be one of the Invisible People, her name for the men and women she befriended at clubs and bars, lonely people no one ever noticed.

"It's McCall, isn't it?" he'd asked. "Because she's back? She won't hurt us again. We won't let her hurt us."

And then it was gone, almost instantly—the focus, the love—making her wonder if it had ever been there. *You see! He doesn't really care. It's just a trick.* That voice had grown stronger inside her head this last year as she realized she'd given up everything that mattered for her father.

Sometimes, she wondered if that wasn't what he'd done to McCall. What he'd done to their mother. It was just Belinda's turn now.

How are you, Lindy? How's your dancing? Belinda twisted the hand towel in her lap, remembering. McCall had asked about her dancing. She'd called her Lindy.

Belinda hiccuped. She stared at the stall door, feeling a little sick from the booze. At the bar, she'd wanted to trust her sister. To be her friend. It was like slipping into a familiar role. All those years she'd followed McCall around, her smarter, older sister. That's why she'd gone looking for her at the casino, thinking about how things had once been between them.

It's not as if you're a soloist with an established dance company. Her father's words crept inside her head, banishing the memory of her sister's warming interest. He'd made it clear that ballet was a meaningless waste of time if she couldn't be a principal dancer, or even a soloist. And Belinda had agreed at the time, tired of being part of the corps de ballet. She'd wanted to do something more important with her life, just as her father had suggested. With him. At the lab.

Now, she worked at Clarke Laboratories as his assistant, a role he'd always intended for McCall. Only, McCall had thought herself too good for the position. She'd abandoned them, then ended up besmirching her family when she'd doctored that data.

Not so Belinda. She was the good daughter now. The one engaged to marry Roger Clarke, the heir apparent.

Only, the better Belinda was, the more she became invisible to her father. The more perfect she became—the able technician, fiancée to the boss's son—her father spent less and less time with her. It was only when she hindered him, becoming a distraction that he seemed to even notice her at all.

And now that McCall was back, she'd lose him again, just as she had all her life.

Couldn't cut it dancing, relegated to a career in the chorus.

She wasn't smart, like McCall. She wasn't pretty enough to keep Roger's wandering eye.

She knew she would gradually disappear, becoming the Belinda of the past. Only now, there wouldn't be even her mother's fleeting attentions or her dancing to fall back on.

But then she remembered her sister at the bar, taking her hand, squeezing it. McCall had asked about her dancing.

Belinda unrolled a handful of toilet paper and blew her nose. She didn't know who to trust, or even if it mattered if she trusted anyone.

She tossed the toilet paper and flushed. She glanced at her watch. Fifteen minutes before the casino riverboat launched for a short harbor cruise. If she hurried, she might find that nice man at the machines again, one of the Invisible People, just like herself.

The silver Ferrari was parked halfway across the driveway, blocking her way.

McCall slammed the door of Stan and Barb's '91 BMW, walking alongside the sports car. Parking was always a problem in the French Quarter, but the driver had managed to squeeze the Ferrari parallel to the curb by nosing up onto the drive. The only thing that prevented the car from going any farther was a wrought iron gate that enclosed the private driveway. Even if she managed to creep the BMW onto the sidewalk and around the car, the Ferrari's position prevented her from opening the driveway gate.

"Damn it." The perfect end to a terrible evening.

There came a soft "tching" behind her. "The Love Doctor has a filthy mouth. What would Sally Jesse and the gang think?"

McCall turned, searching for Roger in the weak light coming from the streetlamp. The Ferrari's appearance fell into place. Roger's new toy.

He'd been lurking under the vine-covered myrtle inside the

courtyard. Now, he stepped onto the brick walkway, positioning himself between her and the door to the eighteenth-century outbuilding where Stan and Barb lived. McCall opened the courtyard gate, hating that he was here, a place she thought of as a refuge.

"Why am I not the least surprised to find you skulking in the shadows," she said. She kept her voice upbeat, but it was almost eerie to meet Roger here, in the moonlight, where the vines and ferns of Barb's courtyard only added to his menace.

He laughed. He stood in front of her, wearing an outrageous turquoise jacket with matching trousers, the fabric, some sort of treated velvet that shimmered as he moved. The exaggerated collar of his cuffed shirt lay open, showing he had no chest hair. The ensemble probably cocked in at a couple of thousand. It was an outfit few men could carry off. With his *GQ* looks, Roger did it with style.

"The famed Love Doctor." His natural drawl only made the name sound more ridiculous. "From developmental geneticist to quack. Hmm, hmm. My, how the mighty do fall. But you did look so yummy in those infomercials. And you sounded downright erudite, you did, peddling your newest client's snake oil. Now, that vanilla stuff a year ago . . . I might have tried that one, darling."

"If you're through with the *curriculum vitae.*"

He snapped his fingers as if just remembering something. "You know, I gave your name to a fellow. Frank Weiss, I think that was his name. He was marketing some sort of male enhancing vitamins. Something to keep your schlong long." The elongated vowels were exaggerated even for a New Orleans native. "I said you had all those pretty titles, Harvard, Caltech, and no one buying his stuff was going to care about your dirty little past. Did Frank give you a call?"

"I must have missed it. Why are you here, Roger? I gave your father the number to my service."

He pouted. The baby-boy look actually suited him, working with the tousled gold-brown curls and full lips. "And aren't you just as prickly as Barbara. She wouldn't tell me where you'd gone tonight. Still trying to protect you from me," he said, alluding to their past relationship. McCall and Roger had dated for a few months. That's when she'd discovered Roger's charm maxed out around week two.

"Gambling," she said. "At your friend's casino, as a matter of fact." McCall had gone to the *River Palace* on Roger's recommendation, primarily because it had given her a kick to take money from one of Roger's friends.

"Win anything?"

"As it turned out, this isn't my lucky night."

Roger laughed again, getting her meaning. He brought out a cigarette from a silver case and lit up, taking a deep drag. "Wow. Look at you, darling." He whistled softly, his eyes steady on her as he blew the smoke through his nose. "All dolled up."

When he handed her the cigarette, she took it, remembering how he'd always done so on their dates together—and how she'd followed suit, smoking, wanting to please him. This time, she let it smolder in her hand, refusing to put her mouth where Roger's had been. That was something Roger always liked to do, get everyone involved in his dirty habits.

"Wow, Roger," she said, raising her gaze to his, mimicking him. "I bet you're still full of the same old crap."

She was about to toss the cigarette when Roger captured her wrist. He jerked her up against him. He smiled, a mean, rattlesnake smile. "You never did take me seriously." His brows lifted. "I thought by now you would have learned better. After Alicia."

For the longest time, she said nothing. This was the kind of game Roger enjoyed best. He'd always denied he'd had anything to do with Alicia Goodman's death, and yet, every once in a while, he would allude to it, fueling McCall's suspicions.

"Is that supposed to frighten me?" she asked, pushing it. "That you might kill me like poor Alicia?"

He grinned. "And you told Daddy you didn't blame us anymore."

"You're the one making threats, Roger," she said, twisting her hand free and dropping the cigarette. "I'm just trying to interpret."

He leaned close enough that she could smell the cigarette on his breath. "You know, darling. I would worry if I were you. I mean, *really* worry. But that night with Alicia"—he winked—"it was just plain bad luck. The car running off the road like that."

"So you claimed. Strange how you were driving Alicia's car, though. I never knew the two of you were close."

"Didn't you know Dr. Goodman had a thing for me? Maybe I was her little secret." He put his finger up to his lips, making a soft shushing noise. "Maybe we were doing the deed and it shamed her, her being so much older." He stepped closer. "You look good in a dress, McCall," he said, letting his voice drop low with a hushed resonance she'd once found sexy, not even bothering to segue away from Alicia's death. "You should have worn more of them back then. Nice tight ones, like this one. Dresses that tell a man exactly where to put his hands."

He fit both of his palms over her buttocks and drew her flush against him. He leaned into her, letting her feel his erection.

She forced herself to smile coyly. "Oh, Roger," she said in a high, breathy voice reminiscent of what she might have sounded like four years ago. She threaded her fingers through his curly brown hair with blond highlights, as if she might actually contemplate kissing him. "I think you're actually going to make me ill. If I were you, I'd step aside. In case I puke on your nice expensive shoes."

His brow furrowed, showing first confusion and then a wicked gleam of meanness. McCall couldn't help her sudden burst of laughter as she stepped away. She wanted to laugh at Roger. She wanted him to be ridiculous. She didn't want to be frightened, thinking about the last four years and wondering just how far he and his father would go to get what they wanted.

"Oh, my. Have I offended you?" She crossed her arms over her chest. "Come on, Roger. I've been down this road already. You didn't really think I'd fall for the lover boy act again?"

"Your sister certainly has."

The words were lightning quick and as painful as an electric shock. A multitude of responses sprang to mind. She wanted to claw his face, to tell him to leave Belinda alone. But she decided indifference was Belinda's best defense.

"My sister's a big girl. She knows what she wants."

Roger nodded, strolling past McCall as if he were leaving. At the last minute, he turned and whispered in her ear. "You almost make me believe you don't care, darling." His mouth brushed across her cheek in a faint kiss. "Almost."

It was Roger's turn to laugh as he opened the gate and stepped out of the small courtyard. He leaned back up through the bars, the moonlight and streetlamp slashing the shadows of the wrought iron bars across his face.

"Daddy sends his love." He pushed back from the railing, digging his hands in his pockets and flashing his million-dollar smile. "By the way. You have a job. We'll see you at the lab Monday morning. Eight sharp, now." He blew her a kiss. "Don't be late, darling."

He hummed tunelessly as he strolled over to the Ferrari. He opened the door and stepped inside. Within seconds, the engine roared to life, waking half the Quarter as he peeled out into the street.

McCall felt sick to her stomach, haunted by the vision of her young sister flirting with a conventioneer twice her age and a balding bartender, wondering just how miserable Roger had made Belinda. Roger and his games.

She searched for her key in her purse. Her hands were shaking worse than ever. "I'm going to save you," she said, already knowing she would extricate her sister from Roger's clutches. She wouldn't let Belinda marry into that murderous family. "I'm going to save you and Daddy both."

Professional blackjack player. Genetics whiz kid. A nice girl.

Jake leaned back on the couch, his feet on the glass coffee table. He was listening to Paul Taylor's *On The Horn* CD, the saxophone player, one of his favorites. He clicked the ice in his glass, staring at the screen of the 36-inch Mitsubishi television. He was watching the black and white image of Mac sitting at the casino's safari bar on the second level. A blonde sat next to her, wearing an outfit that made Mac's little black number look conservative. He'd "borrowed" the tape from surveillance.

A nice girl, Stacie had called her.

He put the glass down, the drink no longer fresh. But even if the alcohol hadn't been watered down from the melting ice, he wasn't particularly interested in finishing it. He watched Mac place her hand on the blonde's. There was something natural about the gesture, almost maternal; she was trying to comfort the other woman.

He'd gone to the surveillance room because he'd thought she was meeting someone else. A man.

"Jesus. I'm screwed."

He raked his hand through his hair, feeling like a voyeur. He'd never done anything like this before. But when Mac had left the table, he'd gone to the ship's hold. There, he'd watched her on the bank of video monitors in the surveillance room, knowing with every passing image that he was becoming obsessed.

Donovan Curse. Nice Girl. Donovan Curse. The words pulsed inside his head with the syncopated beat of the synthesizer coming from the CD player.

Of course, the Donovan Curse didn't really exist. It was just something Dino had made up. A joke. But lately, it was like a big neon sign in Jake's head, warning him that he wasn't ever going to find that elusive happily-ever-after his parents had advertised with forty years of marriage. His sisters, both of them, seemed to be managing the till-death-do-us-part stuff. But not Jake.

He focused on Mac on the television screen, thinking over the day Susan had walked out on him, reminding himself of just how wrong these things could go. One day, you have a wife . . . a career. Everything's marching along like you planned it. Then the whole thing gets napalmed.

He thought about that a minute, forcing himself to remember how it had been that day, how he'd come home late from work at the Attorney General's office in Baton Rouge, thinking everything was right in his world. He was on his biggest case yet, a real break for him. But he'd promised Susan no more all-nighters so he'd come home, leaving the gang burning the midnight oil back at the office. The case was red hot with the press; he'd had a briefcase full of work he'd lugged home.

He'd found his wife packing her bags in their bedroom.

He could still remember breaking out into a cold sweat— knowing, just knowing. "Susan? What are you doing, honey? It's almost midnight."

But Susan, she'd just kept packing her jeans, a couple of blouses, some dresses—one neat pile after another—never bothering to turn around. Until she'd said it.

"I'm leaving you, Jake."

Leaving you, Jake. They'll always leave you. He stared at the image of Mac talking to the blonde, mulling it over in his head, step by step. Marriage number one going down the tubes.

He could picture it perfectly, how he'd dropped his briefcase, taking two steps toward Susan, reaching for her. He could hear their argument, walking back into the scene, playing it in his head like a movie. "Look," he'd told her, "if this is about the Torres deal, I'll tell Gus to take me off the case tomorrow—"

She stepped away. She'd put her blond hair in a ponytail. She looked just like the day he'd met her eight years ago. She'd been crying, then, too. A couple of guys at a fraternity party had scared her . . . Jake had stepped in, doing his knight-in-shining-armor routine.

"This isn't about Torres, or McCarther, or any other of your cases. Jake, I just don't feel it anymore. What was between us. It's like, I'm dead inside. I don't feel anything."

But she wasn't talking about the kind of love Jake believed in. "Okay. So you need some time." He thought about Susan's mom. Her suicide. "For God's sake, your mother died less than a year ago. Maybe you're depressed? And I've been working so hard—"

"I don't want you to blame yourself, Jake. It's me. I swear. It's just me. You're a wonderful man; any woman would be lucky to have you. But I have to find something inside myself again. And I'm not going to find it here. Cleaning the apartment, baking brownies for the office."

"All right, all right. You need to get away. I understand. Really I do. Take some of the money your mother left you. Go to Hawaii or something."

But she was shaking her head. She pulled something out of her pocket and held it up for him to see. It was a check made out to Susan Donovan for eighty-five thousand dollars.

He got this horrible cramp in his stomach. "You never invested it like we talked about with Tom?"

She shook her head. "I know I said I would. But I got to thinking. It's my money. She would want me to use it to save myself." Her eyes looked so cool, all that Nordic blood. Ice blue. "I'm taking it all." She closed the suitcase and stuffed the check back into the pocket of her jeans. "And I'm leaving you."

"Jesus Christ, Susan. Don't do this."

"I'm sorry. I'm so sorry."

I'm sorry. That's what Mac had said walking away from the table tonight. *I'm sorry.*

Jake reached for the controls to the VCR; he froze the image of Mac on the television. He sighed, letting his head fall back against the couch. "Shit."

He'd been trying to put things in perspective, thinking about Susan, reminding himself that he had this really lousy luck when it came to women and he had to be more careful.

But the truth was, all the bad memories in the world wouldn't change how he felt. And maybe that was the true Donovan Curse, that he couldn't seem to hold back those emotions.

He stared back at the screen. He'd watched this particular scene over and over. The blonde spills her drink; she wipes off the booze with a napkin, giving McCall this look. And Mac. The expression on her face told the story. He'd stopped the tape right when the blonde leaves the bar, honing in on Mac's reaction.

It was the same expression he'd seen just before she'd left him at the table. She'd felt guilty because she'd been gambling with his money—and a little pissed, maybe for the same reason. And then there had been that split second, when she'd tensed and he'd thought she might be in some kind of trouble. That's what she looked like now.

He shook his head, thinking that Dino was right. There was no hope for him. Whatever was going on between him and Mac, he had to see it through.

The phone rang, the sound jarring his concentration from the screen. But he let it ring. He told himself she wouldn't know his number; it was unlisted. It wouldn't be Mac.

He turned back to the television, pushing the play button to watch Mac race after the other woman until she was out of camera range. As the phone rang in the kitchen, he pushed rewind, knowing what he was doing was a little off, watching her like this.

The machine picked up.

"Jake? Are you there? Pick up if you're there."

Susan, ex-wife number one. He smiled, shaking his head as he turned off the television using the controls. Speak of the devil. He stood and took the tape out of the VCR, grabbing his glass on the way. He walked behind the granite-topped island that separated the kitchen from the living room.

"Jake?" Susan's voice called out again, sounding impatient now.

He tossed the melting ice from his glass into the sink and threw the tape down on the counter. He had the fleeting thought that he hadn't nailed Dino about Susan supposedly seeing this other guy.

"Come on, Jake. Pick up," Susan continued. "Dino's here with me. We're worried about you."

Jake put his glass in the sink. What the hell did Dino mean Susan was involved with someone? If she wasn't at work, she and Dino were strapped at the hip.

"I know you're there, Jake Donovan. Pick up."

The silence hummed from the machine as Susan waited for him to answer the phone. Jake walked away, turning off the lights as he headed for the master bedroom. He was tired, real tired.

"Call me, okay? We need to talk. I have something really important I need to show you."

Susan Donovan closed her eyes, hanging up the phone.

"He was there," she told Dino behind her. "He just didn't want to talk."

She heard Dino walk up behind her as she picked up the file folder she'd taken to the casino. Only Jake had left before she'd been able to show it to him. On the table, right next to the phone, stood a silver-framed photograph of Jake with Michael.

That could have been our son, she thought for the thousandth time. *That could have been our life.*

Dino reached out from behind her and put the photograph facedown. "This is really stupid, Suzy."

Her hands tightened around the FBI folder, bending the

corners. She didn't want to turn around. She knew she couldn't hide anything from Dino, that he would see the truth in her eyes. "You're his friend. Don't you think he should know?"

"And that's why you're doing this? To help Jake out?"

She braced herself against the pain, the weakness that urged her to argue that she could make Jake happy. They had been through so much together. Why shouldn't she get a second chance?

She forced herself to speak calmly. "I had access to the information. What was I suppose to do? Forget about it?"

"An FBI file? Come on, Suzy. How many favors did you call in to get 'access'?"

"You said she was a problem," she said, defending herself. She turned around, facing Dino, taking him on. Dino was the only person who'd guessed how she felt about her ex-husband. Jake Donovan was the one that got away—the one she threw away. Because she'd been young. Because she'd been foolish.

She cut off those thoughts. The truth was, she'd found a vital piece of herself those years she'd lived off her inheritance in Alaska, building the strength to know that one day she wouldn't be staring at a bottle of pills as her mother had, wondering how many she would need to swallow.

But she hadn't been prepared for how she'd felt when she'd come back, seeing Jake with Hope and Michael. When his marriage to Hope had broken up, she'd thought . . .

"Let me tell you a story." Dino hooked a curl of her hair over her ear, touching her gently, so gently it made her want to break down and weep. "I know this couple, see? They used to be married. Only, things didn't work out, and well, the wife, she leaves the guy and there are all these hurt feelings. A few years later, she shows up again. She's put her act together, has her own business, a nice place in the Quarter. And she realizes what a gem this guy is."

"You work at a casino, Dino. You're not my therapist," she

said, holding tight to the emotions hurting her. Dammit, she was not going to cry.

"She helps him through some rough spots . . . another failed marriage. She's thinking, now she'll get this second chance. Maybe they even sleep together . . . when they get lonely."

"I don't want to talk about this right now."

"But it's not the same. You see, the guy, he's moved on." Dino placed both hands on the table behind her, one on each side of Susan, closing her in so she had to pay attention. "Move on, Suzy."

"I made a mistake." She could feel herself choke on the words. "Do I have to pay for it for the rest of my life?"

"Did you? Maybe the mistake is trying to go back to the past?" he whispered.

His gold-green eyes showed his Mediterranean ancestry. He was an extremely handsome man and very conscious of his appearance. Wearing the right clothes, gelling his hair every day.

At the moment, he had what she called Dino's "come hither" look. She'd seen it before; she even felt its pull. That's why she'd given it a name, so she wouldn't be taken in by him. Dino was a dear friend. They'd even discussed a partnership. But she wouldn't let it go any farther than that; wouldn't ruin it. She wouldn't lose her heart to Dino, the Greek gigolo, a womanizer with notches on his bedpost.

She lifted her chin. "*You* gave me the idea to do a little investigating. I believe your words were, 'She'll take him for all he's worth.' "

Dino shrugged. "Maybe she's not so bad. Her giving him back that money at the table. I think it showed class." He grinned. "Me? I might have kept it, just to let him know what an ass he was making of himself."

Susan slapped the FBI file against Dino's chest, holding it there. Right now she didn't want to hear anything good about McCall Sayer.

On a label across the top of the folder appeared the name
DR. McCALL ELIZABETH SAYER.

"Why don't you read the file and see if you still feel that
way," she said. No matter what, Jake had her loyalty. They
were friends. And if that was the only piece of Jake she could
have—the only part she deserved after divorcing him—then
she would take it.

"Whatever you think my motives may be," she told Dino,
"Jake should know what he's getting into."

Part Two

Synthesis

Age before beauty.
                    —A proverbial saying

Eight

Last night I made love to my Dr. Frankenstein. He has everything I have to give now; my mind, my body, my soul. I never thought it would be like this for me, that I would find someone who would ask me to hold nothing back and that I would give him that power over me. We are ready to enter the second phase of testing.
—Excerpt from Dr. Alicia Goodman's lab book

McCall slid her identification badge through the swipe lock. Hearing a soft click, she opened the door leading into a glass-enclosed booth, the entrance to the high-security area that housed the research laboratories. She stepped into the two footprints outlined on the floor and slid her badge into the metal box containing a small video camera, following the procedure they'd outlined for her at Badge and Lock Control. Eight o'clock sharp she'd arrived at Clarke Laboratories, a compound located on the old River Road twenty minutes outside of the city. It was almost ten now. After Human Resources had finished with her, she'd been sent directly to Security for a photo ID.

At some remote location, a security guard was now comparing the image on the badge with the person standing in the booth. McCall had dressed in a fitted lemon yellow pants suit, her hair crimped so that it appeared permed. She wore big daisy clip-on earrings reminiscent of the sixties. This morning, she'd wanted to look casual, as if she wasn't the least bit impressed by this little summons on the part of Curtis Clarke.

She smiled at the video camera above her, saying, "Cheese."

The light over a second door, this one leading into the lab area, turned green. The guard on the other side opened the door. "Welcome, Dr. Sayer."

McCall glanced at the man's badge, clipping her own photo ID to her jacket as she'd been instructed. "Thanks, Murray."

"Mr. Clarke will meet you at Lab 19. That's down this hall and around the corner on your left."

Lab 19. As in nineteen or more facilities. Curtis Clarke had certainly expanded over the years.

McCall walked down the main hallway. On either side of her, the glass-and-metal-enclosed labs showed technicians in lab coats working at bench-top tables and computer terminals. *Skin Care Lab. Fragrance Group. Microbiology,* she catalogued mentally. The place was completely up-graded from what she remembered, with swipe locks on everything, which was odd. Normally, only specific areas required that kind of security, rooms with radioactivity or climate control. Otherwise, the labs had been open areas.

She couldn't remember the last time she'd visited her father's lab. Certainly enough years had passed to expect changes. But she found the security measures extraordinary. Not to mention that the number of lab facilities had doubled.

She glanced at the framed lithographs advertising Clarke's newest products, from herbal shampoos to skin creams promising a "mini" face-lift effect. Despite these splashes of color hanging from the walls, there was a high-tech starkness to the area. At the university where she'd worked, there had been so much noise—life—and a well-used feel to the labs. Walking down the hall to Lab 19, she felt isolated by the white halls, cocooned by the muffled sounds.

It didn't help that she'd had a difficult weekend. Unnerved by Roger's surprise appearance at the house, she'd argued with

Barb about moving out. Now that she'd accepted a position at Clarke Labs, she thought she should move on, perhaps to a hotel.

But Barb had begged her to stay, explaining that the time wasn't right for her to leave. The stars again. And McCall had given in, thinking about the twins, who woke her every morning laughing and bouncing on her bed until she grabbed one under each arm and gave them "kiss attacks." She knew she would miss the family dinners when everyone sat at the table and talked about their day. Barb and Stan had given her a taste of a life she'd never known. A family. And she couldn't seem to turn her back on that just yet.

Last night, she'd even gone to the casino, looking for Jake . . . unable, after all, to forget him. She'd found Dino instead, who'd told her Jake had taken the weekend off to go camping with his son. She'd ended up playing video poker, drinking ginger ale, and pretending Jake might walk through the double doors at any minute, home from his trip with Michael. It was the first time in years that she'd lost money at a casino, but it didn't matter. She was here now, an insider in the sacred halls of Clarke Laboratories. She didn't need the money. Not anymore.

McCall turned the corner, following the guard's directions, telling herself no more trips to the *River Palace*. With the coming weeks, she vowed she would forget about the Boy Scout. Her life was complicated enough. She had to stay focused.

Just ahead, Curtis Clarke stepped out from one of the labs and into the hallway. He wore a formless beige jacket with matching trousers and a collarless black shirt, an outfit that would have looked superb on a man twenty years younger and twenty pounds lighter. Roger, two steps behind Dear Old Dad, looked like a movie star after a wrap party, wearing sunglasses and bootlegged trousers in white that gloved his thighs, a white V-neck cotton undershirt that said he didn't give a shit, and a body-hugging lightweight tweed jacket that said he did.

Both men were laughing, speaking in hushed tones. An evil version of Tweedle Dumb and Tweedle Dee. But it was the vault-like door just beyond father and son that held her attention.

The familiar symbol of three circles forming a triangle, linked by a fourth circle at their center, warned of biohazards just beyond the door. The lock on the vault appeared to be a swipe and cipher combination. Even at this distance, she could see the key pad was pretty sophisticated, superior to the lower-tech locks used for the other labs. A plaque to the side of the door stated: LABORATORY 20. BIOSAFETY LEVEL-2. AUTHORIZED PERSONNEL ONLY.

The vault door opened with a *whoosh* of air. Just inside the room, she could see a man tearing off the mask and hair net used to protect from contaminants, then kicking off his paper booties. Her father. He disposed of the protective cloth-ing and, like Belinda behind him, donned a fresh lab coat. They both signed off on a clipboard and walked into the hall to meet Curtis and Roger.

A Biosafety Level-2 laboratory. A high-security facility that required protective clothing, used to avoid contamination for sensitive experiments. Highly unusual for cosmetics research.

She thought about Alicia's lab book, her heart pumping double time.

"Ah, the mistress of ceremonies arrives." Curtis waved her forward, while Roger lounged near the door, his eyes hidden behind his sunglasses. *A late night,* McCall thought, knowing entirely too much about Roger's body language.

She walked slowly, her eyes on the welcoming committee, deepening her breathing. She told herself to prepare for the performance of her life.

Before she came to a full stop, Curtis snatched her badge off her jacket, just grazing the side of one breast with his knuckles. He swiped the badge through the lock, his actions implying the mechanism might be too difficult for her to figure out without the demonstration.

The light on the box to the side of the door turned from red to green. There came a discordant buzzing as Curtis opened the door, handing her back the badge. "Enter into your kingdom, McCall," he said, signaling her to proceed.

As she took a step forward, she felt a hand on her shoulder. McCall turned, looking up into the face of the man who'd had the greatest influence on her life. Her father.

"Do you mind?" Donald Sayer asked the others. "I'd like a word with my daughter."

For a moment, McCall couldn't catch her breath. *My daughter.* She couldn't remember the last time he'd called her that.

The buzzer stopped as the door closed behind Belinda, the last one to enter Lab 19. McCall waited, letting her father set the tone. She'd left several messages since she'd arrived in New Orleans a month ago, none of which he'd returned. But perhaps here, surrounded by those he knew and trusted, Donald Sayer would finally have his say.

He raised his hand, then dropped it to his side in an aborted gesture.

"Daddy?"

"I just find it so difficult . . . after all these years . . . with your mother dying . . ." He took a moment, looking just over her head. He was a tall man, over six feet. He shook his head, his handsome face with its hawk nose and wide mouth strained with emotions she couldn't begin to decipher. McCall noticed there was more white in his dark blond hair.

"You shouldn't be here." His changeable eyes met his daughter's. "This is a mistake . . . McCall, whatever you may think, I am not your enemy."

"Enemy? Daddy—"

"Listen." He held up his hand, silencing her. "I know these last years have been difficult for you. Those god-awful commercials, the talk shows. I know in my heart, I should have listened to your mother's pleas. I wish to God I wasn't such an unforgiving bastard. But I can't help how I feel . . . what you did, McCall. What you did . . ."

She didn't bother with denials. He'd heard them all before.

Her father sighed, shaking his head as he met her gaze. "Whatever I've managed to carve out here for your sister and myself. Please. *Please,* I beg you. Don't ruin this, too."

"You'll never trust me, will you?" she asked sadly. "Because I wanted what Alicia had to offer more than this." She glanced around the facility.

"And for what?" he challenged, raising his voice, showing for the first time his anger. "Did she give you anything better than I could have?"

"I wasn't going to be your assistant forever, Daddy," she said, miserably repeating the words he would never listen to. "I was better than that."

"How good are you now, McCall? You and your manufactured love potion? Alicia Goodman ruined you." His eyes appeared a clear cutting blue. "I'm wasting my breath; you made your choice years ago. All I ask is that you don't ruin me completely."

He swiped his badge through the lock. As head of Research and Development, he would have access to any of the labs. He didn't wait for McCall to follow.

McCall stood in the hall, feeling as if she'd just been hit by a train. *End of discussion.* It was always that way with her father. He would never trust her, wouldn't even return her calls, merely granting her a dressing down in the hallway. But if McCall's fears proved true, it wasn't her discredited past that her father had to fear.

She told herself to calm down; the scene with her father was just the beginning. Using her badge, she opened the door to Lab 19, her laboratory. She reminded herself she was here for proof, something her father would listen to. The disjointed ramblings of Alicia Goodman, a woman he'd never trusted, would never sway Donald Sayer against Curtis Clarke, a man who had signed his paychecks for nearly thirty years. But perhaps Alicia could help them yet, leading McCall to the truth.

Taking a breath, she stepped inside the lab. She steeled herself against the memories of another facility. So much would be the same, the glare of the overhead fluorescent lights, the black bench-tops and the metal cabinets with their glass doors. The past four years, all her work had been done in garages and hotel rooms, the equipment, makeshift, research financed by blackjack and appearances on infomercials. Here, at Clarke Laboratories, the home of perfumed body lotions, hydrofirming creams, and cellular energizing formulas, everything would be cutting edge.

The room smelled new—the dry wall fresh, the equipment just out of boxes—as if Curtis, the magician, had erected a fully functioning molecular biology laboratory overnight. Four bench-top tables dissected the chamber; cabinets outfitted with glassware lined the walls, stocked with racks of test tubes, Erlenmeyer flasks, and glass pipettes. McCall strolled around a solid marble table heavy enough to dampen even the smallest vibration. On top, a hanging scale sat enclosed in glass, the mechanism so sophisticated it could weigh the smallest volume. She opened a drawer, glanced at the box of medical gloves and safety goggles inside, feigning an indifference she didn't feel.

Who wouldn't be impressed. *A hood, an ultracentrifuge, a peptide synthesizer, even a DNA sequenator,* she catalogued mentally. And four lab techs waiting, each wearing a white lab coat with the Clarke Labs logo over the heart, a woman kneeling with her hands held up before her to catch the cascade of roses falling from her hair. The stance of the four techs said they would be at her beck and call, bought and paid for by Curtis Clarke. *Just like everything else in the room,* she thought.

"What do you think?" Curtis asked.

McCall leaned her elbows back against one of the bench-tops. "It'll do."

Curtis barked a laugh. "It will more than do. There's only half a dozen companies in this country that could provide this kind of setup. Even that fancy university of yours would be hard-pressed to get a hold of this sequenator," he said, passing his hand over the instrument as if it were a woman. "All right here at your fingertips. Everything you ever wanted to know about guanine, adenine, thymine, and cytosine," he said in a low purring voice, naming the specific molecules that made up every strand of DNA.

McCall turned to Roger. "How long did it take you to teach him those big words?" Like McCall, Roger had a doctorate in developmental genetics.

For an instant, everyone in the lab tensed, waiting for Curtis's response. Curtis Clarke was a brilliant man, a self-made man. A proud man with no formal education. But Curtis only laughed, first softly, then more loudly, ending in shoulder-shaking guffaws.

"You know, girl." Curtis wiped the tears from his eyes, still chuckling softly. "I think we're going to work well together, you and I."

McCall's gaze focused on her father standing behind Curtis. It was impossible to tell what he was thinking. Belinda beside him appeared perfectly bored.

"And now for your side of the bargain," Curtis said. "At the end of each day, I will expect a written report documenting your progress—"

"Is that your definition of autonomy?" She picked up her purse, a bogus Hermes Bolide she'd splurged on. On her way out, she stopped next to Curtis, whispering in his ear, "You want to turn your back on the kind of money I can make you with my formula?" She shrugged and kept on walking.

"Once a week, girl. I'll expect a report once a week."

McCall turned around, trying to decide how far she could push him. It was hard to judge looking into those slate-gray eyes. "All right," she said, returning Curtis's grin. She tossed her purse on the nearest bench-top. "I consider it a waste of time, but if you want the dog and pony show . . ." She crossed her arms and shrugged.

Curtis nodded, getting exactly what he wanted. He motioned one of the techs forward. "Overseeing your progress will be Kyle Woods. And, of course, your daddy, as the head of Research and Development, will be in charge."

Ignoring Woods for the moment, McCall watched her father's face, looking for disapproval but finding only a controlled indifference. She waited for some comment. Donald Sayer had never been good at keeping his thoughts to himself. But he said nothing, just meeting his daughter's gaze straight on.

His silence made her strangely sad. Even to thwart her—the daughter who, in his eyes, had betrayed him—Donald Sayer was willing to swallow a bitter pill, completely under Curtis Clarke's thumb. As he'd always been.

McCall jogged her head toward the waiting techs, assuming the one who'd stepped forward was Kyle Woods, Curtis's man. "What are his qualifications? Other than being your able spy, of course?"

"Damn straight, I don't trust you, girl," Curtis said. "I don't trust anyone. Woods."

Kyle Woods stood fidgeting with a mechanical pencil. He appeared somewhere in his early thirties, with thick glasses, a rumpled lab coat, and slicked-back blond hair just long enough to put in a ponytail. The consummate nerd.

Woods cleared his throat. "I've been working for Clarke Labs over a year now. My degrees are in molecular biology, Chicago and Stanford." He cleared his throat again, nervously clicking the mechanical pencil. "Of course, I skipped the post-doctoral work to come straight to industry. Mr. Clarke sort of recruited me from my previous position. My research was with *Drosophila.* Flies," he added, as if she needed the explanation. "But I've looked over your proposal and I think you'll find

me useful. Particularly in engineering the bacteria you propose
to produce the compound."

McCall said nothing. She could see so much of herself in
Woods. Young, seduced by all the lab equipment money could
buy. A man without the backbone or the vision to see Curtis
Clarke's poison . . . and therefore a perfect foil for Curtis.

"Great," she said at last. She moved away from the bench-
top, ignoring Woods as she stepped around the table. Her heart
pumped inside her chest almost painfully as she approached
her father.

She spoke softly, with all the love she could put in her
voice. "What do you say, Daddy? Do you think we can work
together?"

"Don't do this, McCall," he whispered. "It's wrong. You
know it's wrong."

The way he'd emphasized the word "wrong," she thought
he'd already seen through her, that he'd read the proposal she'd
submitted and realized where it would lead. She held her
breath, fearing that—without knowing how he would hurt
himself in the process—he would tell everyone in the room
the truth about the Omega Principle.

Curtis stepped in between them. "Your father doesn't see
eye to eye with me on your joining the family business. But
I think with time, he'll come around. Won't you, Donald?"

McCall's father sighed, rubbing the bridge of his nose under
his glasses. He looked so tired. "You'll be reporting your results to me. Once in a while, I'll come in and take a look
around, make certain everything is as it should be. It's all very
straightforward," he said.

She nodded, telling herself she couldn't let things hurt this
much. The next weeks, maybe even months, she couldn't let
herself feel the pain so deeply. She turned back to Curtis.
"So. When's the press conference?"

She knew how Curtis Clark worked. He would want to make
her research a media event. She was counting on it. It was part
of the reason she'd worked the talk show circuit last year, earn-

ing the title of Love Doctor. Clarke and his business thrived on such hype and she'd known it would get his attention.

"Thursday," Curtis said, grinning. "Do you think you'll be ready, girl?"

"I was ready years ago, Curtis."

Curtis walked up behind her. In a voice meant to be threatening, he said, "We could really do something together, McCall. I saw that four years ago and I can only say you're lucky life taught you the lesson it did and brought you back here. You can make us all filthy rich, take care of your sister and father. Don't fuck it up. Because if you do, what happened to you four years ago is going to seem like a picnic. You understand?"

"You're coming in loud and clear," she said.

"I think I'm going to like having you here, girl. Looks like the years have done you good." With those words, he left, the door buzzing loudly as he stepped into the hall.

McCall watched Curtis Clarke and his pricey potato sack suit saunter past the windows of the lab. The moment reeked of last week's breakfast meeting. Curtis loved to manipulate people. *The master of ceremonies has quit the room.*

"And here we are. One big happy family," Roger said. He took off his sunglasses, appearing the picture of sincerity. "I think we should all put the past behind us, make the best of things," he said. Good old charming Roger. "With McCall's help, we all stand to make a great deal of money. I'm absolutely certain she's learned from past indiscretions—"

"Indiscretions?" her father interrupted. "That's very diplomatic of you, Roger. Falsifying data. Accused of misappropriating government funds." Donald Sayer spoke as if each accusation hurt him as much as McCall. "Yes, it was very indiscreet."

With the echo of those words and his anger humming through the air, Donald Sayer left, buzzing himself out into the hall.

"Ouch," Roger said once the lab door shut behind McCall's father. "That must have hurt."

"Don't be an ass, Roger," Belinda said, unexpectedly coming to McCall's defense.

Ignoring Belinda with a disturbing nonchalance, Roger glanced at his watch. "Will you look at the time. I'm outta here." Pulling Belinda in his arms, he made a show of kissing her, opening his mouth over hers, taking his time. But his eyes remained on McCall, even as his hand grabbed Belinda's buttocks, squeezing it tight in front of the lab techs. He winked, then put on his sunglasses, releasing Belinda. "Dinner, darling?"

"Whatever," Belinda said.

There seemed a strange lack of reaction on Belinda's part. She appeared detached from the moment of her ill use. This morning, she was stone cold sober, and yet, the placid expression on her face showed she felt as little as she had when she'd been under the influence.

Blowing a kiss to McCall, Roger left. McCall felt a sharp pain stab her chest. She thought this must be what it was like to have your heart break. She knew how Roger could be to someone vulnerable enough not to fight his subtle cruelty.

Her eyes met her sister's. To McCall, tiny Belinda looked completely out of place in the white lab coat, almost engulfed by the white cotton. She imagined her sister in leotards and tights, her torn T-shirt wrapped tightly around her body. How gracefully she'd moved, her features animated and bright with life as she made the music part of her.

"You work here?" McCall asked gently, realizing now what her mother had meant when she'd said she'd given Belinda to her father. "You're not dancing anymore?"

Belinda shrugged. "I'm Daddy's assistant. I help out in the lab."

A technician. McCall remembered her question to her sister at the casino, praying in her heart that her father couldn't be that insensitive, that he hadn't stolen Belinda's dreams to bring her here.

"I gotta go," Belinda said. For a moment, she looked as if she were going to say something else. But then she bit her lip, swallowing her words as she turned to leave.

Someone cleared their throat. McCall pivoted back, remembering her staff of three. Four, if she counted Kyle Woods, Curtis's spy, which she didn't.

"Why don't you all take the rest of the day off?" she said, too tired to keep up her charade much longer. "You all have copies of my research proposal. Go over it, memorize it. I want input before we get started tomorrow."

Woods stepped forward, again fidgeting with his pencil. "But the press conference is Thursday. We really should take advantage—"

"Not today," McCall said, cutting him off.

"I think—"

McCall held up her hand, silencing him as her father had done to her earlier. She looked at Woods, trying to see what made him tick, how to get a handle on Curtis's weapon.

But the guy was so wound up. Fidgeting with his pencil, clearing his throat. It was hard to see him as a threat. Playfully, she snatched off his glasses and lifted them up to look through them.

"Lordy, Kyle. I'd say you couldn't see three inches in front of your nose without these."

He grabbed the glasses back. "Six, to be precise."

"Let's get one thing straight, Woods. When I look at you, I'm going to see Curtis Clarke's eyes and ears. You're nothing but a nuisance to me." She turned to the others, two men and a woman. "I hope that's not the same for the rest of you."

Having made her point, she left Kyle and walked up to the others. Each wore identification badges with their photographs and positions. McCall pulled out a stool, and sat down. She gestured for the others to do the same.

All her life, she had relied on her intellect. It had been

only the last few years that she'd learned to read people, to listen and hone her intuition about their wants and needs. That particular skill had kept her out of trouble while she played the blackjack tables, going from city to city, earning the money she needed to back her research.

"I know what you're thinking," she said, sensing that her own response to this situation would mirror their own. "You're trained to make medical breakthroughs . . . and all this"—she waved her hand to indicate the lab—"appears so frivolous. A million vain women and we're just feeding them hope. Perhaps even a false hope."

She looked at the only other woman in the group. She smiled, reading her name off the badge. "Kate. Are you a *Star Trek* fan?"

Kate had short black hair that grew out of her head in corkscrew curls and pretty blue eyes that reminded McCall of her sister. "Are you kidding? *The Next Generation, Deep Space Nine, Voyager.* I watch them all." She grinned, showing a tiny gap between her two front teeth that made her look ten years younger. "I even went to a couple of conventions."

"Do you remember the episode in the old series about the brides?"

"Sure. Harry Mudd, he gives the women he recruits a pill, the Venus drug, that makes them beautiful and younger. For a fee, he sets them up with husbands in frontier planets in space. Only, the women have to keep taking the pill or the effects wear off. They become old hags."

McCall turned to the other two, both men. One appeared in his early thirties, very thin, with a blond buzz cut and hazel eyes. The other man was a good decade older, taller, with the puppy dog eyes and droopy cheeks of a basset hound.

"In the end," McCall said, "one woman didn't want to deceive the man who'd contracted for her. When the pill wore off, she showed him her older, more tired self, trying to convince him that—despite her looks—she would make him a fine wife."

"He thought he'd been ripped off," Kate said.

McCall stood and began pacing before the troops. She stopped before Woods, who'd remained standing, obviously cut off from the group, as she'd intended him to be. "So she takes the pill, just to show her proposed husband it's a trick. She transforms before his eyes, becoming more beautiful. A younger-looking woman." McCall crossed her arms, leaning back against the table behind her. "Only, this particular pill was a placebo. Nothing but colored gelatin. It was a trick. She just *thought* she was beautiful, and made it so."

She picked up an empty test tube, twirling it between her fingers. "A swipe of blush, a different lipstick color. These things can sometimes transform a woman. Illusions that can sink skin deep and open up the beauty within. I hope no one here will ever belittle that effort. Whether it comes from a tube of lipstick or a spritz of the Omega Principle."

She put down the test tube and made eye contact with each of the three techs. It was something she'd learned to do as she tried to persuade television audiences to buy the products she endorsed. "I'll be here at six in the morning tomorrow. I hope to find you all here working beside me." To Kyle, she said, "Except you." She winked. "You have my permission to sleep in."

There was a snicker from the group. The younger one, the one with the buzz cut, smiled shyly at McCall.

She returned his smile, thinking she'd accomplished one thing. She'd made certain the three lab techs knew who was boss. Though no one could know her true intentions, it would help if she earned some loyalty.

"Dr. Sayer," Kyle said from behind her. "I'm only trying to do my job."

McCall looked back at Curtis's lackey, a little surprised that he'd spoken out loud. She hadn't expected that much gumption from the man.

But now she saw an earnestness in his gaze. He had these strange yellow eyes. Wolf eyes. She hadn't noticed them before because of his glasses. And there had been a tremor of emotion in his voice. Anger, perhaps. It instantly made her regret provoking him. She was letting her hostility toward Curtis and his son make her too harsh.

"We'll be fine as long as you don't get in my way. I don't like people looking over my shoulder, reporting to others about me," she said, giving in that much.

Kyle sank his hands into the pockets of his lab coat, and shrugged. He glanced at the door.

"I guess I can go do some work for your father today. If you don't need me." Obviously, the thought of a day off put Dr. Kyle Woods at loose ends.

McCall watched him walk out into the hall. To the others, she said, "We're going to be working hard here. Late nights. Maybe even weekends. I hope you guys have something better to do with a day off than go look for more work."

"Hell, yes," Tom, the younger tech, said.

"You bet." Kate echoed the sentiment.

All three left. But not before McCall had committed their names to memory. *Tom, Kate, Robert.* She glanced at the folder they'd given her at Human Resources. It contained all the *curriculum vitae* of the people she'd be working beside. She thought of the Biosafety Level-2 lab next door, wondering if any of her people had access.

She sighed, picking up her purse as she headed for the door.

"Here we go," she said under her breath.

Kyle Woods thought he'd actually found someone he liked at Clarke Labs.

Unfuckingbelievable.

Walking down the corridor, he smiled, remembering the rousing show McCall Sayer had put on. At his expense, but he didn't care. Nothing here could hurt him. This wasn't what he was about.

He liked her spirit, though. He liked best that she hated Curtis Clarke. They shared that in common, at least.

No doubt, there were some interesting family dynamics going on here. He, of course, knew all about the brilliant but infamous Dr. McCall Sayer. He'd made it his business to know as much as he could about anyone associated with the labs. When Curtis Clarke had approached him about spying on McCall, he'd jumped at the chance to get in good with the older man.

He needed Clarke to trust him. To let his guard down.

He smiled again, wondering if now—with Clarke's plate full with the challenging Dr. McCall Sayer—Kyle would finally get his chance.

He heard voices, shouts coming from the direction of the Fragrance lab, where Donald Sayer had his office. A split second later, Belinda Sayer careened around the corner.

"Fuck you, Daddy," she said under her breath as she slammed into Kyle.

He grabbed her before she fell, pinning her against him. He could feel her body, lithe and supple beneath the lab coat and the stretchy material of her dress. She was so beautiful, he thought she was unreal sometimes. He had the sudden image of her in Roger's arms, how the idiot had pawed her while he'd been staring at the older sister.

"I'm sorry," she said, not really seeing him, brushing tears from her eyes as she stepped around him.

He watched her walk away. He knew he was invisible to her. A nerd. It made him a little angry, because she wasn't the least bit invisible to him.

He kept walking, warning himself not to get involved. He had a mission here, something that was bigger than figuring out why Belinda Sayer let her fiancé abuse her and cursed her father.

He made his way to the Fragrance Group, determined to make himself useful. He wanted inside that Biosafety Level-2 lab so bad he could taste it, sensing that was where he'd hit pay dirt.

But as he was buzzed into the Fragrance lab, ready to resume his personae of brown-noser—the insignificant Dr. Kyle Woods—he couldn't get the picture of Belinda out of his head.

He thought about that a minute, smiling as Donald Sayer motioned him forward, ready to set him up on his current project. He only half listened to Sayer, his mind on the daughter, Belinda Sayer. *She might be useful.*

Certainly, she was in the thick of things, just like the rest of them. And if he judged matters right, unlike her father who kept his mouth shut, Belinda Sayer was a weak link. A connection that could be explored and exploited.

Only, she would never pay attention to him as Kyle the Nerd.

Kyle Woods smiled, whistling softly as he sat down at the computer terminal, knowing it was time to make some changes.

Nine

Jake picked up the phone on the second ring. "Devil May Care Pizza," he answered, shoving a frozen pot pie into the microwave. "You buy it; we burn it." He shut the door and punched in ten minutes to nuke the food. "Deliveries straight from hell."

"Turn on your television set. Channel fifty-seven."

It was Dino. Getting a bad feeling, Jake forgot his dinner and did as he asked. He sat on the couch and changed the channel using the remote.

It was a local chat show, one where the host, Cyndi—a Barbie clone wearing a fitted white dress and the newest shag hairstyle—walked around the studio audience with a mike and shot questions at the guests like mortar fire. Only, there was just one target this hour. A single woman sat spine straight, legs crossed, in a chair center stage.

"Mac," he said.

"Now that's cute," Dino said through the receiver, his tone overly sweet. "Mac. Short for Dr. McCall Sayer. Gosh, you're already using those cuddly names for each other. Do you know who the *hell* you're involved with?"

It was a little difficult to recognize her at first, though Jake was getting used to her varied disguises. She wore a very conservative blue pin-striped suit, complete with thin tie, her hair pinned back in a tight bun. She had on large tortoiseshell glasses, making him wonder if she'd worn contacts when they'd gone out or if she would truly go so far as to wear glasses she didn't need on television.

Despite the outfit, there was something very sexy about the look. She reminded him of one of those models in the print ads posing as a high-level exec or an intellectual—only, they looked so gorgeous you just sort of rolled your eyes and thought: Yeah, *that's* what my physics professor looked like in college.

"It's her, isn't it?" Dino asked. "That's why you asked me about the pheromones. Jesus, Irishman. You're going out with the Love Doctor. That's what they're calling her on the show. The Love Doctor."

Jake made an noncommittal noise in the back of his throat. He was trying to listen to what Cyndi the talk show host was asking Mac, wanting to hear her answer.

He hadn't made any attempt to see Mac since she'd left him high and dry at the *River Palace,* even after Dino had told him she'd come by Sunday night. It had spooked him, how he'd kept watching that surveillance video of her talking to the blonde, running it over and over until he could antici-pate every move, each gesture. Instead, he'd headed north of the lake with his son, taking Michael camping, trying to con-nect with someone in his life so he wouldn't have this great big void he was trying to fill up with the mysterious Dr. Sayer. He'd worked hard this week, focusing on the casino and Mi-chael, trying to get a little control over the roller coaster ride he'd been on last week.

"I don't frigging believe it," Dino said into his ear. "The Donovan Curse strikes again."

"Gotta go," Jake said, not willing to have the lecture he could hear on the tip of Dino's tongue interfere with the in-terview. "See you tomorrow." Both he and Dino had been working the day shift that week.

"Listen to me, Irishman. Do *not* hang up until I talk some sense into you. I am your friend. You are not to—"

Jake punched the phone off. He collapsed the antenna

against his chest, staring at the set. She looked so composed, sitting there. The perfect scientist. But when the camera came in close, he could see the fire in her eyes.

"Certainly there are products on the market today with pheromones," she said in the metered tone of a woman accustomed to lecturing. "Quite good ones. I give a tremendous amount of credit to the people whose ground-breaking research brought these compounds to the attention of the consumer. But I think you'll find the Omega Principle will be different from what's already available on cosmetics counters and through mail order."

"And what makes it different, Dr. Sayer?"

Mac gave a mysterious smile Jake felt all the way down to his toes. "How I derive the formula, of course."

"Without giving away any trade secrets, why don't you tell our studio audience a little about that."

McCall sat forward in the chair, looking energized by the question. "We've already discussed how pheromones work in animals. Without getting too technical, every human has receptors in their nose specifically designed to detect pheromones."

"One up each nostril," Jake said with a grin, remembering.

"What I have studied is how to make a compound that mimics pheromones. Only, through genetic engineering, I plan to mass-produce something that binds more tightly with those receptors in the nose, creating a stronger response than normal human pheromones would evoke."

"So what can we expect?" the interviewer asked. "We put on the Omega Principle and—look out. Men fall at our feet?"

"Yeah, Mac. I'd like to hear the answer to that one myself," he whispered.

"The Omega Principle is like any other cosmetic enhancement. The formula works with the woman to make her feel more attractive. Only on a molecular level, if you will. It gives confidence, bringing out a person's inner beauty."

"Do you use your product?"

Again, the secretive smile. "The Omega Principle is still highly experimental. But whenever I synthesize a compound, I am always the first to use it."

"And?"

"And?" Jake echoed.

"I'm not often disappointed by the results."

"I bet," Jake said softly. He had to hand it to Mac. Whatever she was using, she'd hooked him good. Even now after a week of cajoling himself that he only needed a little distance from Mac to get some perspective, he could feel himself slipping . . .

"Are you aware that you're known as the Love Doctor?" Cyndi stretched out the name, sounding like a poor imitation of Barry White. There came an answering titter from the studio audience.

"I've heard the title used before, yes."

"How does that make you feel, Dr. Sayer?" Cyndi asked, winking back at the audience.

The camera zoomed in on Mac's face. She appeared to have on very little makeup, or at least the tones the television people had used were natural. But they'd emphasized her eyes behind the glasses, lining the lids heavily in black.

"I take it as the supreme compliment I imagine it was intended to be," she said with another smile. "But I must say, it's a bit of a misnomer. The products I have endorsed in the past were never aphrodisiacs. And neither is the Omega Principle. If I may use an analogy for purposes of comparison. We've all heard about the powers of aroma therapy and researchers have shown that scents such as musk or vanilla can be natural attractants. I believe there's even experimental results that indicate the scents that stimulate a man most are the smells of cinnamon buns and apple pie."

"Talk about getting to a man's heart through his stomach," Cyndi said, pausing for laughter from the audience.

"The Omega Principle works in a similar manner, only the science behind it is a bit more complex."

"And when can we expect to get our hands on this miracle?"

"By the fall, we hope to have the product marketed."

Cyndi held up a bottle. Tall and thin, it was made of red glass capped off by a clear crystal stopper. A gold heart was set into the glass at the throat of the bottle.

"You heard it, folks. Clarke Cosmetics will soon be marketing a compound that mimics human pheromones, engineered for a stronger response. Despite rigorous disclaimers by Dr. Sayer, who is deriving the formula, it is being heralded as the love potion of the future. Remember." The hostess pointed a manicured nail at the camera and flashed a laser-bright smile. "You heard it from Cyndi first. In our next half hour, we'll be hearing the incredible story of a boy who—"

Jake kept staring at Mac. He felt an intense longing flow through him. More than a week had passed since she'd come to his hotel suite, and he could still remember everything about her: her smell, her expressive eyes and their changeable color . . . the touch of her mouth on his. The vivid image of her naked in his bed speared through his brain.

He heard the microwave oven beep, announcing his chicken pot surprise was ready, but the last thing he was thinking about was dinner. She was working for Clarke Cosmetics. He'd heard of them, of course. Nothing good. During his tenure at the Attorney General's office, Clarke and his shady business deals were legend. For Gus Pierson, the head of the Criminal Division, Curtis Clarke was the one that got away. Every time.

When the program cut to a commercial the phone rang. Jake punched the "talk" button on the cordless telephone. "Yeah?"

"Look," Dino's voice piped in through the receiver. "I wasn't going to say anything. I thought Suzy was wrong . . . but hell. Maybe you should take a look at the file, at least."

"What are you talking about?" Jake frowned, remembering he'd forgotten to return Susan's messages. She'd called twice. "What file?"

There was a long sigh on the other end. "Cascade Lounge. Two hours. Be there. I have some interesting reading material for you. Trust me, Irishman. You won't want to miss this."

Stacie Winn turned off the television set. That Cyndi was something, she thought, going to her room to pick out a dress for tonight. That's what she liked about Cyndi's show; if there was anything new in town, Cyndi was there to point at the camera and say, "You heard it from Cyndi first."

Stacie shifted through the clothes in her closet one by one. She had arrived home from the day shift dealing at the casino just in time to catch her favorite show. Now she needed to get down to the business of major repairs before meeting Garrett for dinner. He was taking her to the Grill Room at the Windsor Court.

She picked out the black Donna Karan dress Garrett had bought for her. Everything nice in her closet was a gift from her lover. He was a very generous man . . . and very picky about how she looked.

Dress nice, sweetie, he'd said.

She frowned, remembering how the comment had struck her at the time. That she needed instructions . . . that she might disappoint. The Grill Room was high class.

She looked at herself in the wardrobe mirror. Garrett was always saying things like that to her. *Wear the Chanel suit tonight. Try your hair up. Now don't say much at dinner, because this is business. You just sit there and look pretty.*

Look pretty. She had long black hair and dark green eyes and could still pass for her late twenties in a pinch. But not for much longer. And that frightened her sometimes.

"You should have known better than to fall in love with that Garrett," she chided herself, shaking her head.

At thirty, Garrett Renault was seven years younger than Stacie. A rich New Orleans boy who'd used his granddaddy's money to make himself even more . . . trying to impress parents who would always see him as their wild child.

Sometimes, she worried that was all she was to Garrett; his white trash girlfriend. Someone he could flaunt in front of his society parents, like his flashy hotel and garish casino. But Stacie, she loved him to death.

She sighed, putting the dress on the bed. "Take my word for it, Stacie girl. He is never going to put a ring on your finger. And darling. You aren't getting any younger."

She'd been with Garrett four years now, madly in love with his maverick spirit and his tender heart. Garrett would say things to her—about growing up with his family, how they always expected things from him. She'd seen him cry like a baby in her arms, never holding back, showing a side of himself he hid from others. But sometimes she feared she was giving up too much to be with such a rich and powerful man. Her dream of a white picket fence near her mama's house in Georgia. Children.

She thought about the Omega Principle, remembering that pretty red bottle with the crystal stopper.

"Maybe that's what I need. A love potion. A supersonic one."

The kind that would make Garrett love her forever.

Biting her lip, Stacie padded back into the front parlor of the small house she rented, still wearing her dealer's uniform, a ruffled shirt and fitted trousers. She had a good two hours before Garrett sent his car to pick her up—just enough time to get ready.

She sat down in front of the coffee table, wrapping her arms around her stomach as she stared at the folder lying there. The cover was real shiny, looking expensive. *Money's no problem, sweetie,* Garrett had told her when he'd given her the folder. It featured a line drawing of a woman kneeling with her hand cupped before her, catching the roses that tumbled from her hair.

Garrett had given her the brochure last week, but she hadn't looked through it yet, afraid of what it meant. That he thought she needed a beauty clinic. One that promised to keep its clients young.

But now she picked it up, thinking about the things that doctor had said on Cyndi's show. She seemed awful nice, the doctor. Someone you could trust. The same company making the love potion, the Omega Principle, ran the beauty clinic.

Stacie flipped through the brochure inside the folder. The photographs were incredible. The clinic was on some sort of tropical island called Isla Hermosa. Panoramic views displayed miles of white sand beaches with crystal-clear waters. Other smaller photographs featured women having facials and massages, lavish bedroom suites, and tables laden with tropical delights.

"What the hell, Stacie. You had your boobs done. How different can this be?"

She found a pen in the kitchen drawer and flipped out the application. There were a lot of pages, some forms asking for detailed medical information, but she could at least get started.

She filled out her name across the top of the first page, planning to tell Garrett that she'd changed her mind about the Clarke Spa and Clinic.

After all, it's what Garrett wanted. And above all, Stacie wanted to make him happy.

Jake sat down across the table from Susan. In the background, he could hear the water sluicing down the rock formation that gave the Cascade Lounge its name. "I thought I was meeting Dino?"

"He'll be here later." Susan played with the toothpick speared through her olive, swishing it around the martini. Jake ordered a beer from the cocktail waitress and grabbed a handful of peanuts from the bowl in the center. He popped two in his mouth.

"Sorry I didn't return your message. I took Michael away for the weekend and it slipped my mind."

"It's okay. Dino told me," she said, reaching for her briefcase. She opened it with a quick *click, click,* and pulled something out—he couldn't see what—placing it on her lap. The mysterious reading material, no doubt.

Susan wore a coral suit and a necklace made with tiny seed pearls strung along a gold chain. Jake crunched down a couple more peanuts, thinking she'd done something new with her hair—had she cut it? It fell, soft and straight with long layers, to just below her shoulders, looking sharp. But then, Jake figured hanging around Dino, Mr. Style, might put a little pressure on a woman.

Both his ex-wives favored that tailored look, though Susan looked pretty and feminine in the stuff. Hope, she had a tendency to look like the Queen of Freeze. All those years working to break the glass ceiling could make a person hard.

Mac came to mind, making him smile. Hell, he didn't even know if she'd be a redhead next time he saw her, much less what she'd be wearing.

"Look, Susan." He signed for the drinks, putting them on his account. "Maybe it's a good thing I got a chance to talk to you alone. I promised I'd put in a good word for Dino." He took a sip of the beer the waitress had poured for him. "You know he's hot to get into that business of yours. You have him working there every spare minute as it is. You're not stringing him along, are you?" he asked, meaning more than in the business sense.

"No, of course not. We've talked about it. Taking a partner might be a good idea; I'm spread out a little thin these days. Too many cheating spouses. He's even helped me on a couple of cases already."

Jake put down the glass, remembering. "He says you're seeing someone."

She looked away quickly, making him think Dino might be

right. "Did he? Well, it's not as if I'm dating anyone exclusively. We'll see."

Jake drank his beer, thinking even if Susan was interested in someone besides Dino, it wouldn't work out. She and Dino had something special. Anybody paying attention could see it. For Jake, the most telling thing was how Dino could get Susan riled. And the Greek enjoyed it, primarily because it showed she cared. During the years Susan and Jake had been married, she hadn't so much as raised her voice. Jake thought that might have been part of the problem. Twenty-twenty hindsight.

"So, do you know anything about this reading material Dino wanted to give me?" he asked, prompting her.

Susan took a thick folder from her lap and laid it on the table. He recognized it instantly, because he'd seen them before. The white background, the brown trim. There was a file number, of course, and a place where you could check mark certain notations: armed and dangerous, escape risk, suicidal. Printed across the center were the words UNITED STATES DEPARTMENT OF JUSTICE, FEDERAL BUREAU OF INVESTIGATION.

An FBI file.

Jake stared at it as if it were a snake. Because someone had added a label at the top of the file. Normally, they didn't do that at the Bureau, identifying files only by case number.

DR. McCALL ELIZABETH SAYER, it read.

Slowly, he took his hands off the table, dropping them to his side. "What the hell is this?"

"You know what it is, Jake. I'm sure you've seen them before. It's an FBI file. Dino was going to show it to you, but I thought I should be the one to bring it."

He didn't move . . . he thought maybe he forgot to breathe. He shook his head, trying to snap out of it.

For an instant, he felt dissociated from the moment, almost as if it were happening to someone else. It was one of those television moments. He had zoomed out, panned the room, then focused on the fool seated across from his ex-wife, the

PI, as she handed him an FBI file on a woman he'd been lusting after. *Joke's on you!*

Susan pushed it closer. "Open it. Read it."

When he didn't lift a finger, Susan started to do it for him. Jake pushed her hand away. He grabbed the file and slid it to the edge of the table. Following some long forgotten instinct, he opened it, than began flipping through the pages almost mechanically. It was the typical stuff. Background checks. Interviews with neighbors. Surveillance photographs.

Only, this wasn't some criminal he wanted to prosecute.

He spread the photographs out, lining them across the table, seeing a different woman than the one he'd almost made love to. Not different in the sense Mac was today, someone who could change her look like a chameleon. This woman was . . . a scientist, a nerd. Baggy jeans, hair pulled tight—a braid, a ponytail, a bun—shirts with little Peter Pan collars and wind breakers.

"Where did you get this?"

"I have my sources. I'm sorry. But I thought you should know."

Jesus, there was even an FBI personality assessment from the Behavioral Science Unit. And photocopies of newspaper clippings, though he didn't know if Susan had added these or if they were part of the original file.

Scandal Rocks Local Genius. Professor Found Guilty of Academic Misconduct. US Attorney to Launch Grand Jury Probe.

He set the articles aside, not reading them. He wondered how he could have missed something like this—local girl gone bad. But the headlines were dated around the time he'd been fighting Hope for custody. He'd had other things on his mind then.

He kept turning the pages in the file, catching a sentence here and there, not focusing too long on any one thing, but feeling every word hit like a body blow delivered by a prize fighter.

Communist connection . . . regularly e-mails sensitive material to Dr. Kam Chang of the PRC . . . research possible front for black market designer drug . . . megalomaniac with a devious genius . . . diabolic research prompting ethical challenges . . .

His eyes skimmed over the words, faster and faster, until the sentences became one endless blur. He couldn't focus.

He shut the file. He couldn't remember the last time he'd felt like this. Those days in the lawyers' offices, fighting for Michael, maybe. He couldn't seem to catch his breath.

"Jake. I know what kind of man you are. This woman. Don't try to help her. There's a big difference between someone in trouble and someone who is trouble. You know that, don't you? Please, tell me you know the difference."

He didn't answer her.

"Jake, listen to me. This thing really stinks. Experiments on the brain? Black market designer drugs? She even accused Curtis Clarke of murdering her partner. Now, four years later, she's working for him? It's twisted. You can't seriously involve yourself with someone—"

"Don't." He held up his hand. "Just . . . don't."

They both stood, Jake grabbing the file off the table.

"At least finish your beer. Dino will be here any minute. We can go over it together. You don't have to go through this thing alone."

But Jake wasn't listening to Susan. There was just this roar of sound in his ears, like the ocean was stuck in his head.

"I brought it to help you," Susan said, latching on to his arm when he turned to leave. "Dino said you were getting involved with her. That she was coming to the casino to look for you. Please, let me help you."

"You already have," he said, holding up the file. "Leave the rest to me, Susan."

Leave the rest to me. He almost laughed as he headed for the doors, turning his back on Susan standing there in the middle of the Cascade Lounge. He'd sounded so reasonable. As if he actually knew what the hell he was going to do.

He hiked it to his office, carrying the file tucked under his arm so no one could see what it was. He strode through the hotel lobby and up through the passageway, past the Riverwalk to the gangplank. For the first time, he didn't return the smiles or the greetings from the men and women who worked with him at the casino. The file felt incredibly heavy in his hands.

When he reached his office in the hold of the ship, he shut the door. He dropped the file on the center of his desk and sat down, staring at the cover. He didn't know how long he waited there. Minutes? Hours? Then, just as Susan had asked, he opened the file and began reading. Cover to cover.

He tried to pretend it was just like any other file. When he'd worked for the Attorney General, he would get something similar and he would go over it, putting the pieces together, coming up with the angle. *Just like the old days.*

When he finished, he sat back in his chair, trying to keep it straight in his head. Trying to keep some distance . . . but then he would remember Mac's face on that video.

Jake knew how to read people's gestures, their facial expressions, the fluctuations in their voice. During those exercises for *voir dire,* when they would slip the mock jurors cards telling the volunteers their hidden prejudices, Jake could always find the time bomb waiting to hang the case. At the Criminal Division, his ability to pick a jury had been his greatest strength. Gus Pierson, his boss, had called him the Svengali of the jury box.

How many times had he watched that video, freezing it right at the moment when the blonde leaves Mac at the bar? He knew what he'd seen on Mac's face. Resignation. Fear. Now, he thought maybe it went farther than that.

He picked out the photographs of Mac four years ago, wearing her glasses and her baggy clothes.

She even accused Curtis Clarke of murdering her partner.

Now, four years later, she's working for him? He could still hear Susan spelling it out.

He picked up the phone, punched in the number from memory. "Gus Pierson, please."

Gus had been his superior in the Criminal Division, a man who'd had it out for Curtis Clarke. If any investigation was ongoing involving Clarke Cosmetics, Gus would be up on it.

Jake tried to sound upbeat, talking to his friend on the phone, taking the usual razzing about leaving the office to go work for the bad guys. At the Office of the Attorney General, Louisiana Department of Justice, there was a Gaming Division, specializing in investigating any illegal activity involving the casinos. It had blown a couple of people away, particularly Gus, that Jake had left the office to work as a casino manager. But the *River Palace* was a clean operation. And Jake had been pretty bitter about losing Michael at the time. He'd figured being one of the guys in the white hats hadn't gotten him much in this life.

Jake asked his question, keeping it vague, not letting it become personal. Until he hung up the phone.

He sat at his desk, going over what Gus had told him.

There's a big difference between someone in trouble and someone who is trouble, Susan whispered in his head.

The Donovan Curse strikes again.

But Dino was wrong. This wasn't a game.

Jake leaned forward, propping his elbows on his desk, burying his head in his hands.

Mac was in a shit load of trouble.

"Guess it didn't go well, huh?"

Dino was wearing a nubby sweater in different shades of brown, patched stylishly in places with leather. He'd combed his curls back with pomade to give his hair that permanent wet look. Normally, Susan would have made a joke about his hair, the way he always dressed as if he'd just read the latest issue of *Esquire Gentleman*. Only, right now, she didn't feel much like talking.

She remembered the look on Jake's face when he'd turned those pages in the file, the way he'd handled the photographs. *You've lost him.*

She felt the disappointment settle inside her, dark and bleak and heavy. Who was she kidding? She'd lost him years ago.

"Hey." Dino nudged her foot under the table, getting her attention. "Maybe she's using those pheromones on him, huh?"

"You're not making me feel better, if that's what you're trying to do."

Susan slid the olive off the toothpick and watched it float to the bottom of the martini glass. She jabbed it a couple of times with the toothpick.

"Damn her." She was thinking of Dr. Sayer, of what she'd read in the file.

"Jake's a big boy, Suzy. You gave him the information. It's up to him now."

"And what if he sees her as some big crusade? Like he did Hope? What if he talks himself into helping her?"

"That's the risk you took showing him the file."

But she'd wanted it to go the other way. She'd thought he would recognize the woman's poison and steer clear of her.

"You know what I think?" Dino said, leaning forward across the table. "I think you should forget about the Irishman. And I know just how to work it . . . a night of incredible, wild, *unforgettable* sex. Just wipe him out of your memory." He glanced at his watch. "As it happens, I have a couple of hours to kill."

"I don't find you the least bit attractive, Dino," she lied, knowing his offer wasn't entirely a joke.

"What's the matter, Suzy?" he said, suddenly very serious. "Am I only good for a shoulder to cry on? To fix your security system and help you order from catalogues?"

For the first time, he sounded angry at her rejection. But

he had to know how she felt about their relationship. What they had was special; why risk it by sleeping together?

Still, she wasn't in a diplomatic mood. Instead, she told him, "Dino. You are a womanizer. There's something really unattractive about a man who has notches on his bedpost."

He gave her the sweetest, sexiest smile. "That only means I've had lots of practice."

"Your virility overwhelms me."

She got up and grabbed her briefcase from the floor, angry because she was tempted by Dino's offer. A night of sexual abandonment with a man she trusted enough to offer a berth in her business . . . a friend she spent hours with weekly, sometimes daily. Dino was someone who knew her inside and out. A man who just might erase the pain she was feeling right now, even if it was only for one night.

That's all you need, Susan. From the frying pan into the fire. That would make her truly pathetic.

She glared down at Dino, still seated at the table. He was lounging back in his chair, eating peanuts as if their fight hadn't affected him in the least.

"I'll let you know when I'm ready to become another notch on the belt, Dino," she said.

He popped another peanut in his mouth. "I thought you said it was the bedpost."

"Smart-ass." Dino could always get to her.

She walked away, leaving Dino and the Cascade Lounge. She kept telling herself, it wasn't Dino she wanted. And she wouldn't make the mistake of fooling herself into believing it was.

Ten

We're trying something different with the monkeys. We're administering immunosuppressant drugs along with the injections. My hopes are high. I don't think I could bare to see the type of death suffered by the rats again. Certainly not in the monkeys.

—Excerpt from Alicia Goodman's lab book

Roger jackknifed out of his chair, charging Donald Sayer, almost knocking down a pussy willow basket the interior designer had called art. Personally, Curtis thought the damn thing looked like a trash can growing hair.

"What is your problem, man!" Roger shouted.

"You are seriously underestimating McCall," Donald insisted.

"I'm underestimating her? I'm not the one arguing the Omega Principle is full of shit." Roger stabbed his finger to the middle of Donald's chest. "You haven't even bothered to read the goddamn proposal and you're claiming she can't pull it off?"

"I don't need to read it," Donald answered in that superior tone he loved to use with Roger. "A critical reading of the data has convinced me human pheromones don't exist, much less a compound that mimics them. What she's suggesting is simply not possible. Any idiot can see that."

Curtis wrapped his lips around the eight-inch Romeo y

Julieta, drawing the Cuban cigar into a slow burn as he waited for the dust to clear.

"Well, *this* idiot thinks McCall's on to something," Roger argued, "something that's actually going to make money for this company, unlike the crap you've been peddling the last year, acting as if Clarke Labs is your own personal Swiss bank account."

"Easy, boy," Curtis cautioned, seeing Roger's needle wiggling into the red zone.

Roger grabbed the data Kyle Woods had put together off Curtis's desk and waved the pages in front of Donald's nose. "I e-mailed you a copy of Woods's report. Did you even bother to read it? She's generated the peptide, Dr. Asshole. All she needs is the bacteria to mass-produce it and we're marketing a gold mine."

Sayer puffed up like a porcupine. Ever since the scandal surrounding McCall's research, the man wanted nothing to do with his daughter. It was something Curtis just couldn't figure. He knew his son was an idiot most times, but he loved the fool. Family was family, after all.

"You know what I think, Daddy?" Roger said, dropping into the crimson leather chair shaped like an eggshell. He swiveled back and forth in front of Curtis's desk, giving a smile that said Donald was about to get one right between the eyes. "I think you should offer McCall her daddy's job again, like you did four years ago. I think she'd take you up on it this time, I do. How about it, Donald? Ready to step aside for someone who actually has a clue?"

"You're so blind, Roger."

"Why? Because you didn't think of the Omega Principle first? Come off it, Donald. You and I both know your daughter is smarter than you'll ever be."

Donald rose to his feet, having had enough of Roger's abuse. He shook his head, looking at Roger as if he felt sorry for him. "You could always be stupid, Roger. And you never were much of a scientist."

"Don't you walk out on me. I'm not finished with you, asshole."

In a fit of rage, Roger threw Woods's report at the door as it shut behind Donald Sayer. Curtis watched the pages flutter to the beveled inlaid pattern cut into the carpet in the shape of the company's logo. "Have a seat, Roger. We need to talk."

"Who the hell does he think he is? Fucking idiot." Roger paced in front of Curtis's desk, crushing the pages of Woods's report under his elephant-skin shoes. "He talks to me like I'm a piece of shit. I *own* his ass. This company owns him! He shows me no respect."

"Calm down, Roger. Donald will do as he's told." Curtis clamped the cigar between his incisors, passing a hand through his hair. He'd been trying to get those highlights his son had naturally. He'd have to talk to Stefano, ask the stylist if he could go a little more blond next time. "Have you ever considered the man might have a point? Are we moving too quickly on the Omega Principle?"

"Oh, no. I'm not letting him ruin this." He leaned over the desk, his gray eyes shining, his three-button leather jacket flapping open to show muscle definition beneath his cotton shirt that Curtis wouldn't see in a lifetime of sessions with personal trainers. "Let me tell you a little about the tests we ran this week, in layperson's terms, Daddy, so you can understand."

Curtis grinned behind the cigar. Roger loved to parade his degrees in front of him, implying his daddy was ignorant. But Curtis knew he'd paid for all that schooling. He'd made Roger. It was something he was damn proud of.

Roger hitched his butt onto the corner of the black teak desk and helped himself to one of his father's cigars from the humidor. "We did PET scans on ten male test subjects at a local clinic. That's positron emission tomography. Woods oversaw the whole thing so she couldn't pull anything. The PET scan lets us measure the level of activity in the brain. Guess what? When these guys took a whiff of the peptide McCall synthesized, the nerve centers in their brains lit up like they were watching *Debbie Does Dallas*. We're going to see money on this. Now. Not fifteen years from now, the way Donald is planning."

Curtis sighed, not liking the fact that McCall was on the up and up. He would have preferred that the girl had been scamming them. That would have made sense. He didn't like when things didn't add up.

He swirled the smoke from the cigar in his mouth, savoring it like wine. "How's construction on the clinic coming along?"

"Slow. Very slow. And expensive." Roger plopped into the chair, stretching his long legs before him, stacking one foot over the other. "I had to wire more money to the contractor for bribes. But it will be ready."

Curtis watched Roger use the cigar clippers. He hated to see his son smoke, primarily because he was so bad at it. He puffed like a girl, not willing to get the end good and soggy. Most times, he couldn't even keep it lit.

"I'm worried about your friend, Garrett Renault," Curtis said, thinking maybe he'd slip a couple of bands from his Cubans onto cheap shit cigars for Roger. *What a waste.* "His people called me about the clinic. They want to fly down to Isla Hermosa, see the operation."

"Forget Garrett. I'll take care of him. I'll show him some slides, work up some financial projections." He smiled, trying to light the cigar from the edge and not the bottom. "I let his girlfriend in on BioYouth." He winked. "We're going to keep her young and beautiful for him."

"Is that wise?" Sometimes, he thought his boy courted trouble. Hell, Curtis knew how it felt to come close to the edge, the excitement. But Roger really got off on it. "We can't afford mistakes with this one."

"It's casino money, Daddy. Garrett has cash to burn on this thing. And you're going to want his family's connections when the clinic gets rolling. What are you worried about anyway?" he asked, sounding annoyed. "She's just some piece of ass he picked up. Even if anything happens, they'll never trace it to the clinic. The symptoms just aren't like that. How many times do I have to explain it to you?" He was swinging left and right in the chair, the motion becoming agitated. Roger hated to be questioned.

"Still," Curtis said. "Let's slow down on the investors; keep it in house as much as possible. We don't want too many people in on this . . . too many questions."

"You don't get it, do you?" Roger stood, holding the cigar, ash up, as if it were some goddamn cocktail. "We need lab facilities, medical personnel, bribes for government officials. That takes money. You want to get halfway through this thing and lose everything because we don't have the capital to see it through?"

"All right, all right. But ease off a bit; let me see what I can squeeze out of our people. All we need is an investigation from the DA right now."

"Whatever. I'm the one with the fucking MBA and the doctorate in developmental genetics. Why listen to me?"

"Just humor me on this one, boy."

Roger smoked the cigar like a lollipop, making Curtis wince. He was squinting through the smoky haze, his gray eyes narrowed with a malevolence that jarred even Curtis. He knew his son itched to prove himself, and hell, someday the entire operation would be his. But only when he was ready.

Curtis thought of his own beginnings. He'd been taking care of himself since the age of twelve, talking men into the strip clubs on Bourbon in his teens, watching the girls do their magic backstage, fascinated by that transformation only makeup could give them. But Lord help him, at thirty years old, Roger still needed wet-nursing.

Roger nodded at the pussy willow basket. "Why do you keep that thing, Daddy?" his beautiful boy asked, the son he'd prayed for and managed to get off that weasel-faced bitch he'd married then discarded after she'd served her purpose. He and Roger had been on their own since his boy was two months old.

"It's a one-of-a kind piece. Art. It shows class."

"It looks like shit." Flashing the sweetest smile, a smile that should have warned Curtis, he said, "Here. Let me help you out."

He kicked the pedestal enough to rock the base. The basket tumbled to the carpet, breaking, the delicate pieces scattering to the four corners of the office.

Roger stretched, then walked to the door. "I'll send Woods in to go over the PET scan results with you. By the way, we're getting a delivery tonight from your buncher friend."

Curtis hated when Roger used the term "buncher," the name for dog traders who scoured the streets for animals, sometimes even nabbing them from their own backyards. Which was probably why Roger had said it. Roger and his moods.

"I'll let you know how these dogs turn out," Roger said. *"Adieu,* Daddy."

Curtis shook his head, biting down on the Cuban as he stared at the debris on the carpet. *There goes a few grand.*

Boys and their temper tantrums.

McCall buzzed into Lab 19, surprised to see Kate Mulligan seated at one of the bench-top tables. McCall had just returned from getting coffee and gumbo at the Ragin' Cajun, a roadside diner. She'd hoped to find the lab empty.

"Kate? I thought you'd gone for the day." She came up behind the tech, watching her carefully scrape the bacterial cells from the petri dish. Kate had a rhythm going, placing the cells that looked like bread mold into test tubes, discarding the petri dishes that showed no bacterial colonies had grown.

Kate smiled at McCall, the gap between her teeth making the brunette look Lauren Hutton cute. "I just thought I'd get these done today."

Earlier in the week, Kate had infected the bacterial cells with a virus that carried the gene for their magic peptide—the critical ingredient for the Omega Principle. The next step was to cull out the infected cells, dropping them into a solution rich with enough nutrients to encourage the cells to grow. Robert and Tom, the other two techs, had done the same.

"You're putting in some long hours," McCall said.

"I don't mind. I guess I got the bug as much as these cells," she said, laughing at her own joke. "I can't believe we've already gotten transformation."

"Infecting the cells with the virus was the easy part. The work comes in purifying the compound."

Kate nodded. "Kyle thinks we'll have results by the end of the month."

McCall didn't say anything, hoping he was dead wrong. She was counting on more time than that.

She felt as if she were dancing on a mine field. One misstep, and everything she'd created would rock beneath her, bringing down her house of cards. The PET scan had been her first real test, a turning point that had managed to win over Roger. She'd worked a solid year to pull off that hat trick, and still, she'd practically held her breath until the results came back her way. Even Woods had been fooled.

She pictured Kyle Woods in her mind, his blond hair pulled back in a ponytail, his thick glasses hiding intelligent eyes . . . the nervous way he would click his mechanical pencil. Dr. Kyle Woods. She'd begun to see him as her nemesis at the lab. Roger and the others she could handle—even her father had shown only a cursory interest in her work. But not Woods.

He was a brilliant scientist—very intuitive. And committed, working like a demon on the project. His credentials, the speed with which he labored, it all showed an incredible affinity for this type of work. Left in his hands, it was possible they could isolate the peptide within a month.

She might have to do something about that.

McCall leaned back against the table, picking up one of the petri dishes. This one showed no colonies, devoid of the odd-shaped dots of moldy cells. "I was really surprised to see they'd added the Level-2 lab," she said, trying to make her interest sound casual.

Kate nodded, focusing on the bacteria. "It's been here since I started a couple of years ago."

McCall put down the dish. "I bet the stuff going on in there is wild."

Kate moved onto the next dish. "I wouldn't know. I don't have security clearance."

"Still, you must have heard something."

Kate turned around on her stool, looking McCall dead in the eye. "The last person who got curious lost his job. So I don't ask questions. Just a friendly warning."

Kate got up, carrying the tray of test tubes to the incubator. McCall pressed her lips together. She'd had similar responses from Robert and Tom, the other two techs.

Under her breath, she whispered, "Strike three."

She came up behind Kate and took the tray of test tubes from her. "You get going. I'll finish up here. That's an order."

Kate rotated her shoulders, showing that she was stiff from bending over the petri dishes. "Right, Chief." She shut the incubator and turned to salute McCall, then broke into her characteristic grin. "See you in the morning."

"I'll be here."

McCall waited until Kate gathered her things and left, busying herself with the test tubes and petri dishes. When the door shut behind Kate, McCall glanced down at the bacterial colonies that supposedly held the magic compound she'd promised.

Kyle Woods thought they'd have results by month's end. Purification might take a little longer. But once they isolated the peptide, her time was up.

Kyle listened carefully. Dogs. Definitely dogs.

This was the closest he'd come to confirming the information he'd received months ago. He was in the parking lot, toward the back of the compound of buildings that made up Clarke Labs. A white delivery truck had just pulled up, one with nothing to identify the company that owned it.

He could hear what sounded like soft whimpers coming from inside.

He watched as Belinda signed an invoice, flirting with the oversized hunk of meat packed into jeans and a work shirt. Handing the clipboard back to the driver, she gave him instructions, smiling winsomely as she pointed to a back entrance. The door would lead to the Level-2 lab, where only she and a few others had clearance to enter. She turned around, going back up the stairs.

"Dr. Woods?"

At the sound of his name, Kyle nearly jumped out of his skin. He commanded himself to calm down, turning slowly. He hadn't heard anyone walking up behind him.

It was George, one of the security guards in charge of patrolling the perimeter during graveyard. He looked genuinely surprised when he recognized Kyle. "I thought that was you, Dr. Woods. What are you doing here so late?"

"George." Kyle smiled, grateful that his yen for doughnuts had come in handy for something other than a sugar rush. Every morning, when George was just getting off duty, Kyle showed up with two of the chocolate sprinkle ones, the guard's favorite.

"I just came back to get this report." Kyle held up a file folder he'd brought along. *Just in case.* He needed a plausible excuse for returning at this hour, something that wouldn't end up in a memo on Curtis Clarke's desk in the morning. He nodded his head toward the delivery truck. "Know anything about that?" he asked casually. "Those guys supposed to be here this late?"

"He had the paperwork." George shrugged. "Besides, Miss Sayer is taking care of it."

"Yeah, you're right," Kyle said, smiling. "See you in the morning. Chocolate sprinkles, right?"

"You got my number, Dr. Woods."

Kyle made his way to his Volkswagen Rabbit, the distinct echo of those poor animals ringing inside his head. They would have them muzzled as a precaution, the soft whining the only sound the poor creatures could manage.

A familiar rage rose up inside Kyle, raw and burning. The animals' whimpers had been barely audible from that truck but somehow for Kyle those cries filled the night, becoming almost palpable, a living thing that swelled inside his head becoming a deafening cry for help.

Miss Sayer is taking care of it.

"I just bet she is."

He opened the door to his Rabbit and tossed the file onto the passenger seat. He sat down behind the steering wheel and fitted the key into the ignition, but he didn't turn the engine over.

It didn't take long for her to emerge. The anger pumping inside Kyle shifted into double time as he watched Belinda Sayer skip down the steps, keys in hand. She wore a giraffe-patterned dress that hugged her body, her heels, man-hunting boots that laced up to her knees. In minutes, she reached her premiere parking space, front and center, slipping into her Mazda Miata.

The rage inside him grew hotter, focusing its intensity like a laser. Once she started her car, Kyle pulled out. He slipped in behind Belinda, knowing that—as always—he would be invisible to her.

ROGER

Having typed in the word, McCall punched ENTER, keeping her eyes on the screen as it lit up with a series of listings.

"Gentlemen, we have liftoff," she said, watching Roger's e-mail scroll past.

Like many corporate computer systems, the system manager had set up e-mail accounts so that the user's first name was the default password—unless it was changed. Roger, of course, had never bothered to change his password.

"You were always lazy, Roger."

McCall sat back in the chair, stretching her neck. A couple of hours had passed since she'd sent Kate home. This was the first time she'd dared snoop around the computer files, desperate to make the time she had here count.

Taking a drink of coffee from a Styrofoam cup, she scrolled through Roger's e-mail listing, no small feat. As well as being lazy, Roger was a pack rat. He hadn't discarded e-mail for months. There were almost four hundred entries in his listing, with only two showing in boldface that they hadn't been read.

McCall clicked in on several entries, staying away from the two he hadn't read yet, knowing it would return receipts to the senders if she opened them first. Most of what she found was business or personal—including an XX-rated message to a tech in her father's lab. True to form, Roger was fooling around on Belinda.

McCall choked back her disgust. Earlier today, she'd met Belinda in the employee lounge, convincing her baby sister to take a short break and meet her for coffee. She'd hoped to make up for those first false steps at the *River Palace*. She'd launched into her speech about Belinda's dancing, their father's benevolent interference, trying to make a connection with her sister. She'd wanted Belinda to learn from McCall's mistakes.

What followed was a far cry from the warm and fuzzy moment she'd intended. They'd fought, ending with McCall's ill-considered words. *Don't marry him if he doesn't love you.*

As if Belinda would want to hear that from McCall; as if Belinda would listen.

ENGLISH LIFE.

"Hello." McCall leaned forward, quickly scrolling back up to the listing she'd just passed. English life? The title conjured images of vacations abroad or a slick magazine for Anglophiles—neither meshed with Roger's personality. She clicked the message open.

To: Roger Clarke
From: Martin Burger
Re: English Life
Roger,
Package we spoke about received from England. Damaged!!! Will look for replacements.
Sonia

The message was two days old. Unlike the other e-mail she'd read, this message appeared purposely vague. On a hunch, she opened Roger's "sent mail" folder, checking for any response to Martin Burger or Sonia or whoever may have sent the message, but she found nothing.

"All right," she said to herself, "let's try this."

She searched through the e-mail address listing for a Martin Burger. It flashed on the screen.

MARTIN BURGER 3-L20

"The mysterious Biosafety Level-2 lab?" She frowned. The message had originated from this building, Building 3, from inside Lab 20.

She searched through the e-mail address listing for Sonia, any Sonia.

The system came up blank.

"So why is Sonia using someone else's e-mail address to send Roger messages?"

McCall quickly logged off, knowing she'd browsed too long. She'd been careful with her searches through the file servers and system files, but she'd taken a chance opening Roger's electronic mail. If someone had a tracer on her, they would know what she'd done.

"So much for the Mata Hari act." She'd been trained as a scientist, not a spy. And she was coming to understand that her years at the blackjack tables—hours spent pretending to be someone she wasn't—hadn't come close to preparing her for this.

She thumbed her purse strap over her shoulder and snatched her briefcase off the bench-top. She'd been working at Clarke Labs a week now, and still, she was no closer to discovering any connection between Alicia's experiments and the Clarkes.

She stepped into the hall, immediately aware of the security cameras. Enclosed in a room somewhere, a guard would be watching her stroll to the security station leading out of the labs. It was the strangest sensation, as if a million eyes were watching her. *A fly under the microscope.* The last couple of days, she even thought someone might be following her, getting glimpses of a gray car—possibly a sedan—but she couldn't be sure. Every fifth car in the city was a gray sedan.

Flashing her badge through security, she turned for the nearest exit. She was incredibly tired; primarily because she was having trouble sleeping. The past week, doubts had settled inside her, whispers in the middle of the night that would sneak into her heart and weave into her dreams, making her wonder if the last years she hadn't been deluding herself.

You're wrong, those voices murmured. *Alicia's wrong.*

There were times she wondered if Alicia Goodman hadn't had a breakdown of sorts, her writings, mere delusions of a woman on the edge. Only McCall in her desperation had *made* them into something else . . . something that would earn her back her reputation and the love of the family she'd lost . . . something that would take her away from grading blue books at the community college, the only teaching position available to her now.

Had she converted those rantings into some sort of movie-of-the-week conspiracy? Had she used Alicia's lab book to give herself the green light, coming to hunt down her salvation in the halls of Clarke Labs, where she'd lost it so many years before?

Running out of time. Running out of time. The warning spun around inside her head as she raced through the parking lot in the late-night drizzle, finding the red Lexus she'd leased, a perk from Curtis. Inside, she leaned back against the headrest, breathing hard. She felt as if she'd strapped a vise around her chest. She wasn't even sure what she was looking for. Alicia's lab book spoke in riddles. There was nothing concrete—nothing to give direction. The last few days, she'd been on a fishing expedition.

If he doesn't love you, don't marry him.

Running out of time.

Don't marry him.

Her warning to her sister ran singsong in her head, a children's round with her own misgivings.

Don't marry him. Running out of time. Don't marry him.

McCall grabbed the glasses she wore to drive at night and started the Lexus. She pulled out of the parking space. Today, she'd wanted to show Belinda that she'd changed. She was no longer the sister who acted only from her head and not her heart. She'd wanted to tell her sister everything, how she'd been forced over the years to find something else inside herself besides her IQ—to forget the child applauded only for her gift of intelligence, the girl who had grown into a woman who knew nothing but computers and double helixes.

When her life had fallen apart, Barb had been there, reminding her through their friendship that McCall did have the capacity to care for others. She could forge a connection, could make up bedtime stories for the twins, would remember their birthday and the anniversary of their baptism, the day she stood beside Stan and Barb as the twins' godmother.

She wasn't cold or unfeeling, unable to love. Not anymore.

That's what she'd wanted to share with Belinda. Instead, she'd manage to alienate her sister completely, a task that had taken fifteen minutes, max.

McCall drove down the empty road, her lights on, her wipers fanning back and forth against the light drizzle. It was a warm summer night in June and the rain only made the heat more miserable. In the distance, lightning flashed through purple clouds, igniting the levee to her right, a shadow that hid the river from view. She could remember when her sister was four, the age the twins were now. McCall had been thirteen and in college.

From memory, she conjured the one thing she could never forget: her sister's recitals. Pink ballet slippers and tutus. She'd called her Lindy, as their mother always had, incredibly proud of Belinda's talent. That was the girl she'd expected to find here. The adolescent who'd adored her older sister; Belinda, the teenager, hanging on McCall's every word when she came home to visit during break.

Only the years that had changed McCall had also transformed her sister. Today, over coffee in the employee lounge, McCall had sprung into the apologies she had so religiously rehearsed, hoping, dearly hoping. But she'd fallen short of her mark, lapsing into senseless babblings, unable to help the words pouring from her—until Belinda had cut her off, launching the first salvo.

"Roger says you came back here because you're jealous. He says you wanted to marry him and he wouldn't ask you because he didn't love you."

"Is that so?" McCall had stirred her coffee round and round with the stir stick, feeling her temper buck inside her like a beast, hating Roger, hating that he had this hold over Belinda. "And you're sure he loves you?"

The words had spilled out, spurred by the memory of Roger's smug warning in the shadows of Barb's courtyard. He'd implied Belinda had fallen for an act; that he didn't love her.

"If he doesn't love you," McCall told her sister, "don't marry him. Don't make that mistake."

As soon as she spoke the words, she regretted them. Belinda's laser blue eyes had clouded over. She'd pushed her chair back, too quickly. It had clattered to the floor of the lounge, making the other people in the room turn and stare.

Belinda looked for all the world as if McCall had stumbled across some terrible secret.

"He's right," Belinda had said. "You're a jealous bitch."

McCall had watched Belinda leave, knowing there would be no more chats over coffee now. Everything had gone so wrong.

She turned the steering wheel, braking slightly, feeling sick as she remembered the encounter.

It wasn't enough that McCall had been absent all those years. Now, she'd made Belinda hate her.

Pushing the pedal closer to the floor, McCall sped the Lexus past cypress laden with moss, stark sentinels in the night. Finger-lengths of lightning stabbed at the horizon. For the hundredth time, she wondered if she'd come here because of the Clarkes, convinced by Alicia's writings that they could somehow harm her father and sister by laying the blame for some hideous experiment on her father's door, their head of Research and Development. Or was her return some pathetic attempt to make herself part of a family who didn't want her?

Either way, she was running out of time.

McCall turned onto Governor Nicholls, maneuvering the Lexus down the narrow street. She found a parking space miraculously close to Barb and Stan's house and parallel-parked. Holding her briefcase, she walked down the sidewalk, heading for the gated courtyard, telling herself she would start looking for a place of her own this weekend, no matter what Barb and her stars said.

Tonight, when she'd reached town, she'd had that strange sensation again, that someone was following her. A gray sedan? Though she couldn't be sure the incident gave her misgivings, made her wonder about some nebulous unseen danger. She didn't want to bring trouble here, laying it on the doorstep of the only people who loved her.

She crossed the street, already feeling the loss of leaving

Barb and Stan, the twins, thinking about that—until she glanced up and saw him.

Her mind became a perfect blank, as if she couldn't comprehend what she was seeing. She stopped dead.

Incredibly, he was waiting for her. A familiar figure leaning against the wrought iron gate.

Jake Donovan.

For an instant, she thought the ridiculous, that her fears and loneliness had crafted him from her memories into solid form. But he was really there, waiting in front of Barb's house, illuminated in the dim light coming from a distant streetlamp.

The fact that he was drop-dead gorgeous struck her where she stood almost half a block away. She frowned, walking toward him, a twice-divorced man she couldn't get out of her mind.

She could still remember what it felt like to have his mouth on hers. Something incredibly sweet, like honey coursing through her veins.

She walked right up to him. The drizzle had stopped, but he must have been waiting for some time. His close-cropped hair glistened with drops of rain. It pearled on the shoulders of his jacket.

"Did Dino tell you I came to the casino?" She hadn't made any more attempts to find him after that . . . a monumental show of restraint on her part, she thought.

"He told me."

He was wearing a leather bomber jacket. It looked like the real thing, not a replica, the brown leather covered with patches, soft and worn so that you would want to touch it. It might have belonged to his father, or an uncle.

She thought of Barb and Stan, the twins sleeping inside. "This isn't exactly a good time," she said.

He smiled. "You giving me the brush-off, Mac? What a surprise."

He reached into his jacket and pulled out a thick folder. From inside, he flipped out a photograph like a card dealt from a deck. "You know. I like this look for you." He turned the photograph so she could see it, catching the light from the streetlamp. "You have that sort of nerdy scientist thing going."

McCall stared at the picture, at first confused. But then she focused, realizing who it was.

It was a photograph taken four years ago. Of McCall, standing outside her lab at the university where she worked.

Her heart belted against her ribs. She had trouble catching her breath. "Where did you get this?"

"Oh, I have all sorts of interesting little goodies here. Let's see. He thumbed through a folder, then, as if thinking better of it, extended the entire package to her. "On second thought, why don't you have a look?"

Juggling her purse, McCall reached for the folder. She turned it over.

It was an FBI file. Her name was printed on a label across the top.

"Open it," he said.

Her heart started racing. She had to hold on very tightly to her purse and the folder, afraid she might drop both. She knew exactly what would be inside, a nightmare she had lived through. Only, someone else would be telling the story, would set it out in judgmental language that made her sound like a monster.

"Aren't you going to read it?" he asked.

"I don't have to. I know what it says."

"I bet."

"Where did you get this?"

"A little birdie dropped it in my lap."

She shook her head, feeling cold and hot at the same time. She said the only thing she could think of. "I'm not this woman, Jake. Not anymore."

"Now there's an interesting question. Because, you know what? I was just wondering who the hell you are. For example." He took the file and opened it. "Are you the brilliant scientist ready to cure millions. Or . . ." He flipped to another page. "The devious spy selling secrets to China. Or maybe"— still another page—"you're developing mind-altering drugs using NIH funds?"

She couldn't say a word.

"Do you really want to have this conversation here?" he asked, very softly.

There was something different about his voice. She realized she had never heard him angry before.

She didn't want to be afraid of Jake. Right now, there had to be someone in her life she didn't need to fear. But she wanted dearly to know why he had that file.

"Let me guess." She looked up. "Your place?"

"Give the woman a cigar."

He took her arm, steering her toward a black Jeep Grand Cherokee. She realized that surprised her a little. Somehow, she'd expected him to drive a gray sedan.

Eleven

McCall stopped in front of the Elvis clock. It was a perfect likeness of The King, early sixties, the bottom half swinging back and forth so his hips kept time with the second hand.

The clock was a new addition, doing its thing on the kitchen side of the large hotel suite. McCall hung up the phone and leaned back against the granite counter that separated the kitchen from the living room. She'd been talking to Barb, having called her friend so she wouldn't worry.

"I have Barb's permission to sleep with you," she told Jake, trying to be a little outrageous—even though it was the truth. For some reason, Barb thought Jake was The One. McCall's soul mate. And she'd just given McCall a nice lecture on the subject.

"You know, I really like that Barb." Jake finished pouring their drinks and handed her the ginger ale, the glass packed to the top with ice. He smiled, showing cute dimples. "Never met her . . . but I like her."

She nodded toward the Elvis clock. "Another gift from Dino?" She was thinking of the cow teakettle, the only other object that didn't look like it had been purchased by an interior decorator.

"Nah. You made me want to put my mark on the place; it's been four years. Have a seat, Mac."

McCall followed Jake into the living room. Beyond the floor-to-ceiling windows, she could see the *River Palace,* the floating casino still docked. Its flashing lights rippled across the paddle wheel and hull, making the riverboat look like an enormous Christmas ornament. Lightning glimmered in the distance.

She sat down on the kidney-shaped couch. The FBI report lay unopened on the coffee table, seeming to float in midair on the glass balanced on a granite pedestal. Jake sat down on the couch opposite, the two sofas mirror images of each other.

"I feel as if I'm floating in a big cup of café au lait," she said, looking around the suite.

"Hell in neutral, I call it." He lifted his ginger ale, taking a drink. "Stuff's not bad."

McCall just held hers. "How did you know where I lived?"

"Barbara Rojas, longtime friend and confidant. You met during your undergraduate years at Harvard, where you returned to complete your graduate work after a short stint at another university. Governor Nicholls Street," he said, reciting the facts. "It was in the file."

"Do you always investigate a woman you want to sleep with?" she asked, needing tonight to be about sex and not FBI reports.

"This is a first for me, Mac. But then, you're nothing but special."

"You don't have to try so hard, Jake. Or haven't you noticed? You already have my attention."

She'd kept her voice teasing, but inside, she felt like a combustion engine about to explode. The miserable sense of helplessness she'd endured four years ago was there, a faint echo tapping at her heart, ready to grab a handhold . . . something she wouldn't allow. Not now. Not yet.

On the trip here, she'd gone over the data in her head, making a study of him, sorting through the facts. *Picks up drunk woman at casino and tries to sober her up, even after she blatantly comes on to him. Marries one-night stand when he finds out she's pregnant. Allows card counter to play at casino but with his money.*

These were the things she knew about Jake, that he could

be kind, that he cared enough to take chances. He'd touched her in a way that made it difficult to shrug off Barb's theories about love and soul mates. She didn't want to lump him into some larger conspiracy she wasn't even sure existed.

Boy Scout. The name had come to her that first time she'd seen him seated at the blackjack table. And there was something about Jake—the intelligent brown eyes, the strong nose with its spray of freckles, that dimpled smile, sweet and sexy at the same time—you *wanted* to trust him. Even the way he dressed, so casual, never intimidating. Tonight, he was wearing stonewashed jeans and a tan corduroy shirt over a black T-shirt. He'd stretched his long legs out under the table and to the side, one arm hitched over the back of the low-slung couch, completely at ease. In a room filled with men, he would be the most approachable . . . the one you'd expect to offer his stool to a lady when the bar was full . . . the one you would want your kid sister to date.

"Truth or dare, Mac?" he asked, leaning forward, turning the glass of ginger ale round and round on the coffee table between his large hands.

"Do I have a choice?"

"You most definitely have a choice."

He grinned, egging her on, teasing her into thinking the obvious. *Take the dare; see where it leads.* She put her glass on the table and opened the FBI file, trying to keep focused. She needed answers as much as he did.

She flipped through the first couple of pages. Finding what she was looking for, she read out loud, "Regularly e-mails sensitive material to Dr. Kam Chang of People's Republic of China." She shook her head, dropping the page. "I met Dr. Chang at Harvard. He was part of a cultural exchange program. For three years, we worked in the same lab, sharing data, brainstorming together. It seemed ridiculous to stop when he returned to his own country."

"It says in the file he's involved with the military, doing research on mind control."

"I can't believe that. Not Chang. But honestly I can't be sure . . . I only know the material I sent him had nothing to do with mind control."

She left the file and stood, needing a little distance, taking it in small steps. There was an enormous blown-glass egg in the corner and she walked toward the piece. It was almost three feet tall, sitting upright on a black lacquer stand. A light shown from inside the opaque glass, making the milky color glow faintly.

"The agent who put that file together didn't understand my research," she said, staring at the swirling pattern of the glass. "My partner and I worked with mice. We had genetically engineered brain cells from newborn mice, infecting them with a virus so they would act like stem cells in the brain—cells that can reproduce. Unlike other organs, the cells in the brain can't replenish injured or dead cells. The idea was to find a way to replace tissue that has been damaged by stroke or disease."

She looked out through the window at the paddle wheeler and its blinking lights below, remembering the excitement of those days, when everything seemed so possible. "It could have been a godsend for people suffering from Huntington's or Parkinson's. Stroke victims. It could have led to a cure."

"What went wrong?"

She touched her fingertips to the glass. Warm. Summer nights here could be oppressive with heat and humidity, but the air conditioning kept the room almost cold. "One day, a troop of FBI agents marched into the President's office at the university. The audit trail showed significant gaps, irregularities in the handling of federal grant money, enough that they filed charges and convened a grand jury."

"What about the black market drugs?"

She pivoted around. He had this way about him, as if he could see so deep inside you, it would be impossible to hide anything. She shook it off—that look—and walked around the room, trailing her fingers across the rough texture of the upholstery behind Jake. She watched him from every angle, taking in the details she'd memorized long ago.

Jake Donovan was tall, with lean muscles that showed he probably jogged or worked out. He was *solid*. His shoulders beneath the corduroy shirt, his thighs pressing against the worn denim—they reminded her of that first night, when she'd been allowed to hold him. In the recessed lighting, his strawberry blond hair made her think of his son, a unique shade the genes had somehow carried onto the next generation.

She stopped at the kitchen counter, watching Elvis do his thing. *Almost eleven.* She thought about what had brought her here, wanting desperately for this moment to be about them and not the past. It would be too easy to dream up a plot in which Roger encouraged her to visit his friend's casino, a place where the manager was instructed to keep an eye on her . . . to get to know her.

"Mac?" he said from behind her.

She turned around, leaning back on her elbows, trying to imagine it: Jake Donovan, a Clarke stooge. Only, she couldn't see Roger being that farsighted . . . and she didn't believe Jake was any man's lackey.

Still. "It's not much of a game if only you get to play," she told him. "Truth or dare, Boy Scout?"

He smiled, bringing on the dimples. "All right."

"Where did you get an FBI file?"

"Dino." Jake crossed his legs, ankle on knee, leaning back to perch both arms on the sofa.

Always look them in the eye when you lie, he thought.

He had already decided to tell her it was Dino who'd given him the file. He realized the truth wouldn't sound so good. *You know my first wife, Susan? She's a private investigator now. Has her own business. She looked into it for me . . . checks out all the girls I date. Isn't that handy?*

"He has a friend who works as a private investigator," he said, now on solid ground. "Dino saw you on Cyndi's show

yesterday . . . a couple of bells went off in his head. He seems
to think I have bad luck when it comes to women."

That, at least, made her smile. "Really?"

"So he asked his friend to look into it—came up with the
file. The PI added a couple of things, some newspaper clippings, an address. Dino thought I should read it." Jake
shrugged. "He's like that sometimes. An old hen."

He kept it simple, not telling her that he used to work for
the Attorney General's office—not mentioning his lunch earlier with Gus Pierson, the head of the Criminal Division, his
old boss. He couldn't talk about the investigation, couldn't
compromise it. He wasn't even sure Mac was one of the good
guys. That's what tonight was about. The biggest *voir dire* of
his life.

"Truth or dare, Mac?" He nodded toward the file. "Twenty-
one phone calls to the FBI by anonymous informants? All
accusing you of illicit research for black market drugs. You
can't blame the FBI for being curious. Where there's
smoke . . ."

He slid the folder around to face him, so he could read it.
He flipped through a couple of pages, reading out loud,
"Looking for receptor sites in the brain . . . experimenting
with drug combinations that will bind more tightly with re-
ceptors." He looked up. "Any of this sounding familiar? Be-
cause, I could have sworn you said that's how the Omega
Principle works. Binds more tightly with VNO receptors? Do
I have it right?"

"You sound like a prosecutor."

He grinned, not missing a beat. "Do I? My mother always
did want me to go to law school." No lie there.

"The process is the same, Jake. But with a very different
result. I wasn't looking for the next Ecstasy. My research had
nothing to do with mind-altering drugs."

"But?" he asked, hearing the qualifier in her voice.

She turned away from the counter, pacing the Berber carpet.
"During the investigation, they did find something. Someone

had altered my data . . . making my results appear better than they should have."

"Someone? As in, not you? You're saying you were set up?"

His gaze tracked her as she walked. Hell, he couldn't keep his eyes off her. She was dressed in tight black slacks and this flimsy little sweater that buttoned down the front. Watching her pace, he kept thinking he could see through the shimmering mesh of the sweater when the light hit just right, but he couldn't be sure. The color, teal blue intertwined with metallic silver threads, lit up her eyes in the same iridescent hues. Her hair just brushed her shoulders, thick with a hint of curl to the bottom, making him want to take fistfuls into his hands.

He kept hearing Susan's voice inside his head: *There's a difference between a woman in trouble and one who is trouble.*

And easy as hell to figure it out, no doubt, he thought, irritated because this woman so mystified him. With Mac, he figured he could probably flip a coin and come as close to the truth as he was getting by grilling her.

She circled the couch, nice and slow. When she sat down, she crossed her legs, dangling a backless sandal from her foot.

"It's my turn, Jake," she said. "Truth or dare. Why? Why the interest, the FBI file . . . this confrontation? What do you want from me?"

"Hey, now. I'm just a little casino manager who got blindsided by pheromones. I'm trying to even the odds. I'm learning your game."

"The Pheromones Made Me Do It? Sounds a little like a lap dog."

"I had an Irish setter when I was a kid. Seems like a nice life." He leaned over the table separating them, the devil in his smile. "She licked me all over my face . . . and anywhere else she could get her tongue."

"I never used pheromones on you."

He nodded, a little surprised at his reaction. Relief. Had he actually considered the Omega Principle as a possibility? *Hell, yeah.* What he was doing seemed irrational. Drug induced.

"Thanks for the freebie, Mac . . . but that's not what I wanted to ask." He settled back against the couch, examining her eyes, watching the dark wide pupils. "Truth or dare? You weren't shy about telling people you thought Clarke and his son were behind the FBI investigation. You even accused him of setting up the car accident that killed your partner, Alicia Goodman . . . a death, I might add, that resulted in all charges being dropped against you when they discovered she was behind the misuse of the grant money. You got off with a hand slap."

"A hand slap?" she whispered with just enough force that he could hear the stronger emotions beneath the disbelief. "A faculty panel found me guilty of academic misconduct. I was forced to resign from my position because someone altered my data."

Sitting on the couch opposite him, McCall could feel herself begin to tremble. Deep inside—in a place where she had too little control—she sensed her anger building, coming to life, rising like the bubbles in a lava lamp. *Heating up; heating up.* "I have been in exile for four long years, Jake." She spoke the words slowly, forcefully, surprised by the depth of emotion behind them. She thought she'd moved on with her life. "No one, not my colleagues—not my family—believes I am innocent of altering that data. The FBI left a stain on my soul, one that doesn't wash off."

"Then you were innocent?"

"I was guilty of nothing more than supreme arrogance. A hand slap? Overnight, every door I knocked on was slammed in my face. My own father disowned me. He was ashamed of me. He believed I was desperate and ambitious enough to alter that data."

"And Clarke was behind it all," he said, watching her solemnly.

Too late, she realized how she'd played into his hands. Her

anger—that horrible rage that lived inside her—giving too much away.

"Now you're working for him," Jake continued softly. "Ready to put him at the top of a multibillion-dollar industry with the Omega Principle. Truth or dare, Mac. Why?"

"No." She stood, backing away, nudging against the glass table, almost tripping. She managed to keep stepping back, over to the windows, stopping when her shoulder blades hit the warm glass. "No, Jake. It's my turn now. You keep wanting to skip my turn."

Looking into his eyes, using the intuition she'd honed over the years to guide her, she saw what she needed with a clarity so sudden and sharp, it was almost blinding. The reason she'd come here, the signal she'd been waiting for, it was there—it had been all along.

The truth was, the questions Jake asked, he wanted those answers for himself and no one else.

Barb's words on the phone floated up inside her, easing over the anger to turn that heat in a different direction. *This could be the one, your soul mate. Don't be so angry with the world that you can't see it.*

McCall didn't know anything about a soul mate. She only knew she was alone with a man in his hotel suite, a man she desired beyond anything that seemed rational . . . a man who desired her, caring enough to ask his questions. She had sensed the emotions running deep beneath their game. And now, she wanted to change the rules, take a different risk altogether.

Jake watched Mac framed by the floor-to-ceiling windows behind her, the dramatic view suddenly taking a backseat to the woman as she reached for the hem of her sweater and eased it up over her head. She shook out her hair; the curls, the rich deep red of a burgundy wine, fell back around her face, brushing her bare shoulders.

His mouth went completely dry. The Sahara. He watched, mesmerized as she dropped her skimpy little nothing of a sweater to the floor, then unzipped her pants and stepped out of the black slacks. She straightened, standing before Jake in Victoria's Secret glory.

"I've only slept with one other man. He was my thesis advisor." She unhooked her bra. It slipped down her arms, a wisp of lavender satin that spilled onto the carpet. She had high beautiful breasts tipped with pale pink nipples. "He was married with two children. He told me his wife didn't understand him. She wasn't smart, like me, you see. We made love on the floor of his lab. He was the most brilliant man I had ever known."

She hooked her thumbs over the edge of her matching underwear and pushed the slip of satin down her thighs, kicking it off when it pooled at her ankles. All she had on were her high-heeled sandals.

Jake remembered a book he read as a kid. A Mickey Spillane novel, he thought. In it, our hero is holding the beautiful villainess at gun point. She begins to strip, trying to convince him to put the gun down, to let her go. The hero's comment was something like: She was a real blonde.

Mac. She was a real redhead.

"I only slept with him once," she told him. "Afterwards, he said it was a mistake. Suddenly, he remembered his marriage vows. I felt so guilty, but I told myself that I loved him. I told myself that he deserved better than his ignorant wife, a woman who could never understand him the way I did. I was in love with his mind, you see."

"And me with a C in physics," he said, watching her. Mesmerized.

She smiled. "I'm not in love with your mind, Jake."

Behind her the night was a storm of indigo and churning clouds. Lightning bursts pulsed across the sky, reflecting in the black glass of the river.

"The next year, he published my research under his name. He didn't give me any credit. I guess he was in love with my mind, too."

She stepped out of her shoes, first one, then the other.

"I had to quit the university and transfer back to Harvard. I lost a year. But that wasn't the most important thing he took from me. I've never had a relationship with a man after that."

She stood before him in naked splendor, her soft elegant curves shadowed by the light, her hair shining with it. Venus on a half shell.

"I don't have any experience with seduction . . . I don't know how to be shy or coy or flirtatious. But I know I want this. So very badly. Enough to take the risk. Truth or dare, Jake?"

He didn't make a move. Didn't say a word.

"Did I read this wrong?" she asked. "This is where we were going, isn't it?"

He closed his eyes, but she was still there, a vision burned into his retinas. He glanced down at the FBI file. *Shit. Shit. Shit.* The word went round and round inside his head, telling him he was totally screwed. Outmaneuvered by the better player.

He closed the file and stood. He walked over to Mac. He didn't touch her, just watched her, standing there so very close.

"No. You didn't read this wrong."

He smelled the same spicy scent that was Mac. He walked around her, coming to a stop behind her. He brushed his mouth across her neck as his hand slid up her naked thigh. His palm rounded her buttock. He felt her shiver.

"I have on exactly nine items of clothing," he whispered. He brought both his hands up around her breasts, cupping them. "Do the math for me, Mac." He bit down on her ear gently. "How fast can I get them off?"

"Fast. Light speed."

She turned in his arms, reaching for him as he gathered her to him. She opened her mouth to his, tasting him, breathing with him, mouth to mouth. She was physically warm to the touch. And heating up.

"Do you want to do this on the bed?" His mouth stayed opened over hers, doing all the things he'd dreamed of. Drowning in the taste of her. "See what it's like with real sheets and a mattress?"

"No. I want to stay here. With the clouds and the stars and the lightning."

She unbuckled his belt, struggling. He helped her, his mouth never leaving hers. She had such a cherry mouth, full and sweet. He couldn't get enough of her. How long had it been since he'd kissed a woman like this? With this kind of desperation, as if he'd been waiting a lifetime for this moment?

The answer came from somewhere deep inside, a voice that answered: *Never.*

They peeled off his shirt; he toed off his shoes. The socks and jeans followed, dropping to the carpet. Her hands were under his T-shirt, pressing against the planes of his chest, revving him up with her electric touch.

"I thought it was because of the champagne," she said breathlessly, pulling off his T-shirt. "I thought it was the alcohol that made me want this so badly. But I was wrong," she said, reaching beneath his underwear, digging her fingers into the muscles of his buttocks, as he kicked the briefs aside. "It numbed things. It made me feel less."

She was on fire. He seemed to touch her everywhere at once, her breasts, her mouth, her neck and thighs. She glanced down at his large powerful hands as they covered her breasts, watching how he held her, his fingers so dark against the soft white flesh.

"Hold on, sweetheart," he said. "We're just getting started here."

His thumbs brushed over her nipples, making them rise up, making the lightning bursts beyond the window shimmer inside her with each stroke. She ran her palms up and down his chest. The sculpted muscles were just as she remembered, smooth and hard and covered with coppery hair. She tasted the freckles on his shoulders, kissing him there, then reached again for his mouth.

He had these lips; they were incredibly soft. You had to have lips like these for a proper kiss, she thought. He moved his mouth to her shoulder, her neck, using his tongue to make everything more intense as he tasted every inch. He was much taller than McCall. She could feel his erection against her stomach, hard and smooth. She closed her eyes, letting him kiss her, threading her fingers through his hair. "We didn't take our clothes off, that time in the lab. I didn't feel any of this."

He pulled her down to the carpet, laying her there so she could feel the rough texture against her back and buttocks. He kissed her mouth, again showing her a talent she felt sure few could possess. He made each kiss an experience, a frozen moment to be cherished and remembered.

Wet, open-mouthed kisses. There seemed nothing more intimate in the world. She'd never known a kiss to be like that, to hold a part of a person, making them yours.

"Merit badge number one," she said against his mouth. "Really good at kissing."

"Let's go for number two."

His mouth left hers, trailing down her neck to her breasts. She could feel his weight lifting off her as he opened his mouth over her nipple and took it into his mouth. A sweet melting overtook her, turning her body into syrup. His fingers brushed up and down her side in teasing feathery strokes, then moved to the inside of her thigh. He pressed his erection against her. It was a completely erotic experience, feeling him there next to her, between her legs but not inside her.

"Open your legs for me, baby," he whispered. And when she complied, "Wider, sugar."

He reached with his hand and touched the pad of his finger to her, teasing her there between her legs as he sucked on her breasts.

"That's it, darling," he whispered, "that's it."

She realized she was whimpering. She was spiraling to some sweet death. She thought of the French term for it. *Le petit mort*. The little death. She was dying. Over and over.

"There now," he whispered as the sensations spilled over her, making her shudder. He kept his fingers resting where she pulsed against him. "There now, baby. Now you know where we're going with this," he said, looking deep into her eyes. "Now you won't be in such a rush."

She buried her face against his shoulder, trying to catch her breath. But he didn't let her. He picked her up, cradling her against him. A few seconds later, he kicked open the door to his bedroom and set her on the big iron bed. He started his magic all over again.

"What you just said," she whispered, her fingers finding the nipples beneath the coppery curls, stroking them as he'd stroked hers, "that now I would know where we were going . . . that I wouldn't be in such a rush. How did you know I'd never had an orgasm?"

"A quickie on the lab floor with a married professor?" He kissed her. Again. "Your first time and you didn't even take your clothes off." He grinned that cute, sexy smile. "I must be psychic."

"It could have happened another time. I'm a mature woman."

"Could have. Didn't. I'm wondering why?"

She shook her head, not really knowing the answer to that. "I must have sexual hang-ups."

"No, baby." And then with a grin that could only be called cocky. "You were waiting for me."

"Yes," she answered, perfectly serious. "I think I was. I wanted this to happen. I wanted you to make love to me. I wanted to trust you."

He stilled above her, his body so in tune with hers. His dark brown eyes focused on hers in that way he had, making you feel as if there was nothing else in the world but this moment. As if he could stop time for them. "Me, too."

He took a package from his drawer, a condom, and put it on. This time, his eyes never left hers. He crept over her, entering her slowly, so slowly. Filling every inch, letting her feel him, that connection between them. He gathered her hair in his hands, holding her head so that they looked only at each other. Nothing else existed.

"This is what I wanted," she said breathlessly as he started his rhythm, moving inside her, pulling back to enter her again. "This is why I let you bring me here."

"I know."

He didn't kiss her this time, just watched her. They stared into each other's eyes, moving together breathing together. "Do you hear the music?" he asked. "Do you feel the rhythm?"

It was a pulse inside her, following the beat of her heart, feeding her desire. It gathered force with his movements, faster and faster, then agonizingly slow. He was a magician, this man, and the things he was doing to her, bringing her to the verge, then letting her drop back to build the pleasure, would bind her to him forever. She could only hope he felt the same, that the music he made inside her would crescendo to take him along with her.

At one moment, she closed her eyes, the sweetness almost too much. But his fingers tightened in her hair, getting her attention, making her open her eyes again.

"Look at me, Mac. I want you to look at me."

Her breath came fast, spiraling up inside her with the pulse of her heart. He pushed deep inside her until she curled her legs around him, bringing him even closer.

"Your eyes are changing color." He said it softly, like a promise. "There," he said, as she came, falling like a roller coaster ride into the pleasure of it. "They're completely blue now."

She felt caught by the magic of it, the endless, weightless, consuming magic of him. It was a shivering delicate rite of passage. A sensation of being wound up too tight inside then allowed to release, to fly, to soar up and touch something he'd created for only them. Magic.

"You now, Jake," she said, reaching up for him, kissing his mouth, his neck. Nothing could be the same again. Not ever. It was that complete, that addicting, the sensation of him inside her . . . as if they'd touched forever. "Come with me."

"I'm there, baby. I'm already there."

She knew the exact instant he came, feeling him inside her. He arched up over her, coming incredibly deep. Pulsing, shifting, turning the music into a deafening crescendo that allowed nothing but the moment. And she could see in his eyes that he'd felt it, too, that instant when everything changed and the stars moved and there was only the two of them.

He lay down, covering her with his body, holding himself up by his elbows so she wouldn't carry his full weight. He nuzzled her neck, his chest brushing against her breasts. McCall pressed her thighs against his, feeling somehow that he was hers now, wanting to get closer still. She fitted their hips together as she rounded his shoulders with her palms.

"You know," he said, the heat of his desire coming out in heavy breaths, "for a novice, you're pretty damn good at this."

"I was inspired." She could feel him still part of her, pulsing sweetly. The afterglow. "This isn't about just sex anymore, is it, Jake?"

He brushed her hair aside. He smiled and shook his head no.

"Barb told me that if you were my soul mate, I would know it when we made love," she said, letting the words pour out of her before her better sense could stop her. "That I would feel as if I had found another part of myself, a part I didn't know was missing. That afterwards, I would see the world differently."

She waited, holding her breath. He was still smiling, looking at her as if she were something he'd lost and suddenly found, looking so happy.

"Ditto," he said quite solemnly. "To all the above."

"I'm frightened, Jake."

"Shh." He covered her mouth with his, granting featherlight kisses. "Don't be. I'm here, baby. I'm here."

"Is it always like this?"

He shook his head. "It's never like this. But then, no other woman had the benefit of your magic pheromones."

"Do you really believe I used pheromones on you?"

He nodded. "The real kind, not the ones in a bottle."

"That's exactly what Barb said."

"Barb the wise . . . Guru Barb." He kissed her with each word. "We have great chemistry, Mac."

She cupped his face in her hands. She stroked his straight perfect nose and its freckles with her thumbs. She kissed him, long and hard, trying somehow to make the mark permanent. To make him hers and hers alone. And then, when she thought she was ready, she confessed, "I didn't lie when I said I didn't love you for your mind." She pressed her hand to his chest. "I love your heart."

He didn't say anything. But then he smiled. "Well, that's good, Mac. Because I think I've just wrapped it up and put a ribbon on it for you."

It was the perfect thing to say. It made her feel safe. As if he was telling her he was hers to keep.

Mac turned on her side, cuddling up against him. Jake held her spooned to him, her bottom pressed against his sex, his hand palming her breast. He knew the exact moment she fell asleep. He could feel the gentle rise and fall of her chest, a perfect rhythm.

I wanted to trust you.

He sighed. Without waking her, he pulled away and leaned back against the pillow, mulling it over. After a while, he got up, going to the bathroom to clean up. He didn't feel like sleeping. For him, Mac was a jolt of adrenaline. He wasn't going to get much sleep.

In the bathroom, he thought about his meeting with Gus earlier. The things he'd learned about the investigation rose up like ugly unanswered questions. *We're finally going to nail the bastard this time.* It had taken a little wheedling to get Gus to talk, a couple of promises about things Jake wasn't sure he could deliver. But once he got started, Gus had spoken with great relish. *This one is big, Jake. Clarke is finally going down.*

He thought about it a long time. All the pieces were coming together. The only thing that didn't fit was the woman in his bed.

He padded back into the bedroom. He covered her with the sheets, then settled in next to her. He kissed her on her forehead, whispering softly, so he wouldn't wake her, "Please, Mac. Don't be one of the bad guys."

Twelve

Belinda drank a long swallow of the screwdriver. There was already a haze surrounding her, keeping the neon edges of the casino's carnival world a blur. That's the way she wanted it right now. A sweet numbing cocoon.

She was at the blackjack table, losing twenty-dollar bets. She had come to the *River Palace* straight from work, looking for her sister. She'd wanted to talk to McCall, wanted to finish what they'd started earlier in the employee lounge that day.

Only, she'd been afraid to let her sister know how important that conversation had been to her. If Belinda called and asked to meet, somehow that gave her sister an advantage she couldn't afford. It was Friday night; still too early to go home. Belinda had thought she could stop by the casino, that she might run into McCall like she had that first time.

But McCall hadn't come. Of course, she hadn't come.

Games. Stupid, silly games. Belinda was always doing stupid things.

The dealer tossed her the yellow card that marked the last hand of the four-deck shoe. When the dealer shuffled the cards, it would be Belinda's turn to slip the plastic marker into the deck, showing the dealer where to cut.

She tried to concentrate on her hand. She had sixteen—the dealer was showing a seven. But it was hard to remember the rules. Was she supposed to take a card or stand on sixteen?

Everyone at the table was staring at her. She could feel

their impatience. *Hurry up. Hurry up. It's so obvious!* She was taking too long. *Stupid, stupid, stupid.*

She nodded for another card. The dealer flipped over the king of hearts on her sixteen—twenty-six—then scooped Belinda's chips and cards away.

The dealer moved on to the next player. Belinda felt the lights and sounds of the casino become less distinct, a kaleidoscope shifting into its next shape. Like some strange video looping over and over, her conversation with her sister began to replay itself inside her head.

He's trying to mold you into something you're not, Belinda . . . when you rebel, it will never be the same . . . I know because it happened to me . . . You're a beautiful dancer, Lindy . . . Don't give up dancing to please Daddy; he can't see it, but he's hurting you both . . . I handed him Belinda, letting him steal her from me to take your place . . .

Those final words had hurt the most. Her mother's deathbed confession, delivered by a sister who'd abandoned them both too long ago.

"I didn't know, Mama," she said softly to herself.

She had never known that her mother needed her. Instead, she'd believed Lucinda Sayer regretted having her, the child of her old age. The Mistake. As far as Belinda was concerned, she'd been left with the flawed parent . . . while McCall basked in the glory of their father's love. *No wonder she's smarter, more successful.* Later, when her father had taken Belinda under his wing, she had followed the blinding light of his attention, happy to leave her alcoholic mother to her dark addiction, knowing somehow she'd been waiting her whole life for her turn.

"Blinded by the light," she said to no one but herself.

Behind her, the discordant harmonies of computerized noise shifted up and down the scale. She took another drink of the screwdriver, thinking about moving to the dollar machines. Maybe she would lose her money more slowly there. But the blackjack tables seemed less lonely, especially with a lively crowd. Tonight, the four souls circling the dealer were too quiet. *Welcome to the land of the dead.*

The dealer held out the deck to Belinda. She stared at the cards, wondering what the woman wanted. Then she remembered. The yellow marker. She stuck the plastic card into the middle of the deck, almost spilling her drink as she did it.

"Maybe you'll change the table," the guy next to her said. "We could use some luck. Cynthia here is killing us."

He was watching Belinda shyly. He was blond and good looking, in his thirties. For the last twenty minutes, she'd had the feeling he wanted to talk to her.

Belinda finished her drink, ignoring him. She hated it when the beautiful people were nice to her. What did it mean when someone was kind? What did they want? Roger always wanted something. When he was inconsiderate or vicious, then she knew how to deal with him. When someone was mean, you knew where you stood.

If he doesn't love you, don't marry him. Belinda remembered how she'd pretended McCall's words had hurt, making a scene in the employee lounge. As if she cared that Roger didn't love her. As if that had ever been the point.

She wasn't even sure she'd ever intended to marry him. The proposal had been the goal. He had asked her, and she'd felt special, flattered. A winner. Engaged to the heir apparent of Clarke Cosmetics. Like her father, when Roger chose to shine the light of his charm on you, it could be blinding.

"Is this seat taken?"

Belinda turned to look at the man standing behind her. His name was Dan. She'd met him earlier at the gangplank. They'd been pushed together by the crowd waiting for the *River Palace* to dock. He was here for some convention; she couldn't remember which. He was in sales, a tall and skinny man with thinning hair he'd dyed a dark brown, showing gray roots. She guessed he was in his mid-to-late fifties.

Belinda smiled. "It's got your name on it."

She caught him staring at her breasts. Ah, Danny. Life does have its little thrills.

She put down a bet and waited to be dealt in. She liked people like Dan. They made her feel safe. Invisible People, just like herself. No one bothered to speak to them or flirt with them. They were the background noise. The chorus.

"I was looking for you earlier."

Dan was still standing next to the stool, hesitating to sit down. Belinda crossed her legs so that her dress hiked up almost to her panties. Dan didn't miss it.

"I'm touched, Danny. Really I am." She patted the stool next to her. "Come on. Don't be shy."

Dan's hazel eyes behind his glasses never left her legs. "I thought maybe we could go have a drink?"

Already, she was having trouble keeping her balance. She'd had three screwdrivers, one after another. It was the perfect state for her, when everything seemed bright and possible. Another drink might not feel so good.

She remembered when she'd danced to feel like this, as if she could fly. *You're a beautiful dancer, Lindy.*

Belinda shook her head, confused by the memory of her sister's words.

"Maybe we could just go out on the deck?" Dan said, shuffling his feet. "Get some air?"

Belinda nodded and grabbed her purse. She didn't want another drink, but a little air, that sounded nice. "Sure. Outside sounds okay." And then she would go home. Put another day behind her.

She stood, then stumbled, almost falling off the high-heeled boots that laced to her knees. Dan reached out and caught her, smiling again.

"Whoops," Belinda said, flashing her sexiest smile. "Had an eensie weensie too much to drink."

She could feel herself flush even as she said it. What a stupid way to talk, eensie weensie. She stumbled along with Dan through the crowd. Sometimes, she could be so stupid.

Roger and her father always got on her when she acted dumb. Only the Invisible People like her and Dan didn't care about stuff like that.

She cruised past the tables, thinking about her father. They always fought now. He didn't like her clothes—he disapproved of her drinking. But mostly, he hated that she wasn't McCall.

Oh, he tried to hide it, his disappointment, but she could see it in his eyes every time she forgot something or screwed up an experiment. And now, McCall was here with her million-dollar Omega Principle, reminding him of how little he'd settled for. Belinda The Incompetent.

Fuck him, she thought, pushing past Dan to punch the double doors open with the palms of her hands. The chill of the night hit her bare arms and exposed thighs and she took a deep breath, trying not to cry, telling herself that if she couldn't be smart, at least she could be a smart-ass.

The water was a little choppy, making the deck feel like Jell-O beneath her heels. She grabbed the rail and held on, listening to the jazz band playing on the Texas deck above, the crack and snap of the flags whipping in a frantic rhythm on the wind. When McCall had come back, Belinda had been so afraid she would take their father away.

"Maybe that wouldn't be so bad," she whispered. Sometimes, her father's attention could hurt.

"What's bad?" Dan asked.

"Just talking to myself," she said, liking how Dan's eyes lit up with her smile. Roger never looked at her that way anymore. "Don't you talk to yourself sometimes, Danny?"

"All the time," he said, grinning, showing crooked white teeth.

Belinda touched his lips right over those teeth. Sweet old Danny. Invisible just like her. "You have a nice smile."

He actually blushed, looking surprised. "Thanks."

Belinda stared out over the inky water. They were alone on the deck, watching the lights from the paddle wheeler dancing across the surface in companionable silence. The way those lights shimmered on the water, it reminded her of a production of *The Nutcracker;* the "Dance of the Sugar Plum Fairies." They were little fairy lights twinkling on the surface. Dancing, dancing.

She couldn't remember how many times she'd danced *The Nutcracker.* In those days, her sister used to come to all of Belinda's recitals. When had McCall stopped doing that? she wondered. Had Belinda been ten? Eleven maybe?

You're a beautiful dancer, Lindy.

She blinked hard against the tears, the lights on the water blurring even more, disappearing into the darkness of the river at night. Sometimes she felt like that water, so black inside she wanted to disappear into the darkness. She wondered how it would feel to be swallowed up in it. Sometimes she thought about things like that. Jumping in, falling . . . falling forever.

From behind her, she felt Dan's hand on her shoulder. She was about to brush her tears away and plaster another smile on her face when his fingers dug into her arm painfully. He grabbed her, turning her around, forcing her up against him. She could smell the alcohol on his breath as he tried to kiss her. When she opened her mouth to scream, he jammed his tongue inside her mouth, making her gag. Belinda slapped his back . . . hit him with her balled fists, her purse banging against her side, hanging from its strap. The alcohol made her sluggish, but she tried to push him away, struggling. *Can't breathe!*

"Come on. You've been teasing me all night," he said, reaching up between them to squeeze her breast, hurting her. "You know you want it."

She felt so helpless; she tried to fight him, but then she stopped, letting him do whatever he wanted. It was like she'd jumped into the river, falling slowly to some numbing depth. Soon, it wouldn't hurt anymore. She would close her eyes and disappear and it would all be gone. *I deserve this. I deserve this.*

"What the—"

Dan released her. Belinda collapsed to the ground, choking for air. She felt a hand on her shoulder, and for a moment, she thought it was Dan again, coming for another round. But when she glanced up, she looked into the eyes of a stranger.

"Are you okay?" His expression was strained, showing his concern—his voice, pitched low and soothing.

"Yeah," she said, panting for air. "I think so."

She watched her rescuer stand. That's when she saw Dan, sprawled on the deck, cradling his jaw. *My God. He must have hit him.* She stared, fascinated by the possibility that a man had become violent to help her.

"Get the hell out of here, asshole," the man growled deep in his throat.

Dan stumbled off. Her rescuer turned back to her, crouching down to get at eye level. He had blond hair. Not white blond like Belinda's but a true gold. And his eyes. She'd never seen eyes like his. In the moonlight, they appeared yellow-brown, like a wolf's. Penetrating, as if he could look deep into your soul to let you know things. *I will never hurt you.*

"Are you all right, Miss Sayer?"

He knew her name. She tried to think why he would know her name. She realized she'd drunk too much. She felt sick.

She hitched the strap of her purse over her shoulder and hugged her arms around herself, starting to shiver. She was all tangled up inside, thinking about Dan. That wasn't supposed to happen. The Invisible People didn't hurt you.

"That's right, Miss Sayer," the man whispered. "You cry it out."

She realized she was crying. And the man was holding her, touching her in a way that made her feel so safe.

"You're okay," he whispered. He took off his corduroy jacket and put it around her, the cotton still holding his warmth. "You're going to be fine now." He held her face up to his, and then he smiled, wiping the tears from her cheeks as if it were the most natural thing in the world. "He won't ever hurt you again."

His voice was so comforting. And suddenly familiar. She realized who he was. From the lab. The nerd. The guy who always hung around her father in the Fragrance lab where she worked.

Only he looked different now. *No glasses.* She reached up and touched his face. "You're not wearing glasses."

"Contacts," he said.

He usually wore these coke bottle glasses. They hid his eyes. His wonderful, wonderful eyes that smiled and said he would protect her.

She couldn't remember his name. She was so embarrassed that she couldn't remember. Because she'd relegated him to someone unimportant . . . even more invisible than the people she'd singled out as losers like herself. She realized she'd never really looked at him.

Now, she couldn't take her eyes off him.

"Thank you," she said, not moving. He was stroking her hair so gently. He smiled, then looped a swag of her hair behind her ear.

"That was really wonderful. What you did." She felt herself blush. "I don't remember your name."

"That's okay," he said, not telling her who he was.

"Can I buy you a drink or something?" She'd meant to sound so together. Only, the question came out awkward. The words slightly slurred. She knew she'd drunk too much already.

He shook his head. His hair was long, brushing his shoulder in thick heavy waves. It was cut stylishly in long layers, only, at the lab, he always wore it in a ponytail.

"What I would really like is something to eat." He stood and helped her up, holding her waist until she got her balance. "I haven't had dinner. How about it, Miss Sayer? Will you join me for dinner?"

"Belinda, please."

"Kyle—"

"Woods," she finished, pleased that she'd remembered.

"Thank you, Kyle." And then she smiled, really happy that she'd remembered who he was. "I would love a steak." She didn't know when she'd eaten last. Maybe yesterday. She laughed, feeling a little giddy. "God, I think I could eat a whole cow."

He smiled. "I'll see what I can come up with."

Kyle Woods took her hand. Belinda felt this incredible warmth begin at her fingers where they touched. It glided up her hand, electric shocks that short-circuited up her arm and into her heart.

"You know," she said, walking beside him, letting him guide her through the crowd waiting for the ship to dock. "What you did back there, that's absolutely the nicest thing anyone has done for me."

He turned back to look at her. For an instant, he reminded her of her father . . . because he was angry. But then the lines of anger disappeared, vanishing as if they had never been there. "I think you're hanging out with the wrong crowd."

Under the glow of his smile, Belinda felt suddenly like those sparks of light on the water. She was dancing again. She was flying.

Kyle watched Belinda Sayer seated across the table from him. She stared down at her steak, her hands folded on her lap. She hadn't touched her food, allowing the juices of the rare steak to congeal on her plate.

"I don't know why you're getting so upset," Kyle said, taking a bite of his salad. "You didn't know I was a vegetarian."

"I said I could eat a cow." Her giraffe-patterned dress pressed her breasts together in a way that made her lithe figure look overly voluptuous. There were smudges under her eyes from her mascara. Still, she looked all of sixteen, sitting there, bright pink splotches of color on her baby cheeks, so angry with herself.

"Actually, I said a *whole* cow."

"I didn't take it literally."

She pressed her lips together. She'd bitten off most of her lipstick, but there was still some traces of the vampy red color. "I wanted you to like me." She spoke so softly, he could barely hear her over the noise in the restaurant.

"And now you think I won't?"

She pushed the plate away in a quick gesture that sent her utensils clattering across the china, all her hot temper focused on herself. "I probably disgust you."

Kyle knew that look. She was waiting for him to agree, a woman who was used to being hurt and accepted it as if it were her destiny. It made him incredibly sad, her low self-esteem.

He'd followed her to the casino, thinking only about those dogs in the truck. All night, he'd watched her carefully, waiting for his chance. But when it came, it wasn't what he'd expected.

He'd been surprised by the violence he'd felt, punching that jerk.

Kyle sighed, pushing his own plate away and reaching for his wallet. His job would be so much harder now. He had never turned his back on a hurt thing. "You want to get some ice cream?"

Belinda's face lit up. She wiped her hands on her napkin and put it on the table, already scooting out of the booth. "Ice cream sounds good."

They found a place a few blocks away. They were walking together, holding hands, eating something called Beyond Chocolate on brown sugar cones. She was wearing his coat, which hung down past her knees. After a while, Belinda giggled.

"What's so funny?" he asked, smiling because she looked so happy.

She stopped, standing in front of him. "You have ice cream on your nose. Here, let me."

She cleaned it off with her napkin. And then, standing on her tiptoes, she closed her eyes and kissed the tip of his nose.

When she opened her eyes, her smile vanished. She took a couple of steps back. "I'm sorry."

"Why?" he asked, genuinely puzzled by her reaction.

She shrugged. "I don't know. You just looked, well, sorta mad."

"No," he said, because it was the truth. "I'm not mad. I'm just a . . . a very intense person."

"Okay."

He could feel something between them. For Kyle, things usually worked on this level, messages that came almost subliminally. A kind of instinct. She hadn't figured it out yet, what was happening. But Kyle knew.

He took her hand, liking the feel of those small fingers clutching his—maybe too much. He could almost hear her sigh of relief. She was holding his hand so tight, almost desperately. All through dinner, she had watched him as if he were Prince Charming, afraid she would scare him away.

He remembered how upset she'd been when she couldn't remember his name. She wouldn't know how hard he'd worked to make himself invisible. Tonight, he had changed that.

"Why are you a vegetarian?" she asked. Kyle knew she would want to know everything about him now, her Prince Charming. "Is it because it's bad for your health?"

"It's really bad for the animal's health," he said without thinking.

"Oh, you're into animal rights. That fits. You're someone who wants to fight for the underdog." She peeked down at his shoes.

"All man-made," he said, knowing he should stop. He wasn't supposed to tell her this much. He didn't want to give himself away. "I'm not that strict. I eat milk and cheese. And I've been known to have the occasional omelet."

"But it's nice," she said. "That you care so much. That's probably why you work at Clarke Labs. Because they don't test on animals. Humanity first," she said, repeating the logo they put on their products.

She sounded entirely sincere. It couldn't be an act.

"Of course," she continued, swinging their hands between them as they walked, "Curtis stopped doing animal testing because of the competition. That man has a gold nugget for a heart, I swear." She walked on her wobbly heels, her feet out like a duck's. "My sister used to work on animals. On mice . . . and my dad. Rabbits, too." She made a face. "I'm glad I didn't ever have to see that. Those poor bunnies."

"Rabbits, cats . . . even dogs," he said, stopping so he could see her eyes as he spoke. He knew he was taking a chance. But he also knew that by asking her now, he would get the answers he needed. "Only, the shelters would rather put the animal down humanely, so you can't always get what you need legally. They have what they call bunchers, people who go around gathering up strays . . . sometimes even beloved pets. They steal them right out of your yard, if you're not careful. The animal just disappears. And then they sell them to labs for research."

"My God. That's hideous." There were tears in her eyes.

He saw the truth in her face. *She really doesn't know.*

He frowned. He'd meant to befriend her in a cold, calculating way, to find out what he could about the dogs in the truck. She was the weak link at Clarke Labs. Saving her from the jerk mauling her had been a God-given opportunity.

But now she was watching him worshipfully, like an animal would watch you. Trusting him completely.

"I saw you at the lab when I left," he said, following his instincts about her. "You were signing for a delivery. What was in the truck?" he asked, knowing she would tell him, that she was so focused on him, she wouldn't even question his curiosity.

"I don't know." She shrugged. "Some stuff for the lab. Roger asked me to take the delivery for him because he'd made plans and they were coming so late." Again, she took a few steps back. "Why are you so mad?"

This time, he didn't deny the emotion. But he changed his

focus, forgetting the dogs and Roger for now, going back to concentrate on what was happening between him and Belinda. "Tonight. That man who attacked you. I saw you with him earlier. Why, Belinda? You're young, beautiful. Engaged. Why that guy at the table?"

She looked down at her feet. She shrugged. "Sometimes I do things like that." She licked the ice cream. He could see she wanted to say more; that she was wondering if she should.

"Usually after I've been drinking," she told him, trusting him, waiting for his reaction.

"Do you drink a lot?"

"Maybe. Lately anyway." She'd sighed. "I used to dance professionally. But I quit about a year ago. I guess I miss it, so sometimes I drink. Because it lets me feel loose. Happy. Like when I danced."

"Ballet?" he asked, looking at her feet. The toes were still pointing out, as if she were standing in a permanent first position. "You look like a ballerina."

"Not really. My legs aren't long enough. I'm too tall and my breasts are too big. I wasn't a soloist. I only danced in the corps de ballet."

"Your breasts look just the right size to me."

She tilted her head, watching him. And then she smiled. "The way you said that. You looked into my eyes—you never even glanced at my breasts." She sighed, shaking her head. And then she turned, walking on. "You don't know very much about ballerinas." She bit into her ice cream. After a moment, she said, "Sometimes, I scare myself. Because I like it so much. Drinking, I mean. Not the headache and the queasy stomach in the morning, but that nice safe haze."

"It wasn't safe tonight," he said, stating the obvious.

"Yeah, right." She pitched the ice cream into a waste can. "Look, I've kept you out too late as it is."

He tossed his ice cream in with hers and stepped into the street. "Did you park at the *River Palace?*" At her nod, he signaled for a cab. It had started to sprinkle. "We're pretty far away. I'll take you home."

Kyle watched the light from the street lamps blur past through the rain-streaked glass. It had rained a little, giving the night a nice clean feel. Belinda was cuddled up next to him on the bench seat of the cab, her hands cupped and tucked between her body and his, her head resting on his shoulder. He'd been careful to suggest a cab rather than going back to the *River Palace* parking lot. He knew she lived with her father. He hadn't wanted him to recognize his car.

He looked down at her smiling. He threaded his fingers through her hair, caressing her absently. He thought she was beautiful, with clear blue eyes that tilted up at the corners. Even her eyebrows slashed upward, exaggerating the elfin look of her. And her ears stuck out a little from beneath her white blond hair. She had a full bottom lip.

Because he dearly wanted to, he leaned down and kissed her, being careful not to wake her. She smelled like gardenias.

He dropped his head back against the seat with a deep sigh. He didn't want to hurt her. Too many people had hurt Belinda. But he knew he would.

He hated doing it, taking advantage of her. His reluctance was a pain inside his chest. But he also knew that, no matter what he felt personally, he couldn't lose sight of the greater purpose.

The cab swerved into the curb and slowed to a halt. He nudged her gently. "We're here."

She woke up and rubbed her eyes with her fists, a childlike gesture that reminded him of how young she was, maybe just twenty, or twenty-one because she'd drunk at the casino. She looked up at him, smiling, making that connection again. And then she reached up and kissed him.

It was a wonderful kiss. Sweet and slow, but with the promise of fire. Belinda Sayer knew only how to give everything. She hadn't learned how to hold back.

A light came on inside the house. It was one of those large Victorian homes that made the Garden District famous. The kind people liked to tour. Through the car window, Kyle could see the curtains part.

His heart sped into double time. It was dark; Sayer wouldn't be able to see inside the cab. He wouldn't know who his daughter was kissing unless Belinda told him.

She pulled back, touching his mouth with her fingers. "Do you want to have lunch Monday?"

Lunch. At Clarke Labs. In the cafeteria, probably, where everyone would see them together. Her father, Roger Clarke. He couldn't imagine Curtis Clarke taking his budding relationship with Belinda—his son's fiancée—lightly. Nor would Donald Sayer.

"No. Not lunch."

Her face fell. She was so easily crushed by his rejection. He remembered how dispassionate she'd been when Roger had mistreated her. But she'd given Kyle the power to hurt her.

"Tomorrow night. Dinner," he said. "I'll meet you at the same place. It has to be late, though. Nine o'clock."

She smiled as if Kyle were the sun and the moon. "I'll skip the steak this time."

He looped her hair over her ears, liking the fact that they stuck out just a little. "If you want."

"Yeah. I want."

He sighed, twisting her hair around his finger. He'd known she would be the weak link at Clarke Labs.

Her father stepped outside. Kyle nodded in the direction of the house. Belinda looked a little daunted as she turned and stared out the window toward Donald Sayer. But then she sighed and leaned up to kiss Kyle again, a feathery brush of her mouth against his.

"You were wonderful," she told him. "I'll never forget that."

He grabbed her hand just as she reached for the car handle. He'd meant to tell her not to discuss their time together, to give her some excuse about why she should keep it secret. Instead, he asked, "Do you want me to walk you to the door?"

He couldn't believe he'd just said that. It would go completely against everything he'd planned.

"I'll be fine," she said, getting out of the car. "He'll just hassle you if he knows we went out. Don't say anything at work, okay?"

He waited, watching her walk past her father and into the house. Rather than following her in immediately, Sayer looked back at the cab, as if he might try to figure out who was waiting for her in that darkened car.

"Carondelet," Kyle told the driver.

He could feel himself sweating as the cab sped away, and it had nothing to do with the balmy night. He'd put everything on the line just now, saying he'd walk her to the door. He should have been the one telling her to keep their time together a secret. Instead, Belinda was protecting him.

He put on his jacket, breathing hard. It smelled like gardenias.

He told himself he had responsibilities. Promises he had made. To himself and to others. He would have to be more careful. He couldn't let Belinda derail those efforts. He couldn't let her get to him. No one could.

Thirteen

They die. They just keep dying.
——Excerpt from Dr. Alicia Goodman's lab book

McCall dreamed she was nine years old again, trying her first transformation.

The dream always started the same. She was in her father's lab, completely alone. A light shone from some unknown source, spotlighting the black bench-top table before her. An enormous petri dish, almost two feet in diameter, lay on the tabletop. Everything in the dream was exaggerated in size, test tubes like skyscrapers, a box of rubber gloves the size of a bathtub, as if McCall had suddenly become very small in comparison. Alice in her own fantastical Wonderland.

A thin layer of agar covered the bottom of the dish, the amber-colored gel containing the nutrients essential for the cells to grow. She had already infected the bacterial cells with the virus. Now, using a pipette as long as her arm, she dropped the liquid containing the bacteria onto the plate. *Drop. Drop. Drop.*

Polka dots of cells began to sprout, materializing as tiny pencil points that grew and spread across the amber gel. The transformation happened at an incredible speed. She knew that, like the size of the instruments, this was wrong, that the cells would take days to grow in the incubator. But the dream was always the same, moldy cells growing like jungle vines, bubbling and spewing in the enormous petri dish. Eventually the tendrils of cells overpowered even the dish, exploding from its confines, shattering the glass.

The liquid splattered on her arms and face. McCall looked down at her hands, watching the cells root into her skin, using her now as the growing medium. Like a cancer, the cells spread up her arms; she could feel the spiderweb delicacy of their touch covering her face.

She ran to a mirror, the ground beneath her feet shifting like the floor of a fun house. Reflected in the glass, her face was pocked by white splotches of mold. As she watched, the growth spread across her cheeks, her nose . . . her hair . . . until it blossomed into blood-red roses to cascade down her face, creating a living, breathing symbol she instantly recognized. The Clarke Labs logo.

The face in the mirror changed—shifting, morphing. It crystallized into Alicia Goodman.

Her hair was salt and pepper, falling straight to her shoulders, intertwined with roses. Her eyes were the same hazel green McCall remembered. She was smiling, always so happy. Always so alive.

She held her hands out to McCall through the mirror. "Be beautiful and be sad," she whispered.

The words echoed eerily, making McCall suddenly afraid. The dream had never been like this. Alicia had never been part of it.

"I don't know what you mean," McCall said, stepping backward, away from the mirror. "I don't understand what you wrote in the lab book."

Like a ghost, Alicia separated from the mirror, floating up into the air. She whispered her secrets in unintelligible murmurs, tantalizingly indistinct as she glided over McCall's head. She circled faster and faster, making the dark lab spin until the familiar scene blurred, becoming another.

McCall sat in church. The same blood roses flowed from two enormous urns, each situated on either side of a white lacquer casket. McCall stood and walked up the aisle, an incredible heaviness weighing her with each step. She climbed to the pulpit, getting closer and closer to view the casket.

Alicia lay inside, nestled in white satin. Roger stood over her, holding a syringe in his hand. Like the other instruments in her dream, the syringe was huge, almost the length of his arm. But with the knowledge of dreams, she knew it was similar to the instruments she and Alicia had used, the syringes that injected transformed brain cells into the ventricles of lab mice.

Wake up.

Again, the images of the dream shimmered, changing, floating into something else. Someone else. It was her mother in the casket, her father holding the syringe.

"I'm sorry, darling," he told her. "But you shouldn't have altered that data."

"I didn't, Daddy. I swear I didn't."

Wake up!

Belinda stepped out of the shadows to stand beside their father. They were both smiling. "You shouldn't have altered that data."

Wake up!

"Come on, baby, wake up."

McCall sat straight up in bed, completely awake. She felt incredibly cold. She realized she was naked, the sheets bunched at the foot of the antique iron bed. She remembered where she was, in Jake's hotel suite, gasping for breath, chased by her nightmares.

"Mac?"

She could feel herself shivering. *So cold.* Jake rubbed her arms and kissed her shoulder. Gentle, soothing kisses. Kisses that said she wasn't alone anymore.

Turning on the bed, she folded her legs beneath her, knees bent. She put her palm against the middle of his chest, feeling the crisp hair, the heat, almost as if she were trying to determine if he was real.

"You were having a nightmare," he said, his hand coming up to brush over her back, warming her up.

McCall inched closer, hesitating, then turned and pressed herself to him, heart to heart, as he crushed her against him. "I've dreamed it before," she whispered. "The same thing, over and over. But it's been so long." And it had never been like this, so vivid. It had never gone beyond the strangeness of that lab.

"The dream started when I was nine years old," she said, wanting to talk about it, hoping to clear away the lingering cobwebs. "My father worked for Curtis even then, and he would let me help him in his lab. I spent hours there, watching him. One day, he let me do a transformation. I made up the solutions, infecting the bacterial cells with my virus, just as I'd seen him do hundreds of times. He watched me every step of the way. I was so excited. But something went wrong. The bacteria didn't grow."

She remembered it so well, every detail, each nuance. One of those moments a child never forgets.

Do you know what you did wrong, McCall?

No. Daddy. I don't.

"When he asked me what I did wrong," she said, "I couldn't tell him because I hadn't done the proper controls."

How many times have I told you an experiment isn't an experiment unless you do the controls?

But you saw me. You didn't say anything—

I'm not here to spoon-feed you the answers. You've watched me do this a hundred times. You need to be more observant, to figure things out. Think, girl. Think!

"My father had me do the experiment over," she said. "Twenty times. It took me two weeks."

"That's a little excessive."

She shook her head. "It wasn't a punishment. He was my teacher." She frowned. "More than that, my mentor. He took it upon himself to help me be my best. He always told me I would be the best." She remembered how it used to be between them, how close she and her father had been in those days. "I never forgot about the controls after that."

"But it gave you nightmares?"

She nodded. "I started having a dream where the bacteria grows too fast, overpowering everything in the lab, until it starts growing on me, smothering me."

Jake listened carefully, the lack of emotion in her voice unnerving him. He couldn't imagine what it must have been like, growing up as she had. He pulled her closer, rubbing her back.

"Let's see," he said, kissing the top of her head. He wanted to help her work through this, to chase away the nightmares. "I'm digging back here. Psychology 101. Your father is like that bacteria. Trying to take over your life."

She looked up. The only light in the room came from the bathroom. Her pupils where huge, showing just a rim of green. Her lips parted slightly. He could tell she'd never thought of it that way, her father trying to take over, smothering her.

He brushed a curl of burgundy hair back from her face. "It's kinda obvious, baby."

She pushed away and threw her feet over the side of the bed. She grabbed the afghan he kept folded at the foot and wrapped it around herself as she walked out of the room, leaving Jake to lie in bed by himself. He let out a sigh, pushing his hair back with his hand. He glanced at the clock. Almost one in the morning.

He hadn't told her what had woken him up, that she'd been calling out in her sleep. Calling out his name. Again and again.

He pushed off the bed and padded into the main room. He found her walking around the living room, touching things. She was taking the expensive crap off the shelves, turning it over in her hands, then replacing each trinket.

He came up behind her and pulled her back against his naked body, nuzzling her neck, trying to keep that connection he'd felt earlier.

"There's just so little of you here," she said, reaching back to thread her fingers through his hair.

He stared at the junk on the shelf. Some Baccarat crystal, a Chinese puzzle box, a set of blown glass candlesticks. He had read a whole file that revealed the intimate details of her life and here she was trying to find him on these shelves. Except for the photographs of his son, there wasn't anything that said shit about him.

"I have two older sisters," he said. "Molly, of indeterminate age since she keeps celebrating her thirty-ninth birthday over again. I think this year we're up to number three. Then there's Casey. The dreamer of the bunch. She paints. She's had a few shows, even sold some stuff, though Lord knows, I don't get it. Big blotches of color that she names crap like: 'Abstract Number 16—The Heart.' They both married young and have two kids apiece. God, Mitch, Molly's eldest, just started high school. My mom still teaches literature at Tulane; my dad is retired. We're transplants from California."

"That's why you don't have an accent." He could hear the smile in her voice. "My first year in college, I was thirteen. I was the only one in my class with an accent. I wanted so badly to fit in, so I listened and practiced, until I sounded just like them. But I couldn't change my age. It took me the whole year to understand I never would fit in."

He was holding the afghan around her, his head bent over hers. She was telling him the story behind the facts he'd read, breaking his heart just a little. He could see why she'd been such a sucker for their night together—just as he'd been. The nerdy girl in the photographs never went to her senior prom or homecoming. Never got invited to a campus party.

"Come here," he told her, knowing there was something he could do.

He took her hand and led her to the other bedroom, Michael's room. "Since you have this thing about interior decor. This one, I did myself. With help from the little guy. He

doesn't spend a lot of time here—it's still a hotel room. Bu
we did our best."

McCall walked inside, holding the afghan around her shoulders. The twin-size bed was covered in a colorful comforter
with matching sheets that featured killer whales. The bedside
lamp had T-rex roaring from the stand. A bean bag chair
shaped like an enormous stuffed elephant lounged in the corner. Beautiful posters of dragons flew across the walls, with
crayon versions taped up next to them. Everything was at eye
level for a child.

She stepped around the bed smiling. There was a desk with
a computer. A set of bookshelves where MICHAEL was embla-
zoned in colorful letters across the wood. A coat tree rained
baseball caps—a scooter leaned against the wall.

She knelt down in front of the aquarium. "Who lives in
there?"

"A salamander and a tree frog. Slimer and Mr. Bellows,
respectively."

She looked around, then slipped to the floor, sitting down
next to the bookshelves. "Everything is so neat. I bet it's been
a while since he's slept here."

"Michael and I are a couple of slobs, but the head of house-
keeping takes good care of us. Michael stays with me most
weekends," Jake said, dropping down to sit next to her. He
hadn't turned on the lights, but the glow from the aquarium
and the computer's screen saver were more than enough. "I
wish you could meet him tomorrow. Normally, I would pick
him up in the morning. We could have gone to breakfast. But
this weekend Hope is taking him to one of Dickey's conventions. Hilton Head. She thought Michael would like it. He
won't be back for a week."

"Sounds like you'll miss him."

"Yeah. I always do. But the coast is nice. He'll have a good
time."

She nestled into the crook of his arm and pulled the afghan
over both of them. "Barb and Stan have twins, a girl and a boy.

They're four years old, just like Michael." She laughed. "Only, their room looks like a toy store after a natural disaster."

She remembered her own room as a child. She didn't have many toys, maybe a stuffed teddy, a few Madame Alexander dolls. Her mother had decorated the room with Queen Anne furniture and designer wallpaper. But her father had made it hers. A chemistry set with a fairly sophisticated microscope. An abacus. A clear plastic model of the human body, showing organs and bones, all anatomically correct. Books and books.

McCall watched an angel fish swim across the computer screen, the screen saver, an underwater scene that showed colorful fish and the ocean floor. The soft gurgling of bubbles accompanied the image. She frowned, remembering that everything her father had ever given her had had a purpose.

"You're not falling asleep on me, are you?" he asked, his hand brushing over her breast under the afghan.

"No. I'm not sleepy," she said, reaching up and twining their fingers together. "You call him Michael, never Mike or Mickey? You, a man with a penchant for nicknames?"

She could feel him shrug his shoulders behind her. "He was named after my father. And no one called my dad anything but Michael. I guess I just got used to it."

"Mac." She made a face. "I still hate it."

"Admit it. It's growing on you."

"I admit nothing."

She could feel the rumble of his soft laughter. She sighed, looking across the room, taking it all in. She thought about the twins' room. Barb had let the kids decorate; there was an entire wall covered in colorful handprints. This room was just as Jake had described it, a nice attempt, but still a hotel room.

She stood, walking over to the desk with the computer, trying to discover more about Michael. On the shelf above the computer, Jake had lined up his son's CDs. *Meet the Masters,* she read silently. *Reading Blaster Jr.; Where in the World Is Carmen Sandiego?* She frowned, reading the next title. *Math Blaster Jr.* Pretty sophisticated for a four-year-old.

She turned, still frowning. The shelves behind Jake were stacked with books. The *Eyewitness Books,* a children's picture encyclopedia, *My First Thousand Words in French,* a Berlitz Jr. book. There was even a math workbook with stickers, and a box of flash cards guaranteed—the box said—to expand your child's vocabulary. On the shelf below: Magnetic Map of the United States, Home Planetarium, *Suzuki Violin School, Volume II.*

There wasn't a Disney figurine or an action hero in sight, just erector sets and an art supply chest. She knelt next to Jake, thumbing through the books on the shelf. She picked out one: *I Want to be an Astronaut.*

"He's reading already?" she asked, knowing somehow that he was.

"Michael could spell his name on the computer by two. Hope says he's read over a hundred books." She could hear the pride in his voice.

"He reads French as well, does he?" she said, her finger on the Berlitz book.

"No," he said slowly, hearing the disapproval in her voice. "Hope started him in this class. Kids are supposed to be good at languages. He brought that book to show me. He must have forgotten it here."

On the bottom shelf, there were a set of dinosaurs, but they were nothing like the ones the twins had in their toy chest. Those plastic toys were neon colors, all teeth and spikes and dangerous looking. These dinosaurs appeared to be models, too realistic.

She picked up diplodocus, reading the bottom. "British Museum of Natural History. It's not even a toy."

"Of course it's a toy. Look, what's your point?"

There was a banjo on a stand next to the shelves. She put down the dinosaur and picked up the Suzuki violin book. "He's four years old and he plays two instruments?"

"No, he doesn't play two instruments," he said, taking the music book and shoving it back on the shelf. "I gave him the banjo so he could mess around with it . . . Look. I'm not pushing Michael."

Like a flash, Jake remembered Michael telling him he didn't want to play the violin anymore. How Jake had convinced him maybe he should.

A sense of helplessness he didn't like to acknowledge sparked inside him. He wasn't the custodial parent. He had Michael only on weekends. Hope always called the shots. And most times it was easier to give in to her demands than fight.

The whole situation made him angry, angry enough that he said the first thing that came into his head. "Michael's just a smart kid. He wants to do this stuff. By the age of five, a child's brain is at its peak. If you don't exercise it, their brain power starts to decline."

Jake stayed perfectly still. He couldn't believe he'd just said that. That's the kind of crap Hope always fed him.

For the longest time, neither of them said anything, those words just hanging in the air between them, making him wish he could take them back. The only sound in the room came from the computer, the soft gurgling of the screen saver.

"My father started teaching me the Greek alphabet when I was six," she said, looking at him. "He wanted me to be familiar with the symbols in calculus. By seven, I had the periodic table memorized. He had a poster of it hanging on my wall. He told me to take a little time every night before I slept to look it over, so I could memorize each element and its atomic weight. I counted them, like sheep. Hydrogen—H, 1. Helium—He, 2. Lithium—Li, 3." She waited, letting it sink in. "I guess he wanted to exercise my brain."

"And thank you for your opinion," he said, sounding incredibly defensive. Feeling defensive.

Because he could see her point—had actually started to worry about it lately, that Hope had crowded Michael's life with too many classes and too many rules. He thought of the toys he'd wanted to buy him, all nixed by Hope. No ray guns, no GI Joe, no trucks. Only gender-neutral stuff. Which meant he hid the speedway and its carrying case under the bed—their little secret he'd told Michael—not knowing what would pass muster. No coloring books either, because they stifled his creativity, suggesting that he should color in between the lines.

Most of the time, Jake could see her point. It sounded pretty reasonable. Everyone knew television was bad. Why not give a kid a blank piece of paper and a bunch of crayons? But when she'd forbidden Dr. Suess books because some of the words were made up—when she'd told him not to take Michael to see *The Lion King,* saying it was a racist movie because the hyenas hated the lions—he'd listened to her even then.

He dropped down on the bed. "Look, I'm trying to be the best father I can." The Weekend Dad, that was Jake Donovan. And he loved Michael so much. It hurt, not to be a part of his daily life.

He shook his head, looking up at Mac. "I can't change the fact that his parents are divorced. But for God's sake, he's not memorizing the periodic table of elements."

After a while, McCall sat down next to him. "I'm sorry." She reached over and leaned her head against his chest. "I just remember how it was, being so smart . . . not being allowed to be young." She sighed. "What would your Psychology 101 say about what just happened?"

He smiled, touching her lips with his fingers, feeling the fullness, the curves. "That you were projecting."

"I'm sorry I projected." She kissed his hand. She sat up on her knees, kissing his mouth, dropping the afghan so it slipped to the floor. "I can't imagine you being anything but a great father, you love him so much."

"It's okay," he said, kissing her back, already putting his hurt aside. He wondered what it would be like if Mac were a part of the decisions that affected Michael. To have someone else challenge Hope's benevolent dictatorship. Someone who loved Michael, as he loved him.

They stretched out across the little bed, half on, half off, soothing each other with a touch, seducing with open-mouth kisses. He could feel that connection between them again, how they could weave the fabric of it even tighter. He forgot to be cautious, forgot about the investigation and the things he'd learned from Gus.

He knew he wanted her, all of her, and he was making her a part of his life. And even if he opened himself for the hurt, falling for a woman who could very well be involved in Clarke's scam, he didn't have a choice anymore. Last night, he'd crossed some invisible line. There was no going back. For either of them.

"Aren't you going to answer it?" she asked, still kissing him.

He heard it then. *Brr—ring. Brr—ring.* The phone ringing.

He deepened the kiss. "Only work calls this late. Let them get Dino to trouble-shoot tonight. The machine will pick it up."

The answering machine clicked after the sixth ring. There was a pause to let the outgoing message play, and then he heard Susan's voice.

"Jake? It's Susan. I couldn't sleep and it's your fault so I thought I'd see if you were up. Maybe you're still on graveyard sleep patterns, your schedule is so crazy these days." She sighed audibly. "I'm worried about you. I was thinking about that woman, the one in the FBI file I gave you."

Jake froze.

"Dino told me you met with your old boss at the Attorney General's office—"

He bounded off the bed. He'd never moved so fast.

"—Gus from the criminal division. I think I did some work for him a while back as a contracted investigator. He's a good guy to talk to about this—" Susan was speaking fast, almost as if she could see him coming, getting too many words out. "Remember the Donovan Curse? It doesn't pay to rescue damsels in distress—"

He pulled the machine out of the wall, phone and all. He dropped it to the granite counter. "Shit."

He turned around. Mac was standing right behind him, holding the afghan around her.

"Don't look at me like that," he said.

"The private investigator is your ex-wife. It's not Dino's friend."

"Susan just handed me the file. I didn't ask her—"

"What did she mean, criminal division? You're investigating me?"

"No. It's nothing like that." Even though it was exactly like that. "I used to be an assistant attorney general. When Susan gave me the file, I just thought it wouldn't hurt to check in with my old boss. Look, I only asked him a few questions."

But he could see things were going from bad to worse. There was no good way to talk about this.

"Shit." He raked his fingers through his hair. He shook his head and threw his hands in the air, pleading with her. "I couldn't just ignore an FBI file."

"No. Of course, not. What prosecutor could?" She shook her head. "I even said you sounded like a prosecutor."

She grabbed her purse off the counter where she'd left it last night. She walked past him toward the door. He hooked his arm through hers, swinging her back around. "It's almost one in the morning. You're not going anywhere."

McCall slapped him. Hard across the cheek.

He could feel the lingering sting of it, but it was nothing compared to the pain he saw in her face. Because they had made love, and now they knew they were in opposite camps. "If it makes you feel better, you can hit me again."

She did. Then again.

But then she covered her face with her hand. She stayed like that for an eternal second, with her hand over her mouth and eyes.

He knew then everything was ruined. All he could figure was that he'd been wrong about Mac. She had something terrible to hide. That's why it mattered so much, that he'd been a prosecutor. That he had connections with the criminal division.

"I've never hit anyone before," she whispered, still covering her face. "I shouldn't have hit you."

She pushed past him. Before he could stop her, she was out the door. Jake ran after her, into the hall.

"For God's sake, Mac!" But she didn't listen to him. The elevator door closed behind her.

A man peeked out from one of the rooms. Jake realized he was standing in the hall buck naked. Cursing softly, he returned to the suite, slamming the door behind him.

He turned and punched his hand against the wall, feeling the pain jar up past his elbow and into his shoulder. "Dammit. Dammit to hell."

McCall curled up in the backseat of the taxi. She clutched the afghan around her, the only thing she had to cover herself, having left her shoes and clothes at Jake's hotel suite. But this was New Orleans. The driver had probably seen worse at Mardi Gras.

When you make love to him, you'll know, she heard Barb's voice say inside her head.

"I can't love him." She spoke out loud, as if somehow that could make it true. "I can't love him."

She thought about the girl in the photographs Jake had showed her, the woman she'd been four years ago. She wanted to be that girl again, a woman who couldn't feel pain this deeply—couldn't be this afraid. She wished she could put on one of her disguises, a wig, a dress, and be someone else.

She tucked her knees up beneath her, shaking. She told herself nothing had happened yet. He'd just asked a few questions about her to his old boss.

But she knew. She knew it in her bones, her very cells. Oh, God. She knew.

Because in his heart, Jake was still that prosecutor, a man curious enough to nose around and ask questions. He was already in touch with the authorities. He was investigating her . . . a woman who had a great deal to hide.

She had made a terrible mistake. She'd forgotten to do the proper controls. She'd allowed herself to believe this was all about her and Jake and a moonlit night.

And by letting her guard down, she'd given Curtis Clarke the advantage. If something illegal was going on at Clarke Labs—if Jake alerted the authorities—Curtis would have his scapegoat ready. Not McCall, who was too new to the labs. Belinda, maybe. But most likely, it would be McCall's father, his head of Research and Development. And McCall was so afraid. This time she wouldn't be the one who was hurt. It would be her father and Belinda.

The taxi slowed to a stop in front of Barb's house and McCall stepped out of the cab. The rain started again, making her want to weep with it. *Should have been more careful; should have done the proper controls.*

"McCall?" Incredibly, Barb was waiting for her, dressed in a long cotton nightgown and holding a macramé shawl around her shoulders.

She stepped down the walkway in the rain, meeting McCall halfway. Barb put her arm around her and shuttled her past the tangle of the garden and up the stairs. "He called here," Barb said. "He told me you would be upset."

McCall shook her head, trying to explain. But her throat locked up, all clogged with emotion. And she didn't know what she could tell Barb. She had to keep it all inside. *Do the proper controls. Don't put anyone else in danger.*

"Oh, McCall."

Barb held her under the eaves as the rain dropped from the sky, making the ferns and vines tremble. She spoke in hushed whispers, all the while promising that the pain would recede, that the healing would come. But McCall couldn't see how.

It could happen again, the nightmare of four years ago.

Barb opened the door and guided her inside the house, shutting the door behind them. McCall thought about what Barb had told her, that she had found her other half. Now, it felt as if that half would be missing forever.

Down the street, the same car that had waited half the night outside of the River Palace Hotel—the car that had followed her here—turned on its lights for the first time. Making a U-turn, the gray Honda Accord disappeared down the rain-washed street.

Fourteen

Jake woke to the sound of a key jingling in his front door. Before he could clear the fog of sleep from his brain, forty-two pounds of preschooler landed on his stomach and chest.

"Daddy, Daddy!" Michael screamed. His arms locked around Jake's neck, bowling his father back against the pillows. Jake glanced at the clock at bedside. It was just past seven in the morning. He'd been asleep less than two hours.

"Hey, sport," he said, hugging his son. "What are you doing here?" Over Michael's shoulder he saw Hope standing in the doorway to the bedroom. She had Michael's duffel bag hitched over her shoulder.

"I've been calling you for the last three hours," she said. "Something's wrong with your phone."

"Really?" He must have done something to the line when he pulled the machine out of the wall. "I can call out okay." A fact he'd tested already. After Mac left, he'd used the redial button to reach her friend, the last number dialed on the phone. He'd wanted to know she was going to be okay. That someone was looking out for her. "Why didn't you use my beeper?"

She set Michael's duffel bag on the bed and picked up his beeper from the nightstand. She glanced at it, then held it out for him to see. "You left it off, Einstein."

He sat up straighter. For an instant, his sleep-deprived brain wondered if maybe Mac had tried to get in touch with him. But then he remembered how she'd left. Even if she knew his phone number, no way she'd want to talk to him. "What happened to Hilton Head?" he asked.

"We're getting a baby sister!" Michael wriggled out of Jake's arms and stood. He started jumping up and down on the mattress as if it were a trampoline. "Mommy and Dickey are going to go get her for us. I want to call her Demona," he said, naming one of the gargoyles in the Disney series he watched with Jake sometimes on video. "Demona! Demona! Demona!"

Hope gave Jake a hard look. "You're letting him watch television again? Jake, it's a proven fact that the level of violence—"

He lifted his hand in a silencing gesture. "Save it for a decent hour."

He grabbed Michael under one arm and wrapped the sheet around his waist with the other. He thought about the things Mac had said to him about his son, knowing he'd let Hope and her politically correct view of childrearing call too many of the shots. But he'd always believed Hope had the Mother Gene, that she would know a thing or two more about this parenting thing than Jake. Now, he wondered if maybe he didn't have more to bring to the table.

He set Michael on the floor, crouching down to talk to him. "Why don't you go to your room and dig out your speedway? I bought at least two miles of new track. I bet you can get that thing to go all the way around both sofas."

Michael's eyes grew to the size of softballs. He stared at Jake as if he'd just let the cat out of the bag, then glanced nervously at Hope.

"Speedway?" She said the word as if it were in a foreign language.

"Yeah. Speedway. You know, little cars running around a track." He stood, turning toward Hope. "You have a problem with that?"

He could tell she was thinking about it, bouncing the idea

around in her head. *Go ahead, lady. Have a problem. Make my day—*

"No," she said, actually smiling. "Go on, sweetie," she told Michael. "I'll come kiss you goodbye in a bit."

Michael let out a whoop and raced out of the room. As soon as he was out of earshot, Jake shut the door. "What the hell's going on, Hope?" Just six hours ago, Mac had been tucked up warm and naked beside him. What a charming surprise it would have been for his son if she'd stayed. Leave it to Hope to use her key and not even bother to knock.

"We're adopting," Hope said. "They called us in the middle of the night. It's a young girl in Texas. Apparently she wanted an older couple. Somebody established who would know their heart and take good care of her baby. The ultrasound showed a little girl," Hope said with a trembly smile. "She picked us because she wants the baby to have an older brother." She shook her head. "It's so crazy. We just talked to the attorney a few weeks ago."

It surprised him a little, the adoption; he thought she'd been dead set against it. And there was a softness to Hope today. It reminded him of how she'd looked when she'd given birth to Michael.

"I don't have much time if we're going to make the plane," she said. "We may be gone the whole week."

"The week?" He remembered the things he'd set into motion. "Hope, this isn't a good time—"

"I know, I know," she said, turning to leave already, the decision a *fait accompli*. "But we just all have to pitch in to make this work. For Michael's sake. You do understand, don't you, Jake?"

What he understood was that Hope wasn't giving him a choice. But maybe she was right; this was for Michael. A new baby might lighten Hope up a little, take that Klieg-light glare off Michael.

"Okay," he said, raking his hand through his hair as he

followed her into the living room, already thinking over the logistics.

"I'm sorry to drop him off like this, but I really do have to go."

"It's fine." He could get Mindy, his regular sitter. And sometimes Stacie helped him in a pinch; Michael loved Stacie. "Michael and I will work it out."

She stopped abruptly. "And it's not like you have a real job, anyway. Not since you left the Attorney General's office," she said, getting in that last zinger.

"Right," he said, nudging her toward the door.

But Hope didn't get the hint. She turned and smiled, really smiled, in a way he hadn't seen in years. "This is it. I'm going to be a mother again. She's already in labor. It could be any minute, though they're saying not until tonight. I haven't even had time to talk it over with Michael."

"I'll handle it. Just call me to give a status report, okay?"

"Of course." She watched him a moment. "You know, I don't believe I ever told you . . . Michael. I owe you so much for giving him to me . . ."

Before he knew what she intended, Hope kissed him, full on the mouth. It was a reminder of other times; when they hadn't fought, when Michael had been the focus of their lives together.

"Thank you," she said, stepping away. "And forgive me. For Dickey. For the custody nightmare. For everything."

"Jesus, Hope," he said. "Of all the times to go soft on me. He's my son, too. I'm happy we have him."

"Dickey is downstairs with the motor running. Wish me luck?"

He couldn't help smiling, she was so happy. "Bring home a baby."

She said goodbye to Michael, who was counting out track in his room. Jake had to give her credit, she made the proper fuss over the speedway, even though he could guess she would have mixed feelings about it.

He almost had her out the front door when she turned back to face him. "Oh, Jake. I don't think I have to say this, but don't take Michael to that sleazy casino where you work. It's such a bad influence. And no more television. I really believe it teaches children to detach. I don't want him to have social problems later in life."

"Wouldn't dream of it," he said. And when he shut the door behind her, he continued, "Because you see, Hope, I'll be sitting right there, watching the video with him, rooting for the good guys. In fact, the whole thing will be like one big social event. No detachment. No social problems." Leaning back against the door, he shook his head. "Jesus. What a day."

He checked on Michael, then headed for the bathroom. Tossing the sheet back on the bed, he padded barefoot onto the bathroom tile and turned on the faucet. Thinking about his meeting today, he splashed water on his face, wondering if he could pull it off—knowing he didn't have a choice.

Garrett Renault thought he owed Jake. Maybe it was time to see just how thankful Garrett could be.

Jake leaned both hands on the edge of the sink, watching the water flowing down the drain. He focused on the eddies twisting past the gold stopper of the posh bathroom, recalling his meeting with Gus his old boss from the criminal division.

"This is big, Jake." That's what Gus had told him during their lunch yesterday, after Jake had convinced him he could help with the investigation. "Interpol made a request through the legal attaché in London. FBI headquarters contacted the local guys. You know those frozen embryos in England? The ones they're planning to destroy and those ProLife people are making such a fuss about? Welcome to the twenty-first century. Someone is trying to steal over a hundred of them."

Jake kept staring at the water. He'd called Gus to talk about Clarke Cosmetics. He hadn't mentioned Mac or even the FBI file. Thank God, he hadn't mentioned the file.

"And guess where they traced it? Right here, to a girlfriend of Roger Clarke's. She works at a fertility clinic. Only, this isn't like the accusations against those doctors in California. No one thinks these embryos are going to be given away for donation to infertile couples. It looks like she was trying to sell them to her boyfriend for research."

Jake remembered the chill that had gone through him when Gus had talked about it. Because he'd read the file on Mac.

Stolen embryos. It sounded like Clarke Labs needed a geneticist. A damn good one.

"So why steal them?" he asked. "Are these embryos difficult to get legally?"

"If you're an established program affiliated with a hospital with a review board, they're available"—Gus smiled—"but not if you're some insignificant cosmetic company. And then there's the question of what the hell they're doing with frozen embryos. It doesn't sound like lipstick or perfume to me. And they're trying to get their hands on over a hundred of them."

Gus had gone on to explain that the FBI was working with the local authorities. The Office of the Attorney General had been called in on a Request for Assistance, basically because everyone at the District Attorney's office knew Gus had been trying to nail Clarke's ass for years. His investigators were on it now. But nobody wanted to jump the gun. They had a sense there was something bigger going on. They wanted to see where the thing would lead—and that's where Jake had convinced Gus he could help, a private citizen, acting on his own. Someone the Clarkes wouldn't recognize, because Jake had never worked in the division trying to prosecute Clarke.

"You have to let me in on this one, Gus." During their lunch, Jake had been putting it together in his head, feeling the juices flowing, just like in the old days. That's when he'd remembered Garrett. The brochure he'd seen. "I know I can help."

Jake looked up in the mirror, seeing his reflection, the blood-shot eyes and the stubble. He reached for his shaving kit. He was meeting with Garrett today. Two o'clock. Jake's office in the hold of the riverboat casino. And he had a hell of a favor to ask the casino owner.

When he leaned forward, ready to scrape away the stubble with his razor, the face in the mirror changed. Maybe because he was tired—maybe because he couldn't get her out of his mind—he pictured Mac, the round soft eyes that changed color with mood and light, the cupid's bow mouth. He remembered how she'd looked when she'd heard that telephone message. Betrayed. Frightened.

He shook his head to clear away the image. Right now, he had other things that needed looking after.

He finished shaving, then grabbed a towel and dried his face. He put on a pair of jeans and walked into the living room, needing to check on Michael before he stepped into the shower. He found his son setting up track on the carpet. Michael was halfway around the first sofa.

Taking up a piece, Jake knelt down beside him.

"I can't believe you told her about the speedway." Michael grinned up at his dad. Jake could tell his son had enjoyed razzing his mom a bit.

"Yeah? I figured we got her at a weak moment, press our advantage. Besides," Jake said, laying down another piece of track. "This week I'm getting you an Easy-Bake oven. Even it up a bit."

Michael's mouth dropped open dramatically. "That's for girls!"

Jake smiled. So much for Hope's politically correct upbringing. "Gotcha."

"Dad!"

"Look, I made a mistake. It was stupid of me to ask you to keep the speedway a secret. You shouldn't have secrets from me or your mom. And besides, I have an equal say in your life."

"You do?" he said looking skeptical.

Ouch. "Sure," Jake said, trying to sound confident, gaining some ground. "Don't your mom and I fight all the time?"

"Yeah."

"Well, there you go," he said, as if that answered the question. "I'll always fight for you, sport," he added, going with it. "And your mom wants you to be happy. That's number one for her. Like the violin. If you want to stop, it's okay with me. I'll talk to her, make her see our point. I can be a very persuasive guy."

Michael thought about it. Then, looking so much older than his near-five years, he said, "I think I'll give it another year, Dad. See how it goes."

Jake felt those words twist up inside his chest. For a minute, Michael had sounded just like him. "All right. But you let me know. Okay?"

"Sure."

"So," he said casually. "What do you think about this baby stuff?"

Michael didn't bother to look up, just snatched another piece of track and fit it into the piece Jake had put down. "I think it's way cool. I'm going to be a great big brother. Why don't you have a baby, Dad? Mom says you don't have to adopt or anything."

An incredible heat rushed through Jake. He had the sudden image of Mac pregnant, round with his child. What would it be like to try the family thing again? Only with Mac.

Those cozy thoughts shattered at the memory of her face when she'd slapped him, then raced out into the hall with only an afghan to cover her. She'd looked so hurt. So scared.

He grimaced. He might have to get her to talk to him again, before they started that family.

He shook his head. It was impossible to believe she was in on it with Clarke. But he'd seen that fear in her eyes; she had something to hide. And that's why Jake was getting involved. He needed the straight scoop—before Gus and the rest of them just labeled her guilty because of her past.

Come Monday, whether she wanted it or not, Mac was in for a big surprise.

He felt a pain in his hand. He glanced down and saw he

was holding the piece of track so tight, it was going to bend. Handing the track to Michael, he let his son take over, watching him put his track together. Jake brushed his hand through his son's strawberry blond curls lovingly. He was a great kid. Jake knew he was lucky to have him in his life.

Maybe this was all you get in this world, he thought. The one chance. And he'd used his up with Hope.

The thought depressed the hell out of him. Because, despite everything he'd learned about her—or maybe because of it—he didn't want to let go of that dream of Mac and him together.

He glanced at the clock. He thought about what Hope had said to him. *Don't take Michael to that sleazy casino*. He turned back to his son. Michael was looking up at him expectantly.

"So, sport," he said with a grin, "you want to go see where your dad works? My office is in this really cool place, at the bottom of a ship."

Roger held up a plastic test tube, oddly cone-shaped, about an inch in length. He was dressed in green scrubs, wearing rubber gloves. Like Curtis beside him, he wore a hair net and paper booties over his shoes. Roger had called his father a few hours ago. It was Saturday, but Curtis didn't mind coming in. Not for this. Roger had been working in the Level-2 lab all afternoon.

"It's beautiful, isn't it?"

The mask covering Roger's mouth muffled the words slightly. Curtis wished to God he could rip off his own mask. The thing made him feel as if he were suffocating.

"BioYouth," Roger said, saying the name they were considering for the product. "Daddy, I think he's done it."

"Let's hope so . . . for all our sakes," Curtis said. Sometimes, he really wished he hadn't listened to Roger about the clinic. Damn thing was beginning to feel like an albatross around his neck.

But then he looked at the cloudy solution frozen in the test tube and smiled, feeling the old excitement. If they succeeded, their little operation would leave every damn pharmaceutical company in the dust. They would be playing with the big boys, no longer some peon cosmetics firm that grossed a measly hundred million, but part of a multibillion-dollar-a-year industry. Curtis had learned a long time ago that for the big payoff you had to take the big risks.

He watched Roger lift the freezer lid. Smoke-like tendrils curled down the metal sides, the condensation pooling toward the floor as Roger placed the test tube inside. The freezer was filled with racks and racks of similar tubes, all labeled with dates and experiment numbers. The hope was that this generation of the inoculation would prove less toxic than the others.

"Come on," Roger said. "I need to check on Friday's delivery."

They stepped into the hall. *Damn place gives me the creeps,* Curtis thought. Their paper-covered shoes made strange scuffing noises as they walked down the empty corridor. It looked exactly like a hospital, sterile halls flanked by little rooms, reminding him too much of his angiogram last year. Only, there was a slight animal stench in the air.

Roger swiped a card through the lock, pushing down on the door handle. You needed a special card to access these doors . . . even to use the elevator to get to this level. The animal room required the highest security possible, allowing for only a skeletal staff. It would kill Clarke Cosmetics if word got out that they were testing on animals. Animal rights activists, questions from the FDA about their product, USDA inspections of the lab facilities, these were complications they had managed to dodge the last years by keeping the research under wraps.

He felt a sudden fear that they were taking too many chances, that he could lose everything, end up as he'd started, that poor slob hawking the strip clubs on Bourbon Street. For a moment, he couldn't catch his breath and he thought about the little pills he always carried to put under his tongue, nitroglycerin. But he took a couple of deep breaths, commanding himself to stay calm.

Dammit, he'd planned for every contingency, even failure. He'd socked away enough cash in the Caymans—money his capital-hungry son didn't even know existed. Even if this whole thing with Isla Hermosa and the Clarke Spa and Clinic blew up in his face, he could spend the rest of his life on a beach sipping umbrella drinks. And he was just enough of a risk taker to see this one through.

"Look at them, all healthy. All within the stats we requested."

Curtis glanced around the room anxiously. It wasn't very large, allowing for only eight cages, four stacked on four. The cages were made of stainless steel and clean—Roger insisted on that. There were two feeding bins and bright, white, fluorescent lights. Inside each, a middle-sized dog lay waiting. Roger also had monkeys, rabbits, and mice, each species housed in its own separate room.

Curtis knew the monkeys were the most dangerous to work with. Certain viruses, like Monkey B, while mild in the host monkey, could kill humans. One bite, and in just four days, a researcher could find himself dying a hideous death that Roger described as "having your brain burned." Curtis never went into the monkey room. Just thinking about it made him check his gloves and mask nervously.

All the animals here would be inoculated with the BioYouth solution produced for that particular species, the results carefully monitored. But it was the dogs that interested them most right now, the animal of choice for experiments testing motor functions.

Curtis grabbed the clipboard with the paperwork from Roger. At five hundred a pop, he wanted to make sure he was getting his money's worth. *Eight dogs,* the papers said. He glanced down at the signature at the bottom.

"Belinda took the shipment?"

"Sure did," Roger said, opening one of the cages on the bottom row, the one with a decent-looking golden retriever inside.

"I thought we'd decided to keep the girl out of this."

"Out of what?" Roger knelt down in front of the cage. He pulled off his glove and held out his hand, coaxing the dog to come out. "She hasn't a clue what's down here or what was in that truck. And even if she figured it out, who cares? Look, I was busy meeting our supplier for the embryos." He smiled, as the dog sniffed his outstretched fingers. "It was very tricky business, requiring a delicate hand."

From his son's tone and choice of words, Curtis knew the "supplier" was a woman. The Clarke men had a prodigious sex drive. He doubted the skinny little ballerina, despite her big boobs, could keep up with his son.

Curtis shook his head. If Roger wanted a hold over Donald Sayer, Curtis wished he'd picked the smart daughter. But instead, Roger had done his damnedest to piss off McCall— probably because she was smarter. He'd gone for the girl with her brain in her panties.

"This supplier. Are we on for that shipment from England?"

Roger played with the dog, petting it. It made Curtis uneasy to watch him. The dog wasn't exactly here for R and R.

"Shake," Roger said. The dog put his paw in Roger's hand, executing the trick as if he'd done it a thousand times. He knew immediately the damn thing was somebody's pet.

"Dammit, boy. Will you leave the dog alone and tell me about the shipment?"

"There might be a problem," Roger said, repeating the trick with the dog. "It doesn't look like the English supply is coming through. But Sonia thinks she has another source. We're scheduled to discuss it tonight."

Tonight? Shit. He was sleeping with her. "I don't like it," Curtis said. "The English thing sounded damn good. No records, no mess-ups. Nobody to care. Don't take a chance with this, Roger. We're talking about extremely sensitive material."

Roger shrugged. "The first shipment was damaged and now they're holding out for more money—which we can't afford. We're already short. As it happens, I'm meeting with a potential investor—"

"What the hell are you talking about?" Curtis raged, feeling his blood hit the boiling point. "Look here, this is not for public consumption. Isn't the money I got us last week enough?"

"That's your problem, Daddy," Roger said in his most ingratiating tone. "You keep thinking small. The spokesmodel alone for the Omega Principle cost more than that."

"Shit," Curtis said. "If you bring the goddamn government down on me, boy—"

"What did you think, Daddy? That this was going to be easy? No risk? It's not like we can write up a prospectus and get an influx of capital. I worked my ass off to find the right kind of people for the Clarke Spa and Clinic—I personally selected every woman getting on that island, every man who handed us a dime. I know what the fuck I'm doing, so just back off. Besides, what are you so worried about anyway? So what if we're investigated?" Roger stroked the dog's sleek floppy ears. "We pay a couple of fines and move the operation. Or if it gets really ugly . . ."

He turned, looking up at his father with his smart good looks and an angelic smile. "How could we have known? A trusted employee like that. Of course, Donald Sayer always was overly ambitious, a man who lived in his daughter's shadow for years," he said, as if quoting newspaper headlines. He shook his head. "Imagine, Dr. Donald Sayer using our facilities for his own hideous purpose. And what he did to Dr. Goodman." His smile deepened the grooves bracketing his mouth.

"Donald Sayer isn't going to jail for me."

"Well, then, maybe he'll just have to go somewhere else," Roger said, his expression becoming hard, alluding to a deadlier solution. "If this thing goes south, we won't need him anyway. Remember Alicia. It's easy to take the blame when you get yourself dead. Sit," he told the dog.

The dog obeyed immediately.

"Isn't she beautiful?" he said, scratching the dog's head. "So well cared for, she could have been a beloved pet. Such a cute little doggie," he said in a baby voice that had the dog's tail thumping. "Gonna give your all for science, aren't you, girl?"

"Stop it, Roger. You're giving me the creeps." Because they both knew what would happen to that dog if the inoculation didn't work. Curtis had seen it firsthand, a collie, before they put the poor animal to sleep.

Unbidden, the thought of those women came into his head. The ones they'd recruited for their island paradise, Isla Hermosa, and the Clarke Spa and Clinic there. For one horrible instant, he imagined them suffering the same fate as the dogs.

He couldn't catch his breath. *Not enough air in here!* Panicking, Curtis ripped off his mask, cursing. Fuck the damn rules anyway. A guy had to breathe, didn't he! "This *place* gives me the creeps."

"Jesus, Daddy," Roger said, laughing as he put the dog back in the cage and closed the door. "They're just a bunch of dogs. Come on, you look like you need a drink." He put his arm around his father, leading him out the door. "Monday, I meet with this guy. If my information is correct, and I'm solid it is, he represents a very lucrative group. He just might be the shot in the arm we're looking for. And if he comes through for us, I promise—no more investors."

Curtis walked beside his son, thinking about the dog, how Roger had played with the retriever, holding it so lovingly, then blithely sentencing it to possible death. He thought maybe he'd done something wrong with Roger. Twisted him a little.

Being the son of Curtis Clarke couldn't have been easy; he had big shoes to fill and Curtis had always been demanding. Or maybe he shouldn't have divorced his mother so soon and told her to get the hell out of their lives. Who the fuck knows.

The plain truth was, Curtis didn't give a rat's ass if his son was a sick son of a bitch. As long as he was a successful one.

Sierra settled down inside the cage, her muzzle resting on her two front paws. She whimpered softly.

The dogs had been brought to a room that looked as if it was part of a hospital. Everything smelled of chemicals and animals, making the dogs nervous. And the cages were small, a great deal smaller than the dog runs where they'd first taken Sierra.

The retriever looked out from between the bars of the cage at the world of white walls and gray metal. Beside her there were several stacked cages. Inside each cage, another dog waited, looking just as cramped within the confining space.

They had brought her here in a truck. The black German shepherd lay hunched over in the cage next to Sierra. Hardly able to move in the close quarters, the retriever just managed to turn. The German shepherd touched his nose to hers, the only thing familiar in their new sterile world.

A man in a white coat came inside the room, followed closely by a woman. He had a clipboard on which he jotted notes. He checked the cages and the papers hanging there.

"Get the black German shepherd ready," the man said. "We'll start with him."

The woman opened the door, stroking the dog. "Poor thing. Come on, fella."

Sierra watched as they took her friend away.

Part Three

Regeneration

The serpent beguiled me, and I did eat.
——Genesis, 3:13

Fifteen

We've had a breakthrough. One of the monkeys. It's extraordinary, beyond anything I ever imagined. I feel like Superwoman, without limits. Invincible. He was right—it's worth any risk.

—Excerpt from Dr. Alicia Goodman's lab book

McCall watched Curtis tilt open the humidor. "Would you like a smoke? I understand it's all the rage now, even for a little lady like you."

The box looked as if it was made out of zebrawood, an exotic wood McCall knew was scarce. Curtis sat behind an obscenely large desk, made of another exotic wood, this time covered in stainless steel from the lip down.

The room was ultramodern—to the point of bad taste, McCall thought. Everything looked misshapen, almost surreal, a style that might have fared well in a minimalist setting. But Curtis had crammed every nook and cranny, even leaving a pedestal near the center of the room waiting for the next *objet d'art*. The crimson leather chair where she sat reminded McCall of a giant clam, with her nestled inside like dinner.

"No, Curtis. I do not want a smoke. But I would like to know why you called me here."

Curtis slipped the humidor back to its spot next to a large oblong stone. The polished rock was seated in a round wooden stand. Together, they formed a linga and a yoni, Curtis had been quick to explain, religious objects symbolic of a phallus and the female form.

McCall's lips pressed together. The way he kept playing with the cigar, passing it beneath his nose, almost caressing its length, you just might wonder how many phallic symbols a man needed.

"I thought you should know," Curtis said, swiveling in his chair, lighting the cigar. "I'll be meeting with Woods tomorrow." He smiled, accentuating his double chin. "That boy's giving me a progress report on you. And he's sharp, McCall. Hey, now. Maybe even as smart as you. I've asked you here because, despite what you may think, girl, I'm a fair man. I want to give you the opportunity to get anything off your chest—before I hear Woods's version, that is."

"How incredibly subtle of you, Curtis. Unfortunately, I don't have time for your paranoia today." She stood. Then, batting her lashes and speaking in a patently ingenue voice, "No, Curtis. There is nothing I want to confess." *End of meeting.*

"Have a seat, girl. I'm not finished with you yet."

"How disappointing," she said, falling back into the clam chair. "Do you think we could wrap this up soon? I'm keeping your precious Dr. Woods waiting and I'd hate to get a tardy slip."

Curtis puffed on his cigar, the light in his gray eyes showing that he found her amusing. He was dressed in a white suit with a white tie, all contrasting with a burnt orange shirt that turned his complexion muddy. She felt like telling him he should use better lighting when he applied his foundation in the morning, but held her tongue.

Curtis allowed the smoke to curl in his mouth, savoring it. "Have you ever heard the saying, 'Don't get between a man and his money'? We're sinking a hell of a lot of capital into the Omega Principle. I just want you to know what I'm going to do to you if you're not dealing square with me."

"I would say this is just about where we left off four years ago. 'You'll be sorry, girl,' " she quoted from memory, mimicking his drawl. " 'I do believe your ill-considered decision could be the death of a fine career.' "

"And imagine. It all came true."

"I'm a smart girl, Curtis. Cross my heart and hope to die, I learned my lesson. Why don't you take this up with that son of yours, your brilliant scientist?" she said, hoping that Curtis, at least, perceived Roger as such. "Both he and Woods thought the PET scan results quite remarkable. Ask Roger if he believes I have a winner. Now, if you think you've wasted enough of my time . . ."

She rose from the clam chair, but instead of leaving, she picked up the linga. "What an interesting rock. Siva the Destroyer?" she said, naming the Hindu god Curtis had said the stone symbolized. "How appropriate." She lay the stone flat on the desk rather than returning it to the stand. "You know where to find me if you feel like another chat."

"Just so you know, girl," he said, as she reached the door. "I'll eat your heart this time."

McCall pushed past the door, the soles of her flats clapping hard against the marble floor to the beat of her anger. "And I hope you choke on it," she said under her breath.

She hated these confrontations, mostly because they sapped so much of her energy. She had to be another woman when she met with Curtis, someone fearless, someone who could take him on, as well as his minions, and come out the winner. *I'm going to beat you, Curtis,* she threatened in her head. *I won't let you hurt me or mine ever again.*

But after only one week, she was already weary from the battle. She'd been working through the weekend; they all had. Functioning on little sleep and lots of caffeine, she had too many emotions raging near the surface. She hadn't spoken to Jake. *But I miss him.* And it hurt not to call him, to shut him out. To think of him as a threat.

She shoved the pain aside, knowing she had to concentrate

on the task at hand. She didn't take Curtis's warning about Woods lightly, despite their banter in his office.

Kyle Woods was a machine. Tireless, unrelenting. Over the weekend, she'd kept her eye on him, watching him make short work of procedures that would eventually lead to the information they wanted. Left to his own devices, he could very well purify the peptide as quickly as Kate, her tech, had suggested. Only, McCall hadn't left it all in his hands.

She'd noticed the only time he'd disappeared was for a late dinner, saying he was meeting someone. She remembered how he would glance at his watch, the single distraction he'd permit himself in a near fourteen-hour stretch at the bench-top tables. She wondered if he was meeting a woman. It was difficult to imagine, that he could unbend enough to be involved emotionally with someone.

It was during those precious hours, after Woods left the lab, that McCall had started her undercover work. She'd browsed through the computer system, searching out any interesting files. She'd come across something in the system file servers. A file she couldn't get into as a guest user—which she found odd in and of itself.

But it was in those hours alone, with only the soft whir of the machinery for company, that she was most susceptible to her emotions. Jake would sneak into her head, breaching her defenses. She'd tried to be strong, not to remember their night together and the words she'd heard coming from his answering machine. *Gus from the criminal division . . . he's a good guy to talk to about this.*

McCall turned down the hall leading to the laboratories, glancing at her watch as she headed for the security booth. Falling in love with Jake Donovan was a disaster on every level. She had come here to help her family, afraid that Roger Clarke might be involved in the sort of diabolical experiment alluded to in Alicia's lab book. The addition of Lab 20 only fueled her suspicions. It was the perfect place for Roger to execute his crimes.

But if something illegal was going on at Clarke Labs, something that could bring down the Clarke empire, Curtis wouldn't take the fall—and McCall knew the most likely candidate to bear the blame was her father. He was their head of Research and Development. He had access to Lab 20. And Curtis had sold him out before, offering McCall her father's position four years ago without so much as a thought for her father's welfare.

McCall slashed her card through the lock at the entrance to the security booth, preoccupied by her grim thoughts. Stepping inside, she flashed her badge. When the light turned green, she clipped her badge back on and walked past the buzzing door into the hall.

And now, rather than helping her family, McCall may have facilitated the very things she'd feared for them. Because of her FBI file and a curious ex-assistant attorney general, she might have brought closer scrutiny—an examination that could paint her father with the same brush as it would Clarke and his son.

What I've managed to carve out here for your sister and myself. Please, she heard her father's voice beg her, *don't ruin this, too.*

McCall walked down the hall, the sound of her shoes striking the floor becoming a rhythm in her head. A ticking clock. *Running out of time. Running out of time.* Woods had completed the gels. He was screening the transformants for the gene they wanted. Jake and his connections at the criminal division were looking into her past.

She remembered the day the FBI agents had charged into her office, flashing their badges and waving federal warrants. Imagined it happening again, only to her father this time.

"McCall!"

She groaned, recognizing Roger's voice. It was almost six. By now, Roger should be long gone or locked up in the Level-2 lab, where he spent a considerable amount of his time. She was tempted to keep walking, not knowing if she could take father and son confrontations on the same day.

"McCall. Hold up. There's someone I'd like you to meet."

She turned, knowing she wouldn't get away with ignoring him. She had a ready excuse on the tip of her tongue . . . until she saw who was walking right next to him.

Her heart stopped. Stopped. Not a breath . . . not a pulse. Nothing.

The hall fractured. The images shifted, twisting oddly. McCall wondered if she might actually faint. But then the corridor righted itself and everything focused with incredible clarity on one man.

Jake Donovan strolled alongside Roger, one hand tucked into the pocket of his trousers. He'd slicked back his hair with some sort of pomade that made the style look both wet and salon-studio chic. He was dressed in black, a long jacket with a narrow lapel and perfectly draped trousers that showed the power of his thighs with each long-legged stride. The shirt beneath was the most beautiful shade of jewel green, a color that gave an almost artistry to the ensemble.

He wore a very thin tie in iridescent blues and greens and very thin sunglasses. The glasses reflected the overhead fluorescent light like black mirrors.

Next to Jake's vibrant green and black, Roger's patterned black and white jacket and form-fitting white pants appeared stylish but subdued. Jake was the sleeker of the two, looking almost foreign despite his reddish blond hair. A Ferrari compared to Roger's pricey DeVille.

"This is Jonathan Donovan," Roger said as both men came to a stop. "He's a friend of a friend. I'm taking him around, showing him our facilities. We just came from your father's lab in the Fragrance Group. But Mr. Donovan here was particularly interested in your work on the Omega Principle."

Jake tilted his glasses down, peering over the top of the lenses. As if liking what he saw, he swept the glasses off alto-

gether. "Please, call me Jonathan. I saw you on Cyndi's show.
I couldn't resist meeting the Love Doctor while I was here."

He held out his hand.

She hesitated for a fraction of a second then placed her
hand in his, watching as hers disappeared within his grasp.
Irreverent images flooded her head with the warmth of that
touch. Jake, cupping her breasts, his skin so dark against the
paleness of her own. Jake's hand covering her mouth, his fingers dipping inside.

McCall stared at the back of his hand—the near invisible
freckles, the reddish brown hair—completely lost.

He squeezed her fingers, extra tight.

"Are you okay, Doc?" He grinned at Roger. "I hardly ever
have this effect on women, really." He leaned down to
McCall's eye level, smiling. "I think I left the doc speechless.
But that's okay, because—heck. She's got my pulse racing."

McCall closed her eyes. *Oh God.* "I'm sorry—Jeremy, was
it?"

"Jonathan," he corrected, flashing his dimples.

She took her hand away. "My mind wandered a bit there.
I've been thinking about the number of transformants I should
expect given the concentration of the viral particles containing
the gene we're looking for. The incorporation of foreign DNA
into the bacterial genome can be tricky sometimes."

"Whoa, Doc. You're scaring me." He nudged Roger.
"Sounds like she knows her stuff."

"McCall is probably the most brilliant scientist in her field.
That's why we recruited her for Clarke Labs. Now that we
found you, McCall," Roger said, "why don't you give
Jonathan a tour?"

"This isn't a good time," she heard herself say.

Jake remained standing next to Roger, looking incredibly
relaxed, as if they weren't walking a tight rope together, watching each other's moves, countering.

Roger smiled as he insisted. "Jonathan represents a group
of investors who are thinking of coming on board in a very

big way. And as I told him, the Omega Principle promises to be quite lucrative."

"We're labeling the probe," she said. Then turning to Jake. "That means we're using radioactivity. So, I strongly suggest that, unless you want to put your sperm count at risk, you postpone your tour for another day."

Roger laughed. "The levels of radioactivity aren't nearly high enough to be dangerous. Besides, Dr. Woods told me you labeled the probe yesterday." To Jake, he added, "We have a highly trained staff of scientists working round the clock on the Omega Principle. We're planning to hit the stores before Christmas."

"I'm trying a new technique, Roger," McCall said, knowing she wasn't going to spend the next hour performing a dog and pony show for Jake. "As it turns out, the levels of radio-activity have proven very high. Jonathan, right now, it just might be dangerous to your health to push this," she said, knowing he would get the double meaning.

"Hey"—he raised both palms up, taking a step back—"I'm not putting my boys at risk. Another day, Doc. It's been a pleasure."

He strolled away, forcing Roger to follow . . . which Roger did reluctantly.

"So, Roger," Jake said, slipping on his sunglasses as if the overhead lights might be too much for him. "You were talking about this Japanese Group? That sounds like something I should know more about."

"It's right this way." Roger glanced back at McCall, looking furious. Everything in his expression let her know there would be hell to pay for defying him.

Jake smiled, half turning as he walked. He pulled those ridiculous glasses down again and winked at her. "That doctor—boy, she's hot," he said to Roger loud enough for McCall to hear. "Do you know if she's seeing anyone?"

"No," Roger said, looking back at Jake, distracted again. "McCall is very dedicated; I don't believe she dates. Now, our new Japanese Cosmetics Group is just up ahead, in Lab 14. Most everyone working there has gone for the day, but we can peek in for the moment. It's not my field, but I'll fill you in as best I can."

McCall started to breathe again, watching both men walk down the hall. They were of a height, Jake perhaps an inch taller. His solid form made the slighter Roger appear almost delicate in comparison. But while Jake's eyes gleamed with his lighthearted grins, almost as if he were laughing at his own tongue-in-cheek responses, Roger's eyes showed a visceral ability to hate. To hurt. To get even.

They were dealing with pure evil. And Jake Donovan appeared completely oblivious to it, following her here, hunting her down . . . acting as if she and not the Clarkes were the danger. He was putting her and her family at great risk.

"And it has to stop," McCall said to herself.

Jake walked down the steps, nodding every once in a while to let Roger know he was hanging on the man's every word. He'd just spent the last two hours with Roger Clarke courtesy of his own boss, Garrett Renault, who had made the introductions. Roger was now walking Jake out to the parking lot at Clarke Labs, getting in his last pitch on the potential profits to be made by investing in Clarke Cosmetics.

"Nice shirt," Roger said. "Mossimo?"

Jake almost said *Gesundheit* before he realized the guy was talking about the shirt's designer. Shit. He should have paid more attention to what Dino had told him. "Right."

They stopped in front of a candy red Lamborghini Diablo VT. Jake opened the door, watching it lift skyward like the wing of a bird. He was thinking about Mac. She was going to kill him. Which, of course, had been the point.

He grinned, remembering her expression when he'd called her "Doc," razzing her out of her deer-in-oncoming-traffic daze. He thought he'd done a fair imitation of Dino.

"Jesus, this is cherry," Roger said, genuinely impressed as he walked around the car. He leaned down to look inside, admiring the champagne leather piped in red. "I was thinking of trading my Ferrari for the new Diablo Roadster."

"What can be more fun than driving two hundred miles an hour when you're going topless?" Jake answered, repeating something he'd read in a magazine on exotics, an ad for Meade Lamborghini. Which was the extent of his knowledge on the convertible coming out that summer.

Jake had prepared for today's meeting carefully. Garrett Renault and Roger Clarke had been childhood friends, the bad boys of the social registry set in town, and Jake had gleaned as much information as he could from Garrett about his old pal, Roger. While Stacie took Michael on a tour of the decks, Garrett had given Jake the lowdown. Roger was a man who lived by the three C's: cars, clothes, and cunt.

Jake had made two trips to gather his props before tackling Roger Clarke today. He'd dropped by Dino's, and he'd raided Dickey Harper's garage.

"Wanna go for a spin?" he said, tossing the keys to Roger. He wished Dickey, Hope's husband, could see him now. The man would have an embolism.

Roger caught the gold keys in one hand and stared at them as if tempted. "Not today. I've staged a rather delicate experiment for the next few hours." He smiled. "The lady won't appreciate it if I'm late."

Jake winked, snatching the keys Roger tossed back. "Catch you next time, then."

He eased down into the car and shut the door. He lowered the window after he slipped the keys in the ignition. Roger leaned over. "So, what do you think about my suggestion?"

Jake smiled. "I'll give you a call."

He peeled out of the parking lot, stopping at the security booth. But once he hit the road, he punched it, yanking off the tie he'd borrowed from Dino. He couldn't wait to get home and wash this stuff out of his hair. He smelled worse than a perfume shop on Royal Street.

Jake zipped along Route 44, feeling as if he were hovering mere inches over the road, the ride was so low. He could see the draw to these cars, but hell—give him his Jeep any day. He smiled, remembering Dino's reaction when he'd told him about his plans for today.

"Have you lost your mind?" The first words out of Dino's mouth.

"Why?" Jake had answered, sitting back on Dino's couch. They both had Sunday off, which was good, because what Jake had in mind was going to take most of the day. "You think only you and Susan can have fun with this spy stuff?"

Dino had called to tell Jake he'd "scored"—Dino's word. Not in the bedroom but in the pocketbook. He and Susan were having the papers drawn up for their new partnership in the PI business. "What's so crazy about it anyway?" Jake asked. "As far as I can see, I'm dead on with this one."

He'd told Dino everything. He'd even asked Dino to go over Mac's FBI file as he listened to Jake's ideas about her involvement. He'd wanted Dino's opinion on whether he believed Mac could be in on the things he'd learned from Gus about the embryos. Jake thought not—but then, he wasn't exactly unbiased. It was a relief to see Dino agreed.

"I think you're right," Dino had said. "She's here for revenge. She gets them to invest a bundle in a dud love potion, and poof. The company goes belly up—or at least she hurts them, bad. She gets the last laugh."

That's how Jake figured it. Now, it was up to him to make sure Mac didn't get her butt tossed in the Big Muddy for her troubles. The first step had been talking to Garrett Renault—a meeting that had gone better than he'd expected. Garrett had literally picked up the phone on the spot and called Roger Clarke from Jake's office, telling him that Garrett was coming in on the deal at Clarke Cosmetics only if Jake's group got a shot at it with him.

Jake checked the rearview mirror, recalling how great Garrett had been about the whole thing. Sure, the guy had his rough spots, but he never forgot a favor. As far as Garrett was concerned, Jake had turned his life around. In gratitude, he'd agreed to serve as a reference for Jake and his mysterious group of investors . . . without asking too many questions. Which was good. Jake wasn't about to tell the casino owner he was part of a criminal investigation of the Clarkes.

"That boy always did hang out with the wrong crowd," Jake had told Dino, sipping beer with his friend as they compared notes.

"You really think you're going to get away with this." Dino had shaken his head, looking at Jake as if he'd finally lost it. "You know," Dino added. "Maybe you should consider taking medication?" He snapped his fingers. "How about that woman Suzy sees about her mom's suicide?" He actually picked up the phone. "Why don't you give Suzy a call and ask for the number? Don't these guys take 911 cases?"

"Are you going to help me or not?" Jake asked. He needed Dino if he was going to fool Roger Clarke into believing he was a player. You could probably play touch football in everything jammed inside Jake's closet right now. And the Greek was the only guy he knew who actually subscribed to *GQ*.

Dino sighed dramatically. "How much time do we have and how much money are you willing to spend?"

"Atta, boy," Jake had said, standing. "We'll put it on the plastic. Who knows. I could get lucky at craps later this week."

"Right," Dino said, knowing Jake didn't gamble.

Jake turned the Lamborghini onto the 61, smiling at the memory. Dino, who always complained about Jake's wardrobe, had finally gotten his wish, picking out the weirdest shirt for Jake to wear. A bright green shirt? Give me a break. Like he was a leprechaun or something.

Later, that day, Jake had hit Susan up for some of her surveillance equipment. But he'd skipped discussing her middle-of-the-night phone call, knowing he wasn't going to get her cooperation if he started in on the trouble she'd caused him.

As things turned out, he hadn't needed the camera Susan lent him. Today's meeting with Roger hadn't yielded much. Everything had been aboveboard. No mention of the clinic . . . no illicit shipments of frozen embryos lying around for a look-see.

Jake signaled, heading for the 10 into the city. That's when he'd asked Roger to show him Mac's lab, thinking to accomplish at least one of his objectives. Though he'd been less than excited about the look Roger had given Mac when she'd refused to give them a tour, he knew one good thing had come out of the encounter.

He smiled. He could almost imagine the steam coming out of her ears. He glanced at the car's clock and pushed the gas pedal.

If he hurried, he might get a shower in before she storm-troopered his front door.

Kyle Woods pushed away from the light box where he'd been examining the films he'd exposed earlier. He'd set the light box down on the bench-top, finding a free spot between a box of gloves and a rack of pipettes someone had forgotten to put away. A water bath incubator lay just across the way, but Kyle focused on the light box. He frowned. He couldn't believe the results staring him in the face.

They'd busted their butts all weekend, trying to get the films ready for today. They had isolated the bacterial DNA from the transformants they'd grown, then digested it, treating it with an enzyme that cut it into smaller pieces, running the gels. The gels were a jelly-like substance placed between two glass plates to which they added their samples of digested DNA. Yesterday, he had transferred the gels onto filter paper, had hybridized the filter paper with a probe. The probe was radioactively labeled so they could see it on film. When he exposed the filter to film, the radioactive probe would show the particular lanes where the probe found its complimentary DNA strand.

It was the only way to find out which of the forty transformants contained the gene for the peptide they wanted. Once they knew that, they could purify the peptide, the key ingredient for the Omega Principle.

Only, of the forty transformants he'd tested, none carried the gene they needed.

It was incredible. Forty false positives. It was a disaster.

He rubbed his eyes, then glanced at his watch. Six o'clock. He was set to have dinner with Belinda later tonight and he didn't want to be late.

He stood and got himself another cup of coffee, knowing he couldn't leave until he went over these results with McCall. He hoped she got here soon. He'd planned to go home and change before meeting Belinda at their restaurant.

Kyle stirred the powdered creamer into his coffee, watching it turn from black to near white. *Their restaurant.* That's what Belinda called it . . . because they'd met there three nights in a row.

He thought about how much he'd enjoyed Belinda's company. He'd learned a lot about her these past days, about the years she'd grown up alone, the sister she'd idolized but didn't understand, the dancing she'd given up—and her strange relationship with her father, a man she both worshipped and cursed.

But Belinda wasn't all about the problems that plagued her life. She had an incredible sweetness to her. And she was a hell of a lot of fun, with a silly sense of humor that made him laugh—and Kyle had been told he distinctly lacked a sense of humor.

She even persuaded him to go out dancing. Dancing, for God's sake. He hadn't danced since high school.

And he wanted to sleep with her so badly, he'd almost crossed the line several times. But he knew if he made love to her—if they forged that bond together—then ultimately, he'd damn them both.

He took a sip of the coffee, knowing he wasn't a saint because he'd settled for heavy petting, like a couple of teenagers, in his car parked a block from her house. He'd meant to befriend her, not seduce her into helping him. Still, he smiled with the memory of those stolen moments, the feel and taste of her mouth. Her smell and touch.

He leaned back against the bench-top, the mug warming his hands in the air-conditioned room. He and Belinda definitely had something together. And he knew why.

Kyle's eyes unfocused, his mind wandering back to the events that had set him on this path, bringing him here to Clarke Labs.

Sissy, of course, had been the initial step.

The big yellow Labrador had been the first dog he'd rescued. He remembered the day perfectly, a particularly bad one. Kyle had worked on flies in both his undergraduate and doctoral work. Only, he'd been given an opportunity to do postdoctoral work in neural networks. It was a prestigious lab and he'd jumped at the chance.

The trouble had started with the rats. Mammals.

He couldn't seem to convince himself that—even though he'd medicated the rats with a dissociative drug during the procedures—they didn't *feel* pain. Every day, it got worse. He'd break into a sweat; his hands would shake. The work he did required the steadiness of a surgeon. He *was* a surgeon, operating on the brains of tiny mammals, dissecting the cerebellum for analysis.

He'd tried everything to get over it, knowing his career was at stake. He'd become a vegetarian. He'd given money to PETA. But in the end, it only made him feel like the hypocrite he was.

Animal rights versus people's needs. He knew there were no easy answers. AIDS, cancer—animal experiments were a vital part of the research into cures. And computer models weren't nearly sophisticated enough to do the job.

But that day, he'd seen the end of his career in experimental biology. His lab partner had walked in on him just staring at the rat, unable to make the first incision. The guy had taken one look at Kyle and stepped in, taking the scalpel, telling him to go for a walk.

He'd left then, considering what he could do if he quit science. That's when he'd heard a colleague discussing the dog. The voices came from a neighboring lab, saying things like Sissy wasn't going to make it "on the outside." Kyle knew the university had a program where laboratory dogs and cats were rehabilitated and sent to caring homes as pets. They were animals with special needs because of their experiences in the lab.

He had stepped inside the door. He remembered distinctly the instant the big, yellow Labrador and he had locked eyes. He couldn't tell how long he'd knelt there, in front of the dog's cage, only that Sissy had inched forward and licked his face.

"Hey." A man he didn't recognize had dropped down beside him, smiling. "Want a dog?"

That had been the beginning. The day he'd decided what to do with the rest of his life.

He'd had Sissy five years before she had died from complications caused by her years as a lab animal. Now he had Hercules, another graduate of the program.

He thought of Belinda, knowing that was what she'd first reminded him of: an abused animal. And when he'd knelt down beside her at the casino, their moment had been a little like that instant with Sissy. He could read it on her face: She had found someone to trust. Someone who wouldn't hurt her anymore. After only three days, he'd seen the changes, how she'd blossomed with just a little loving care.

The lab's door buzzed open. Kyle turned, the sound snapping him out of his reverie. McCall walked through.

"You're late," he said.

"It couldn't be helped," she said, making her way to the light box. "I had a command performance in Clarke's office. I understand you're next. I hope to God you have something nice to say about us, Woods. How do the films look?"

"The news isn't good."

McCall pulled up a stool and sat down. He pointed out the lanes even though he knew it wasn't necessary, that McCall would immediately recognize the problem.

"My God," she said.

"That about sums it up. How do you account for every single transformant being a false positive?" he asked. "In fifteen years of doing this, I've never seen results like these."

"It must have been contamination." She stared at the films, her face showing the strain of the past few days.

"But Kate, Tom, and Robert each did separate transformations. About twenty each. We had forty transformants from those. You honestly think they could all be contaminated?"

"It must have been in a solution they used in common. It's the only explanation." She sighed heavily, shaking her head. "This means we'll have to start over."

He pressed his mouth shut, figuring that's what she'd say. It was, after all, a possible explanation. But he was a little disappointed that he'd been right about McCall.

Kyle gathered his things, stuffing the paperwork he needed into his backpack. He had his answer.

"I'll see you tomorrow," he said walking to the door as he swung the backpack over one shoulder. "No one's going to be happy about this."

"It can't be helped. Hey, try not to be too discouraged when you see Curtis. I'd hate for him to pull the plug on us."

"Don't worry," he said, opening the door.

McCall heard the door buzz shut and watched as Kyle Woods stepped into the hall. She let out a slow breath, then slowly collapsed against the bench-top, clutching her arms around her stomach.

This was the moment of truth, the inevitable confrontation she'd dreaded. She was pitting herself against Kyle Woods, a man she'd come to see as a formidable opponent.

She remembered what Curtis had told her in his office. *I'll be meeting with Woods tomorrow . . .*

She could feel sweat pooling between her breasts. She was still shaking from her encounter with Jake in the hall, a toxic mix of anger and fear. And now Kyle.

She told herself that he hadn't seemed particularly suspicious, just upset about the results. She glanced back at the light box. *Please, God. Don't let him suspect.*

The films showed exactly what McCall had expected—because she'd switched the test tubes in the incubator, replacing them with ones that didn't contain the gene they were searching for. She'd known all along that when they probed the filters, it would look like contamination. That they would be forced to start over.

She'd been trying to buy herself more time . . . and Woods had scared her into cheating. The instant they purified the peptide for the Omega Principle, they would test it again. And they would know she was a fraud.

McCall took a deep breath, straightening in her chair. Jake was investigating her, showing up here to do God-knows-what. Curtis was making threats—Kyle, breathing down her neck.

She grabbed her jacket off the back of her chair. She would have to take them on one at a time. Snagging her purse, she headed for the door, tired but determined. She would be using precious hours—the only time she had the lab to herself—but she had no choice. She would come back later tonight. After she had it out with Jake.

Kyle made his way through the parking lot to his Volkswagen Rabbit. He thought about the explanation McCall had given for the false positives. *They must have used a common solution.*

The problem was, Kyle himself had overseen the transformations of all three technicians. There was no solution they'd used in common—he'd made certain of that. And just to be on the safe side, he'd done his own transformation.

Out of the fifteen transformants he'd gotten, twelve had the gene for the Omega Principle peptide.

He'd kept his transformants in the Fragrance lab. McCall never even knew they existed. What he'd discovered today wasn't contamination. It was sabotage.

Kyle opened the door and threw his backpack onto the passenger seat. And he knew who was responsible. Oh, she thought she'd fooled him, but there was no way she would have accepted those results so calmly, coming up with the lame excuse that there had been contamination.

Kyle shifted into gear, pulling out of his parking spot. Which probably meant the Omega Principle peptide didn't work. It was the only reason why she would ruin the cultures. Once they purified the peptide, it would become perfectly clear the Omega Principle wouldn't produce.

Kyle drove past Belinda's parking spot. He frowned when he saw her Miata. Apparently, she was running late as well.

He thought about Belinda, getting that uneasy feeling in the pit of his stomach. But he shoved his guilt aside as he steered the Rabbit toward the security gate. He didn't have the luxury to worry about Belinda's big sister. He had to keep focused on what counted. His mission was more important than any one person or how he felt about them.

Tomorrow, he planned to meet with Clarke about the Omega Principle.

If he told Curtis his suspicions, he would divert attention from himself and earn the man's trust. He would be just like Alex Pacheco, the man who started PETA by taking a job at a research center, ingratiating himself to the institute's chief research scientist, and later, exposing the center's incredible abuses against their animals. It had been the turning point in the animal rights movement.

And Kyle knew that if he handed McCall up to Curtis Clarke, exposing her flawed formula, he might buy himself the one thing he wanted most: a security pass into that Biosafety Level-2 lab.

He turned onto the road from the parking lot. "Sorry, McCall. But this is business."

Sixteen

Belinda swiped the card key through the lock to Lab 20, trying to remember the dumb code. They changed it every month, and sometimes she got the numbers mixed up. She kept a cheat sheet in her desk drawer, under the pencil tray, figuring no one was going to get in without stealing her card *and* the code—which she carefully kept apart, like her ATM card and the PIN number.

The door clicked and Belinda smiled, glad that she hadn't had to run back to her desk to check the number. Her father was still there, working in the Fragrance lab, and he was the last person she wanted to see right now. All day, he'd been ragging on her. He'd sent her to restock stuff they didn't need, hovered over her when she did the tiniest thing, making smart remarks the whole day that made her feel dumb. *Belinda, did you remember to* . . . On, and on, and on.

She knew he was punishing her because of Friday night. When she'd come in from the taxi ride with Kyle, her father had grilled her until she'd admitted she'd been out with someone other than Roger. But she'd made it sound like some guy she'd picked up at a club. A nobody. Nothing her father could say or do would make her cough up Kyle's name.

She stepped into the room she referred to as "decon" because she would have to load up with clothing to protect against contamination, then strip the stuff off later to decontaminate. She sighed, putting on a lab coat and the rest, the hair net, the paper booties. The gloves and mask she just brought along. Roger had asked her to meet him in a small office he kept here. She only needed the other stuff inside the actual labs.

She couldn't figure out why Roger had asked her to meet him here, in the Level-2 lab. But she could tell she wasn't going to get out of it. Which was okay, she just didn't want to be late for dinner with Kyle. But Roger had said it wouldn't take long.

Belinda signed in her name and nodded to the guard sitting outside of decon. He was reading a magazine, his feet up on the desk. It was probably pretty boring work, just sitting there. Not too many people were allowed in here, Belinda knew. Because they worked on such sensitive stuff, her father had said. She wasn't really sure what went on here, she was just glad she didn't have to come very often. The mask, the booties, the hair net . . . it was such a big deal.

She hurried a little. Roger had told her to meet him in his Level-2 lab office just after six. She knew he was a little mad at her, like her father. Two nights in a row, she'd told him she'd made plans and couldn't go out.

But it had felt good to say no for once, instead of jumping into line whenever he whistled for her. She didn't do that often enough, she knew . . . say no. To Roger. To her father. She thought he might even be a little jealous, might have figured out she was meeting another guy. It actually surprised her, that he would care enough to be jealous. But then Roger could be funny about stuff like that.

Don't marry him if he doesn't love you. She remembered her sister telling her that. Belinda frowned. Maybe McCall was right and it was time to give Roger back his ring. She'd been putting it off knowing he would get mad. That he would take it out on her somehow.

Belinda stopped, hearing a noise coming from Roger's offices. Voices? It seemed kinda strange that someone was here with Roger. Belinda knew she wasn't much of a technician.

She figured Roger had asked for her help because no one else was available.

She walked hesitantly toward the office door. The sounds grew louder, more distinct . . . until she realized what she was hearing. The soft whispers of a man to a woman, followed by a low female moan.

Belinda recognized the man's voice instantly. She'd heard those same somnolent whispers, had fallen asleep to them long ago, when Roger was still nice to her. And she knew what they meant.

She pushed the door open and stepped slowly into the room. Illuminated by a single desk lamp, Roger leaned over a table, his back to the door. A woman, her skirt pushed up over her hips, her breasts exposed by her opened blouse and lab coat, lay on her back on the table. The floor was littered with shoes, paper booties, gloves.

Roger had his head between the woman's legs. His arms stretched over her body so that he teased her nipples. The woman groaned softly.

Belinda felt like a zombie, just standing there, watching them. She should turn around and leave. *Leave!* a voice said inside her head. *Don't let him do this to you!* It sounded like her sister's voice—McCall warning her.

The woman saw Belinda first. She gasped and sat up awkwardly on the table, closing the lab coat she was still wearing. Roger took his time as he straightened and turned to face Belinda.

"Hello, honey," he said. He took a handkerchief from his pocket and wiped his mouth. "You told me you were busy tonight, so I made plans."

"Jesus, Roger," the woman whispered.

The woman scooted off the table and started gathering up her things from the floor. But Roger stopped her, making her stand up. "Where do you think you're going? We still have unfinished business." He pushed her roughly back against the table.

"What is this, Roger?" Belinda asked. "Why did you ask me here?" There were tears in her eyes, and she couldn't figure out why. She didn't love Roger. She knew she didn't love him. "Is this some kind of mind-fuck because I wouldn't go out with you tonight?"

"Roger, I want to leave," the woman whined behind him. "I can get you that shipment you wanted. This week. Tomorrow, maybe."

"Sonia, I'd like to introduce you to my fiancée, Belinda Sayer. Sonia here is one of our suppliers, a very important part of our future at Clarke Labs. We had a little mishap with a shipment from England, but this resourceful lady thinks she can make up for it."

"I told you I would try." The woman sounded like Belinda felt. A little scared.

"But you know that's not all I want from you, darling." Roger walked around the woman, standing behind her so he faced Belinda, watching Belinda over the woman's shoulder. Sonia was very pretty, a brunette with big brown eyes and a knock-out figure. Roger reached around her, slipping his hand inside the lab coat the woman still clutched. Belinda could tell he was touching her breast.

"Belinda understands I have needs that she can't even come close to satisfying. You see, Sonia, my fiancée isn't particularly good at much. From sex to science." He laughed. "Does that about cover it?" he asked Belinda, his hand moving inside the lab coat.

"I think you're sick," Belinda said, trying to fight back. "I think you're both sick."

He smiled, then kissed the woman's cheek. "Of course I am, darling. And think of all the sick things we've done together."

It was true. She'd let him do stuff, things she didn't like—things that made her feel dirty inside. Things that made her hate herself afterward.

"You should see her, Sonia. She doesn't even know how

to go down on a man. She putters around the lab, pretending she knows what she's doing. But half the time, she screws it up, like everything else. Wouldn't you say that's true, Belinda? About half? Or is the math too much for you, sweetie?"

She told herself she didn't care, that Roger was cruel and she was a fool to let him hurt her. She tried to think about Kyle. That he liked her.

Only she wasn't so sure anymore. When she kissed him, he was always the one to pull away. He was the first to stop, telling her it was time to go home. And Kyle was so smart. Why would he like her? Dumb Belinda.

"Belinda's never enough for anyone," Roger whispered. "So I have you, fair Sonia. A real woman. I was thinking just the other day what a good thing it was for your daddy that McCall is back. Because you can never take her place. That's something your daddy will figure out real soon."

His words tore into her heart, confirming all her doubts. *Never enough.* Not enough for Kyle, for her father. Not even for her mother, who eventually turned to alcohol for companionship. All the insecurities she'd tried to hide in a secret corner inside herself came creeping out, unfurling their wings, exposing her flaws.

You're too dumb. You're not beautiful enough—not special enough. For anyone.

Belinda tore off her ring, the marquis diamond Roger had given her for their engagement. "You're right, Roger," she said, stepping over to his desk. "I'm just not enough for you."

She put the ring on the desk, proud of herself because she hadn't broken down completely. And then she ran out of the room.

She raced down the hall, choking on her tears. She told herself this was for the best. Roger had gotten his little revenge—and she was finally free of him. But she knew that wasn't true. Because his voice was still inside her head.

You're not enough . . . you're not enough . . . for anyone.

She stumbled down the hall, the tears making it hard to

see. Her doubts roared inside her head like some great beast. *You're too dumb. You're not beautiful enough—not special enough.*

She thought about Kyle, waiting for her at their restaurant. That's where she wanted to be right now—this instant—with Kyle holding her, a man who truly cared about her. Who at least treated her with kindness and patience.

In decon, she threw off her lab coat, kicking off the booties and tugging off the hair net, mask, and gloves as she put each in the special waste receptacles. She wanted Kyle to love her so much it hurt. And she prayed, prayed with all her heart that he could.

Please God, for once in my life, let me be enough.

"Mac?" Jake said, opening the door wider. "Imagine. You coming to find me."

"Don't even try to act surprised," she said, stepping past him. "And get that smug look off your face."

"Smug?" He closed the door, following her inside the hotel suite. "I'm just happy to see you. You taking care of that blanket you wore out of here? I hate to be picky, but it's sort of a family heirloom."

McCall ignored him, throwing her purse on the counter and tossing her jacket across one of the stools. She had on plaid pants with a black stretchy top, the zipper on the shirt pulled down low enough to make it interesting. Jake had just come out of the shower. A warrior preparing for battle, he'd donned his best armor: his favorite bowling shirt and chinos.

"Why?" she asked in that clipped voice, her hands on her hips.

He didn't even pretend he didn't understand. "Come on, Mac. You sound like you want to take that radioactive probe to me."

"What a tempting thought."

He smiled. She was pacing now, back and forth, couch to

couch, her curls bouncing with each step. She'd pulled her hair up in a ponytail so that it tumbled down in burgundy fire to the tops of her ears.

He pictured the woman in the photographs he'd found inside the FBI file. Mac was as far as you could get from that image of egghead scientist. He thought about that a minute, watching her.

"I wish I'd been there," he said, speaking his thoughts out loud, because he wasn't scared of being honest with her. Not about this. "I wish I'd known you in the tough years, the ones that chiseled away that inflexibility I saw in those photographs, making you the way you are today."

"Don't," she said, stopping her pacing, fisting her hands at her sides.

"I wish I could have made it easier for you somehow."

She shook her head, turning to face him. "You don't want to make my life easier, Jake."

"Maybe you're right," he said, considering it, remembering his own struggle the past four years. "Because you know what? Sometimes the pain of change is necessary. A butterfly coming out of its cocoon. If you try to help, cut the cocoon open, the creature that emerges is only half formed and dies. The butterfly needs the struggle to be whole. The woman in those photographs was like that butterfly, too focused, half formed."

Suddenly, she came at him. She slammed both palms into his chest, a good attempt at a shove.

"Stop it. Just stop it!" she said. "Why are you doing this? Why were you at the lab? Are you investigating me? I have a right to know." She pushed him again, putting a little more into it this time. He obliged her by taking a step back. "Or is this some sort of demented attempt at your Donovan Curse? Just another damsel in distress for you to mess up her life? Answer me!"

"It looks to me like I'm screwed no matter what I say," he

said, matching her tone. "The answer is none of the above, Mac. This isn't about games."

"You come to the lab, looking like . . . those clothes. Where did you get those clothes you were wearing?"

"Just some stuff I had lying around."

"And that name. Jonathan?"

"Jonathan Patrick Donovan," he said, stepping closer, smiling when she took a step back to keep some space between them. "Jonathan is my real name. It's sort of a thing in my family. Nicknames."

Before she could stop him, he reached out and grabbed her around the waist with both hands and pulled her up against him.

"Like Mac. Maybe you don't like it, that I call you that. But it suits you. McCall was the woman in the photographs. The one who looked like she should wear a button on her chest that says I LOVE SCIENCE." He brushed the hair from her face, liking the feel of it.

"Let go of me." But there wasn't enough conviction there.

He thought about letting her go, really he did. The voice of reason in his head even said it might be for the best, to let her walk out of his life. *The smart thing.*

But there was something else he heard louder. Mac, calling out his name in her sleep.

He shook his head. "Maybe I wasn't there four years ago, when the world turned upside down for you. But I'm here now. I won't let them hurt you again."

"What business is it of yours?" she asked. But her eyes glistened as she said it, as if maybe she was fighting back tears.

"Now that's a good one, Mac. Two nights ago, you were lying buck naked in my bed. When we made love, you couldn't get enough." Jake pressed his finger over her mouth, feeling the softness of her lips. "And now you're asking me if it's any of my business?"

She closed her eyes. "Please, don't do this. I'm not strong enough for this."

"You remember that night?" His fingers kept tracing her mouth, the full lower lip, the curves at the top, knowing what she meant, feeling it just as deep. "Those memories make my bed so cold at night now. It makes me keep the clothes you left behind, like I'm some obsessed idiot, because they smell like you. I want you back there, Mac. Beside me on that bed."

"This is a mistake." But when he pulled her arms up around his neck, she didn't fight him. Instead, she stared at his lips hungrily.

"No, Mac. The mistake is walking away from it." He lowered his mouth to hers, granting small, teasing kisses, waiting for her protests. Hearing none. "That night, with your nightmare. You were crying out in your sleep and you woke me. Do you know whose name you were calling? My name. Only mine. Over and over."

She kissed him then, her hands combing into his hair, pressing him tighter as she opened her mouth beneath his. He pulled back, smiling when she pressed up on her toes to reach for him. "You can't ask me to forget that," he said.

A key opened the front door. Mindy came in with Michael. A coed from Tulane, Mindy was his mother's all-time favorite student. She was a sweet kid who looked like a young Vanessa Williams, and the only baby-sitter he trusted with Michael at night. Good old Mindy. An education major with a penchant for literature. Responsible, strict but fun.

And staring just as hard as his son, transfixed by the movie trailer image of Jake and Mac's bodies pressed so close, they practically occupied the same space.

"Wow," Michael whispered, his fingers tight around his Happy Meal.

"Whoops." Mindy held up the McDonald's bag and smiled sheepishly. "We're a little early, but we thought maybe you wouldn't get a chance to eat before you had to go to work."

"Excuse me," he said to Mindy.

He swung Mac up into his arms, cradling her against him. "She's feeling a little faint," he told his son, trying to sound perfectly serious. "I think she needs to lie down for a minute."

Mac's eyes stayed on Michael, who stood equally mesmerized. Jake figured the shock was keeping them both quiet. Not one to miss an opportunity, he carried Mac bodily toward his bedroom. "This will only take a minute," he said over his shoulder.

"Wooow!"

Michael's exclamation followed them all the way to his room. Jake kicked the door shut behind him and locked it. He dropped Mac on the bed, following her there so she couldn't get away. He leaned into her, both hands on either side of her face, lowering himself slowly so that she could feel his body molding into hers, no longer holding his weight off her with his arms.

"Your son is here," she said.

"Yeah. I recognized him. The baby-sitter looked familiar, too."

"I should leave."

"Didn't you hear?" He kissed her. Once. Again. "You're feeling very faint. You have to rest."

She pressed her forehead against his. And then she was holding him, her hands coming around his back, clutching at him as if he might disappear. "He's even more beautiful in real life."

"Yeah. I know."

There were tears in her eyes when she looked up at him. "I wish he were ours." She whispered it like a secret.

He brushed away the tears, then kissed her eyes. "You getting emotional on me, Mac?"

"I can't help it," she said, laughing a little. "I think I've slept a total of six hours since I left here."

"See? You do need your rest."

But he knew how she felt. Because he was feeling it, too. The soul mate stuff. "My missing half," he said, meaning it.

"Oh, Jake." She brushed her fingers through his hair. "We just can't be right now."

"I think we already are." He moved a little, a slow dance of his hips against hers. If they had their clothes off, he could nudge inside her. He could make her a part of him right now. "Do you remember how it was with us?"

The connection called out to him seductively. If he made love to her, he would have a greater say in what she did next, even if it was just for tonight.

"I happen to be a very old-fashioned guy," he said against her mouth.

"This from a man with two ex-wives?"

"Details." He held her face in his hands. "Friday meant something to me. I don't want to walk away from it. Do you?"

She closed her eyes. "What terrible timing," she whispered.

"I don't know, Mac. I thought my timing was dead on."

Her eyes widened just a bit as she realized what he meant. He could tell the exact moment she remembered their love-making.

"Yes," she admitted. "You have exquisite timing, Jake Donovan."

"You're in with some very bad people," he said carefully, guiding the conversation. "People that you have some history with. But maybe you don't know as much about them as you should." He couldn't imagine her involved with the stuff Gus had talked about. And the FBI file. *Fuck it.* His instincts told him that mad scientist routine wasn't Mac.

"Curtis Clarke," he said. "I could tell you stories," he added cautiously, so tempted to confide in her.

She was looking at him, but something must have been off about the connection he was feeling, because she scrambled out from beneath him.

She sat up on the bed, her back turned to him. "You want to tell me he's dangerous?" she said, not looking at him as she spoke. "That he's capable of murder? You want to protect me from him?"

"Yes."

She was silent, not giving anything away. At first, he wasn't sure he'd played it right, her turning away like that. But then he sensed it, that subtle change in her posture, just like in the old days when he'd been prosecuting. Intuition was everything to him. And right now, at this moment, Mac was with him. Trusting him.

"I think Roger killed my partner, Alicia Goodman," she told him. "I don't know how Curtis is involved, but it wouldn't surprise me."

"I read the file, Mac. There was an investigation. Accidental death. No charges were filed."

She turned, her eyes very green. "And you think Roger Clarke can't buy himself out of murder charges?"

"You tell me."

She leaned closer to him on the bed, even the movement of her body willing him to believe her. "The night of the accident, Roger was driving Alicia's car. Roger loves cars. Fast ones. He had a Maserati then. I kept thinking, if it was an accident, why wasn't he driving his own car? Why would he be behind the wheel of Alicia's car? But if he was going to kill her, if he had planned it, he wouldn't have taken the Maserati. He wouldn't have sacrificed it."

The words came out fast, one rolling over the other, gaining momentum, as if she'd held it inside too long. She sounded almost out of breath, a marathoner with the end in sight.

"He said the brakes gave out," she continued. "That he lost control and hit a tree. The car spun out, going over the embankment into the bayou. Roger is excellent behind the wheel—I've seen him do 360s in the rain just to scare me. I think he could have managed it. The accident. I think he could have planned to kill her."

"Okay. All right," he said, because so far, it was a just a story she was telling. There was no proof. "But, Mac. The facts—"

"I know the facts, Jake. He said he thought she was dead

from the impact of the tree, that he almost didn't save himself. Only, he didn't call the police right away. He claims he fell unconscious." The anger came creeping into her voice now. "He was conscious just long enough to get himself out of the car and make it to the embankment. And then he passed out."

He could see how much she wanted him to believe her. "Not impossible, but suspicious."

"I'll never forget when he told me about the accident. His voice. It was ringing with this mock sympathy, almost as if he were acting out a script. I swear to you, he was enjoying himself. There were tears in his eyes, but he was smiling, as if he were proud he could shed those tears. He looked at me and said he thought she was dead before the car hit the water. How would he *know* that?"

"He thinks she's dead?" he said, still hearing a lot of maybes. "Sounds like an opinion to me. A mistaken one as it turned out. The autopsy showed she drowned; it said so in one of the newspaper clippings. Motive, Mac. Talk to me about motive."

Whenever he interviewed someone, there was always a critical moment when the person wanted to trust him, but was afraid. He could almost fill in the words for them, he could see them so clearly on the tip of their tongue. But to play the moment right, he just had to wait, hoping the silence would tip the scales in his favor.

He saw her hesitate. She looked away, for just a second, her breathing becoming more shallow.

"He implied they might have been lovers. He was her little secret," she said, whispering now, "because he was so much younger than Alicia. You don't know Roger. He's twisted. If she spurned him . . ."

He shook his head, seeing that she was keeping something from him. "Ah, come on, Mac. Don't disappoint me now."

He came up very close to her. He tipped her face up to his. "Did you know, Dr. Sayer, that when a person lies, there are all these neurological responses? The most common is in the pupils. They widen, just a fraction of an inch. Anybody can miss it. If you want to be really convincing, you'll have to work on that."

She shook her head. "I don't know—"

"The eyes, Mac. The eyes." His finger pressed against her mouth in a gesture of silence. "Let's go back to that game of truth or dare. You said someone set you up, altering your data to make it look like you cheated, siccing the FBI on you with anonymous phone calls. You said Curtis was behind it. You think Roger killed your partner. Fit it together for me. Motive, Mac. Give me the motive."

She wanted to trust him—but she was scared, he could see it in her face. And this wasn't a *voir dire*, a job where his emotions weren't involved. He could tell she was weighing it inside her head. But Jake wanted her to trust him with her heart.

He took her hand in his. "Trust me," he whispered. "Just this little bit more."

She seemed to collapse at that touch of his hand. She stared down at their linked fingers, then squeezed them together. When she started speaking, he almost couldn't hear her, her words were so soft.

"Four years ago, Curtis Clarke came to me with a job offer." Her voice grew stronger, surer. "He wanted me to take over my father's position as head of Research and Development at Clarke Labs." And then she looked back at him with her beautiful eyes. "I refused and he said I'd be sorry. Two weeks later, I'm at the center of a federal investigation, my research questioned, my reputation ruined."

Bingo. He thought about Gus, the frozen embryos. Maybe Clarke had needed a geneticist even then. So he'd tried to recruit Mac. Only she didn't play along. "Your partner dies two weeks after that," he said, finishing the story for her. "She could have found out about it, the setup—she could have even been part of it. The bastard thinks you don't work for him, you don't work at all. But your partner, she had second thoughts. A change of heart. You were friends, after all. Maybe she even threatened Clarke to make him stop. Maybe he thought she knew too much?"

"That's what I believe."

"Shit." He released her hand and pushed his fingers through his hair. "Shit!"

The raw burning in his gut that always nagged him when a case went bad flared inside him. He slumped back against the pillows, knowing just how possible the scenario he'd just mapped out could be. Mac was on to something. And she didn't know the half of it.

He let out a breath, thinking she was like a ball of lightning. Something he couldn't control. He sat up again, coming at her, afraid to let her out of his sight until she understood the danger. "And now you're back for revenge. It took you years to plan it. You needed money to research your love potion, the bait you thought Clarke couldn't resist. Only, you're out of the science business as far as the established community is concerned. So you take up blackjack, a game that gives you enough money to get you up and running, no questions asked. And you're good at math, maybe even have a photographic memory."

It all made sense. And it scared the shit out of him, what she was trying to pull. "They wanted you and now they're getting you. The Omega Principle is a dud that's going to cost them millions," he said, giving her his theory. He grabbed her shoulders, pulling her to him, needing to have a say in this. "Listen to me, Mac. You can't take these guys on."

"You think that's what I'm about? That this is some sort of vendetta?"

"They ruined your career; they turned your father against you. You said so yourself. All because you wouldn't play their game." It fit the bill. And it was a hell of a lot better than believing she was in on it with Clarke.

She looked up, her eyes blue with a thin rim of green. "That's what you see in my heart? Revenge?"

"I hope to hell I know what's in your heart." Because he couldn't afford to be wrong about her. "Look. I can handle the Clarkes for you. But you need to step out of this. You need to stay safe."

"You see me as one of your damsels in distress, don't you?" she said, sounding tired as she reached up and stroked his cheek. She shook her head, looking at him. "And you're going to save me. Aren't you, Jake?"

For a minute, he didn't say anything, sensing another one of those quicksand moments opening before him. But then, he thought she was going to kiss him. It was so clear in the way she watched his mouth, the desire she made him feel with that look. Only, the emotion didn't jive with her mood or her voice and what she was saying. He waited, seeing where she was going with it.

And then he got it. Right between the eyes.

"If I ever see you at Clarke Labs again," she said, "I'll tell Roger you were a prosecutor. He'll look very carefully into your phantom investors. I imagine that would be a big problem for you."

She moved so fast he actually lost his balance. One minute she was there in his arms—the next, he was holding only air.

At the door, she said, "Stay away from the lab, Jake. I'm not there for revenge. I'm there for survival. And no one, not even you, is going to stand in my way."

Her words hit hard, hard enough that he just kept staring at the empty space where she'd been sitting, letting her go. *I'll tell Roger you were a prosecutor.* Just like that . . . she'd turn him in. Because he was trying to help her.

Slowly, he got to his feet, so mad, mad as hell. He stood there for a while, trying to figure it through. By the time he made it out to the living room, the only thing he saw was the front door closing behind Mac.

Michael pointed to the door. "She went thattaway, Daddy."

Jake stared at the door, hearing her threats, remembering her eyes. How the pupils hadn't changed. But he told himself to calm down, not to let his emotions muddle his thinking. He analyzed her response a little, trying to keep it straight— and despite his anger, he didn't buy it. That she would turn him in like that.

"She said her name was Mac," Michael said, still lit up with the excitement of it all. "And she's bringing me a coloring book next time she comes."

Jake turned toward his son. "She said *Mac?*"

"Yeah. You know, like a Big Mac."

"Well, what do you know." He glanced at the door. "I guess she got used to it."

Looking back at Michael, he saw his son the way Mac would see him. A beautiful four-year-old boy with his father's coloring, a precocious and bright child. He remembered how she'd acted in Michael's room, touching everything, then attacking like a lioness when she thought Jake rode Michael too hard.

She'd said she'd been projecting from her childhood, but he thought there was more to it than that.

He came and knelt down in front of Michael's stool at the counter. "She said she'd bring you a coloring book, huh?" And she'd taken the time to talk to Michael, not just running out.

"Yeah, 'cause she noticed there weren't any in my room."

Jake smiled, the anger gone, finally getting the picture clear in his head. "You know, sport. I don't believe she's turning us in to anyone."

"I guess," Michael said, looking puzzled. He took another bite of his Chicken McNuggets. "I like her name though. Mac, Mac, the Big Mac."

"Yeah," Jake said, standing. "My favorite."

He turned to the baby-sitter, who'd been watching every move like this week's installment of her favorite soap opera. "I gotta go."

"Sure," Mindy said. "Michael and I are set."

He went to the hall closet and grabbed his bomber jacket.

"You have my beeper number. Call me for anything. He needs to be in bed by eight," he told Mindy. "He can watch a video. But make sure you watch it with him. Discuss the story line . . . he's real good at it. I'm telling you, my kid is the next Spielberg."

He glanced at the Elvis clock on the way out. He was due at work in an hour, the graveyard shift. He hoped to God Dino could cover for him.

McCall leaned her head against the steering wheel.

I'll tell Roger you were a prosecutor . . .

"Right," she said out loud. She sat up and checked the rearview mirror, staring at her eyes reflected in the mirror. "How did I do that time, Jake? Did my eyes give me away?"

She reached for her glasses in the glove compartment. She had been lying, of course. She would never hand Jake up to Roger, making him or his beautiful son a target. But Jake was a man too used to rescuing women. A man who would step in, unthinking of the danger. So it was up to McCall to think of it for him.

She jammed the key into the ignition, angry all over again. As if she didn't have enough to worry about. Now Jake was stepping in, taking chances, aligning himself with her in a way that put him directly in Roger's sights.

And that precious little boy. What would become of him if something happened to Jake? "I'm not leaving Michael to the fate of a man named Dickey," she said, shifting as she backed out of the parking spot.

The instant she'd seen Michael, she been struck by how badly she wanted to make them a family. It came to her whole cloth, the vision of them together, always. Michael was a smart child, already reading when most kids could only recite the alphabet. She could teach him how to live with that intelligence, how to be happy despite its burden.

It was during the power of that moment that everything

about Clarke Labs had slipped away. All she had thought about was forging a life with Jake and Michael. Just like Barb and Stan and the twins. She'd seen the picture of it so clearly in her head that it had brought tears to her eyes.

McCall drove through the parking complex, winding her way down to the exit, remembering how in the wake of that moment, she'd confided in Jake, despite her resolve to push him out of the equation. She shook her head, realizing how blind she'd been, believing Jake had come to the lab today to investigate.

She should have known—she should have guessed Jake would try to protect her. Now, it was Jake she needed to protect. Because he loved her. And she'd seen it so clearly in his eyes.

He wanted her safe. He was going to rescue her.

That's why she'd said those awful things, hoping she could make him hate her—even if only for the few days she needed. That's why she hadn't told him about Alicia's lab book.

She took a deep breath, feeling more in control. He must have been very good as a prosecutor. The scenario he'd painted of her life the last four years was dead on, wavering only at the end, when he'd talked about revenge.

Steering around the parked cars, McCall turned onto the street, knowing she needed to get back to the lab. Tonight, she vowed she wouldn't leave until she found something, some tangible proof. And then, she would go to her father. With her father's help, she could beat the Clarkes and finally put the past behind them.

As McCall slipped out into traffic, a gray Honda Accord followed. It prowled several cars back, careful to keep out of sight.

"Will you lock up?"

Sonia Baxter glanced up from her seat behind her desk at

the fertility clinic. One of the physician's assistants stood in the hall, looking tired.

"Long day?" Sonia asked, though she didn't give a damn. She'd been waiting for the bitch to leave for an hour.

"I'll say. See you in the morning."

Sonia listened for the *snap click* of the front door closing. Quickly, she changed files on the computer.

She'd just done the paperwork that afternoon. Roger was riding her so hard for those embryos. He scared her a little with his threats. He could be so ruthless, like today with his fiancée.

She couldn't disappoint him—not after the considerable amount of money he paid for those embryos. She would have to make another contact in England, someone who wouldn't back out at the last minute.

By the end of the summer, the English government planned to destroy thousands of frozen embryos. Sonia had thought she'd procured at least a hundred—but her source had run scared. She'd told Roger the package had been damaged in shipment, which wasn't true. When he'd pressed her for another shipment, she'd hedged by suggesting the supplier wanted too much money. He wouldn't like it if he found out the truth, that she wasn't sure she could ever get her hands on those embryos.

What a waste, she thought, typing as fast as she could. They were just going to destroy them anyway. Who cared if a hundred or so slipped through to some lab for research?

"There," she whispered, finishing the transfer. In the meantime, she would get Roger off her back with this dozen from the fertility clinic.

She was always careful when she took embryos from the clinic, making certain they were donations that would later be classified as failed pregnancies. She forged the paperwork and fixed the files to show that thirteen frozen embryos belonging to various couples would be scheduled for donation at another clinic. But she had to take a few chances to get enough, changing some of the embryos for donation even though they weren't classified for it.

Later, she would notify the doctor she worked for that the procedure of implantation had failed. She'd done it before. No one ever asked questions. Like in England, people just stored the embryos for years, then forgot about them.

Sonia Baxter waited as the paperwork printed out. Despite the ugly scene in the lab earlier—or perhaps even because of it—she knew she wanted to see Roger again. But she liked him best when he was happy.

She gathered up her things and headed for the embryo nursery, smiling to herself. She thought Roger would be quite pleased with this baker's dozen she was delivering.

Seventeen

Kyle pulled up to the curb, ready to hand his car over to the red-jacketed valet. But instead of a man opening the door, Belinda peeked into the car from the driver's side.

"Scoot over," she said. "I'll drive."

He took one look at her face and did what she asked. It was clear she'd been crying.

He watched her maneuver into traffic, her expression set with a focus that defied conversation. She reminded him of the day she'd slammed into him in the hall, cursing her father.

"What's wrong?" he asked.

"Just a change in plans."

She glanced at him. She looked incredibly young, nowhere near her twenty-one years. She'd scrubbed off her makeup, leaving her skin perfectly clean, her cheeks pinked. But the image of sweetness was garishly set against her short black dress. Crisscrossing laces held the plunging neckline loosely opened to her navel, showing she wasn't wearing a bra.

"Where do you live?" she asked.

"Garden District. Carondelet."

She braked the car into a screeching halt. In the middle of the street, she made a U-turn to a chorus of car horns, heading in the opposite direction, toward the Garden District.

"Pull over," Kyle ordered. "I'm not letting you drive like this."

"I'm doing just fine," she said, zipping past a red light.

He wasn't going to grab the wheel or slam his foot on the

brake to stop her. He decided to play it cool, to try and calm her down a little.

"You want to talk about it?" Something had gone very wrong since he'd seen her at work earlier today.

"I don't want to talk at all."

"Then do me a favor and slow down."

She glanced at him anxiously. "You're mad at me."

"I'm not mad. I just want you to slow down."

She did as he asked, staring straight ahead. But after a while, he saw her tears.

"Belinda—"

"I don't want to talk right now."

"All right. When we get to the house, then."

They drove in silence, Kyle quietly giving directions when necessary. It bothered him to see her this upset and not know why. He felt cut off. He realized he wanted to *fix* things for her somehow. When they reached his house, he jumped out of the car and walked around to the driver's side. He opened her door, smelling the odor of burning rubber from the brakes.

She made a show of stepping out of the car, her dress hiking to display black stockings held up by lacy garters.

"You're such a gentleman," she said.

The way she spoke, she sounded like an actress. She'd made her voice huskier. But the sexy tones were forced; there was only a veneer of sincerity. It was nothing like the young woman who had charmed him the last three nights, making him laugh, making him forget the burden of his responsibilities, if only for a few hours.

She danced up the steps to the double where he lived, swinging her hips, turning on her heels to give a sexy smile over her shoulder. Her hair was pinned up loosely so that soft tendrils swept down the curve of her cheeks to brush her chin.

When he took out his keys, she grabbed them from him playfully. She leaned up against the door, and opened it from behind her back. "I hope you live alone."

"I do."

"That's good." She bit her bottom lip, the look full of sweet seduction, playing the baby-doll vamp to the hilt. She grabbed his hand, tugging him into his house. "Come on."

Once inside, she shut the door and dropped her purse and the keys. She wrapped her arms around his neck and kissed him deeply, then began swaying her body against him. "Do you have music?" she asked, biting his bottom lip gently. "And something to drink." She reached down and caressed his erection, making him grow even harder as her fingers pressed around him. "I would love something to drink."

He pulled her hand away. "I think you've had enough," he said, realizing she had been drinking. He could taste the sweetness of alcohol in her mouth.

"What's the matter? Don't you want me?"

The way she spoke, he could see that she was desperate not to be rejected. But before he could do or say anything to reassure her, she stepped away. Her smile began to tremble, as if it took a tremendous effort to keep it there.

"Of course you don't want me," she said, taking another step back. "Stupid Belinda. Why would you want me?"

She picked up her purse from the floor and headed for the door. Not knowing what else to do, Kyle let out a sharp whistle. He heard the back door rattle, the clicking of nails against the floor boards. Seventy pounds of Doberman came flying into the room, beating Belinda to the door.

Hercules planted himself in front of Belinda, barking his fool head off. Belinda stood paralyzed, watching him.

"Make him stop," she whispered. "He's going to bite me."

Kyle snapped his finger once and pointed to the floor next to him. Herc immediately stopped barking and came to sit at his side. Kyle ran his fingers over Herc's coat. "What the hell is going on?"

Belinda stood by the door, staring at Herc. "Is he going to attack if I grab the knob?"

"In a heartbeat," Kyle said, though Herc would never hurt anyone. This was just a game they played. Kyle's whistle signaled they were going for a walk. Herc always waited barking at the door excitedly while Kyle grabbed the leash. Not that Belinda would know that. "You'll have to do exactly what I say."

She nodded, stepping away from the door. Kyle snapped his fingers twice, letting Herc know he could do as he pleased. The Doberman immediately walked over to Belinda and sniffed her hand, then nudged it, impatient for her to pet him.

After a while, she knelt down, putting herself at Herc's level. Kyle could see she was holding her breath, as if this were some sort of test of bravery on her part. The dog began licking her face.

Belinda wrapped her arms around the Doberman and started crying. "He's just a big baby." She was laughing and crying at the same time. "He's just a big baby."

Kyle knelt down beside her and Herc. "He won't hurt you," Kyle said. "Neither of us will."

Belinda dropped to the floor, crossing her legs, the tears filling her eyes to slide down her cheeks. As he often did, Herc lay his head on her lap, letting her pet him.

"Tell me what happened," he asked, surprised that he sounded almost pleading. He'd never asked anybody to confide in him. He let people make those decisions for themselves. But it was different with Belinda.

"Tonight, Roger asked me to meet him in his office inside the Level-2 lab. I found him there with some woman." She sniffed back her tears. "I don't give a shit. I mean, I guess it just sort of freaked me out. Seeing him like that with her. And then he started saying stuff. About me. That I wasn't enough woman for him." She looked up, her eyes still luminous with tears. "Or for anybody," she added softly.

Kyle didn't say anything, but silently he was calling Roger every name in the book. He pulled her to him, holding her. Herc just lay down beside them, letting out a soft sigh as he rested his head on his paws.

"Your dog's really great," she said, leaning her head against Kyle's chest, still combing her fingers through Herc's coat.

"He likes you," Kyle said. He pulled her face up to his. "You're not going to marry Roger."

She shook her head. "No. Never."

Kyle kissed her. For once, he just let himself feel . . . trying not to think of the consequences of what he was doing. She tasted so sweet. She gave so much with each touch of her hands and her lips, holding nothing back.

"I think I'm falling in love with you," she whispered.

"Yeah. Me, too."

Funny how he didn't mind saying it. How naturally it came. Just like the rest of it, picking her up and carrying her into his bedroom. He lay her in the middle of his bed, being very careful with her, thinking she was fragile and all his. He knelt over her and slipped his hand into the peekaboo laces, holding her breast, watching her face as the nipple puckered beneath his fingers.

"My dad cheated on my mother," she told him. "I was thinking I was just like her. A loser."

"I won't cheat on you."

"I've slept with a lot of guys," she said. "Even before Roger."

"Well, since it's time for true confessions. I haven't slept with any guys," he said, smiling as he shifted the wide lapels of her dress so that he could fit his mouth over her nipple, kissing her there.

She looked puzzled and then she grinned. "You made a joke."

"Not a very funny one, apparently," he said, kissing her mouth, opening the laces enough to slip her dress off her shoulders.

"No, it's not that. It's just that, you don't say very many jokes."

"But you do. Funny ones that make me laugh." He brushed the silky blond hair from her face. "And you know every single piece of music they play in the restaurant, who composed it and what year. I like that. I like that you cry sometimes when you tell me the story behind the music and what the musician is trying to say with each note. I like the way you move your hands when you talk, that you're incredibly graceful. That you don't mind that I'm not."

"You're going to make me cry again."

"And I like that you feel things so very deeply. You have an artist's spirit."

"Kyle." She closed her eyes. "Those guys. I did it because I knew that's what they wanted. I guess I needed them to like me." She looked at him. "But that's not why I'm here. Make love to me, Kyle."

He hadn't made love to many women in his life, but nothing they did felt awkward. With Belinda, it was like a dance, slow and smooth and reaching somewhere deep into his soul. With every touch, every kiss, she let him know how important he was to her. She was incredibly expressive with her body, turning him on in ways that got under his skin. Making him feel things he knew he would never forget. And he knew he did the same to her. He could see it in her expressive face, hear it in her sighs.

When they lay in the bed together, their arms and legs intertwined under the sheets, Belinda whispered in his ear, "I love you, Kyle. I'll never love any other man. Only you."

Those words echoed inside his head as she fell gently to sleep in his arms. *Only you.* They kept whispering softly to him as he crept out of bed and covered her with the comforter.

"Stay," he whispered to Herc when the Doberman lifted his head from the foot of the bed where he'd draped himself.

Only you. Only you. Only you.

The cadence of her words, their sweet seductive pull, stayed with him as he walked into the kitchen where he saw her purse on the floor near the door. He picked it up and put it on the kitchen table. Pulling up a chair, he sat down, staring at the brown leather bag.

Only you.

With a sigh, he opened the purse and searched through it. He pulled out her wallet and took out her security card, the one that would open the door to her father's lab, the Fragrance lab, where she worked as Donald Sayer's assistant. The one that would let him into Lab 20, the Biosafety Level-2 lab, if he could find the code.

He turned the card over and over in his hand, remembering the feel of her in his arms and the strength of the emotions he'd felt when she'd whispered her words of love.

"Yeah. Me too," he said.

He stood. He put the card in his own wallet and walked over to the bedroom door. She was sleeping soundly in the bed.

For once, he didn't feel the thrill of the chase, of bringing the bastards to justice. He only felt a deep longing not to carry this burden anymore. To live a normal life again. To lay back down on that bed next to Belinda and forget the opportunity she'd just handed to him.

But it was a luxury he didn't have.

He dressed quietly. He wrote her a note. *Forgot something at the office. Be right back.*

When he left, he left dreading what he would find. Knowing that if his suspicions were correct, he would have even more difficult choices to face come morning.

FILE NOT FOUND.

"Come on," McCall whispered staring at the computer screen. "I know you're in there somewhere."

She continued running the search program, this time typing in the French word for beauty, *belle,* hoping to find her needle in a haystack.

She'd given up hacking into the protected files in the early going. As far as she knew, there were only two ways to break into a file: look for a weakness in the operating system, which was beyond her capabilities, or guess the password, which might tip off the system administrator if she made too many unsuccessful attempts.

When she first arrived, she'd taken a stab at one of the file servers reserved for the Biosafety Level-2 lab group. It was a promising file that wouldn't allow her access as a guest user. She stopped after two attempts, believing another miss at the password would generate a message to the system administrator that someone was attempting unauthorized access.

FILE NOT FOUND, the computer screen flashed.

"Brother." She stretched her neck and looked at the clock. It was a little past ten. She was incredibly tired. And her concentration was off. She would read through a file and her mind would wander . . . she would start thinking about Jake.

She pictured his face when she'd told him she'd give away his cover. She'd hurt him, making him think she would betray him to Roger. But she needed Jake to back off. McCall wasn't a damsel in distress. Nothing so simple. The things she feared were much too dark, a nightmare Jake couldn't twist into a fairy tale, giving them a happy ending. It was something Jake didn't understand, coming here, involving himself. She couldn't allow him to get hurt because of her.

McCall pushed her bangs from her face and focused once more on the computer screen. She was tired, yes. But she was also determined. Tonight, she would stay here until she found something—anything—that could at least put her on the right track.

The search program she was using scanned the entire computer system. She'd been using key words to look for possible clues into new product research. Eventually, she'd chosen "beauty" for her search, a word that Alicia had written over and over in her lab book.

But beauty wasn't exactly a rare commodity in a cosmetics company's computer files. It had taken her over an hour just to weed through the files of familiar product ads, clinical data, and benign project development.

That's when she'd gotten the idea to try foreign words. She remembered how she'd come up with the name for the Omega Principle, choosing Greek to give the product a certain cache. She was familiar with the names of most of Clarke's products and avoided those. She'd started with Greek and Latin, then moved on to French. But so far, each had received the same response. FILE NOT FOUND.

"Let's try another stab at the romance languages," she said, typing the Spanish word for beauty into the search program. She knew that, no matter how careful Curtis might be about covering his tracks, even the most secretive research would leave some trace in the computer's files.

She pushed ENTER and waited as the search program scanned the files for the key word *hermosa*. She picked up her cup of coffee, taking a sip.

APP.DOC

McCall almost choked on the coffee, staring at the computer screen. She blinked, putting the coffee cup down as she leaned forward, completely taken by surprise that the search program had found something after so many hours of coming up empty-handed. Fingers trembling, she clicked into the file. It appeared to be a word-processing file, generated by a secretary, containing what looked like an admission form or application for some sort of spa. The file had come up because "Isla Hermosa" was the name of the island where the Clarke Spa and Clinic was located.

A spa? McCall drew closer to the screen, skimming. She'd been working over a week at Clarke Labs and she hadn't heard any mention of a spa.

The form explained a little about the luxuries and amenities a client could expect to find at the Clarke Spa and Clinic. The pages that followed asked the usual questions about sex, age, and marital status. It included a medical questionnaire, the kind of History and Physical that any weight loss clinic might request.

Only later, the questions changed focus. There was page

after page attached to the document . . . all asking detailed medical questions that had little to do with the applicant's general health.

"Oh, my God," she whispered, reading on. *Have you ever undergone general anesthesia . . . Has any one in your family suffered a stroke . . . Is there a family history of disease of the brain . . . have you ever had a seizure?*

McCall sat up in the chair, incredibly uneasy. Mixed in with mundane inquires about skin allergies and special dietary needs were requests for information dealing with the human nervous system.

It didn't make sense. Not for a beauty clinic. No way.

She sat back, frowning, thinking about the clinic's location, a remote island somewhere in the Tropics. The thought came unbidden, how a company might avoid stringent regulations at home by setting up a lab overseas. She knew that, since the dismantling of the Soviet system, some European firms had done something similar in Eastern Europe.

Teasing wisps of memories slipped through her head, allusions in Alicia's lab book. Alicia's greatest frustration had been the quest for the perfect experimental model, an animal that would accurately reflect the effects of their testing on a human being.

McCall jumped to her feet, her chair falling backward to the floor. She stared at the questionnaire. A laboratory overseas, disguised as a beauty spa.

It would be simple, really. Clarke was a legitimate name in cosmetics. And women would be desperate for any of the "youth and cosmetic" secrets mentioned in the form.

Plastic surgery, silicone breast implants, liposuction . . . they could make it sound so easy, so safe. *Just a little cosmetic surgery* . . . How many women could they talk into participating in human trials with such assurances?

Be beautiful and be sad. The quote from Baudelaire echoed eerily inside her head.

She could feel herself shaking. Incredibly, her first thought was to call Jake. But what she was thinking was too far-fetched. Instead, she punched the keys to print the document, then grabbed her jacket and bag. A beauty clinic established to cover up experiments on humans? It sounded like a plot straight out of a science fiction novel. Hardly something she could run with to Jake or the authorities.

But she couldn't get the possibility out of her head. She needed to find out more about the clinic. She knew it was too late to show up on her father's doorstep. But tomorrow—tomorrow she would take him Alicia's lab book and the form she'd printed out. Surely, he would know something about the clinic. And even if he didn't believe it was a cover for illegal human experiments, the questionnaire was suspicious, possibly enough to put him on his guard. He might believe her enough to help.

Buzzing out of the lab, McCall hurried down the empty corridor. She'd stuffed the questionnaire into her purse, a tote bag. When she got home, she'd read it over more carefully. What she needed now was sleep . . . and a clear head. She knew she would have to keep sharp if she was going to argue with her father about Curtis.

A flash of light caught her attention. Aware of the video cameras monitoring the corridor, McCall slowed her pace only marginally. The light flashed again, almost invisible against the white walls of the hall.

She stopped, digging through her enormous purse as if searching for her keys. The pretext was for the benefit of the security cameras should anyone be watching. But she kept her head up enough to scan the labs down the hall.

It was gone in an instant. But she'd seen it, a tiny flash of light slicing through the darkness, the kind that might come from a narrow-beamed flashlight.

Someone was inside her father's lab, taking a look around.

McCall walked slowly, still foraging through her bag. "Where are those keys?" she said, more for her benefit. There was no audio on the surveillance equipment. She dropped

down to the floor, now digging in earnest through the big tote
bag. Not until she heard the lab door buzz open did she fish
out the set of keys. She stood, facing her father's lab, watching
as Kyle Woods stepped into the hall.

"Kyle?" She called out his name as if she'd just seen him.
She smiled walking toward him. She was dead certain Kyle
Woods didn't have clearance high enough to get inside her
father's lab. She knew she didn't.

"Hello, McCall," he said, waiting for her to catch up.

She glanced at her father's lab. All the lab windows began
at waist level and the lights in the corridor were dimmed at
night. It made it almost impossible to see anything if the lights
were off inside the lab. "Did you find anything interesting?"

"I forgot a file earlier." He held up a folder. "A colleague
was kind enough to lend me their badge so I could get it."

"Really? Who?"

He grinned. "I don't want to get anyone in trouble."

She remembered what Jake had told her about the neurological responses when someone lied. "And it couldn't wait
till morning?" she asked, pushing it.

He shrugged. "Sometimes I have trouble sleeping. I thought
I'd get some work done, but I needed my file."

She nodded, as if she believed him. "So, what is it?" she
asked, reaching for the folder. "I'm having a little trouble
sleeping as well. Maybe I can help?"

He pulled the file out of her reach, his eyes meeting hers.
She saw he wasn't wearing his glasses and his wolf's eyes
looked more yellow than brown without them. She noticed
the other differences, then. How he was wearing his hair loose
so that it just brushed his shoulders. And his clothes. A decent-looking shirt and jacket. He didn't appear anything like
the nerd who haunted the halls during the day, trying to in-
gratiate himself to everyone.

She thought about her own attempts to disguise herself over
the years at the blackjack tables.

"Maybe we should go inside your lab to discuss this?" he asked.

He meant because of the security cameras. The cameras were at an angle high above them, focused specifically on the corridor. They couldn't record anything beyond a few feet inside the actual labs. She nodded and they walked back to Lab 19. She swiped her badge through the lock and stepped inside, Kyle walking closely behind her.

Once the door closed, he grabbed her. McCall dropped her purse, her heart slamming up into her throat as he pushed her up against one of the walls, pinning her there by her shoulders. She'd left the lights off and they'd traveled far enough inside that only the amber glow of a nearby computer lit his features. For the first time ever, Kyle Woods looked menacing.

"What are you doing?" she asked, wondering if she hadn't found Alicia's Dr. Frankenstein after all.

"Tomorrow, I'm set to meet with Curtis," he said in a low voice. "I know you sabotaged those cultures. I did my own transformations and I have twelve transformants with the gene for the Omega Principle peptide. I can show those to Roger. I can tell him my suspicions that you sabotaged your own work to slow our progress. When we test the peptide, it isn't going to work, is it?"

There was something in the way he spoke, letting her know that they were negotiating. "What do you want?"

"I'm going to take a chance here. Because I am so fucking tired of this place and what it's turning me into. Maybe we can help each other," he said. "I know you have a little history with the Clarkes. How about it, McCall? Are you and your fake love potion on the same wavelength I am? Do you want to see the Clarkes shut down as badly as I do? Because I think I may be able to do just that. And I could use some help."

She didn't know if she could trust him. But if he told Curtis his suspicions, her very life could be in jeopardy.

"Maybe we can help each other," she said, still hesitating.

He leaned forward, smiling. She saw him suddenly as truly handsome, marveling at how he could change his appearance with just a hair style and glasses. "I think Clarke Cosmetics is full of shit with their HUMANITY FIRST—NO ANIMAL TEST-ING. I think there are ongoing experiments using dogs in the Biosafety Level-2 lab," he told her.

She shook her head. "That would be commercial suicide. Why take such a risk . . ." But the denial trailed off into silence. She was thinking about Alicia's lab book. Of course, there would be animal experiments.

"That's right," Kyle said, seeing that she was considering the possibility. "And now I have a way inside."

He held up a badge, the one he'd used to open the door to her father's lab. McCall recognized her sister's photograph smiling from the plastic card.

In his other hand, he produced a slip of paper. "They change the code every month. I searched Belinda's desk, thinking she might write it down."

"How did you get her badge?"

"I stole it from her purse. She doesn't know it's missing."

McCall looked at the slip of paper and the code.

"How about it, McCall?" His eyes flashed with a sudden excitement. "Do you want to have a look around?"

Fifteen minutes later, McCall and Kyle had dressed in scrubs. They'd found everything they needed inside McCall's lab, where working with radioactivity and dangerous compounds required the occasional use of protective clothing. They had covered their hair with bulky hair nets, using two each to cover up any hair color that might show through. Because of the nature of the work done at the labs, many experiments required supervision at odd hours. A couple of techs arriving in the middle of the night would be a common occurrence; it shouldn't trigger the notice of whoever manned the security cameras.

Kyle entered the code and the door opened with a soft *whoosh*. Inside, there was an antechamber with lockers and bins. They each grabbed a fresh lab coat.

"Ready?" Kyle asked.

McCall nodded.

They opened the next door and stepped through the antechamber into the corridor beyond. Never so much as looking at the guard sitting at his desk, they took the clipboard and signed in, McCall using her sister's name and Kyle her father's, as they'd agreed beforehand. McCall was wearing her sister's security badge; Kyle had his carefully turned at an angle.

McCall's heart lodged in her throat as she followed Kyle down the corridor. The Biosafety Level-2 lab turned out to be a warren den of smaller laboratories. Most appeared empty at this hour, though she could see a man and a woman up ahead, speaking in hushed tones outside one of the doors. She didn't recognize either one; they wore the same camouflaging clothing as she and Kyle. Still, she was fairly certain these two didn't work outside this facility.

A independent staff, she thought. One established to work only in the Level-2 facility. McCall glanced at the glass-enclosed labs, a few with the lights still on. Her gaze followed the scaffolding of black shelves to the artery work of exposed pipes built into the ceilings. The equipment on the counters made it clear these were molecular biology labs, outfitted with the sophisticated machinery used for analyzing genetic material.

Kyle grabbed her hand, squeezing it through the latex gloves. The man up ahead had started walking toward an elevator at the hall's end; the woman stepped back inside the lab behind her. McCall saw the man take out a card key and swipe it through a security lock attached to the elevator.

None of the labs here had swipe locks. But the elevator did.

Without exchanging a word, McCall stepped ahead, walking

directly toward the elevator. She and Kyle stopped behind the tech, waiting as the elevator door opened. She noted a second door on the opposite side of the elevator, which meant you could enter or exit the elevator from either side. *There's another hall behind this one,* she thought. All three stepped inside, their paper booties making soft scuffing sounds against the floor.

Immediately, McCall smelled it. The sharp musk odor of animals. The intensity of it startled her. It had been a long time since she'd been in these types of facilities. She didn't remember the smell being so strong that it could permeate an elevator moving between floors.

The tech pushed a button. The door began to slide closed. "Hold the door, Dr. Sayer!"

The voice was coming from down the hall. McCall and Kyle exchanged glances. The only person who knew they had signed in as Belinda and Donald Sayer would be the security guard. He would have checked the clipboard.

The tech in front of them reached out and braced his hand against the closing door. Her heart slamming against the wall of her chest, McCall watched the door slowly open. In seconds, the security guard would step inside, expecting to see her father and sister.

She searched the elevator panel, spotted the separate buttons for the front and back doors. She punched the button to open the door behind them.

Mumbling that she'd forgotten something as the door slid open, she and Kyle backed out of the elevator.

Kyle grabbed her hand and pulled her into the nearest lab. They ducked down, scrambling below the bench-top tables and cabinetry. McCall pointed to a door that looked like the entrance to an enormous freezer. A cold room.

She opened the door and they eased inside. The miniature lab was designed for experiments that required temperature control. This was a zero-degree room, kept at freezing. With the door closed, it would be colder than a meat locker.

It didn't take long before they heard it, the guard's voice calling out, first faintly, and then stronger as he approached. "Dr. Sayer? Miss Sayer?"

Cold. So cold. And completely dark. She clenched her teeth to keep them from chattering, the cold and her nerves making her shaky. She was leaning against one of the counters, the corner biting into her side. She held her arms around her waist, willing the guard to leave, not to look inside the cold room.

It seemed an eternity before Kyle opened the door, looking through the crack into the darkened lab beyond. He held his finger to his lips and pointed to the floor. McCall nodded and followed his example, dropping down to her hands and knees.

Crawling on all fours, they made their way through the lab. Her breath coming in short, shallow breaths, McCall crept forward, following Kyle as her eyes adjusted to the low light. Like the elevator, the labs on this side accessed either hall. She could guess what Kyle planned. Double back and try to beat the security guard to the only exit.

They stepped into the empty hall. She could hear the blood rushing through her ears, pumping with the force of a jackhammer in her chest. They managed to log out and step into the antechamber without incident, but she kept expecting to hear that guard's voice calling her sister's or father's name. Quickly, they discarded their lab coats, keeping the rest of the protective clothing, the masks and hair nets that would disguise their identity.

Once in the hall, they carefully returned to McCall's lab where they ditched the doctor greens they'd worn over their clothes, dumping them into a bin set for that purpose. There were no security cameras inside the labs themselves, making it safe for the moment as long as they stayed away from the windows. Together, they sat in their street clothes facing each other in a far corner, their backs to the door, taking a minute to catch their breath. After a while, McCall leaned forward, burying her face in her hands.

"You smelled it," Kyle said, the excitement clear in his voice. "That elevator must go down to an animal room of some sort." He took Belinda's badge from the bench-top where McCall had set it down. "Did you see that card the guy used, the one that operates the elevator?"

She nodded. The elevator wasn't activated by ID badges; it was part of a separate security system that required separate card keys. Kyle looked triumphant, waiting for her response. But McCall felt only drained by their close call.

"He's doing it," he said. "Experimenting on animals while advertising products tested only on human volunteers."

"Do you work for a competitor?" she asked, because he sounded so victorious. She'd been right all along—Kyle was a spy, only he wasn't Curtis Clarke's man. If any information leaked about animal experiments, the publicity alone would kill Clarke Cosmetics.

"You might say so," he answered. "Jesus, between the money they've invested in marketing the Omega Principle and the bad publicity from the animal testing, Clarke will be wiped out." He shook his head, watching her curiously. "I'm right, aren't I? The peptide is no good."

She nodded. "I tried for years, but I couldn't synthesize anything that acted like a pheromone, much less intensified its effects."

"How did you get those PET scan results?"

"I paid twenty-five men a hundred dollars a week to watch pornographic videos while smelling vanilla. It was in the test sample along with the peptide when you ran the PET scans."

"Conditioned reflex. Pavlov's dogs."

"Exactly. At the end of the year, I picked the ten that showed the strongest response to the smell of vanilla. I entered their names on the volunteer roster in the computer system. I made certain when the time came, their names would be first up."

"Impressive."

"But you were still suspicious. You ran your own transformations."

He smiled. "I'm always suspicious."

"You really do want to destroy Clarke?" She wanted to believe the passion she heard in his voice when he mentioned Clarke's downfall.

"Maybe as much as you do."

She doubted that, but she held a healthy amount of respect for Kyle Woods. She wanted them to be on the same side. "What do you know about the Clarke Spa and Clinic?"

He shook his head, looking puzzled that she would ask. "Very little. It's Roger's baby—they're doing a trial run to see if they can make it profitable. But it's purely a commercial concern. A service. It's not connected to anything we do in R and D. Why?"

"I'm not sure. I came across an application for the clinic. It seemed . . . curious," she said, not ready to show all her cards just yet. "Now what?"

He grinned, a smile charged with electric energy. "Now we think about how we get into that animal room. With a camera. And we have to do it soon, before they realize anyone is on to what they're doing—"

The lights switched off, throwing them into near darkness. She heard it then, a soft *snap-click*.

She felt Kyle's hand on her shoulder, then groping for her hand as their eyes adjusted to the loss of light. A bottle crashed to the floor not far from where they were sitting. A sharp, choking odor filled the air.

Acid.

Kyle grabbed McCall's collar and lifted it up over her mouth. Getting the idea, she held it there, using the jersey material like a mask. "Can anyone get inside the lab without sounding the buzzer?" she asked, coughing now, the burning sensation closing off her throat, making it difficult to breathe.

"Shit," Kyle said. "Some sort of acid. We have to get out of here."

They had both worked around enough corrosive substances to know that, depending on what had been spilled, they could lose consciousness or even die from exposure to the fumes. McCall felt her way around the bench-tops, trying to avoid the spot where she'd heard the bottle crash. If it was acid, even a simple touch could burn through the soles of her shoes to her skin.

Finding the light switch, she clawed at the lights, flipping the switch. Nothing. She was coughing for each breath now, her eyes watering from the fumes. *Impossible to see.*

Suddenly, the lights flickered on. She turned around. An enormous bottle lay shattered in pieces on the lab floor. The label read SULFURIC ACID.

Both she and Kyle stumbled to the lab door. McCall grabbed the handle and turned. Locked!

She pounded on the window as Kyle kicked at the door then used a heavy water bath to hit the handle, trying to break it off. She could feel herself getting weaker from lack of air, but if she took a breath, the fumes would damage her lungs.

She grabbed Kyle's hand. "The hood."

The hood was the lab's ventilation system, a compartment built into the cabinetry. It resembled one of those refrigeration units that kept soft drinks cold in a convenience store, only smaller. The mechanism functioned like a hood above an oven, sucking up the fumes from experiments placed inside. Following her lead, Kyle crawled up inside the hood with McCall. The space was just big enough for the two of them to step inside and lower the glass door, blocking out most of the fumes. But not for long.

"Stay here," Kyle said after catching his breath. Filling his lungs with air, he opened the hood's door. McCall pulled the door back in place and watched through the glass as he picked up a stool and banged it against the lab windows. On the third try, the glass shattered.

They both crawled out through the broken glass and ran for the safety showers. Huddled under the wide shower head, they pulled the cord that sent down a torrent of water. They stripped off their clothes, leaving only their underwear. A siren wailed overhead, red lights flashing. In seconds, security guards surrounded them.

"Block off the area," McCall shouted. "There's been an acid spill!"

As the hall ignited into chaos, McCall and Kyle remained huddled together under the shower, letting the water strip them of the dangers of the acid.

"My God," she said, one hand braced against the wall to keep from falling. "Someone just tried to kill us."

Eighteen

We can't seem to repeat our results. Thus far, every alteration we've made only increases the toxicity level. We have to do better.
        —Excerpt from Dr. Alicia Goodman's lab book

It was near midnight when Kyle drove up to the house on Governor Nicholls Street. After they had filled out the incident report with security, Kyle had insisted that he drive McCall home. She'd been too shaken up to argue with him.

Kyle turned off the motor, making it clear he intended to walk her to the door. She was about to protest when he turned and asked, "How deep do you think your sister's involved in this thing?"

"Belinda?" Instantly, McCall's guard came up. "My sister has nothing to do with what happened tonight."

He was silent for a moment, staring ahead. And then he sighed, getting out of the car.

They walked up the brick path to the door, the moonlight flickering off the jungle growth of ferns and crepe myrtle. McCall caught sight of the curtains to the parlor shifting, as if someone had just peeked outside. Probably Barb, worried about her and waiting up.

As she searched her purse for her keys, McCall noticed her hands were still shaking. She thought of Alicia, wondering if this is how she'd felt when she'd written those frantic last entries in the lab book. It almost seemed odd, even possibly hysterical, to believe someone had tried to kill her tonight.

Security had looked into it. Apparently, there had been an electrical short in the system, causing a temporary loss of power. That's why the lights had gone out. According to security, a short could have easily screwed up the locking mechanism, jamming it. It had happened before.

The whole thing had been chalked up to a "freak accident." And it did seem possible. When the lights went out, she might have hit something from the shock of sudden darkness. It was the explanation Kyle had given—primarily because he didn't want a lot of questions asked. He'd told the head of security he'd noticed the bottle's precarious position earlier, but had forgotten to put it away. Later, he explained to McCall why he hadn't wanted anyone too curious. Close scrutiny of the security video wouldn't be good; not when their own activity in that corridor could be a little noteworthy.

Reaching the top step, Kyle turned to wait for her. "Look. About your sister. I care what happens to her. Do you understand?"

McCall folded her arms protectively around her waist. "No, Kyle. I'm not sure I do understand. Why don't you spell it out for me?" She wasn't going to be tricked into hurting her family.

Under the glow of the porch light, his eyes appeared a translucent gold. "Right now, your sister is asleep in my bed, waiting for me to come back."

The shock of the news slammed through her. She remembered how at the lab he would glance at his watch anxiously, waiting to meet someone for dinner. Belinda. "My God. The badge," she said, realizing what he'd done. "You seduced my sister for that badge?"

She shook her head, disbelieving that he could be so cruel. But she saw the truth in his face. She remembered how he'd been before the acid spill. So triumphant.

Instantly, all the passion and excitement she'd heard in his voice gained a personal edge. This was more than corporate espionage. "Who the hell are you, Kyle Woods?"

He watched her as if he was considering what he should say very carefully. And then he told her, "We call ourselves Scientists Defending Animals. We were once research scientists, like yourself. Only, we couldn't stomach the things we saw . . . and did. I started the organization six years ago. This isn't the first lab I've targeted."

McCall took a step back, the pieces falling neatly into place. The leader of some radical animal rights organization, someone devious and methodical enough to infiltrate Clarke Labs. Someone willing to seduce her sister for her security badge.

"I know about groups like yours," she said. "I've read the letters sent to colleagues. 'If you and your associates do not desist your research effort and release the animals under your abuse, we will respond with acts of physical violence,' " she said, remembering the tone of those letters. " 'We will harm, even kill, you and members of your family.' "

"You know what goes on in those research labs. I don't have to spell it out to you."

She shook her head. "Biologists don't set out to hurt . . . that's not why we go into research. We want to save lives. To help through greater knowledge and understanding."

"By sacrificing those who can't defend themselves?"

"Groups like yours focus on a few extreme cases. Most lab animals are well treated."

"How about you, McCall? When you operated on those rats, how did you convince yourself they didn't feel every cut, every slice of the knife?"

"I only did dissections," she said automatically. "Not vivisection."

"Ah," he said, nodding. "Well, then. You don't know, do you?"

She could see the passion in his face. He was one of them, those activists who lived by one creed: The end justifies the means. "And what about Belinda? Road kill on the path to achieving your goals?" she said, stricken that Belinda had fallen victim to yet another man.

"She doesn't know I took the card; she doesn't know a damn thing about me. She thinks I'm just what I appear to be at Clarke Labs, and that's the way it should stay for now. Before you jump to any conclusions, I think I'm falling in love with her—and I'm not sure what I'm going to do about any of this."

She felt her mind overloading with the information. The parts didn't fit in any neat pattern by which to gauge her reaction. He sounded so sincere, as if he might indeed care for her sister.

"If you have any decency at all," she told him, "you'll leave Belinda out of this. Think, Kyle. Someone tried to kill us tonight. I don't believe that garbage about electrical shorts and neither do you. We weren't alone in that room. I heard someone. Do you want her to be the next target?"

"And if she's already involved? Look, it's not going to help Belinda to ignore the obvious. I have certain obligations, McCall. People who are counting on me."

"You don't know my sister if you think she's part of some secret experiments on animals," she argued. "She's not even a biologist—"

"She's your father's assistant. If there is something going on, we both know that your father would be in on it."

This was exactly what McCall had wanted to avoid. She didn't want Curtis Clarke's poison to rub off on her family. "For God's sake, Kyle. My father disowned me—his own daughter—because he believed I falsified data. His reputation is everything to him. He wouldn't be involved in anything like this."

"My information is pretty solid," Kyle said. "I think he might be."

"Your information?" she asked, challenging him. She knew

how these things slipped out. "A disgruntled employee looking for trouble?"

"They make the best whistle-blowers. After what we saw
tonight, you can't deny something is going on. I just need to
know how much to protect Belinda."

McCall shook her head, adamant in her beliefs. "She and
my father have access to the Level-2 lab, but I've never seen
either of them with that card key for the elevator. There's no
evidence they're involved. My family isn't a part of this."

"Are you sure that's not blind faith speaking?"

She thought about it for an instant, allowing the possibility
to take shape in her head. But the thought was too painful,
too complicated. She turned away and fit the key to the lock.
"Believe what you want."

But Kyle held her back, pulling her close to him to whisper,
"Don't shut me out because you're afraid I'll hurt your family.
We can help each other."

She felt paralyzed with indecision, and very much afraid.
Blind faith or not, what if her father was somehow involved?
Curtis Clarke could be very persuasive. And manipulative.

"You said you were meeting with Clarke tomorrow," she
said. "Are you going to turn me in? Hand me up to him like
some sacrificial lamb?"

She didn't know what she wanted from Kyle, to show how
ruthless he could be—or how honest.

He looked away, focusing out toward the street. McCall
could hear music coming faintly from Bourbon Street and the
rumble of delivery trucks scrambling down the arteries of narrow streets.

"I considered it," he said. "I thought it could help me gain
his trust and get me inside the Level-2 lab. But I want you
to know this: After tonight, I would never have done it, and
not because you can blackmail me into silence. I'm not here
to get anybody killed."

After a while, McCall said, "If you have a decent bone in
your body, you won't hurt Belinda by making her part of this.

You've already put her at risk. Roger isn't going to take your relationship lightly."

"I'll take care of Belinda. And forget Roger. He already had his petty revenge. I won't let him hurt her again."

She met his eyes in the near dark. He was a man of great intensity. *Maybe, just maybe* . . .

With a sigh, she twisted the key into the lock. "I pray to God you can." She turned the knob, having said her peace. "We'll talk more about this tomorrow. For now, I need to think some of this through."

McCall stepped inside the foyer and leaned back against the door. There had been a fire in Kyle's eyes, letting her know he was a fanatic when it came to those animals. Scientists Defending Animals—he was a man dedicated to achieving his own ends. He had incredible talent and credentials, years of schooling . . . all of which he'd given up to pursue a different purpose. And yet, that same passion had been in his voice when he'd spoken about her sister.

"Dear Lord, what do I do?"

She dropped her purse, folding her arms around herself, trembling inside. She was wearing scrubs and her throat still felt raw from inhaling the acid fumes, reminding her how deadly the game had become. She could still hear that soft *snap-click*. Someone had been inside that room with them when the acid spilled.

"McCall?" Barb walked in from the parlor, parting the beaded curtain that separated the room from the foyer. She was still dressed in a colorful caftan that somehow suited her maternal figure. She wore her braid to one side, emphasizing an earthy quality that McCall had come to associate with her. She remembered Jake's name for her, Guru Barb, thinking that indeed it seemed to fit.

"What's wrong? What happened to your clothes?" Barb asked, giving McCall a critical once-over.

"I changed at work. I was running some gels and ruined my clothes." She wanted to confide in her friend, to let Barb fold her into her arms the way she'd done the night McCall had arrived practically naked from her fight with Jake. But she didn't dare. The danger had to be hers alone.

"I'm sorry I've been getting home so late. Barb, it's time I get my own place—and I don't want to hear what the stars say," she told her, thinking she would just go to bed and wrap herself up in Jake's blanket as she'd done the previous night. Tomorrow, she would move to a hotel. She didn't think it was safe for Barb and the kids if she stayed here anymore, not after what happened at the lab.

Barb touched her shoulder. McCall turned back to face her.

"Now what?" she asked, seeing from Barb's expression that something was wrong.

"He's waiting for you in the parlor. He's been here for a while."

McCall knew immediately who "he" was. There was only one "he" in her life.

"Jake? At this hour?" It was almost midnight.

She turned to face the parlor, the mixed-up emotions of the evening channeling into a different direction. Anger. Anticipation. Desire. "What on earth does he think he's doing here?" she asked, focusing on the anger.

"He was standing outside waiting. I saw him and told him to come inside." Barb hooked her arm through McCall's when she tried to walk past her. "He said he was worried. You stormed out of his place. He wanted to make sure you were all right."

"Don't you go siding with him," McCall said, hearing that tone in her friend's voice. She needed Barb to be in her camp alone. "You know nothing about Jake." And McCall hadn't told her, thinking to keep those details to herself until she could sort through her own complicated emotions. "Did he mention that he's been snooping around behind my back? That he has an FBI file on me. He was a prosecutor, Barb. He's not here for my health."

"No," Barb said, perfectly calm. "I believe he's here because he is in love with you."

"Stop right there. I know what you're thinking. This isn't the time for all that."

Barb gave McCall one of her I-can-see-deep-into-your-psyche looks. "Sometimes, we don't get to pick the time. Just so you know. I did a star chart on the two of you while he was waiting. It's dynamite."

"I'll bet," McCall said, committing to nothing, thinking that dynamite pretty well covered her situation right now.

"You're going to have to see this one through," Barb said cryptically. "There's no running away this time."

McCall met her friend's dark brown eyes. She saw there all the love and loyalty that anyone could ever expect. And something more. A sort of anticipation, as if Barb were the mother bird about to see her baby chick take flight.

"I'll handle it," she told Barb.

Barbara Rojas smiled, making her plain face light up with a beauty that could have launched a thousand ships. "Of course you will." And then she turned and walked up the stairs. "I won't expect you back until morning," she said.

"Funny," McCall said to herself, parting the curtains to step inside the parlor. "I wasn't going anywhere."

The instant she saw him, she knew the confrontation ahead wouldn't be easy. Jake stood near the fireplace, his arms crossed over his chest, his bomber jacket folded over one of Barb's antique chairs. But despite the languid pose, there was something too tense about him; the lines of his face were set, hiding something.

"So, who's the guy?" he asked.

"The guy?" she asked, actually confused.

He pushed off from the mantel, walking toward her. "The one who was entertaining you on the front step for the last twenty minutes?"

She was still wondering what he was talking about when it came to her—Kyle. He was talking about Kyle Woods. "Oh, this is great . . . this is just great," she said, throwing her hands up in the air, then crossing them tightly over her chest. "You're jealous? What do you think I was doing?"

Jake walked slowly toward her, circling her, coming up behind her to whisper, "Did you kiss him? Standing there under the moonlight like a pair of teenagers?" He stepped even closer, his lips almost brushing her ear. "Was it nice?"

She turned, raising her chin as if daring him to think the worst. "Oh, yes. After a night of incredible, wild sex, we couldn't get enough, so we started necking on the front porch. What did you expect? Did you think this was exclusive?"

"Let's see. You left my house"—he glanced at his watch—"let's call it . . . a little over five hours ago? Maybe you could have stayed exclusive for that long?"

She shook her head, giving him a look of utter disgust. "I don't believe this. Do you really think I was kissing some other man out there?"

His expression didn't change, but she could tell he was starting to calm down, understanding just how ridiculous his accusations sounded. And still, he asked, "Just tell me what the guy means to you."

She slammed her palms up into his chest. "You big idiot! You were supposed to leave me alone. I threatened you! Don't you have the sense to hate me for it!"

He grabbed her up, pinning her against him. "Hate you? No. But let's just say I was really pissed."

His eyes were so dark, it was impossible to make out the pupils. He held her hands trapped against his chest, so she couldn't move.

She shook her head, refusing to go where he wanted to lead them. "How long have you been here making a nuisance of yourself?"

He still held her, making it impossible to move. "I checked the house for your car every hour since you left my hotel suite. Luckily, the casino's docked. But around ten, I got antsy. Guru Barb must have checked her stars and figured something was up. She saw me hanging around and asked me in. By the way, she said you exaggerated my big muscles." He grinned. "But that you were right. I do have nice eyes."

She felt herself blush, remembering exactly what she had told Barb. "You are such an ass."

"Did you really think I would let you threaten me, then disappear?" he asked, his voice dropping low. "You tell me you're in deep shit and then you want me to get lost?"

"Jake," she said, so tired she could weep. "This isn't helping anything. I think you should leave."

His expression changed, becoming unreadable. The prosecutor calculating his next move. And then he smiled. "You're right. It's definitely time for an exit."

He grabbed her hand and reached for his jacket. He dragged her past the beaded curtains, heading for the door.

"What are you doing?" she asked, grabbing her purse off the floor.

"I'm taking you home where we can finish this."

"I am not going to make love to you."

"Liar."

Incredibly, she realized he was right. No matter how strong she wanted to be, she felt utterly weak. The acid spill, the clinic application, the things Kyle had told her—the drama of the night had drained her. And Jake was the one person she trusted right now. It was too tempting to lean on his strength. To follow him, knowing how badly she wanted to be in that big iron bed, with Jake holding her, keeping the nightmares from getting too close.

Letting him pull her down the walk, she told herself little lies—*I won't let them hurt him; I can keep him safe*. She didn't protest as he hauled her past the gate. She realized that, try as she might—despite her best intentions—she just couldn't be rational when it came to Jake Donovan. She needed to be with him right now.

He stopped in front of a candy red Lamborghini. "Get in," he said, opening the door.

She stared as the door floated upward, a little shocked by the expensive sports car. "What happened to your Jeep? This isn't your car."

"It is tonight," he said, urging her in. McCall sat on the butter soft leather seat, too confused to argue.

"So what's with the outfit?" he asked, looking down at the doctor greens as he eased behind the steering wheel.

"I was working on something in the lab and ruined my clothes," she said, giving him the same excuse she'd told Barb.

He turned on the ignition, glancing down at her. He grinned. "Kinda sexy."

She frowned, looking down at the oversized clothes. "What?"

"Makes me think of playing doctor." He pulled the V-neck collar forward to peek down the top. "And the view's not bad."

She slapped his hand away. "Who does this car belong to?"

"Dickey Harper," he said, putting the car into gear. "After you left Saturday, I had a little surprise visit from Hope." He peeled into the empty street and turned at the corner. "I'm dead asleep, and I hear her use her key to let herself in. Next thing I know, Michael's throwing a body blow my way, using the bed as a trampoline."

She realized the implication immediately. She could have been in that bed when his four-year-old arrived, unannounced. "You told me he was going to be out of town for the week," she said, making the connection of Michael's surprise appearance at the hotel with his baby-sitter. "What happened?" And then she frowned, realizing that Hope would always have this hold on him, dropping into his life, using keys without knocking. Taking his son away or dropping him off at her convenience.

"What did she need this time?" she asked, unable to keep the resentment from her voice.

"Jealous? Don't be. Both Hope and Dickey are off to Texas. A private adoption. Michael is staying with me until they get back with the baby." He flashed a smile, both dimples armed and dangerous. "Hope insisted we have a set of keys made for each other. For Michael's sake. You know, unless one of us has to cover for the other. Lucky for me, I know where Dickey keeps the keys to the Lamborghini."

"You're borrowing his car? Without asking?"

His grinned. "Oh, yes."

"Won't he mind?"

"You bet your ass he'll mind." He downshifted, slowing the car. She caught him watching something in the rearview mirror. For a while, he was silent, glancing back every so often at the mirror as he wound his way through the French Quarter.

He made a quick turn, the wheels actually screeching. He looked back into the rearview mirror and frowned. "Do you know if someone's been following you?"

"Me?" She forced herself not to turn around. Instead, she peered into the mirror, as Jake had done. There was a gray Honda Accord a hundred feet back.

The car was more visible now that the streets were empty. The sight of it nudged at a memory. "Yes." She felt the prickling of fear again, the sensation of danger. "For over a week now. But I could never be certain; I thought maybe I was imagining it." She thought about tonight, the acid spill. The locked door.

"That car was at your house," Jake said. "They pulled out just after we did. I've been making a few turns, to see what they'll do. Whoever is driving; they're following us, all right. And they're not even bothering to hide it very well."

"It's probably your ex-wife," she said a bit hysterically, disbelieving of everything that had happened the last few hours. "The first one. Susan. The private investigator."

Jake had this strange look. He peered into the rearview mirror again. He cursed under his breath.

McCall turned around in her seat. It *was* a woman driving

the Honda. She stared back at Jake, seeing the truth on his face.

"It is your wife! Why is your wife following me?"

"My ex-wife," Jake corrected. "She's my ex-wife. Hold on."

Jake stepped on it, turning on the next street to head up-river. The car fish-tailed as he straightened it. He glanced at the mirror, seeing she was keeping up. He turned onto the next boulevard and passed the lights of the Hilton and then the River Palace Hotel. He made a left on Julia, knowing the street would be empty at this hour.

As soon as he saw the Honda, he made his move. He turned the wheel in a sudden 360-degree turn. The street was wide enough that he was able to clear the Honda, getting around it so that it was now trapped in the dead end.

"Stay right here," he said.

But Mac wasn't a woman to take instructions easily. She grabbed his wrist. "Jake, what is going on?" she asked.

"That's what I'm going to find out," he said, turning to get out of the car.

Susan stayed behind the wheel as he walked up to the Honda. He didn't recognize the car and realized it was new. Business must be good, he thought. Or maybe she'd bought the Honda with the money Dino had paid for his share in the partnership.

He was still shaking inside from his confrontation with Mac. He couldn't believe how he'd reacted. He didn't consider himself the jealous type, and yet, when he'd looked through the curtain and caught her with that guy, he'd seen this misty cloud of red. Something he wasn't sure he wanted to get in touch with had taken over. Every minute she'd stayed out there had seemed like centuries.

He'd always been easygoing about stuff like that. He couldn't even believe the accusations he'd made. It had been insane. And yet, the insanity of it had swept him along, so by the time Mac had come inside, he'd been working on a different level. Reverting to some caveman ready to drag his mate by the hair to their cave.

He'd never felt anything like that before. And it scared the shit out him. Mac could be in a lot of trouble. Now was not the time to start thinking with his dick.

He knocked on the window. Susan lowered the glass, apparently refusing to get out. He took a couple of deep breaths, telling himself to calm down, not to take it out on Susan.

He leaned down on the window. "What the hell do you think you're doing?"

She was staring straight ahead, acting as if he hadn't said anything. Her lips were pressed together. But he was willing to wait her out, if that's what it took.

"I've been following her," Susan whispered. And then she looked up. Incredibly, there were tears in her eyes. "I can't believe you would be *stupid* enough to sleep with her, Jake. After what you read in that file."

"Shit." He pounded his fist on the car, remembering the night she'd left the message on his machine, talking so fast, almost as if she could see him running to cut her off. Susan was a PI. Snooping on people wasn't exactly a foreign concept. "I don't fucking believe this. That night. The message you left on the phone machine—"

"I followed her to your place; I saw your lights go off and I waited. I know which window is yours. You can see it from the Riverwalk. When the lights came on again, I called from my portable."

"You guessed I wouldn't pick up that phone, that she would hear the message about the file and my meeting with Gus." His voice was getting louder as he realized how calculating Susan had been. "You wanted her to know I'd worked at the Attorney General's office; you wanted her to hear about the Donovan Curse. You set me up."

She waited in silence. And then, "I thought she might be listening, yes."

"Jesus, Susan. Why?"

"You didn't take the file seriously. Someone had to protect you."

"Protect me?" He shook his head. "I'm a big boy, Susan. I—"

But then he stopped, remembering what Dino had told him. That there was another man in Susan's life. That her heart wasn't free to fall in love with Dino. But when Jake had asked her about it, Susan hadn't mentioned a name.

Now he knew who the man was.

"No, Susan. Tell me it's not what I'm thinking."

The words hung in the air between them like an accusation. He couldn't believe it. She looked so hurt, acting as if he'd cheated on her.

"I can't stand that you're sleeping with her," she whispered, choking on the words.

He shook his head. "This is crazy. This is fucking nuts. You and I have made our peace. We both have our own lives."

"I suppose it cramps your style to have your ex following you," she said, sniffing back her tears, wiping them impatiently. He could see she was having a hard time keeping it together. Her lips actually trembled. "Finally, you get your revenge," she said, smiling bitterly. "Now, you've hurt me as much as I hurt you when I left, after my mother died." The tears were flowing now, falling silently down her cheeks. "Now I'm the one completely humiliated."

"What an asinine thing to say. Is that what this is about? Humiliation? Getting even? What are you hanging on to, Susan? Some dream you've cooked up in your head? I never made you happy; that's why you left me in the first place. Don't make it something it wasn't because you think you can't have it anymore."

He realized she was totally ignorant of the fact she'd fallen in love with Dino. That she was hiding it from herself—maybe even protecting herself—by focusing on some myth she'd created in her head about the possibility of their getting back together.

He leaned down low, getting close to her. "Don't lose a chance at something better because you're stuck in a past that never satisfied you in the first place."

She looked at him then, those Nordic blue eyes swimming with tears. "What's that supposed to mean?"

He shook his head. "You're a smart girl. You figure it out. But just in case, here's a hint. I've seen you and Dino together and I *never* made you look like that. Open your eyes." He stood up, stepping away from the car. "Open your eyes."

Susan sat behind the wheel of the car, watching Jake drive away in Dickey's Lamborghini. She leaned both arms against the steering wheel, collapsing against it, feeling ridiculous and completely humiliated.

Somehow, it had all seemed so different, following that woman. She'd assumed she was protecting Jake. Even when she'd made that call from the Riverwalk, watching them with her binoculars through those huge picture windows, she'd still rationalized her behavior, saying it was for Jake's sake. He was too good. He wouldn't know how to protect himself.

But seeing the dawning comprehension on Jake's face, the things she'd done seemed a little off. Jealous and crazy.

She thought about her mother. About her suicide.

She cried quietly in her car, worried that—despite years of therapy—she could fall into some sort of sick behavior. That it had taken this confrontation with Jake to shed a big bright light on it.

Open your eyes.

He'd been talking about Dino. He thought she was in love with Dino.

"Sure," she said to herself, wiping the tears from her eyes

with her hands. "Sic me on the Greek gigolo. As if my heart isn't broken enough."

She turned on the car and steered down the street. *I've seen you and Dino together. I never made you look like that.*

Maybe, she thought. But she was smart enough to guard herself against someone like Dino, a man committed to his sexual prowess. They were friends. And partners, now that they had signed the papers. Loving him would ruin all that.

But fifteen minutes later, she found herself parked in front of Dino's shotgun house, thinking about what Jake had said.

I've seen you and Dino together . . . I never made you look like that.

Dino was the kind of man who broke your heart into itty bitty little pieces, leaving nothing behind. But Jake, she'd always thought he was safe. He'd loved her once. He would never hurt her. Or so she'd thought. Now Jake was suggesting she was hanging on to the past to protect herself. Because she was afraid, afraid to go on with her life—to love again.

She wiped the last of her tears, working it through her head.

Open your eyes, Susan.

She sniffed and got out of the car. She didn't want to love Dino. She didn't want him to hurt her. But Jake seemed to be saying you couldn't protect yourself from that sort of thing. Maybe if you tried, it only made things worse, causing you to do something crazy . . . like follow your ex-husband's new lover around town.

Susan rang the doorbell and braced herself as she waited. She didn't know why she'd come, perhaps because she always ended up here at Dino's door when she had a problem. She didn't even know what she was going to do exactly. But when Dino opened the door, she felt it, that sweeping desire she always tried to control.

His hair was wet from a shower. He had these gold-green eyes, eyes that never failed to make her melt a little inside. And then he smiled, his special smile that told her she was welcome at any hour. He would have just gotten off his shift. She could smell something delicious in the kitchen, probably his dinner. She knew he loved to cook.

"Suzy?" he said, using his special name for her. And then he frowned. "Hey, *mati mou,* what is it?" he said, his voice full of concern.

"Am I interrupting something?" she asked, stepping inside and closing the door behind her. It surprised her that she expected him to be alone. Hadn't she just accused him of having notches on the bedpost from all the women in his life? And yet, other than watching him flirt occasionally, she'd never seen him with another woman. Not in the last year.

"Nah. I was just finishing dinner. It's your favorite. Mousaka. Want me to dish you up some? I even have that wine you liked so much—"

She took off her jacket, dropping it to the floor, knowing then what she wanted to do. "I'm not hungry." She started unbuttoning her blouse, trying not to analyze, just accepting it. That's what Jake was trying to tell her, that she couldn't force her heart to do the safe thing.

His eyes watched her every move, almost willing the buttons to open. He hadn't moved, but she could see how much he wanted her.

She felt the desire building inside her. She wondered how she'd managed to suppress it, to delude herself for so long. And she knew it felt good to face this . . . almost freeing. It was a step forward, almost as if she was admitting that she was strong enough to face the possibility of the heartbreak that might come.

But Dino stepped forward, stopping her hand as she reached for another button. "I don't know, Suzy. Maybe this isn't such a good idea."

She froze, wondering if she misunderstood. But then she saw the desire in his eyes, and she knew that he was just as afraid of taking the next step as she was.

Somehow that made things easier, better. She smiled.

"Dino, for one entire year, you've been trying to get into my pants. Now, you're having second thoughts?"

He took a step back, giving himself a shake, as if he were coming out of some trance. "You're right. It must be some freak form of performance anxiety."

His eyes grew smoldering. She could feel that look deep inside her, warming up all the places she'd thought to keep safe from him. But now, he made her feel more alive than she had in years. *Open your eyes.*

She mentally thanked Jake, knowing she'd needed that lecture tonight, no matter how painful. She walked toward Dino.

"Suzy, about those notches on the bedpost—"

She held up her hand, stopping him. "I know, Dino. I'm the love of your life. The others meant nothing. In no time at all, we'll be going down the aisle of some fabulous Greek Orthodox church. Do I have the picture right?" she said, letting him know she wasn't falling for any fantasy.

"Actually. My people are Roman Catholic."

"I give it six weeks."

"In that case," he said. "We better make the time count."

She slipped off her blouse and threw it on the couch. She had his full attention now. "Let's just take it one step at a time."

"Works for me," he said, sweeping her into his arms.

Nineteen

Jake paid Mindy, Michael's baby-sitter, and walked her to the door. When he came back, he found Mac pacing around the living room, darting glances at the door to Michael's room.

Jake came up behind her, taking her into his arms. She sighed, leaning back against him.

"I don't think I should be here," she said, "with Michael home."

He turned her around to face him. "I've never brought a woman here when Michael was staying over," he said.

She nodded, knowing what he was saying. That she was special. "Okay."

"Come here."

He took her to Michael's room and opened the door slightly, so that she could peek inside. Buried under his killer whale covers, Michael was asleep in his bed, his face lit by the glow of the computer's screen saver and his night-light, his mouth slightly open. He was sleeping soundly, as only children sleep.

"He's so beautiful," Mac whispered.

She was looking at Michael with such longing. Jake realized she did that a lot, examined things, wanting them from afar, as if she could never have the normal stuff that people took for granted. Love. A family.

Mac wouldn't take anything or anyone for granted, he realized. In her eyes, he could see so much of his own feelings for his son. What a miracle he was . . . the frightening responsibility of loving him. Michael was young, fragile—capable of falling ill or having an accident. And so incredibly precious, the thought of him hurt or sick could drive Jake insane.

Watching her, he could see all that and more in her eyes.

"Do you think it's wrong," he asked, "if his father has a life? If I bring a woman here, someone I care about a great deal?"

"No," she said, accepting those things about them. She turned and hugged him, pressing her cheek against him, her gaze still on Michael asleep in his bed.

Jake brushed his fingers through her hair, remembering the first time he'd seen her as herself, a redhead. How he'd thought her hair could spark Fourth of July highlights under the chandeliers. The shade was very dark, the color of a full-bodied burgundy wine. Now, standing outside Michael's door, he took in every inch, each angle, just as he had the first time he'd seen her.

If Mac left him, it wouldn't be like Hope or Susan. The missing half . . . what would it be like to lose that after finding her?

But he knew it was too late to be afraid. She was part of his life now. He wasn't letting her walk away.

"What did you tell Susan?" she asked. They had talked about Susan on the way over, Jake letting her know his opinion, that Susan had been following McCall in some misguided belief that she was a danger to him . . . and that he and Susan might get back together.

"I told her she was in love with someone else."

Mac looked up. "Is she?"

"Yup. Only she's afraid. Because she knows how much it will hurt if it doesn't work out."

"And you're not?" she asked, watching his eyes like he'd taught her, looking for lies. "After two failed marriages, you're not frightened about any of this?"

He smiled. "Yeah. I'm afraid. In fact, I think you could scare the piss out of me sometimes, Mac."

She smiled faintly. "Mr. Romance."

"No doubt, I have a way with words." He tucked her head under his chin, holding her closer. "Look, Mac. Here's how it is. You're like this roller coaster I happened on to. From the day we met, you've never looked the same twice. You have enough brain power packed in your head to add an alphabet of letters to your name, but you're gutsy, making a run at the tables at the casinos. Not to mention you're sexy as hell. So even though I'm riding the damn roller coaster with my heart in my throat through every dip and twist, it's a hell of a ride."

"I don't know who you're talking about," she said. "I'm none of those things."

He smiled, tipping her head up to his. "Baby, you're all that and a bag of chips."

He took her hand, still smiling in that way of his, a smile that came from the eyes, that made you want to smile back. He took her to the master bedroom, to the big antique iron bed that had nothing to do with the man who slept in it. Because he hadn't brought anything of himself here except for a few photographs, a cow teakettle, and an Elvis clock.

He took her clothes off, slowly, one piece at a time, his fingers stroking, his lips touching. Everywhere. McCall did the same, running her hands through the copper brown chest hair, her palms lingering on his shoulders, wanting to taste the freckles there. He always smelled of the sun and salt and lemons.

They stayed on the bed, a gentle exploration, taking their clothes off until they knelt before each other, naked on top of the covers.

Jake followed the curve of her breast with one hand, making her shiver with need and anticipation as he caressed her waist and the small of her back. He leaned down and kissed her, kneeling before her . . . until he pulled her up in a sweep of his arms, crushing her against him as he deepened the kiss.

"You smile when you kiss me," she said, her mouth on his, her hands in his hair.

"That's because I like to kiss you," he told her, pulling her down with him as he rolled down to the bed. "A very enjoyable act."

"If you let it grow, does your hair curl like Michael's?"

"Nah. That's all his, those curls. Maybe when I was a kid."

He lowered his mouth to her breast. She held him there, feeling the sensation in places so deep inside her. His mouth, his tongue. "You have a wonderful mouth."

His hands cupped her buttocks, turning her so she was beneath him, looking up at him. He watched her, entering her, slowly, slowly, bringing them together.

"Do you see how it is between us, Mac?" he asked, moving inside her, bringing her legs up over his hips as he eased forward.

"Yes." She didn't take her eyes off him. She couldn't.

"This is what I'm afraid of . . . that I won't be able to touch you like this," he said, reaching for her breasts, cupping them in his hands to stroke the tips with his thumbs, still moving inside her.

"We didn't use any protection," she whispered.

"I know," he told her, kissing her mouth again, bringing them closer as his fingers tested the skin at the back of her thighs. "I wanted to better my odds. A guy can't always count on the damn things breaking, you know."

"Oh, Jake," she said, incredibly happy and scared and turned on, all at the same time. "What does this mean?"

He held himself perfectly still, then pushed up on his hands, leaning over her. "I thought it meant we loved each other."

"Yes," she said, giving in, because she wanted to, with all her heart. She wrapped her legs around him and pulled his shoulders down to hers, her hands reaching to stroke his long strong back, to make him hers. "I do."

They made love for hours trying to make it last then starting all over again. She accepted everything they did, knowing Jake was right, that losing him would be more frightening than loving him. His mouth, his wonderful, delicious mouth, took her places she could never have reached on her own. Because he loved her. And he wanted only to give and give and give.

When she lay curled up next to him, the sun had already pinked the room, bringing on the morning. She thought of how safe he made her feel, even though she wasn't safe. And she didn't want to leave the bed, or Jake, or any of the dreams he'd just created for them.

His hand curled around so he held her breast in his palm. He kissed her shoulder. "You know, when I saw that guy coming out of the car, taking you up the walkway, staying half the night out there doing God-knows-what, where I couldn't see you, I thought I was going to go frigging nuts."

"It's because we don't trust each other," she said, turning to look at him. "It shouldn't be like this, so fast and intense, it's combustible." She leaned her forehead against his chin. "Oh, Jake. What are we doing?"

He breathed in her special scent, knowing it was time to set things straight between them. He pulled on a heavy curl of hair from the pony tail at the top of her head. "Maybe that's what we should be talking about, then. The trust part. Clarke Labs," he said. "Whatever it is you're doing, I can help you."

She shook her head, looking up at him as if she was scared. Scared for him. "Please, Jake. Think of Michael. I don't want you to rescue me. It's not the same; it's not the Donovan Curse where all you have to worry about is a broken heart."

"Because you're worried someone could hurt me? Even kill me?"

"Roger and Curtis." She spoke only the names, leaving the rest of it unsaid.

Jake nodded. "So I'm supposed to be okay with that? Leaving you to it," he said, wanting her to focus on the worst, to be prepared. "I keep remembering what you said about Alicia. How she died like that—no questions asked. Maybe next time,

Curtis won't settle for ruining your reputation. Maybe he's looking for something more permanent to get you out of the way?"

She started to shake, uncontrollably. He wrapped his arms
around her, holding her. "Jesus. What is it?"

"I'm cold. So cold."

He cradled her against him. An intense need to protect her
came over him. He knew why she was shaking, and it had
nothing to do with being cold. She was afraid. He cursed
softly, feeling her trembling in his arms. "Mac?"

"There was an accident at the lab," she whispered. "That's
why I wasn't wearing my clothes. They were ruined. A bottle
of sulfuric acid spilled. The door to the lab jammed. The man
you saw me with outside, he works with me, on the Omega
Principle. He was trapped in the lab with me."

He was trying not to overreact, but he felt consumed by
the same primal urge that had crept over him earlier with his
jealousy. "That's it. It's over. You're not going back there."

She didn't look at him. "The acid spill. It wasn't anything
like what happened to Alicia."

"Why? Because it didn't work? Because you didn't die?"

She huddled closer, holding him tighter as she whispered,
"Hush. I'm frightened enough. Just hold me."

He stroked her back, not saying anything, but he knew she
didn't believe it was an accident. Not for one minute. Someone was suspicious about what Mac was doing, enough that
they were willing to—if not kill her—at least scare the shit
out of her to get her out of the picture.

"Okay," he said softly. He thought about what he was doing, the investigation he might be compromising. But he knew
he didn't have any choice. He couldn't let her go back there
without knowing everything. "Here's the deal. What you heard
on the message machine from Susan the other night, how I
met with my old boss at the Attorney General's office. We
didn't talk about you. I wanted to know about Curtis Clarke.
Gus told me there's an investigation going on. It's big. Interpol

is involved. The FBI. They think someone at Clarke Labs is trying to buy frozen embryos."

She stiffened. "Human embryos?"

"That's right. Over a hundred of them, to be exact. Apparently, you can't just go to your friendly neighborhood convenience store and buy a dozen. These were set to be destroyed in England. Maybe someone thought a few wouldn't be missed?"

She sat up. She stepped out of the bed and padded over to his closet. She put on one of his dress shirts and left the room. When she came back, she had her big tote bag with her. She sat on the bed next to him and dug through the purse for some papers, then handed them over to him. "I printed it out from the computer at work. It's an application for some sort of spa."

He glanced over the pages, remembering. "Yeah. I know about this. Garrett was happy as a clam because he got his girlfriend signed up for it. Do you remember the dealer the night we played? The one with the nails that you kept handing twenty-five dollar chips? That's her. That's Stacie. She didn't want to do it, but Garrett will get her to change her mind. He wants her on board."

"I'm not sure that's such a good idea." She took the pages and flipped to the back. "Look at these questions."

He turned on the lamp and read them to himself, not sure what she was getting at. "Seems like pretty typical stuff. But Jesus," he said, frowning as he read further. "I've seen insurance applications with a lighter touch."

"Exactly," Mac said, standing to pace in front of the bed. She stopped, biting her thumbnail, then turned to face him. "Jake, you thought I came back to Clarke for revenge. But that wasn't it."

"Then tell me," he said, putting the papers down. She looked worried, enough that he knew to pay attention.

"A year after Alicia died, I received a key to a safety deposit box from her attorney. It was my legacy from Alicia and it took a while to track me down. Inside, there was a lab book. Alicia used it like a diary, writing strange entries that talked about being under the influence of her lover, a man she described as a mix between Svengali and Dr. Frankenstein. But she never gave his name."

She walked slowly toward him. "They were involved in a series of experiments. She never said what the experiments were exactly. She was careful about what she wrote, as if she was afraid to put it down on paper. Evidence. But there was enough there to let me know it concerned beauty."

"Clarke Labs?"

She nodded. "I came back because those things I read in her diary, they frightened me. I wondered if someone had continued the experiments after she died. I dreamed of those experiments . . . the images she wrote about. That's why I came up with the Omega Principle as a cover. I thought I could fool them long enough to find out if there was anything to that lab book—then I would disappear again."

"And what did you find?" he asked, knowing there would be something.

She wrapped her arms around her waist as if she was getting cold again. "Clarke Labs has a high-security facility. A Biosafety Level-2 lab. It's the perfect place for research, the kind you don't want a lot of people to know about."

"My God," he said, putting it together. "The clinic. Garrett told me they were promising something that would make DHEA and alpha-hydroxy look like the stone age."

"A youth formula?" She thought about it. "That would agree with the entries in Alicia's lab book. But I have no way of being sure. In fact, I'm not at all certain what kind of experiments Alicia was working on before she died. I only know the animals they used . . . they died horribly."

"And Garrett has Stacie signed up for the damn thing. Do you think they're going to experiment on these women?"

"I don't know. Human trials? It seems so far-fetched. But those questions, Jake."

He flipped back to one page in particular. "Have you ever undergone general anesthesia?" he read out loud. He scrubbed his face with his hands, thinking. "I've got to show this thing to Gus. He'll know what to do——"

"No. Please, Jake. Not yet. Give me a little time. Maybe I can find something else, something more helpful." She came over to the bed, kneeling before him. "Really, what does this prove? A lot of strange suppositions on my part. And the embryos . . . honestly, I don't see the connection." There was a strange edge to her voice. She was desperate to persuade him. "There's really very little research you can do on embryos. It wouldn't be the tissue of choice for testing toxicity from a pharmacological point——"

"My God," he said, looking down at her, for the first time getting it, seeing the complete picture. "I've been so stupid. Missing the obvious. Your father. He's the head of Clarke's Research and Development. You think he's involved. You're trying to protect him. That's been it the whole time."

She jumped to her feet, her whole face and stance changing. She was angry. "You can't give me a week? I just want a week."

He stood, coming at her. "I can't give you a day. I'm not letting you back there." He grabbed her shoulders. "They tried to kill you."

She pushed him away. "My father has nothing to do with this! But if you send the authorities in there now before I can get proof of that, Curtis will make it look like he's running the whole thing."

"You can't know that——"

"I *know*. I of all people know!" she said, her eyes showing she believed what she was saying. "That's what he did to me. He ruined me. And he'll do the same to my father."

"How can you be certain," he asked gently, "that your father isn't involved?"

"Because he's my father. Jake, he's my father."

It broke his heart to see her like this, so desperate and

pleading. *He's my father.* Which meant he couldn't be involved. Because she loved him.

She turned away, walking to the corner of the bed, her arms crossed protectively over her chest. "And if you need a better reason than that, then you should read Alicia's lab book. She was in love with the man behind the experiments. My father detested Alicia Goodman; they couldn't even stay in the same room together for more than five minutes. They would never have been involved."

"And why was that?" Jake asked, coming up behind her. "Why did he hate her?"

She shook her head again. He could see she didn't want to talk about it, the possibility that her father was involved. That it was tearing her apart, trying to trust him but keeping her father safe at the same time.

"Why Mac?" he asked again, insisting this time.

"Because of me," she said after a while, her voice so low, he wasn't sure he heard her right. "Because I left for Harvard to work in her lab rather than staying here in Louisiana to become his research assistant," she said, making it clear. "He accused Alicia of seducing me with dreams of the Nobel. And when Alicia and I both left Harvard for LIT, when we became partners after my postdoctoral work, he hated her even more." She turned, looking up at Jake, trying to get him to see things her way. "They were never lovers."

"I don't know, Mac. Whoever this man was, this Dr. Frankenstein she wrote about. In the end, accident or not, Alicia Goodman turned up dead."

"That's it exactly. Dead. My father wouldn't kill anyone." She was so earnest, believing what she said passionately. "But Roger. He was driving that night. Just a few weeks ago, he baited me with the possibility that he and Alicia were lovers. It's Roger who is the villain here. He's the kind of man who could love a woman to death—use her up and kill her when she got in his way or wasn't useful anymore. It has to be Roger."

"You love your father," he said. "He disowned you, and you love him."

She closed her eyes, seeming to crumble just a little. She dropped down to sit on the bed.

He tried to imagine how it was between Mac and her dad. What it would be like for someone to have a child who was so gifted and brilliant. The temptation to mold them would be enormous. And he remembered how she'd reacted in Michael's room, seeing that Hope was trying to give Michael some sort of edge—to make him the best he could be. Maybe Mac's dad had taken it a little farther than educational toys and a few classes for toddlers.

"I don't blame him as much as I blame myself." She rubbed her eyes with the back of her hand, looking tired—the night, catching up to her. "I betrayed his dreams. I left him alone, after he'd dedicated his entire life to educating me, giving me every opportunity, any experience if he thought it might help me understand something."

"I thought that's what parents were supposed to do. Help their kids. I didn't know there was supposed to be a payoff."

"It wasn't a payoff, Jake," she said, still fiercely protective of her father. "It was a partnership. Like when a man has a business and he gets to add "and Sons" after his name. But I chose Alicia over him. After Harvard, we still spoke, but it wasn't the same. I hurt him terribly." She stared down at her hands, opening and closing them on her lap. "When the FBI made their accusations, he was prepared to believe the worst. He saw it as a second betrayal. My mother told me my father couldn't abide weakness in a person and she was right. He would see my tampering with test results as the ultimate weakness. Something unforgivable. I can't blame him for what he did."

"Really," he said, smiling but not feeling it. Because what he heard was the story of a man who wanted to live his dreams through his child, sensing that she could attain the things that had eluded him all his life. A man who would give his child nightmares about bacteria growing out of control, suffocating her . . . as he most certainly had tried to do before she escaped him.

Jake knelt down before her, placing his hands on her knees. "Why did you leave?" he asked softly, knowing it wouldn't have been for Alicia's dream. He did something, her father. Something that drove her away.

She shook her head, holding her arms around herself. "I'm tired," she whispered, her voice cracking on the words. "I'm so tired, Jake."

Too tired to talk. Too tired to face all this. He saw that and more in her expression.

"Come here," he said, holding his arms out to her.

She dropped down into his embrace. He held her, kissing her gently. "It's okay, baby," he whispered. "We'll make it all right."

"I want to go to sleep."

"Yeah," he said, pulling her to the bed. "You need to sleep." He threw back the covers and watched her crawl in, then slipped in beside her. Holding her, he pulled the covers over them. After a while, he whispered, "But you'll let me help you."

"Yes," she said, her voice already languid, her breathing even beneath his hand. She laced their fingers together and nuzzled back against him. "Yes."

They brought the German shepherd in after midnight.

Two technicians loaded the dog into his cage, the animal, a dead weight. The shepherd had been on and off the treadmill most of the day, his heart rate monitored, his reflexes checked periodically, noting any changes. When it happened—the blindness, the loss of motor skills—it tended to be quick. It was a good sign the dog had lasted another day, but he was exhausted.

As the cage closed behind him, the dog's eyes opened listlessly. He didn't rise up. The golden retriever, Sierra, nudged at his paw through the cage bars.

"Do you think he'll make it?"

"Who knows. We'll find out soon enough. God, I hate it when they go."

"Yeah. Me, too."

"What about the golden retriever?"

The tech scanned through his clipboard, then flipped the page. "Surgery. Tomorrow night."

Twenty

"Wake up, Mac." The voice was a soft whisper tickling her ear. "Wake up."

McCall roused from a deep sleep, expecting to see Jake. Instead, she found a set of lovely brown eyes, the lashes, femininely long, and a mop of strawberry blond curls . . . all at eye level to the bed.

She smiled, happy that he was curious enough to wake her first.

"Good morning, Michael," she said softly.

Jake's son grinned back, showing a set of milk-white baby teeth. "Hello, Mac."

McCall put her finger to her lips. Checking on Jake, she saw that he was still sleeping soundly. She crept out of bed and took Michael's hand. Together, they slipped out of the room, Michael beginning to giggle softly.

As soon as McCall shut the door behind them, Michael began to laugh in earnest. He pointed at her clothes. "You're wearing my dad's shirt."

She looked down at the white dress shirt hanging to her knees. "Silly me." She covered her mouth as if shocked. "I forgot my pajamas."

They both burst into peals of laughter, McCall loving the sound so much she began to tickle Michael, remembering the kiss attacks she would give the twins most mornings. The boy fell to the floor, rolling around, laughing all the harder as he tried to avoid McCall's hands.

When they finally stopped, they lay down on the carpet together, catching their breath, their heads together. This was how she felt most mornings with the twins, this joy of being part of something bigger—something better. Part of a child's life.

Michael sat up and looked down on her. "Are you going to be my new mother?"

McCall caught her breath. "I don't know," she said, caught off guard enough to be honest. She thought about last night, what she felt for Jake. "I think that's up to you and your dad."

"Don't worry. My dad's real good about stuff like that. He gives me anything I want," Michael said. "Come on." He grabbed her hand and tugged her into the next room.

McCall thought of how trusting Michael was, a beautiful and happy child who exuded confidence. She knew she had to give Hope credit for that, which was a shame, because she didn't particularly want to give Hope any good qualities. She watched as Michael scrambled up on one of the stools. He braced both elbows on the counter, looking incredibly cute in a set of red thermal underwear. McCall waited for his next move.

He cocked his head, looking at her as if puzzled. "Aren't you going to make breakfast?"

"Yes," she answered, immediately walking around the counter. Apparently, mothers made breakfast. She opened a couple of cabinets, then looked back at Michael. "What am I making?"

He gave a long-suffering sigh and clambered down from the stool. He found a box of cereal—Lucky Charms. McCall took a quart of milk out of the refrigerator but he shook his head, setting the bowls and spoons on the granite counter. "We don't need milk."

"We don't?"

"Nah. It's no good with milk."

He poured a lot of cereal into each bowl, then glanced over at McCall. "Can I have your marshmallows?"

McCall put the milk back in the refrigerator, giving the four-year-old an assessing look. Obviously, Michael knew an easy mark when he saw one.

"You can have *some* of my marshmallows. I pick which ones. But not the rainbows."

"Ah, man!"

By the time they were halfway through their cereal, she had learned that Michael's favorite color was purple, his best friend's name was Lauren, and he wanted marbles and a bicycle with training wheels for his birthday, which was coming up real soon. Michael was going to be a musician when he grew up. And he loved Lucky Charms—especially the rainbows, which he always ate first. He managed to persuade her to hand over most of hers.

And he knew his way around Jake's sound system, having taken a break from his Lucky Charms to put on some music. Druha Trava, the Czechoslovakian bluegrass group his father had already acquainted her with, played softly in the background.

"Did you bring me my coloring book?" he asked, talking around a mouthful of cereal.

"I'm afraid I haven't had a chance to get it," McCall said, eating one of the marshmallows, thinking longingly of the milk in the refrigerator.

"S'okay." He was looking her over. "Your hair is red like mine."

Mac smiled. She could just imagine what she looked like, her hair sticking out of the ponytail she'd worn all night. "Just a lot darker."

"But you don't have any freckles."

She wrinkled her nose. "Only the really special redheads get freckles."

He nodded, as if that made complete sense to him. He took an enormous mouthful of cereal, chewing contentedly. Watching him, McCall's heart about doubled in size inside her chest, nudging up to her throat. She felt like a thief, stealing this precious moment, trying to believe that somehow, she might be able to be a part of it forever.

I thought it meant we loved each other. She smiled, remembering Jake's words of love.

"With all my heart," she whispered, brushing back one of Michael's curls.

Michael glanced up at her. "Are you going to use one of my toothbrushes? You can, you know. I won't mind. I even have some that glow in the dark. And one that's really cool because it has the Gold Ranger on it. My mom doesn't let me have Power Rangers stuff, but Dad says it's okay."

"Why won't your mom let you have a Power Ranger toothbrush?" McCall asked, thinking of Barb's twins and the barrage of merchandise that always cluttered every inch of the house.

"Mom says I'm too young to know the difference between fantasy and reality. Dickey, that's my stepdad, he says Mom worries too much but we have to follow her rules anyway. Power Rangers are too violent."

"Oh," McCall said, understanding. But then she realized what he was saying, how adult-like his speech. "Something tells me you're pretty smart. That you would know the difference between make-believe and what's real."

"Yeah. That's what I told Mom, but she still said I couldn't have Power Ranger stuff."

For a moment, she thought of how awful it must be for Jake, living from weekend to weekend, letting Hope set all the rules. Somehow, she knew Hope was responsible for the overkill of educational books, the lack of coloring books, the structure to Michael's life. She realized suddenly she didn't like Hope or Susan very much, women responsible for the Donovan Curse.

"My Mom and Dickey went to Texas," Michael said, filling in the silence. "They're getting me a baby sister. I asked my dad if he could have a baby. I'm going to make a great big brother. My mom says so. So I won't mind."

A tiny hope sparked inside her as she remembered the possibility that she and Jake had made a child together last night. It would be wonderful, to forget the things that had brought her here and step into this fantasy of family, complete with Jake and Michael as the grand prize. She didn't want to think about the spill at the lab or the application she'd printed out. But most of all, she wanted to forget Jake's accusations that her father might be involved.

She heard the door to the bedroom open. Jake came out of the room, yawning. He had on a pair of jeans and a white T-shirt, and his hair was sticking out in different directions, as if he'd run his fingers through it a number of times. His face was covered with auburn stubble. He looked utterly adorable.

He gave both McCall and his son a kiss on the top of their heads, then turned his back to his son as he lingered over a second kiss on McCall's mouth. Stepping back, he smiled, flashing his dimples. "Good morning."

"Good morning," she said, thinking no man should look this incredibly good straight out of bed.

He yawned again and walked around the counter. He opened the refrigerator and took out the carton of milk. Without saying a word, he poured some into Michael's bowl.

"Ah, man," Michael protested. "You ruined it, Dad!"

Jake poured milk into McCall's cereal next. "Did he talk you out of the rainbows, too?"

"Yes," she said, looking down at Michael. "As a matter of fact, he did."

"It's no good with milk," Michael grumbled.

"Eat," Jake told him, putting the milk back in the refrigerator. He started setting up the coffee maker, filling it with water and coffee grounds. "How are you feeling?" he asked McCall.

"A little tired." She glanced down at Michael, eating his cereal. "Incredibly happy."

Jake smiled, tousling his son's hair. "Hey, sport. You wanna watch *Gargoyles?*"

"Yeah!" Michael jumped down from the stool with a whoop.

Jake followed close behind, taking the bowl of cereal Michael had left on the counter. He set him up in front of the television with his breakfast, then turned off the CD before he popped in a video. He walked back to McCall at the counter.

"Boy, those things are damn convenient," he said, nodding toward the video. "No wonder Hope didn't want me to get him started." He shook his head. "It's a slippery slope from here."

"He'll be fine," she said, taking Jake's hand in hers. "It's a great show."

"You're a *Gargoyles* aficionado?"

"And *Batman, The Mighty Ducks, Rugrats, Doug.*" She sighed, pulling his arm around her shoulders. "I love cartoons, probably because I was too busy to watch them when I was little."

"Ah. Deprived as a child. Obsessed as an adult."

"Something like that."

Jake glanced at Mac in his shirt. She'd done up too many of the buttons, probably for Michael's benefit, but the slits up the sides were nice. He shook his head. "I'm never going to think of this shirt the same," he said as he walked past, his hand lingering on the curve of her hip. "You want some coffee?" he asked, pouring a cup.

"Yes, please."

He came back with coffee for both of them and set the mugs on the counter. Standing behind Mac, he pulled her against him. He knew this is what he wanted, Mac here, every morning.

"So what do you think?" he asked, nodding at Michael. "You want to sign up and join the team?"

He thought maybe he was holding his breath, waiting for her answer. Because he loved her, and he knew she loved him. And life could be such a mess sometimes, that those simple truths might not be enough.

McCall turned on the stool, looking up at him. In her eyes, he could see all the longing he was feeling. And the doubts.

"My mother was an alcoholic." The words came out as a breathy whisper. "My sister is eight and half years younger. I never made myself part of her life because no one ever taught me that might be important. She grew up resenting me. With reason. My father. He was my family. The one who scolded me, loved me, taught me all I knew. And then even he was gone. I was thirteen when I started at Harvard."

Listening to her, Jake had this weird image in his head. It was almost as if she were describing one of those strange isolation experiments. Like maybe her father had kept his little girl apart from others, making sure only he counted . . . a father who taught his daughter to focus on his needs and what he believed was important. But he kept his thoughts to himself, believing Mac wouldn't appreciate such a twisted image of her life.

She was watching Michael now. He could see that it scared her, that she wouldn't be good enough.

"Last night," he said, "Guru Barb and I had a little time on our hands, you know, waiting for you to show up. She told me you're the twins' godmother. She said you're real good with them, that she's never seen anybody with so much love to give. That maybe you stored it up all those years and it's kind of bursting out of you."

But he could see he wasn't getting through. Her lips pressed together, she still had that look, as if she could see only the lack in herself and none of the good.

Well, shit. He was pretty good at manipulating when necessary.

He walked around her and sat down facing her. "Look, I didn't want to say anything, but I'm pretty torn up about this and I need some advice." He glanced over at Michael, watching the milk dribble down his son's chin as he watched the television, mesmerized. "Hope had Michael tested. His IQ," he said, shaking his head, lying through his teeth. *Let's see. What would be bad enough?* "It was pretty much off the charts and she thinks we should send Michael away to one of those academies for really bright kids," he said, making it up as he went along. "I'm really going to miss the little guy, but Hope thinks this is a great opportunity and I don't want to hold him back—"

"Send him away? For school? He's four years old, Jake," she said, looking at him with utter disbelief. "If that isn't the most insane idea—"

She stopped. Her mouth snapped shut. But then she smiled, getting it. "You must have been a great prosecutor."

"I wasn't bad." He said, taking a drink of coffee.

"Why did you quit?"

He thought about it, turning the cup on the counter between his hands. "Maybe because I was tired of being one of the good guys—maybe because I wanted a job I could walk away from at any time . . . or maybe I blamed my job for all my personal woes."

"You loved it, didn't you?"

"Pretty much." He picked up her hand and kissed her fingers. "I might go back someday. I think I've learned some things about balance and keeping my perspective. So what do you think about the team part? Look, I think we Donovan boys are kinda screwed if you walk away from us now."

She looked at him as if he'd just voiced an alien concept. "I wouldn't."

"No," he said, seeing that, unlike Susan and Hope, Mac was going to stick around. "You wouldn't."

She looked over at Michael. She smiled, a tiny little curve of her mouth. "Maybe you guys do need me."

Jake folded her into his arms. They stayed that way, with their arms around each other in silence, watching Michael. And then, Jake whispered, "Please don't go back there today."

"I have to." She looked up at him, her expression telling him just how much she needed to return. "One day. Just one day."

One day to prove that her father was the innocent man she needed him to be. One day to make up for the past four years. He shook his head. Somehow, he'd figured that—being Mac— she wouldn't make this easy.

"All right," he said, because he'd known all along it was a long shot even to ask. "But I need to know you're okay. So here's the plan."

Stacie sat on the couch, staring at the brown, white-capped bottles lined up on the coffee table.

Garrett sat down beside her. It was still early morning, not even eight o'clock. He crossed his legs, his ankle on his knee, and sipped his coffee as she examined the bottles.

"Are you just going to stare at them?" he asked after a while.

Stacie picked up one bottle, frowning as she read the label. The printed instructions said she should take one capsule, twice a day. "Garrett, honey. I don't like it." She showed him the bottle. "It doesn't even say what's inside." She put the bottle down, standing it up next to the other four. "Why do I have to take these pills? I'm not even going to the clinic till the fall."

"What are you worried about? They're probably just vitamins, darling."

He pulled her back so she leaned against his shoulder, playing with her hair. He started kissing her neck. "I love it when you pout, sweetheart," he said, biting her bottom lip. He put down his coffee mug and pulled her under him on the couch, kissing her deeply, in that way that made Stacie just melt.

"Why don't we just take the day off and go to St. Francisville? Hell, we could blow off the week at one of those bed and breakfast joints you like so much."

Stacie held his face in her hands, losing herself in those blue eyes. "Oh, Garrett. Why are you always saying things you don't mean?"

"Maybe I mean it this time."

But she could see he was already flinching away from the idea of taking a week off from the casino. Garrett loved the *River Palace,* first, last, and always. Thirty years old and he was already the consummate workaholic.

She kissed the tip of his nose, wondering how a broken nose could make a man look better. But maybe Garrett would have been too cute otherwise with his brown curls and bad boy blue eyes. The bump on his nose made him look more of a man somehow. Older, which Stacie thought was a good thing. She felt those seven years between them as if each were a century.

She sighed. "I told Jake I'd watch his little boy today."

"On your day off?"

"You have a better idea, Garrett Renault?"

"Yeah," he said, his eyes on her mouth, looking as if he could just eat her up. "I do. How about you and me taking him to the zoo together. I hear them albino alligators is something. Like pieces of white chocolate floating in the water."

"Really?" she said, her voice breathy with anticipation. "You mean it, Garrett?"

"I do," he said, kissing her.

It was a long slow kiss, the kind that always managed to give her hope, making her think of white picket fences and babies. But she was crazy to dream she would ever pry Garrett from his Garden District mansion and casino for a simpler life. She would always be his older, white trash girlfriend.

"So is it a date?" he asked, kissing her softly, his hand reaching to stroke her between her legs.

"Yes," she said, really happy, because she couldn't wait to

spend the day with Garrett and Michael, dreaming of how it might be if fairy tales came true and they had their own family.

He sat up, smiling. He nodded at the bottles. "You know, darling. I'm sure those things are just fine. Clarke Cosmetics has been around since before I was born. They wouldn't give you anything dangerous. It would be bad publicity." He reached over and picked up a bottle. He opened the top and took out a pill. "Look, I'll take them with you."

He handed her a capsule and popped one in his mouth. "Okay?"

"All right," she said, smiling as she, too, swallowed the first pill.

Part Four

Scientific Method

When you get to the point where you cheat
for the sake of beauty, you're an artist.

Art Poetique, Max Jacobs, 1922

Twenty-one

The insanity of what we are doing seems a far-off consequence. My Dr. Frankenstein still mourns his lack of a perfect model. At times, I want to offer myself up to him. That I should be the final vehicle to his success.
— Excerpt from Dr. Alicia Goodman's lab book

"Twelve transformants tested positive for the Omega Principle gene," Roger said. He placed both hands on the armrests of the chair where Kyle Woods was seated in Curtis's office, giving Woods a smile that didn't reach his eyes. "I'd say we're right on target. Don't make problems where there aren't any, Woods."

Curtis sighed as he watched Woods squirm in his chair. Kyle Woods might be brilliant, but the boy had the backbone of a jellyfish.

"Let the man have his say, Roger," Curtis said, cutting the cigar with the clippers. "That's what we're paying him for, after all."

Woods adjusted his glasses, pushing them back up the bridge of his nose. He glanced nervously at Donald Sayer, who sat in the corner of the room watching the proceedings without comment. "I'm concerned we won't make our time-table." He cleared his throat and flipped through a few pages on his clipboard. "We had too many false positives." He shook his head. "We have to incorporate some wiggle room. It might take longer than a month to isolate the peptide. And then with further tests—"

Roger threw his arms in the air. "Fuck this shit. We already tested the peptide. It works!"

"But not the mass-produced equivalent," Woods argued.

"Why would the results be any different? It has the same amino acid sequence, asshole."

Woods blinked up at Roger. "You don't have to be abusive."

Curtis Clarke champed down on the unlit cigar, staring across the table at the dweeb he'd hired to keep an eye on McCall. He could see Roger was going to lose it. He wished his boy would show some patience. "So what do you advise, Kyle?"

"A second look at the timetable. Perhaps slowing down the publicity campaign to let science catch up with our promises." Woods adjusted his glasses again. "I don't want to discount the enormous strides we've made with McCall's research, but a great deal is at stake here."

"You want to buy a little time?"

"In a sense," Woods said. He clicked his mechanical pencil nervously. "The timetable set for this project is extremely tight."

Curtis leaned back in his chair. "What do you think, Roger?"

He asked the question more for show. He knew where Roger stood on the subject of the Omega Principle, a product the boy was counting on to finance his other baby, BioYouth.

Roger dropped down into the red leather chair in front of Curtis's desk. He put both his boots on the armrest of Woods's chair next to him, stacking one foot on top of the other as he smiled lazily, daring the other man to make a comment. "We're talking about cutting back on a project set to make millions annually. Maybe more. I say balls to the wall and full speed ahead. McCall will deliver."

"Donald?" Curtis asked, bringing Sayer into the conversation. The entire meeting, the man had lurked in the shadows like some sort of ghost.

"You already know my sentiments on the subject, Curtis."

"Right," Curtis said, biting down on the cigar. Damn Sayer was starting to get to him with his doom and gloom. "Well, Kyle. Why don't you leave your analysis here for Roger and Donald to go over. We'll talk again next week."

"Thank you, sir," Kyle said, gathering his papers, adjusting his glasses.

"Oh, and Kyle," Curtis added as if it were an afterthought. "What about that acid spill last night? Everything all right?"

Kyle straightened his shoulders under his lab coat, juggling his papers to situate them in his other hand. He frowned. "The damage was fairly contained," he said. "They've already installed a new window and cleaned up the lab. I don't see that it will significantly slow down our work."

"I was looking over the security report. Do you suspect any sort of foul play?"

Kyle blinked again, as if confused by the question. "Are we speaking about a competitor sabotaging the project? Extremely doubtful, given the minimal damage. Quite honestly, I may have pushed the bottle over myself. McCall and I were discussing how to avoid contamination on the next set of transformations." He shook his head, clicking the pencil. "I was very wound up about the false positives. When the lights went out, I'm fairly certain I jumped out of my chair and hit something. Possibly it was the bottle." He frowned again. "I'll speak to whoever left it in such a precarious position. The more volatile substances should always be locked in the cabinets if not in use."

All three men waited until Kyle walked out of the room, shutting the door behind him. Curtis smiled and said, "And there you have it, gentlemen. It was an accident."

Roger looked irritated and bored, glancing at his watch as if he had better things to do with his time. In his corner, Donald remained silent.

Curtis didn't like it, Sayer just sitting there, watching them as if what was happening couldn't touch him. His fortunes were tied to Clarke Labs, dammit. Always would be. Maybe it was time to remind him of that.

Curtis lit the Cuban cigar and glanced over at the papers Kyle Woods had left behind. "What do you think about the Omega Principle now?" he asked Donald. "That girl of yours has just about delivered. She's going to make us all very rich."

Roger smiled along with his father. "Twelve transformants positive for the gene. I'm not worried about the false positives," he told Curtis. "Contamination is something we can control. We'll have the thing bottled for market by the end of the year."

Donald bent down to retrieve his briefcase and balanced it on his lap. From inside, he pulled out a batch of papers. He walked over to the table and dropped them on the blotter in front of Curtis. "Take a look. See just what the Omega Principle is worth." To Roger, he said, "You're stupid, Roger. I've said it before and now you've proven it. I'm actually pleased Belinda returned your ring."

"What the hell was that about?" Curtis said, sitting forward as Donald left the room. He frowned. "That little ballerina leave you, boy?" Belinda Sayer might not be much, but at least she might squeeze out a grandson or two.

But Roger wasn't paying attention. He'd slammed both feet to the carpet, glaring at the papers Donald had left behind.

"I always thought you should have gone for the other one, Roger. The smart one," Curtis grumbled. "So what the hell were you thinking, spilling that acid last night?" he asked, puffing on the cigar. He'd tried to play down the incident with security, afraid someone would go over the video. It wouldn't look good to see Roger coming out of that lab, into the hall. Curtis hadn't watched the tape, but there was only one person who could have caused the spill.

"What are you talking about?" Roger said, leaning forward to snatch the papers off Curtis's desk. "I had to meet with our supplier for the embryos last night. I wasn't anywhere near the lab at that hour.

That surprised Curtis. He glanced back at the security report on his desk, picking it up. *The locking mechanism appears to have jammed after a loss of power. Dr. Woods believes he saw the bottle of acid near the edge of the table, that he or Dr. Sayer may have hit the bottle when the lights failed, startling them both.*

Maybe he was getting a little paranoid in his old age, Curtis thought, reading over the report. Could be, it was all an accident—

"Shit!" Roger was flipping through the pages Donald had left on the desk, reading fast.

Curtis dropped the security report. "What is it?"

His son remained seated, but he'd closed his eyes. As Curtis watched, the pages Roger held fell from his lax fingers, scattering to the floor. He'd never seen Roger look like that, as if he'd just taken a punch to the gut.

"Fucking bitch." Roger opened his eyes. "I sank millions into that campaign." He laughed a little. "And she took me. She fucking took me."

"What does the damn thing say?" Curtis demanded, alarmed by Roger's tone.

"It's a fake." He glanced down at the papers on the floor. He shook his head, as if he couldn't quite believe it. "Donald tracked down the ten volunteers from the PET scans for the Omega Principle peptide."

Roger's voice was surprisingly monotone. But then, Curtis thought maybe the boy looked distracted, as if he might be thinking about something else. Something that had his whole attention. And Curtis had his suspicions who that something might be . . .

Roger smiled, the kind of smile that always worried Curtis. "She conditioned their response. The PET scans were rigged," Roger said. "The Omega Principle isn't going to work."

* * *

Kyle took a cup of coffee from the server and placed it on his cafeteria tray. He didn't know if the caffeine was more help or hindrance. Between what had happened at the lab and returning to Belinda last night, he'd had no sleep. And then there had been the meeting in Clarke's office.

He had spoken to McCall before the meeting, convincing her it would be best to show the results from his twelve transformants and claim some victory. Later, they could drag out the purification process, saying it was taking longer than expected to isolate the Omega Principle peptide.

But he had to admit, it had felt good watching Roger Clarke dig a deeper hole for himself. The man was spending millions on the Omega Principle campaign. And it was all going to blow up in his face. Because Roger Clarke was, above all, a poor excuse for a scientist. A fool. A man who couldn't be bothered to look beyond his greed and ambition. He'd underestimated McCall and Kyle both . . . and it felt better than it should to take him down.

"Kyle! Over here."

He turned at the sound of his name. Belinda was seated in the far corner, waving to him.

He couldn't help smiling. They'd made love again early this morning before he'd taken her home. She'd even made him breakfast and fed it to him in bed, although Herc had eaten half of it.

It still astonished Kyle how they had come together despite the circumstances that had brought him here. But he didn't question it. He believed in those kinds of connections. He only hoped that, in the end, he could protect Belinda from that bastard, Roger Clarke, just as he'd promised McCall.

He sat down beside her. "Don't smile so beautifully at me," he said, grinning just the same. "People will get ideas." She'd told Kyle she'd given Roger back his ring. He wondered how long it would be before she would be wearing a simple gold band, the kind of ring Kyle would give her.

"I can't help smiling at you," she said. "You look so different when you're here." He could tell she wanted to touch him. He felt the same. Instead, they both clutched their coffee cups, knowing they still had to be careful about keeping their relationship a secret. "But I like it," she whispered, leaning forward. "That way, other women will leave you alone."

"Are you saying I'm unattractive?" he teased.

She frowned, the light in her clear blue eyes dimming. "You're right. I'm the one who's been blind."

"Kyle?"

Both he and Belinda looked up, watching McCall make her way to their table. He could see something wasn't right and he braced himself for the worst. Last night had been a wake-up call for both of them.

"May I speak to you?" she asked, not bothering to take a seat.

"Sure," Kyle said, already standing, seeing from the urgent look she gave him that whatever was going on, it was serious.

He followed McCall to an empty table, his heart pounding in his chest, the adrenaline coursing through his system giving him a bigger jolt than the caffeine. She chose an empty table where they could have some privacy. It was pretty late for lunch. Only a few stragglers lingered in the cafeteria.

"What is it?" he asked, sitting down close to her.

"I just talked to Roger. I convinced him to ask Jake back for a tour of our lab. He's coming later today."

"But that's great." McCall had told him what happened after they parted company last night. Apparently, Jake Donovan had an in with a friend of Roger's. Donovan thought he could get inside the Level-2 lab.

"He's coming here today, posing as an investor. He says he has equipment that will allow him to take photographs without Roger knowing." She kept her voice down, leaning close to him. "I think between the two of us, we can convince Roger to give him a tour of the Level-2 lab right after we finish up with the Omega Principle."

"What about the photographs?" Kyle asked.

"Anything that shows animals or proof of animal testing is yours. He promised. Your organization can break the story." She reached across the table, squeezing his hand. "But I don't want you there, okay?"

"Why?" he asked, ready to give all the reasons why he should be part of this.

She shook her head. "Something about Roger today. I don't know, he was just too accommodating. Almost eager. I keep thinking about the acid spill last night. It could have been Roger. It had to be Roger."

Kyle thought about it. "At the meeting, he was champing at the bit to go forward with the Omega Principle. In his words, 'McCall will deliver.' I don't know if he was behind the spill or not, but I don't think he meant to hurt you. It could have been some sort of sick practical joke. I checked this morning; there wasn't enough acid in that bottle to do any permanent damage from the fumes. Roger would know that." He shook his head, trying to figure it out. "Whatever was going on last night, he's still one hundred percent behind the Omega Principle and he can't get it without you. Now if this man, Jake Donovan, is there today—a witness, I think we'll be okay."

"What about the security video?" she asked, still worried. "If someone looks close enough, they can figure out we were inside the Level-2 lab."

"I have some good news about that. I talked to George this morning. He's one of the guards who works graveyard. I always bring him donuts just as he gets off shift. And he can be very accommodating with a donut in his hand." He grinned. "He said no one has even looked at the video—no need to. They're convinced it was an accident. It said as much in the incident report on Curtis's desk. I think we're in the clear."

But he could see she was still troubled. "Just humor me, Kyle. It will be hard enough to get that tour from Roger when we finish with the Omega Principle lab. In any case, I think only Jake will get inside. We'll meet directly at your place afterwards. Jake won't back out on his promise. The photographs are yours."

He pressed his lips shut, then nodded. "Though I hate to admit it, you may be right. The fewer people there, the better. Do you think he can do it? Do you really think he can convince Roger to take him to the animal room?"

"If it can be done, Jake will get in," she said with confidence.

Kyle leaned back in the chair. She had told him about the forms she'd found and her suspicions about the Clarke Spa and Clinic. McCall had a good motive to bring these idiots to justice. He trusted her. "Did you get any sleep last night?" he asked.

"Yes. I slept." But her eyes had a glazed look to them. She shook her head. "I thought I would have weeks more. I didn't think things would fall apart this quickly. But after last night . . ." She looked up. "I think we just ran out of time."

Belinda watched Kyle sit down next to McCall. Not across from her, which would have been the normal thing. But right beside her, pulling the chair closer so they could huddle together.

She could feel herself hyperventilating as she watched the two of them. There was something incredibly intimate about their hushed whispers. They didn't look like two scientists comparing notes. Kyle was leaning forward in his chair, bringing his face next to McCall's. And then McCall reached across the table, taking Kyle's hand in hers. He, in turn, leaned his shoulder into hers.

It made Belinda's heart race to watch them. It made her feel sick, as if she couldn't catch her breath and wanted to throw up at the same time.

She told herself she was being ridiculous. That she couldn't be jealous. For God's sake, she'd made love to Kyle just a few hours ago. McCall and Kyle worked together. Of course they would have a close relationship.

But the truth was, everything she'd ever had in her life had been McCall's first. Roger had dated her sister . . . and he'd always let Belinda know she was second choice. And her father—he'd only noticed Belinda after McCall had left them.

Kyle had been the only person in Belinda's life that belonged only to her.

A tray clattered onto the table next to her, startling Belinda. She glanced up, a little dazed, watching as her father sat down beside her.

"Hi, Daddy," she said. She didn't want to, but she found herself glancing over at the table where Kyle and McCall were still speaking.

"Hello, Belinda." He took his food off the tray and set it aside. Spreading his napkin on his lap, he followed her gaze to the adjoining table. He ate silently for a while. Belinda drank her coffee, feeling miserable with every look she gave McCall and Kyle. *Please, please, please, Kyle. Be mine. Be only mine.*

"I told you she would hurt us."

The words were barely audible. Belinda jerked her gaze back to her father. He stared at her, looking as if he felt sorry for her.

He sighed, then peered at McCall and Kyle. He shook his head again and picked up his coffee cup, taking a sip.

"What is it, Daddy?" she asked anxiously. "What are you thinking?"

"I know who brought you home this morning." He spoke in his quiet sure voice, putting down his coffee cup to give her his complete attention. "I saw you together. But I had already guessed he was the man in the cab from the other night. And Roger told me you gave him back the ring, so I know you're quite serious."

He reached over to take Belinda's hand in his. He squeezed it tight. He had her sister's eyes, sometimes more blue than green. But now they appeared very solemn. His pupils were tiny dots, making his gaze look more focused. Piercing, even.

"She uses people, Belinda. Kyle is a brilliant young man. She needs him desperately to make her formula work. I just hope she doesn't destroy him when all this comes to an end."

"I don't understand. How can she hurt Kyle? It's her idea, her research."

"The Omega Principle won't work. If Kyle Woods hooks his reputation on it, he's doomed. I just came back from a meeting with Curtis and Roger. Your Dr. Woods was presenting his report on the peptide." He glanced over to Kyle. "She's fooled him. She's fooled them all."

Belinda didn't say anything. She openly watched as McCall stood to leave the table and Kyle followed her. He didn't even look at Belinda. He hadn't even said goodbye.

"I already know her analysis is flawed," her father continued. "Soon, everyone will know the truth. That she cheated again, fixing her data. And we both know she can't afford to fail again."

Belinda could feel tears starting to fill her eyes, she was so scared. *I can't let her hurt Kyle!*

"Do you understand what I'm saying, Belinda? McCall will do anything to come out on top. She can't afford another failure."

Belinda bit her lip, not wanting to cry. "Not Kyle."

"Kyle. Me. Anyone. I'm not wrong about this. When the Omega Principle is discovered to be a fraud, she'll be merciless in finding her scapegoat."

Her father calmly pulled his handkerchief out of his pocket and handed it to Belinda.

"She can't hurt Kyle," Belinda said, staring at the handkerchief miserably. Because she could see how much Kyle respected her sister, that he would trust her. Because she was so smart.

"She's taken so much from us," her father said. "I wish I was wrong. But I'm not." He glanced back at the doors, where

Kyle had just left with McCall. "Don't let her break your heart, Belinda. She broke mine years ago."

Jake watched Stacie playing with Michael on the floor next to the two couches. She was helping him cut out the gargoyles he'd been drawing while Jake dressed. The living room floor was covered with colorful renditions of the paper monsters, all different shapes and sizes. Mac had suggested they could tape them up on Michael's wall. Jake and Mac had even contributed a few before Mac had left that morning, taking a taxi back to Barb's house.

"You sure about this zoo thing, Garrett?" Jake asked. Garrett had surprised him, saying he was tagging along, taking Michael to the zoo with Stacie.

"He's a cute kid," Garrett said, watching Stacie and Michael together. "I've always liked Michael. And I was thinking it would give me a chance to try out the father role." He turned his back to Stacie as he whispered, "I'm going to ask her to marry me."

Jake didn't say anything. He'd always known Garrett and Stacie were crazy about each other. But personally, he thought Stacie had done a lot to make Garrett happy and he wasn't so sure the same was true for Garrett. Garrett had money and he was essentially a good person at heart, but he could be selfish. Jake thought he had a lot of growing up to do.

"You know that beauty clinic you told me about?" Jake said. "You're not still trying to talk Stacie into doing that, are you?" He tried to make his interest sound casual.

"Hell, yeah," he said, smiling as he turned to watch Stacie with Michael. "It will be great for her, even if the stuff doesn't really do everything Roger promised. Three months of fun in the sun."

"Three months?" Jake said, feeling the wrongness of it. Knowing. "That seems a little long."

Garrett shrugged. "It's a special program. Hell. Don't they

do that for those fat clinics? I'll miss her, sure. But it sounds like it will be worth it. And she'll be tanned and buffed when she comes back to me."

Jake was watching Stacie. From what he could see, Jake didn't figure she needed improvement.

He thought about what Mac had told him. It made him push a little. "Are you sure this clinic is safe?"

"What do you mean?" Garrett frowned. "Of course it's safe."

"You mentioned something about Clarke making DHEA and alpha-hydroxy obsolete. That sounds pretty high-tech. Are we talking drugs?"

"How do I know? Well, yeah. There's some stuff she's taking before she gets there. Maybe vitamins or something. Look, there's regulations covering this stuff. Clarke isn't going to try anything that's not aboveboard. The publicity alone would ruin him. Not to mention the lawsuits."

"Sometimes companies take chances. If they think they can make money in the short run. And you said yourself they're trying something new. Lots of times, they don't even know for years what the fallout might be."

"Hey, look," Garrett said, his voice full of self-importance. "Roger and I go way back. He's not going to do anything to hurt my girlfriend."

"Maybe he doesn't know how much she counts," Jake said, arguing now, knowing that Garrett didn't treat Stacie that well. You would have to really know him to see how much he cared.

"What are you talking about? Besides, Stacie's a big girl. She'll take care of herself. She wouldn't do anything that wasn't smart."

"You'd be surprised what a woman might do if she thought it would please the man she loves."

Jake could see he was finally getting through to Garrett. He was frowning, mulling it over. How Stacie would damn well sell her soul if she thought it would make Garrett happy.

But then he said, "Stacie isn't like that. She has her head on straight. She knows I love her no matter what."

Jake watched as communications shut down, the moment of doubt disappearing in a puff of self-delusion. Garrett might by savvy enough to one day reach the pinnacle of the business scene in this town, but he could still be that dip-shit rich kid who wanted everything his way.

Jake thought about Mac, how she'd reacted last night when he'd suggested her father might be in it with Clarke. He sighed, thinking how people could fool themselves.

"Stacie's going to be fine over there," Garrett repeated, squelching any lingering doubts. "It'll be like three months at Club Med."

Club Med. Jake remembered those questions on the application. *Have you ever undergone general anesthesia?*

Suddenly, that self-assured tone of Garrett's got to Jake. He grabbed the man's jacket, anger pumping through him as he crushed the silk in his fist. "Just be sure of that, Garrett," he said, standing close. "Be very sure."

Garrett glanced down at his sleeve. His gaze drifted back up to Jake's. "What the hell do you think you're doing?"

"Just a friendly warning, Garrett. From one friend to another."

"Maybe it's time you get going." The way Garrett said it, he wasn't giving Jake a choice.

Jake stepped back. "Whatever you say." He walked over to Michael. "Hey, sport," he said, bending down to kiss his son goodbye. "See you later, 'gator." To Stacie, he said, "Mindy has a key. She'll be here at five sharp. Michael and I really appreciate this."

"Michael's my pal," Stacie said, smiling at his son. "I would have been disappointed if you hadn't asked."

"If I miss dinner," Jake told Michael, "we'll go for ice cream later, okay?"

"Sure, Daddy," Michael said, finishing up his gargoyle.

Jake stood, thinking about what lay ahead, hating it. But

he'd promised Mac. And it would be better for Gus if Jake got lucky and found something.

But at the door, he looked back at Garrett. "Just remember when the time comes, that I was there for you again. That I warned you." He glanced down at Stacie, who was watching both men cautiously as Michael continued to cut out his monsters. "Take care of them, will you?"

Jake stepped into the hall, walking toward the elevator, still fuming despite his smiles to Garrett and Stacie. "Fucking idiot."

He knew he wasn't just mad at Garrett. He was thinking about Mac and the chances she might take for her father's sake.

He'd bet anything that whatever had driven her to choose Alicia and Harvard, the incident could put a big fat hole through her theory of daddy's unflappable integrity—which was probably why she didn't want to talk about it. Didn't want to look at it too closely.

He thought about that a minute, hoping he was wrong. Because he knew her father's unbending ethics was the only reason Mac could come up with to justify his turning his back on her all those years ago.

He punched the elevator buttons, remembering his thoughts about the isolation experiments, seeing Mac as the little white lab mouse going up and down a maze of her father's making. The years of manipulation.

Jesus. He hoped to hell he was wrong.

Twenty-two

Waiting outside the door to the Fragrance Group lab, McCall was thinking about Jake.

She would get these images through the day. She would see his smile, picture the way his eyes would crinkle in the corners with it. Or how he tended to worry his hands through his hair. His dimples. But mostly, she remembered his question about her father. It was something she'd tried to put out of her mind, but couldn't.

All day, it had crept into her head, disdainful of her attempts to brush it back into some dusty corner of her mind to deal with later. It was a song weaving through her consciousness, its melody inescapable. *Why did you leave for Harvard?* She could picture his face when he'd asked her that last time, the suspicion there, making her suspicious—which was why she didn't want to think about it right now.

But the memories came just the same, flooding her with the images of that day . . . the day she'd called Alicia to tell her she'd decided to attend Harvard University.

She recalled best the incident that had triggered everything, could remember that Curtis Clarke had been there that day, congratulating her father in what had been his lab at the time. Early clinical testing showed her father's new product, the Keratin Dose, was highly successful, rating well with women using the shampoo and conditioner.

Both products contained a modified form of keratin. The basic structure had been chemically modified so that the keratin would better coat the human hair shaft, making the user's hair appear thicker and more manageable. Donald Sayer's discovery was sure to make the Keratin Dose Shampoo and Conditioner one of Clarke Cosmetics most successful hair products ever.

Only, her father hadn't made the discovery. McCall had.

She remembered waiting for her father to turn to her, to involve her in some way, giving her the credit she deserved. But Curtis had left without so much as a mention by her father that she had been part of the product's development.

Afterward, it became clear to McCall that the discovery was no longer hers. It belonged to her father now. It was his alone. And it would always be that way. Every discovery, every breakthrough, would carry her father's name. And she, as his assistant, would have to be content with that.

Only she wasn't. She'd called Alicia that night, telling her that she'd changed her mind about the school she would attend in the fall. She would like very much to work in Dr. Goodman's lab at Harvard and would be informing Tulane of the fact. She hadn't discussed her change of heart with her father or the reasons behind it.

McCall peered across the hall, watching lab techs maneuvering past the bench-tops of the glass-enclosed lab across the way. She was waiting for her father. He was running a little late, but would be with her shortly, able to spare a few minutes if it didn't take long.

It had given her time to think, the waiting. And she was tired enough that the memories took over. She knew she could have handled things differently that day with her father. She was young, too arrogant, believing that she'd been wronged and worried about only the slight to her. She had never stopped to consider her father's motives, how it might look to Curtis if McCall and not Donald was responsible for the Keratin Dose. Her father was the head of the family, recently promoted to direct R and D at Clarke Labs. The financial welfare of the family rode on his shoulders, not McCall's. All that pressure would influence him. And he was, above all, a proud man.

And she could see how he might justify what he'd done. He was her mentor. He had taught her everything she knew. He perceived McCall, his daughter and assistant, as an extension of himself.

But sixteen years ago, she hadn't understood so well.

In true teenage fashion, she'd saved her revelation for the dinner table, announcing dramatically over her mother's lamb chops that she would be leaving for Boston. Her mother had cried, pouring herself another glass of wine. She had thought it was settled, that her darling daughter would stay home. Belinda, too, had wailed miserably, barely four years old at the time. McCall remembered how she'd held Belinda on her lap, quieting her tears with promises of frequent visits—visits that had never materialized after McCall became swamped with work.

But that day, despite everyone's tears, McCall had been happy, full of the adventure of it, feeling gloriously free. And her father had said nothing. He had only eaten his dinner silently.

Down the hall, her father turned the corner, calling to her as he headed toward her. Looking distracted, he buzzed them inside the lab and together they maneuvered past the benchtops toward his office at the back. It seemed odd to see him now, after imagining him as he'd appeared so many years before, his blond hair, without the gray; his eyes, brighter. She followed him, seeing the changes, how he'd aged over the years. Gracefully, yes, his hair still thick, the wrinkles deepening the character to his face—but aging him nonetheless.

Shutting the door behind McCall, Donald Sayer told her to have a seat as he walked around the large oak desk. It surprised her that, despite the new labs, he had kept his old desk.

He looked incredibly tired, dressed in a white dress shirt, slacks, and a lab coat with the Clarke Labs logo over the heart. Watching him, she wished she could somehow turn back the clock, become that teenager again, make wiser, less painful, choices.

But she knew that wasn't possible. So instead, she'd come here first. To McCall, this was a show of faith. She hadn't been that teenager again, letting him believe she'd chosen Alicia's dreams over his—allowing him to imagine his daughter capable of turning her back on the father who had taught her everything he knew . . . an image that fit nicely with that of an overly ambitious woman who altered data to suit her needs.

Today, she'd vowed things would be different. It was up to her to prove her father wasn't part of Roger's schemes. To Kyle. To Jake. But most of all, to herself.

"Thanks for meeting with me, Daddy," she said softly.

"Why don't you just tell me what this is about? I have a great deal to do still and it's quite late."

Quietly, she took out the application for the clinic she'd found last night. She placed it on his desk, believing she was doing the right thing by confronting her father. She'd promised Jake that she wouldn't speak to him until after Jake's visit to the lab today. But she found she couldn't wait after all. She had a sense that it was all coming to a head. She needed to know that, this time, she had taken the time and consideration to tell her father her fears, to let him explain, to bridge that chasm she'd opened so many years ago.

"I printed it out from the computer," she said, nodding at the papers on his desk. "It's for the Clarke Spa and Clinic. Are you familiar with it?"

He frowned, picking up the forms. "Vaguely. The clinic is really Roger's project. It doesn't seem to affect us much here at the labs." He spoke as he scanned through the papers. She could see his surprise as he reached the last few pages.

"Daddy. The Omega Principle. It's a fake."

She had his attention now. His eyes, so much like her own, appeared intensely blue. He put down the forms on his desk and steepled his fingers in front of his mouth. "I know that, McCall."

"I needed a reason for Curtis to accept me here, a carrot big enough to let him overlook the past."

He shook his head, thinking he understood. "McCall, how could you? After everything you've been through—"

"It's not what you think," she said, speaking quickly, getting it over with. "After Alicia died, she left me a diary of sorts. In it, she wrote about experiments she worked on with a man. Only, these experiments . . . there was something off about the research. I think it concerned some sort of beauty product, something highly toxic. It killed most of the test animals. They had only one success. A monkey. But I believe it was enough to spur this man into pursuing the possibility of human trials."

He frowned. "What nonsense is this—"

"I think that man is Roger Clarke. I think he's continued the research, conducting animal tests here. In the Biosafety Level-2 lab. The elevator, Daddy. The one with the swipe lock. Does it lead to an animal testing facility?"

Suddenly, she saw he understood. That he knew. He didn't stop to question how she'd gotten inside the lab or that she was familiar with the elevator and its swipe lock. The comprehension dawning in his eyes was too clear to miss. So was the fear.

"I don't know where the elevator leads." He spoke slowly, as if he was thinking about what she was saying, analyzing the data. "I don't have a card key to the elevator. They never gave me access and I never asked for it."

"Look at that application, Daddy. The questions at the end. That beauty clinic. Do you think it's possible that Roger is using it as a cover for human trials?"

"McCall, what you're suggesting—"

"I know. I know, Daddy. But you understand how simple it would be. The Clarke name gives a sense of legitimacy. Women might be desperate enough to try a little surgery. If it was disguised as a simple procedure, a little more than liposuction. Everyone wanted to believe that the Omega Principle was real. Because it would be so wonderful, to believe that we could make ourselves irresistible with a little dab of perfume. What if Roger promised something just as seductive?"

He kept his eyes carefully on her, seeming to try and understand everything she'd just paraded out for him. He shook his head.

"Daddy," she said, pleading with him now. "I thought you would know the truth. I thought you could help me stop them."

He leaned over his desk, his shoulder falling forward, his forearms pressing down on the edge. He didn't speak for the longest time.

"I've had my suspicions, of course." His voice was barely above a whisper. When he peered up at her, his expression bore the weight of everything he knew. "I would have had to be blind not to know Roger was up to something. There was even the smell of them sometimes, the animals"—he shook his head again—"lingering in the air when I walked past the elevator. But I didn't want to know. God help me, I didn't want it to be true. So I didn't ask." His eyes remained carefully on McCall. "Can you understand that?"

"Yes."

He looked away. "I was going to retire next year. Half of my savings is invested in this company."

"Daddy. I understand."

She stood and walked to her father's side of the desk. She dropped to her knees in front of him. She put her head on his lap, as she used to do all those years before she left him. "I understand."

Her father's hands hovered over her hair, and then he lay both carefully on her head, stroking her hair.

"I think Roger is behind something awful, Daddy," she whispered. "I'm afraid for you. That if anything goes wrong, they'll make it look like you're to blame."

"Yes, of course they will. That's what they would do." He

lifted her face up to his. "What they did to you. Only, I chose to believe you were the culprit. Because I was so very mad about Alicia."

"Daddy," she whispered. "Do you believe me?"

"I don't . . . yes. Yes, what you're saying. The elevator . . . the clinic. There have been indications for some time, the fact that they wouldn't give me access to the elevator. The Biosafety Level-2 lab, which I questioned from the first. And other things I won't go into right now. Roger Clarke has always been a fool. Capable of anything. But these forms." He pulled her up by her shoulders. "I swear to you, I have never seen these forms. I would have questioned them. And yes, what you suspect. It could be true."

She could see he was telling her the truth, just as Jake had taught her. His pupils remained the same, showing he had nothing to hide. "I'm glad you're not involved," she said, realizing for the first time that she'd had her doubts.

He shook his head. "You came back because of me? To help me?"

"When I left for Harvard, I never told you why," she said. "I never explained how I felt. I've always thought that's why you believed those awful things about me. I should have told you why I left for Boston."

"Don't," he said, giving her a shake. "Don't say anything about that now. I don't want to talk about that. Oh, God." He jumped to his feet. "Oh, dear God."

He pulled her to stand before him, his eyes wide with fear. "McCall, what have I done." His fingers dug into her shoulders painfully. "I've just put you in grave danger."

He turned from her and picked up the application for the clinic, reading it again, thinking.

"What is it, Daddy?"

He shook his head. And then he sat down in his chair, scrubbing his face with his hands. "I know about the PET scan, McCall. I spoke with each of the volunteers you sent here. It wasn't difficult to get a few to admit what you'd done."

He looked up at her. "I had them write it all down. How you conditioned their responses. I gave Roger those results today."

Her heart belted against her chest. She'd known there was something wrong. She'd sensed it. Roger had been so accommodating, agreeing that today would be a good time to ask Jake back for a tour.

"McCall, you must listen very carefully. I think you and Dr. Woods are in grave danger. You must leave here and never come back." Her father stood again. He hugged her, holding her with affection for the first time in over a decade. "We'll go away together. We'll take your sister. She doesn't love Roger. I don't think she ever did. We'll go somewhere safe. Someplace where the Clarkes can't hurt us."

"It will be all right," she said, trying to put him at ease. "There's an investigation." She felt safe enough to let him know that much. And so happy. Incredibly happy to have her family back again. "If the Clarke Spa and Clinic really is a cover for illegal human trials, Curtis won't be able to hide everything. Something will come out during the investigation."

"Perhaps I can help," he said. "Who are you working with?"

But for some reason, she hesitated. Even to her father, she didn't want to reveal Jake's involvement. "I don't know exactly. I've worked through an intermediary. But don't worry. It's all under control."

"All right. But promise me you'll leave today. That you won't come back here, no matter how safe you might think you are. Do you promise?"

"All right, Daddy," she said, holding her father. "All right."

"And there you have it," Roger said as Jake stepped out of Mac's lab, joining him in the hall. Mac followed close behind. "The makings for the most successful women's cosmetic ever. The Omega Principle will make a woman irresistible." Roger turned to Mac. "And it has the potential to bring millions annually to Clarke Cosmetics. Dr. Sayer is making certain we'll hit the stores in time for Christmas."

"Yes," Mac said, digging her hand into the pocket of her lab coat. "Perhaps as early as the fall."

Jake nodded, giving Roger a thoughtful look. So far, things had gone pretty much as he'd anticipated. Roger had called him at the *River Palace,* telling him that Mac had relented on the tour and did he have time to come by? Jake arrived early enough for Roger to take him around to a few of the other buildings. On Jake's request, he'd produced a few marketing strategies that Jake thought looked pretty impressive. If the Omega Principle worked.

But there was something different about Roger today. He was still that too-perfect pretty boy with the *GQ* clothes and attitude but the energy had changed. He wasn't so focused on giving his sales pitch to Jake. His gaze and smiles targeted Mac. And not in a good way.

"Garrett was telling me about a beauty clinic you're starting," Jake said, getting on with it, chalking up the bad vibes to nerves. He spoke as if off the cuff, but every word was carefully orchestrated. He and Mac had talked it over that morning, how after the tour, they would stand outside the lab, near the Biosafety Level-2 facility. Jake would bring up the clinic.

He turned to Mac, following the dialogue they'd come up with for Roger's benefit. "How about it, Doc? Will the Omega Principle be a part of that?"

Mac looked at Roger, her face showing perfect surprise. *Atta girl,* Jake thought. Give the woman the Oscar. "I'm afraid I don't know anything about a beauty clinic."

Roger grinned, still watching her with those cold gray eyes. But Mac gave as good as she got, bringing her chin up, her gaze just as hard as she waited for his response.

Jake got that feeling again. Something wasn't quite right here. Something he was missing.

"Actually. It's a pet project of mine," Roger said. "I play it pretty close to the vest with the clinic. It's not a part of Clarke Labs, per se. So far, I've only approached investors we've dealt with in the past about that particular opportunity. We want to keep it low key for now."

"Really?" Jake said, doing his best to look unhappy about getting cut out of a lucrative business deal. "Garrett said you're working on something that's going to put alpha-hydroxy and DHEA out of business."

Roger laughed. "I hope I didn't put that in writing. Jesus, that's asking a lot . . . but I think we have a few promising products for the clinic. But right now, we're focusing our efforts on the Omega Principle. That's the real money-maker here."

"Well. Like I said. We're interested." Jake took out his sunglasses and put them on. "And send me the stuff on the beauty clinic. I think the men I represent would want to know about *any* future investment possibilities here."

He turned, as if getting ready to leave, then pivoted back, staring straight at the door of the Biosafety Level-2 lab. He whistled as if impressed, lowering the sunglasses. He took a few steps closer to the vault-like door. "Where does that lead?"

"It's a high-security facility. Something we're quite proud of really," Roger said. He glanced at his watch. "Would you like a tour?"

Jake didn't even look at Mac. They had talked about what would happen at this point, when Jake would ask to go inside the Biosafety Level-2 lab. They'd worked out an entire routine on how they would gently pressure Roger into letting Jake inside, maybe even bringing Mac along, if they could manage it.

But in all the different scenarios they'd come up with, they had never anticipated Roger agreeing to show them Lab 20 from the get go.

Jake kept a smile on his face, not letting his expression

show his hesitation. But he didn't like it. The tension between Mac and Roger. Roger being so agreeable.

Following his instincts, he looked at the watch Susan had lent him. He shook his head. "Maybe some other time. I thought I'd be out of here by now. But the doc, she had me mesmerized with all that stuff about genes and gels."

"But you're here now," Roger said, smiling. "And we have a window of opportunity. The facility closed down for the day so we won't be disturbing anyone if we have a look around." Roger took a few steps toward the lab, making it clear they should follow. "As a matter of fact, I was about to ask Dr. Sayer if she wanted to see the lab. She's been here over a week and I haven't had an opportunity to take her in. You shouldn't miss this, Jonathan, really. It will take fifteen minutes, tops."

Jake stopped himself from glancing at Mac. But he knew her. She wanted this bad . . . enough to take chances. If he left now, she might go inside that lab without him. "Lead the way," he said, seeing no option but to follow Roger.

But it felt off, stepping up behind Roger. It was like walking into a James Bond film—only the villain was leading the good guys into a trap and the audience was holding their collective breath, thinking: *Don't do it, man. Don't go in!*

Jake stood before the vault-like door, his heart pumping hard in his chest, thinking about Mac standing beside him as Roger swiped his card through the lock. The problem was, Jake couldn't be sure it wouldn't be more dangerous to cut and run now. So he watched as Roger finished entering the code, triggering the locking mechanism, a combination cipher and swipe that was as high tech as they came.

The door opened with a soft *whoosh.* They stepped inside, entering a sort of antechamber. The movie changed from James Bond to *Outbreak.* Any sound was muffled, giving a surreal feel to the room. Roger gestured to the scrubs piled on top of two tables.

"Just put the doctor greens on over your clothes," he said,

tossing a set at Jake. "There's no danger, really." He shrugged. "But I'm a bit of a stickler for the rules."

Jake took off his jacket and donned the protective gear, including a hair net, mask, and gloves. The suit he wore was a remnant of his prosecutor days. He'd kept it for the occasional meeting with the high rollers at the casino. Thankfully, the clothes had passed muster with Dino. He hadn't looked forward to sinking another small fortune into a second leprechaun outfit.

Beside him, Mac took off her lab coat, showing a sort of baby doll dress that just skimmed the tops of her knees. She wore her hair real wavy and loose. It still amazed him, how she managed to look so different every time he saw her. Out of the corner of his eye, he watched her put on the scrubs, uncharacteristically quiet. But then, he figured she was probably just as antsy about this tour as he was.

"After you, Doc," Jake said, motioning her to follow Roger's lead.

Outside the antechamber, he and Mac trailed behind Roger as he waved to the guard and signed them in. Roger launched into his pitch about the high-tech focus of the research facility in Lab 20, introducing Jake and McCall to anyone who happened by.

"So what exactly goes on in here?" Jake asked, taking in the polished stainless steel equipment as they toured one of the four empty labs that fed into the hall. Here, the doors were labeled with letters. Lab 20a, Lab 20b, and so on.

"We're preparing for the future," Roger said. "It's a very special microbiology lab. Hell, if they can genetically engineer a tomato to give it a longer shelf life or make a strawberry frost resistant, someday soon, genetics will play a big role in cosmetics. At Clarke Labs, we want to be prepared."

Mac was walking around the room, touching some of the equipment. She stopped in front of a machine the size of an industrial cappuccino machine. Little brown bottles were suspended from the front, the letters AGCT AGCU written on pieces of tape above the bottles.

"A DNA/RNA synthesizer," Mac said, naming the machine. She turned to another device. Made out of metal, it looked like a supersonic syringe with knobs and a needle.

"It's almost as if you were working on some sort of gene therapy," McCall said.

Jake could tell from the way Roger's mask moved that he was smiling. "Like I said, we want to be prepared for the future." He turned. "Right this way," he told them, leading them into the next lab.

As they toured the facilities, Mac asked more questions, looking around carefully. Jake knew what she was searching for, something to prove there were ongoing animal tests or, if they were lucky, the embryos themselves.

He fingered the watch he wore on his left wrist. He didn't like how it was going with Roger. Though he couldn't make out the guy's expression behind the mask, he could tell Roger was enjoying Mac's questions, almost egging her on. Mac's reaction was to turn up the heat. She was barking questions like a drill sergeant.

As they continued on to the next lab, the two scientists walked ahead. Jake seemed almost superfluous, Roger and Mac were so focused on each other, rarely coming up for air to bring Jake into the discussion. It made him nervous . . . made him wonder if the situation didn't call for a timely exit.

He was just thinking about how to accomplish that when they stepped inside the third lab. Instantly, he sensed a change in Mac. And he knew what it meant.

The machine gleamed of steel and was shaped like a giant milk can. There was a tank strapped to the wall behind it. "Liquid nitrogen," Mac said, her hand on the tank. "Is this some sort of cryotank?" she asked Roger, walking around the steel tub the size of a small washing machine. Jake stepped back to get a good angle, guessing what a cryotank might have inside.

"Our newest addition." Again, that smile from Roger beneath the mask. "Specially designed for us."

"What's it for?" she asked.

"Embryos," he said. "Frozen embryos."

Jake felt the adrenaline rush through him. He snapped a couple of photographs, using the watch like Susan had taught him. But he knew this was too easy. Sure, Jake—a man who wouldn't know the implications of this equipment beyond the dollar signs Roger flashed in front of him—might be okay to show around. But letting Mac see it without any prompting from Jake, the investor? It didn't make sense.

"I've been doing some work," Roger said, coming up alongside Mac. "I told myself, we use the placenta, why not try to be creative?" He turned to Jake, bringing him in on it. "Embryonic cells are genetically naive. That means, they can become any kind of tissue, a neuron, a liver cell, a skin cell, making it the perfect medium for gene therapy." He laughed. "Though this is all blue sky right now, so I better keep my mouth shut. As it is, I seem to be promising too much these days if Garrett believes I'm working on something that's going to replace alpha-hydroxy."

"May I?" Mac asked, her hand on the cover at the top.

Jake held his hands loosely crossed at the wrist in front of him. Pointing the lens of the camera constructed to look like a wristwatch, he continued to take the photographs.

"Of course," Roger said. "If you're that curious."

Mac twisted the handle at the top and pulled. The round hood lifted like a spaceship, gliding upward. Condensation billowed over the lip of the tank in clouds of thick fog, making Jake think of a boiling cauldron. Six round canisters were attached to the center column coming up from the hood. Each showed individual slots perfect for test tubes.

Of course, the tank was empty.

"As you can see, we don't have any embryos at the moment," Roger said. "Actually, they're quite difficult to get, unless you're affiliated with a hospital. It was an expensive piece of equipment; I shouldn't have indulged myself. But sometimes, you just have to follow your gut. And I believe gene therapy could be very useful to the future of Clarke Labs."

"How?" Mac asked, too focused on Roger, reminding Jake of the way she played at the tables, calculating her odds, taking risks. "You can't possibly compete with pharmaceutical companies."

"That's right," Roger answered. "But I told you. I have a few theories." He stepped to the cryotank and pushed the top down. The hood floated back home, cutting off the smoke of condensation rolling down the sides of the steel tank. When he turned the handle, it snapped into place with a click.

It was a game, Jake thought. Roger had brought them here—lured them to the lab—dangling the bait. But the joke was on them. There was nothing here, no evidence to send to Gus at the Attorney General's office . . . only photographs of an empty tank. And he didn't like it, the fact that Roger was playing games.

As they stepped back into the hall, Jake knew it was time to get Mac out of here. He sensed that he wasn't involved in Roger's little show. Mac seemed to be the target, which was bad, telling him it was time to steer things in a different direction.

Stepping up alongside Roger, Jake asked a few questions, keeping things light. *How about that new Diablo? He was looking to trade up himself.* But he kept remembering Roger's eyes when Mac had popped the lid on the tank. Oh, yeah. The guy had gotten off on showing her the empty canisters.

Which meant, he was on to her.

"Where does that lead?"

Jake stopped dead next to Roger. *Shit!* It was McCall talking from behind them. Jake had purposely cut her off, making her lag behind while he steered Roger toward the exit, wanting to get them out of here.

But he hadn't anticipated Mac's reaction—and he should

have. He could have guessed she might try to go for the brass ring, not wanting to leave empty-handed.

"The elevator," she said, pointing behind her as the two men turned to face her. "Can we take it down?"

Jesus. Jake was the one who was supposed to ask those kind of questions. That's how they'd decided to play it. He tried to catch her eye, tried to get her to understand.

"It's just another exit," Roger said. "There is a storage area below. You need a special key to get in, for security reasons. Though we don't exactly make it difficult from inside the lab." He walked back into one of the rooms, looked around, then opened a couple of drawers. "There's probably one here somewhere. Ah. Here it is."

Like a magician, Roger lifted the card key from the drawer. As Jake watched, Mac stepped forward, ready to take it.

"Hey guys," Jake said, getting their attention, having had enough of Mac's game of mental chicken. He knew she couldn't win here. "I hate to cut this short, but I've got to run." He hitched his thumb over his shoulder, looking back. "The exit's thattaway, right?"

"Right," Roger said, returning the card to the drawer. He stepped back out to the corridor, stopping right in front of Mac, watching her in a way that made Jake nervous. "After you," he told her, gesturing down the hall.

"So when did you say the Omega Principle will hit the market?" Jake asked, immediately stepping up to Roger, letting him know through his tone and body language that he'd felt cut out.

Roger caught on real quick, focusing on the customer now. The two men trailed behind McCall. "We're estimating clinical trials in two months. By then, we expect a viable product."

"What about the FDA? I know they're looking real hard at some of these love potion products."

"Not an issue. We're careful about what we promise. But if in the future they become interested, given what we think our clinical tests will show, we can deliver. And there may be

ways around the FDA," Roger said, following Jake's example
and keeping Mac out of the conversation.

They stepped into the antechamber leading back out. Jake
took off his mask and gloves and dumped them into the same
trash bin as Roger.

"So what do you think?" Roger asked him.

"Why don't I get back to you?"

"I wouldn't wait too long," Roger said, adding the typical
sales pressure. "Understand, you're getting special treatment
because you're Garrett's friend. But I can only keep this thing
under wraps for so long. And it will be the first investors
who benefit most."

"Trust me," Jake said, giving a wink to Roger and Mac
both. "I'm a man who makes his mind up quickly."

Sierra woke up in the cold cage.

At first, the retriever didn't know why she had awakened.
But then she heard the noise again, distinguishing it from the
hum of equipment and other dogs moving in their cages. It
was a thrashing sound. And it was coming from the cage next
to hers.

The German shepherd was sprawled out on the floor of the
cage, his tongue hanging from his mouth, his legs twitching.
He emitted a low growling sound deep in his throat.

Sierra began barking, louder and louder. All the dogs in
the lab joined in, the sound becoming deafening.

The German shepherd tried to stand. But the dog collapsed,
panting, trying to catch his breath. A foaming mucus dripped
from his mouth. And then nothing. No sound, no breath.

A man rushed into the room. "Dammit," he said. He called
back into the hall. "Deb. Get in here. We lost the shepherd."

A woman ran in. "Shit. This is worse than ever. Help me
get him out of here."

After they left the room, Sierra raised her head and howled.

Twenty-three

Be beautiful and be sad . . . all beauty comes from beautiful blood . . . beauty is vain . . . beauty is only skin deep.

—Scribbles found in the margins of
Dr. Alicia Goodman's lab book

"The embryos are there, Jake," McCall argued. "Why else would that cryotank be filled with liquid nitrogen? You don't have a tank like that sitting around prepared, just in case you might start some research someday."

They were seated around Kyle's kitchen table, having agreed to meet at his house after the tour of the Level-2 lab. Kyle had been waiting impatiently, eager to know what they'd found. He hadn't been happy to hear the results.

"Look," Jake said, "I don't know what's going on. But my best guess is that Roger just put on one hell of a show. If the embryos are in that lab, he wasn't going to parade them out for us to snap a couple of pictures with him standing there saying 'Cheese.' Now I don't know who he's on to—you, me, or both. But he knows something." Jake shook his head, raking his fingers through his hair. "I think it's time to hand this over to Gus and the FBI."

But Kyle jumped to his feet. "What good would that do us? If Roger suspects anything, we need to move tonight or those animals will be gone. I don't give a shit about stolen embryos that were scheduled to be destroyed. Clarke Cosmetics advertises HUMANITY FIRST—NO ANIMAL TESTING. I want them nailed. I need to get in there. Tonight. I need photographs of the animal testing facility."

"Gus can move faster than you think. All he needs is a warrant," Jake said. "I have photographs of a cryotank I was told would hold frozen embryos. Combine that with your knowledge that they delivered a truck full of dogs, and those forms from the clinic Mac printed out. Yeah," he said, nodding. "There could be probable cause. But I think you're right. We need to move fast, or Gus is going to find the place empty."

Kyle dropped down into his chair. He folded his hands together and leaned his forehead against them, shaking his head. "A year's worth of work and it could come to nothing."

"We don't know that," Jake told him. But he sounded subdued.

McCall sat very still in her chair. She knew exactly why Roger had acted so strangely in the lab. And it had nothing to do with Jake or Kyle's quest.

Only, if she told Jake—if she let him know she'd spoken to her father—she could guess what his reaction would be . . . because she would feel the same. Betrayed. She'd acted on her own; she hadn't trusted him to handle it. It would be that same gut-wrenching pain she'd experienced when she'd heard Susan's message playing on his answering machine.

And still . . .

She stared at the two men seated at the kitchen table. They looked so defeated. Kyle huddled over the table, seeing his dreams of victory against the Clarkes fading fast. Jake stared across the room, his gaze intensely focused, thinking of the night ahead.

She knew then she'd waited too long, keeping her secrets. It was time to act, irrespective of how it might affect her relationship with Jake.

"Roger knows the Omega Principle is a fraud," she said quietly.

Both men turned, their attention on McCall now. Kyle in particular appeared startled by what she'd said.

"I can't believe that," he said. "Today. At the meeting with your father. McCall, I could swear he knew nothing."

"My father told Roger I fixed the PET scan, Kyle. He probably told him after you left Curtis's office." She looked at Jake. "It's me Roger suspects. Not you, not Kyle. He wouldn't know about the investigation. He's only worried about the Omega Principle. There's no need to act prematurely."

"Back up," Jake said, standing, taking a chair closer to McCall. "PET scan?"

"Positron emission tomography," Kyle said. "You inject test subjects with a radioactive liquid and put them in a machine that helps us map the brain. The first week McCall came to work at the labs, I ran PET scans on ten male volunteers at a small clinic we use. Each man wore a mask with drops of the Omega Principle peptide on the cloth. The data showed that, while they were exposed to the peptide, they exhibited a strong response in the nerve centers associated with sexual desire."

"Roger needed proof that the peptide for the Omega Principle would work," McCall said. "So I conditioned a sexual response to the smell of vanilla in the volunteers. Using my blackjack money, I paid several men to watch pornographic movies while smelling the scent of vanilla for one year. When we ran the PET scans, I made sure vanilla was mixed in with the peptide. Later, I doctored Clarke's computer files so that my conditioned volunteers would be the ten men tested."

"What I don't understand is how your father figured it out?" Kyle asked, looking mystified. "You fooled me . . . you fooled Roger."

"He tracked down the test subjects. Maybe he paid them, I don't know. But at least more than one confessed. He gave their statements to Roger."

Kyle nodded, understanding now. But Jake. His lovely

brown eyes centered on McCall. He had this fierce expression, the prosecutor putting the evidence together in his head.

"And you know all of this because?" Jake prompted.

But she could see that he already knew. "Because I spoke to my father today. And he told me himself."

She waited for his reaction. Jake understood clearly what she was confessing. This wasn't just any talk. It was *the* talk. The talk she'd promised she would hold off until after she had spoken to Jake.

She saw the disappointment . . . and the understanding. That was the part that hurt the most. That he could be understanding.

He reached out and took her hands in his. "You shouldn't have trusted him, baby."

"Jake. He's my father."

"He sold you out."

"He thought I was cheating. He didn't understand the danger."

"The hell he didn't."

The vehemence in his voice startled her. But then Jake hadn't been there today. He hadn't seen her father's reaction when he'd realized what he'd done. "You didn't see him, Jake. He was frightened for me."

"Then it's just McCall that Roger suspects," Kyle said, interrupting. "There's no need to change our plans."

But Jake shook his head. "I still don't like it. Look, we have the photographs of the equipment. Let Gus handle it."

"No," Kyle argued. "It's not the same. Let me go in and finish what I started. The danger is to McCall only—the acid spill, Roger. She was always the target. There's no danger to me. If there were, I never would have gotten out of that meeting today with Roger and Curtis. Use me. They can't possibly know I'm involved."

Jake seemed to think about that. And then he nodded. "Okay. Maybe." He stood. He walked to where Kyle kept his telephone. There was a pad of paper there for messages. Jake wrote something down, then ripped off the top sheet.

"I have to go home and check on Michael, maybe take him and Mindy over to Hope's house. Just in case. I'll call Gus from the hotel. He's going to want to meet with us." He turned to Kyle. "You'll be working with the authorities now, no longer a private citizen, so the rules will be different if you want the evidence to hold up for trial. He'll probably want you to wear a wire. Here's my beeper number," Jake said, handing the piece of paper to Kyle. "If you need me, punch in the number and add 911." He turned to McCall. "Mac, you come with me."

McCall frowned. Something Kyle had said struck a chord inside her. But she couldn't figure out what was bothering her.

"Mac?"

She shook her head, still thinking. "I need to go home and warn Barb. I don't think she and Michael are in danger, but I think you're right. We should at least take some precautions."

"All right. But don't take long. Pack whatever you need and come to my hotel suite. I don't want you alone for too long. I'll leave instructions at the front desk to let you in, in case I'm still out with Gus." Jake crouched down in front of her. "I just want one promise from you. You're going to stay the hell away from Roger, do you understand? Your butt stays out of that lab until I get back to you and Kyle with what Gus says." And when he saw he didn't have her full attention, he steered her face up to his. "No more fudging on this. You stay put. Okay?"

"Yes," she said, her voice sounding too breathy. "Yes, you're right."

McCall watched Jake leave. She caught herself breathing too fast. She tried to calm down. Because she'd just figured it out. What Kyle had said. What it might mean.

She heard the door close. She stood, needing to leave. To do something. Anything.

She grabbed her purse from the table. She could feel her stomach twisting into knots.

"Are you leaving?"

She looked distractedly at Kyle. She realized he'd asked a question. That he would expect her to answer. "Yes. I have to leave. To go see Barb."

"Call me when you get to the hotel." Kyle stood. He walked her to the door. But at the door, he hesitated, shaking his head. "What I don't understand is the dogs. Why dogs? If you're testing a beauty formula that uses gene therapy, the experiments would run through mice to monkeys, mammals more in line with the human immune system."

"Yes," she said. "It's curious. Maybe we'll find out more later."

"Remember to call me as soon as you get to the hotel."

"Of course."

McCall waited until he shut the door behind her. She couldn't seem to take a full breath. The muscles in her chest wouldn't expand right and the air just stayed trapped in her lungs. It hurt every time she breathed.

She walked down the steps. She dug through her bag for her keys, but her hands felt numb. She couldn't keep a grip on anything. She thought about what she'd read in Alicia's lab book.

The man Alicia had written about was a confusing and sensual figure. A man who would gamble with human lives and hide mistakes to forward his own ends. He had no scruples. No conscience.

That wasn't her father. It couldn't be.

But she remembered what Kyle had said.

Use me. They can't possibly know I'm involved.

Jake stood outside Kyle's double, waiting next to Dickey's Lamborghini. He watched Mac step outside. She walked down the stairs, searching for something in her bag. Her keys, probably. She looked really upset, even more upset than when he'd left.

Which was why he was standing here, like an idiot, waiting. Waiting for her to trust him.

Right then, she glanced up, catching him staring at her. She slowed down, like maybe she was thinking about something real hard. She pulled her keys out of her bag, still walking toward the street.

Come on, Mac. Trust me.

She lifted her hand and waved. He gave her a short salute, making like he was getting into the car, watching her . . . watching her walk away toward her Lexus.

He stared at her back, seeing that she was leaving, that she wasn't going to trust him, after all. What he felt was more than disappointment . . . it was as if someone had just ripped a chunk out of his heart.

All his life, he'd tried to give one hundred percent. But this time, he wanted just as much back. He'd wanted the whole enchilada. The till-death-do-us-part stuff. He hadn't wanted to strike out again.

He'd known right away something was wrong. During Kyle's little speech, Mac had frozen up, acting as if she were in this trance of concentration. But Jake had wanted it to be different between them. No more secret talks with her father . . . no more going behind his back. He'd wanted her to come to him, to tell him.

And now, he was staring at her back as she walked away.

Maybe he was being too hard on her. It was her father. But he hated it, that she was still that little white lab mouse, letting her father manipulate her. That she would still put his sorry-ass first. The Donovan boys needed her. But they needed all of her. Not just some of the pieces.

Still, he couldn't seem to help himself. He kept his eyes on her, almost willing her to turn around. *Trust me, Mac. Trust me.* Because for once in his life, he wanted to be right about a woman. He'd wanted to beat the Donovan Curse. *Trust me!*

Incredibly, she stopped. She turned around.

She was looking at him . . . and then she was walking toward him. Fast. Faster. Running now.

He met her halfway, both of them stopping in the middle of the empty street. She looked up at him, and it was all there. Her fear, her pain, and her trust.

"My father," she said. "Jake, it's my father."

He took her into his arms, holding her. "I know, baby. I know."

Curtis blew a smoke ring. He watched it flutter toward the ceiling, dissipating into a formless cloud as it rose. "Well, Donald tried to warn us. Actually, I'm glad she's a fake. I never did trust that she was on the up and up. It didn't fit."

"We were set for clinical trials in October." Roger was seated in the leather chair in front of Curtis. He had his feet propped on the desk, which bugged the shit out of Curtis. But he let it go. Because he knew how this thing with McCall had affected Roger.

His boy was staring into the distance, occasionally talking to himself. Now he shook his head. "I've worked years—a lifetime—for something like the Omega Principle."

Curtis sighed. "Forget the damn love potion. The problem is, how much does the girl know? Is she here for money? Revenge? Or did she come back because of the clinic and Alicia?"

Roger looked at his father, his eyes focusing again, not looking so distracted. "As a matter of fact, I'm conducting a little experiment to find out. I've set a trap. One I don't think McCall can resist, not if she suspects anything about BioYouth."

Curtis puffed on the Romeo y Julieta cigar, waiting. His boy did like his experiments.

But instead of elaborating, Roger dropped his feet to the floor. "I've been thinking about going forward with the Omega Principle." He stood and paced, changing gears, winding up to try and dig himself out of the great big hole where he'd dumped Clarke Labs. Not Curtis. He was thinking about the Caymans, wondering if it weren't time for a fast retreat with his boy. But he figured he'd broach the subject later, when Roger calmed down a bit.

"The formula will have enough science behind it to make people want to believe it will work," Roger said, still pacing. "And a good marketing campaign will go a long way to making it profitable. Of course, it can't make anywhere near the money I was hoping."

"As long as she's not on to us about Alicia and BioYouth," Curtis said, biting down on the cigar. "So how does this little experiment of yours work?" he asked, prompting Roger when he saw the boy was going to skip over the good stuff.

Roger smiled again. It made Curtis shiver a little, that smile. Made him picture Roger with that dog, thinking that his boy wasn't right in the head.

I gave McCall a tour of the Level-2 lab today. I showed her our cryotank and where she could find a card key for the elevator. The tank, of course, was empty. I kept the embryos Sonia delivered in the animal labs. But McCall is a resourceful girl. Given the right incentive, I think she'll find a way into the Level-2 lab."

"And if she goes back, looking for that card key?" Curtis asked.

"As the saying goes, Daddy. Curiosity killed the cat." Roger sat down and stacked his feet on Curtis's desk once again. "Now what are we going to do about Donald? He's not going along with anything that puts his genius offspring in jeopardy. And though I hate to admit it, we need his cooperation."

"I wouldn't be so sure about Donald cutting out on us if we get rid of McCall," Curtis said.

He turned toward the television set built into the cabinetry behind him. Taking up the remote control, he pushed a button. "I had security deliver this to me after our meeting. I got a little curious. If you weren't behind that acid spill, maybe somebody else was."

Both men watched the screen. It showed a man fidgeting with the security lock to McCall's lab. Soon thereafter, the lab went dark and the same man stepped in and out of the lab, again hovering over the lock. He turned and walked off.

Curtis pressed the controls, working them until the picture rewound, then froze on a single frame.

Donald Sayer.

"To answer your question, boy—daughter or not, I do believe Donald means business."

McCall took her sister's hands in hers. "Belinda, I know everything I'm telling you is difficult to believe. But Daddy could be in real trouble. Please. Help me."

Belinda stared at her sister. She had said such awful things, that Daddy was involved in strange experiments. Experiments that could be dangerous . . . maybe even deadly.

"I think he's acting under some sort of duress," McCall said, trying to persuade her. "Do you understand? Maybe there's something that Curtis is threatening—maybe even you or me? Please, Belinda. I think if I know what's going on, it will be better for Daddy."

"Is Kyle involved?" Belinda asked.

"He's helping me. But he doesn't know I'm going back tonight. I didn't want him to take the risk of going there, and Jake will be with me. Once I know the truth, how much Daddy is involved and why, I'll know what to do. What's right."

Jake. That was the man McCall had said was waiting outside, the one with the connections at the Attorney General's office. McCall had explained there was an investigation. That maybe Daddy could be in trouble because of Curtis. McCall said she had talked this Jake into letting her confront Daddy first. That if Daddy had done something wrong, she wanted to give him the chance to turn himself in—that things would go better for him if he did.

Only, Belinda kept thinking about what her father had told her in the cafeteria earlier. Danger? Wasn't McCall the danger?

"And you need my card key?"

"To get into Daddy's lab. I think I can find my answers there."

Belinda nodded. McCall said she was working with the authorities. Belinda should help her. She stood, feeling like a doll. An automaton. She reached for her purse. She took out her badge. Stared at it. "Will this hurt Daddy?"

McCall came up behind her. She turned Belinda around. "I don't know, Belinda. I just don't know. But I have to find out the truth."

Belinda handed her the card. "I don't think we should do anything to hurt Daddy."

Her sister took the card from her. She nodded. "I promise you . . . I'll do what I can to help him. I'll call you when I know for sure."

Belinda watched McCall leave. She sat down, feeling numb inside and very cold. She shut her eyes. She tried to hear music in her head, to picture herself dancing, but she couldn't. Instead, she heard her father warning her. *Her research is doomed. When it all falls apart, she'll be looking for someone to blame.*

It could all be a lie, McCall's story about the investigation. What if this was all about the Omega Principle, that it didn't work? What if McCall and not their father was the one in trouble?

And Kyle. McCall had told Belinda she'd just come from Kyle's house. Belinda remembered how they had huddled together in the cafeteria. How Kyle hadn't even said goodbye to Belinda because he was so engrossed in what McCall was saying. He trusted McCall. She could use that against him.

Not Kyle. Please not Kyle.

Tears fell down her cheek silently. With her hand shaking, Belinda picked up the phone. She dialed.

"Daddy? It's Belinda. I think McCall is up to something."

Twenty-four

"I remember when I was nine years old," McCall told Jake. "I learned to watch my father very closely."

She and Jake were in the Fragrance lab, inside her father's office. Jake had called his old boss at the Attorney General's office—they were set to meet later tonight. But first, he'd come here with McCall, letting her search for her truths.

She was seated behind her father's chair, staring down at the safe built into his old desk. "I was always very observant as a child. But after the incident with my first transformation, when I forgot to do the controls, I became more so. He was so angry with me that day," she said, remembering, "making me repeat the experiment."

"Your nightmare," Jake said gently, standing in front of the desk. "The dream about the bacteria attacking you."

She nodded. "After that, I listened and watched him so carefully, walking around his lab, virtually unnoticed. I would pretend I was invisible, taking it all in. I even remembered the day I began to criticize him in my head, second-guessing his decisions, making my own." She pressed her hands into fists, then opened them again. "Planning for the day it would be my lab."

She stared down at the combination lock to the safe. It was a small safe, built into the desk where normally there would be a drawer. From memory she dialed the numbers she'd watched her father use over and over through the years. The locking mechanism snapped into place with a soft *click*.

"I was always good remembering numbers," she said softly.

She opened the door and stared down at the card key inside, the one that would open the elevator in the Biosafety Level-2 lab—the card key her father had told her Roger had never given him. She lifted the card key, giving Jake a small, painful smile. "It's the key to the elevator."

"I'm sorry, Mac."

Feeling numb, she reached inside the small safe again, searching with her fingers for the top. She found the piece of paper taped there and stripped it from its hiding place. There was a series of random numbers and letters written in her father's hand.

"All those years, watching him." She could feel tears filling her eyes, blurring the numbers and letters on the paper. "I learned his habits . . . was as familiar with them as if they were my own."

She looked at the paper again. She felt frozen up inside, too numb to hate him. She should hate him.

"What is it?" he asked gently.

"It's a password." She took a deep breath. "And I think I know what it's protecting."

She turned to her father's computer terminal and brought up the file she'd tried to hack into the night before. When the computer asked for the password, she typed in the random numbers and letters her father had printed on the slip of paper and pressed ENTER. The file came up.

She stared at the screen, reading, scrolling. She thought she was prepared for anything. But not for this. God. Never for this.

She shook her head. She couldn't look away. She wanted to look away. She realized then she did hate him.

"Are you okay, baby?" Jake asked, wanting to help. To make it better. But this was something he couldn't fix for her.

"It's all based on my work," she told him. "From four years ago. He stole my data. And he used it to hurt people."

Jake closed his eyes. She could see all the pain she felt on his face. And it hurt. It hurt so very much.

She looked back at the computer, seeing that it was all there, the answers she'd come to find. Four years ago, McCall had injected genetically engineered brain cells into the ventricles of mice, trying to make these new cells act like stem cells—cells that would regenerate themselves in the brain. She'd been working to save lives . . . but her father and Alicia had taken it one step further. With disastrous results.

"I can still hear his voice from all those years ago," she said, her own barely above a whisper, "when I spooled my threads of DNA. He said, 'If we could learn its secrets, McCall . . . perhaps we could live forever.' "

He thought he could make them live forever.

The genetically engineered cells McCall had injected into mice were meant to eventually function as normal brain cells. Once injected, the stemlike cells would differentiate and become neurons or other brain cells, depending on where in the brain they settled. After differentiating, the cells ceased dividing—just as normal brain cells would.

Working with Alicia, her father had devised a way to engineer embryonic cells to continue to reproduce, replacing aging or injured brain cells, stimulating new growth in the old brain. The engineered cells never lost their ability to regenerate new cells. Once these engineered cells were introduced into the brain, her father had discovered something extraordinary. By continually reproducing and replacing cells, keeping the brain young, the brain in turn arrested the aging process.

It was an incredible discovery. Current theories showed that aging was a cellular process—each cell determined its own age. But her father's findings refuted that. If we could keep the brain young, it acted like the body's commander in chief, ordering the body to stop aging.

Only, in most of the test animals, there had been a terrible side effect. Just as Roger had explained to Jake, embryonic cells were genetically naive. They could become anything,

from skin cells to liver cells. Some of the altered cells her
father injected in the brain had become super immune cells.
They acted like macrophages, attacking the myelin that insu-
lates neurons in the brain, resulting in a complete loss of motor functions and, eventually, death.

"That's why he needed the dogs," she said after she had
explained her father's findings to Jake. "The animal of choice
for motor skill function tests. The immune cells destroyed the
parts of the brain regulating motor functions."

"He was playing God."

McCall turned away from the computer. She stared at her
hands, remembering how her father had taught her to hold
her instruments, contrasting that image of benevolent teacher
with the years of lies.

She could feel her throat closing up with emotion. "When
we left Kyle's house," she said, struggling with the words, "I
wasn't going to tell you . . . I was going to come here, by
myself. I was going to try and *fix* things for him. I didn't
believe he could—" She choked on the words. She shook her
head, biting her lip.

Jake came around the desk. He knelt down beside her, turning the chair so that she faced him.

The tears slipped down her cheeks. "I was walking to the
car, and I remembered all the things I read in Alicia's lab
book," she said, "how she would do things for her Dr.
Frankenstein—for her Svengali. Things she questioned; things
she didn't want to do. And Belinda, she left behind her dreams
of dancing, becoming his assistant. I . . . I had to make it
stop. I didn't want to be his creature anymore."

He smiled, wiping her tears away. "And you're not, baby.
Are you?"

She shook her head. But it hurt so much to think of all
the years of blindness. Of believing him, thinking it was her.
That she was the one who had betrayed his dream. "I came
here to find out the truth. I wanted him to turn himself in."
She glanced back at the computer, touching the screen with

her fingertips. "But the man who's doing this—he will never turn himself in."

"Very good, McCall."

She and Jake turned, caught off guard. They wouldn't have heard the buzzing of the lab door, not from this far back inside her father's office.

"Very observant," her father said from the door. "And very correct."

At the sight of him, the coldness of anger slipped into her heart, the strength of her reaction surprising her. How different he looked now. Older. Meaner. She had always thought Roger Clarke was evil. But Roger could never have hurt her as her father had.

"That's a neat trick you have," she said, her voice cool and controlled. "Opening the door without the buzzer sounding."

He nodded. "Yes, I knew I had slipped when I mentioned the danger to Dr. Woods. That you would realize I had over-heard the two of you before I spilled the acid." His eyes, so like her own, remained on McCall. "I learned how to circum-vent the security system. Sometimes, it pays not to be an-nounced."

"Given what you've been up to all these years, Daddy, I would think it's downright handy."

She felt the incredible anger that could sometimes take over building inside her. Her father had hurt Belinda. He had killed her mother with his neglect. And Alicia. Now she believed he'd killed her as well.

"You should have stayed away. I told you never to come back."

"Why?" she demanded. "Why would you do this!"

"Come now, McCall. You must at least see why? The pos-sibilities. The incredible possibilities."

"Are not there," she said flatly. "Not the way you want them to be. You can't just launch into human trials, using an inoculation that is killing lab animals."

"And that's where you're wrong!" he said, adamant in his

belief. "You were always so shortsighted, McCall. Too careful and conservative. I told Alicia as much."

"You were Dr. Frankenstein," she whispered, picturing Alicia's smiles, envisioning her friend and partner, now dead because of her father. "You manipulated us, all of us. We gave you our minds, our hearts. And still it wasn't enough. One of the greatest discoveries of our time—that the brain can control the aging process. And it wasn't enough?"

"I needed the product. I needed BioYouth. And I am so close, McCall. Can you understand what this means? I am competing with the giant pharmaceuticals, developing my own inoculation against aging. We can still do it, McCall. The two of us," he said in that same voice she remembered so well. The voice of the man who had taught her everything. His words vibrated with his excitement, making her feel it with him. He could do that, use the fire in his eyes and the passion in his heart—just as easily as he could cut you out of his life.

"The plan all along was to use homeless women," he continued at his evangelistic best, "women with no life to speak of. We would pay them, make them comfortable. Don't you see? It was worth the risk to these women. And we can still do it. Together. I can convince Roger and Curtis that we need you," he said. "Curtis wanted you four years ago. He'll agree to let you help us again."

She smiled. "You still need me, Daddy? Yes, I suppose that, with Alicia gone, Roger hasn't been nearly enough. I can almost guess what you're thinking. 'With McCall's help, I can do it.'" She shook her head. "But all I see is an inoculation that is going to kill every woman you inject. You're a horrible man, Daddy." She said it quietly, without inflection. "A monster."

She turned in the chair. She started foraging through his desk.

"What are you doing?"

Her father stepped forward, but Jake stopped him, standing in front of him so he couldn't reach his daughter.

She pulled a disk from inside one of the drawers. She jammed it into the computer drive. "I am copying this document. It's evidence. And I plan to walk out of here with it in my hand. It's over, Daddy."

"I can't let you do that." Donald pushed Jake aside and reached into his jacket. He pulled out a gun. "Stop right now."

"Put the gun away, Sayer," Jake said, keeping his voice calm, seeing the situation escalating out of control. "You don't want to do this. You're in enough trouble as it is. The FBI already knows what's going on here," he said, telling him the truth. "I called the authorities. They know I'm here. If McCall and I fail to check in soon, they'll be on it."

The cold look Sayer gave him sent a chill through Jake. It was amazing to see those eyes. He had Mac's eyes—but all the warmth was gone.

"She's your daughter," Jake said, maneuvering around him, positioning himself, because he could see it was going to take more than talking with Sayer. Shit. For the first time in his life, he wished he carried a gun. But with Michael, he didn't feel safe keeping one. And he'd thought they had more time. He hadn't expected someone to tip off Sayer. Who the hell had tipped him off? "You don't want to hurt her."

"Stop what you're doing!"

McCall took her hands off the keyboard at her father's command. Looking almost regal sitting behind his desk, she asked, "Are you going to shoot me, Daddy? Are you going to kill me? Like you killed Alicia? Oh, yes. I know you killed her."

He lowered the gun marginally, but it was still pointed at McCall, making Jake hesitate. "Dear God, it was an accident. I loved that woman! With her at my side, I would have finally achieved what you had denied me. A willing partner. Someone with the imagination and the faith to follow my vision. But no, you had to go off on your own, seeking your own research rather than becoming my assistant at Clarke Labs. I groomed you to be what you are. And when I needed you, you left me behind. Don't you see? That's where it all went wrong. When you left for Harvard. Everything was fine until you turned your back on me."

"And Alicia?" she asked. "How did she ruin things?"

"She wouldn't listen," Donald Sayer said, deaf to the sarcasm in her voice. "When it came to the difficult decisions, she wouldn't listen. She wanted to stop . . . she begged me to stop. We fought and I hit her. I was so angry, I hit her too hard. I swear it was an accident. She fell backward and struck her head. I didn't mean to kill her."

McCall turned back to the keyboard. She was staring at it. Jake could tell what she was thinking, could see the determination in her eyes. He swore under his breath as she started to type on the keyboard once again.

"I'll shoot, McCall!"

Jake stepped closer, hearing the soft whir of the drive, admiring McCall's guts but wishing she'd picked another time to push like this. He edged in front of Sayer.

"You're going to have to shoot me, Daddy," she said, her eyes on the screen.

Before anyone could react, Sayer pushed Jake aside and pulled the trigger. There came a *pop,* like a lightbulb exploding. The computer monitor blew up, shooting sparks as smoke trails eddied through the air.

Donald pointed the gun at McCall, his hands shaking.

McCall stood behind his desk. "Go ahead. Shoot me," she said, her voice too calm. "Shoot your own daughter, you coward."

"Shut up!"

"Calm down," Jake said, ready to grab the gun. But he didn't want the gun pointing at Mac when he made his move.

"I didn't see it, but you were always the weak one," McCall said, her fury in her eyes and voice. "Hiding behind the women who loved you. Manipulating us. Go ahead. Shoot me! You can't hurt me anymore, Daddy. I won't let you hurt me."

Right then her father turned the gun on Jake. "I'll shoot him. You'll have an innocent life on your conscience."

"Yeah," Jake said, smiling, seeing his chance. "Right."

He struck Sayer's hand with his fist, flinging the arm up. The gun flipped barrel over nose, arcing through the air to crash to the floor. Sayer lunged for it, but Jake was on him. Both men struggled, each trying to reach the gun just a few feet away. McCall jumped from behind the desk, running for the gun, grabbing it.

"Hold it right there."

Jake felt the blood freeze in his veins. Because he recognized that voice. And he knew what it meant. He turned, edging up on his elbow.

Roger Clarke stood in the middle of the room. He had a Luger pistol in his hand with a five-inch cylinder on the end. A silencer. He was pointing the muzzle at McCall.

"Well, if this isn't a surprise," he said in his most facetious manner. "Jonathan?" He smiled, enjoying the moment. "Don't tell me you're involved in all this?"

He gestured with his gun. Getting his meaning, Jake stood up and walked over to Mac. "The police are on their way," Jake said, bluffing. "It's no good, Roger. It's over."

"I don't think so," Roger said, looking too relaxed. He waited as McCall's father stood and took the gun from her hand. "I left a message at security," Roger said. "They called me as soon as McCall came in tonight. I made good time getting here, but I had a little bit of a holdup. And I had a hell of a time convincing security nothing was going on in here. They're waiting for my report. A shame about the computer. But then, didn't you tell me just the other day, Donald, that it was acting up."

"You can't cover this up, Roger," Jake said. "There's a fucking bullet in that monitor."

"Just watch me." He grinned. "Daddy has fixed bigger messes than this. Hasn't he, Donald?" Roger nodded toward the door. "Why don't you step this way. The fair Belinda and the love of her life, Dr. Woods, await us in the Level-2 lab."

* * *

He took them to the Biosafety Level-2 lab, clearing them through security. He held the Luger inside his lab coat, where it wouldn't be seen. But he'd instructed them very carefully. If McCall wanted to see her sister alive, she would do exactly as she was told.

They rode the elevator down to where it opened onto a hospital-like environment. Only Roger wore the protective clothing used in the facility. As instructed, they proceeded Roger down the white narrow corridor. The air smelled sharp with the pungent odor of the animals. Beyond the small square windows built into the swipe-locked doors that lined the corridor, McCall caught glimpses of the cages, the animals.

Belinda was in a small room at the end of the corridor, tied to a chair. Kyle sat beside her in a second chair, slumped forward against the cords holding him in place. McCall could see from the bruises on his face that he'd taken quite a beating. He was breathing in short shallow breaths.

There was a single cage in the room. A crab-eating macaque screamed from inside, the monkey disturbed by their entrance.

"Hush, Sarah," Roger said to the monkey. He pulled the pistol out from beneath his coat, knowing it was no longer necessary to hide the weapon. Her father, too, removed his gun from his coat pocket where he'd hidden it.

"Oh, dear," Roger said, looking at the single chair, the only empty seat in the room. "It seems I'm not prepared for so much company."

He walked toward Belinda. Standing behind her, he pointed the gun to her temple. "Let's see. Donald, you tie up McCall. I'm going to need her to be very still." He pouted. "I'm afraid you'll have to stand, Jonathan."

"Think, Roger," Jake said. "I'm a government informant. The cops are on their way. You can't get away with any of this."

Roger shook his head. "No one gets into this facility without a call to me first. You'd be surprised how many places you can hide a body here. So keep your mouth shut, Jonathan, or it will be all over sooner than you think." He turned to McCall's father, watching as Donald jerked McCall into the empty chair. "Though I hate to look a gift horse in the mouth, what brings you here at such an opportune moment?"

"Belinda called me," Donald said, putting his gun in the pocket of his jacket. He grabbed McCall's hand and began tying it to the arm of the chair. McCall couldn't take her eyes off her sister and the gun Roger held to her head.

"Daddy told me the Omega Principle was doomed," Belinda said, her expression full of apologies, her words half-mumbled, as if it hurt to talk. McCall could see her lip was swollen, that she, too, had taken a blow to the face. "He made it sound as if you would look for a scapegoat. I was afraid you would do that tonight. To Daddy . . . or maybe to Kyle. Only, I got so scared." Belinda started crying. "I didn't know who to trust, so I called Kyle."

"I tried to stop her," Kyle whispered. He could barely raise his head to look at McCall. "I tried to talk her out of coming to warn you. But she wouldn't listen. The best I could do was to follow her here. But Roger found her first."

"Last night's security tape had a few surprises," Roger said. "Daddy missed it, but I saw Kyle coming out of the Fragrance lab. I did a little checking. I figured out he used Belinda's card. And I knew the bitch was sleeping around on me."

Roger tested the knots on McCall's wrist when her father was done. "Very good. You get a gold star, Donald," he said, watching her father begin to tie her other hand to the chair. "I need it nice and tight. Now Jonathan," he said, walking toward Jake, "I believe it's your turn."

McCall watched as Jake locked eyes on Roger. "You know what I think? I think you're a sick son of a bitch." Jake turned to McCall's father. "You can't let him do this. Think, man! They're your daughters!"

Without seeming to look at Roger, Jake pivoted around,

kicking Roger in the gut. Roger flew backwards with the blow, hitting the wall and falling to the ground. Jake lunged, throwing himself on top of him. McCall pulled one hand free of the ropes and jumped to her feet, but she couldn't move. Her father was holding her down on the chair where her other hand was tied fast. The gun fired.

Jake rolled off Roger, moaning, blood pouring from his shoulder. Belinda screamed as Roger aimed and fired again, shooting Jake just above the knee.

"I swear I'll kill him," he screamed, seeing McCall grab for the gun in her father's lab coat. "I swear the next bullet goes through his heart!"

"Daddy, please," McCall begged. "Please don't do this! Jake is right. The police know everything," she said. "The forms I showed you, with all the medical questions for the clinic, they'll get their hands on a copy. You can't get away with it anymore. It just won't work."

Roger stood, wiping the blood from the side of his mouth where Jake had hit him. Jake remained slumped on the floor at Roger's feet. Blood covered his shirt at the shoulder and seeped through his jeans at the knee.

"Great work," her father said, shaking his head disapprovingly as he finished tying McCall's hand in place. "Now we'll have to drag him out of here between the two of us. He won't be able to walk."

"You still don't get it, do you, McCall?" Roger said, ignoring her father to hone in on McCall, stepping over Jake. "Clarke Labs owns your father. We own him. Oh, he and Alicia tried to pull a fast one. She skimmed off money from your federal grants, just like the FBI said. And Donald was doing the same. To Clarke Labs. Only, we caught him. It wasn't hard to persuade him to let us in," Roger said, enjoying himself thoroughly as he watched McCall's father tie her ankles to the chair. "The night he killed Alicia, he called Daddy to clean up his mess, just like always. And this time, it was a really big mess. I made it look like an accident, losing control of the car. I saved your father's ass and I've owned it ever since."

Roger walked to the back of the room, approaching the monkey cage. There was a stainless steel table next to the cage. Several syringes waited there. "The deal was, they cut us in and all was forgiven. That's when I started to work with them, with Donald and Alicia. Only, my daddy didn't think we were quite up to your level. He convinced himself we needed you to make it work. So he tried to recruit you." He shook his head, looking at her as if she were a fool. "And you turned us down. You know, I enjoyed all those anonymous calls to the FBI, telling them shit about you. I personally doctored that data to make it look like you were bettering your results." Roger pursed his lips and blew her a kiss. "Surprise."

"Why, Daddy? He's an animal," McCall said, not caring what Roger did to her, but thinking desperately of how to save her sister and Jake. "How can you be like him? How can you be his pawn?"

"I don't have a choice," he said. "I thought you understood that."

"We'll start over." Roger came up behind McCall's father. "We'll disappear for a bit, let the heat cool off, then set up somewhere else. At a new clinic. Daddy will help us."

But suddenly, her father didn't look so convinced. "Those forms," McCall's father said, sounding angry. "We were supposed to hire street people, not recruit from your society friends."

"Come off it, Donald." Roger gave her father a disgusted look. "Did you really think it would work to pay homeless women? That's not what we need to test BioYouth. Drunks and drug addicts. The clinic was built for women of money and influence, the kind of woman who can afford the BioYouth treatment. A woman who can spread the word about our success."

"It's always been about the money with you, Roger," her father said quietly. "Always the money."

McCall closed her eyes, realizing that's why her father had

sounded so convincing in his office, his eyes not giving him away. He really hadn't known about the applications for the clinic. Roger had gone behind his back, taking chances.

"It's all in the name of science," Roger said. "And I was careful, Donald. I screened the applicants. They're all single or divorced. No husbands, no children, no close ties. If they should die suddenly of a debilitating illness, no one could trace it back to Clarke Labs. Just a sad little event. And the ones that survive will be very, very happy, recommending our pricey clinic to all their friends until we get the kinks out of the formula or get around the FDA and market the stuff openly."

"Daddy, do you hear how insane this sounds?" she said, hoping, praying he would understand. "It can't work."

"Insane?" Donald shook his head. "I'll tell you what's insane. The years you wasted with your research when you could have had so much more. Everything I ever did was based on breakthroughs you developed. You can't play God and not have a few false starts. These casualties are acceptable. They're for the greater good. I thought you realized that, McCall. They were your breakthroughs."

She shook her head, seeing again the monster her father had become. "But never to be used like this. Never."

Roger grabbed the syringe from the steel table. "And now this charming chapter must come to a close, I'm afraid. Ever hear of Monkey B?" He grinned down at Jake, who appeared to be fighting to remain conscious. "Let me explain for the benefit of the laypeople in the room," he said, balancing the gun while manipulating the syringe. "It's a wonderful virus that lays dormant in monkeys. Sarah here will test positive for it. Only, poor McCall and Kyle, working without their protective gear around a macaque. How careless."

"You're going to let him kill your daughters, Sayer?" Jake said, panting on the floor, struggling to get up, then collapsing. "You're just going to stand there and let him do this?"

"Of course he is," Roger said. "Donald and I will be long

gone, sipping drinks on some exotic beach as Daddy uses his influence to clean up any loose ends. Just like he did with Alicia. Fixing that autopsy report. Later, they'll find McCall and Kyle suffering dreadfully from Monkey B, their brains on fire with their fever. They will have to be heavily sedated." He raised the syringe, still holding the gun awkwardly, pushing the plunger to allow a drop of fluid to slip out. "But unfortunately, there's no cure for this deadly disease. Their brains will literally melt inside their heads. Jonathan here will be swimming with the fishes when they find him, a bullet through the head. A casino is such a terrible place to work. All those shady sorts. And Belinda." He smiled, "She's going to be our first volunteer for BioYouth."

"Think what you're doing, Sayer," Jake said. "You can't let him kill your daughters."

But Donald shook his head. "There's no other way. Here," he said to Roger, "give me the gun before you prick yourself with that damned needle. I'll keep him covered."

"All right," Roger said, handing her father the gun, unnerved enough by the syringe he was holding that his hands were shaking. He smiled, his gray eyes narrowed on McCall.

A pulse-pounding terror gripped her, squeezing her heart as if an enormous fist were closing around her chest, making it impossible to breathe. She tried to think of what to do, how to stop him. "Help me, Daddy," McCall said, barely able to say the words, she was so frightened. Pleading for her life, for the lives of Jake and her sister. "Please. Help me."

Her father looked at her. He stepped back, lowering the gun.

When he pointed the gun, he aimed directly at Roger.

"You were always so *stupid,* Roger," he said.

He fired two shots. One after another. Roger's body jerked with each shot. He stared down at the blood gushing from his chest, his mouth opened in surprise. He dropped the syringe, then fell to the floor.

Belinda began crying softly. McCall didn't know what to think, what to expect next.

Donald Sayer stepped over to Roger, looking down as the younger man struggled for a breath, his lungs filling with blood. And then Roger's eyes glazed over. He slipped to the ground, blood trickling from his mouth, his eyes staring lifelessly.

"He ruined everything with those applications for the clinic," Donald said, standing over the now very dead son of Curtis Clarke. "They were supposed to be homeless women."

"Daddy. Daddy, please untie me," McCall said, watching Jake bleeding heavily. She thought maybe he was unconscious.

"The acid spill." Her father spoke quietly now. "I was only trying to scare you. I wanted you to leave. But then today, you came to me—you told me about the application for the clinic. And I knew he'd ruined this, too." He stepped back, staring down at Roger. "I thought maybe I could get you to understand. That we could leave here and start over, the two of us again. Without Roger and Curtis. That I would finally be free of them." He shook his head.

"Daddy, please untie me. Please!" she begged, not knowing what he would do, who he would hurt.

"I'm not a monster," he said, acknowledging that fear in her voice. He sighed, still holding the gun, looking so tired. "At first, you understand, I hated Alicia, because you chose her over me. I thought, what better revenge than to steal her from you. But later, I did grow to love her."

He put the gun in his mouth.

"NO!" McCall screamed. Belinda looked away, sobbing. Donald Sayer pulled the trigger.

Twenty-five

Stacie put the iron down, frowning at the television set. She'd switched the channel to watch Cyndi's show, as she usually did every day at this hour. Apparently something really big had happened in town. Something that involved Clarke Cosmetics.

She turned up the volume and sat down on the couch. She listened as Cyndi introduced her guests, two men and a woman. They were members of an organization called SDA, Scientists Defending Animals. All three were young and somber-looking. They had once been accomplished biologists, according to Cyndi, but had turned to fighting for animal rights.

"Our people discovered Clarke Labs was conducting animal experiments," said the woman, "despite their claim that their cosmetics were free of animal testing. Our leader infiltrated Clarke Labs, eventually working with the authorities to uncover the company's hideous scheme. We had no idea there was a separate investigation that involved the animals."

"Is it true that they were planning to experiment on women?" Cyndi asked, using her voice and face to express deep concern. "Luring unsuspecting victims who thought they were going away to stay at a beauty spa?"

All the air left Stacie's lungs. "My God."

"That's right," The woman reached down to pet a dog sitting beside her chair, a golden retriever. "It's surprising how many women signed on, even taking medications to prepare for their stay, no questions asked."

Stacie covered her face with her hands, remembering the pills. Those pills.

"Looking-glass upon the wall," Cyndi said dramatically, turning back to the studio audience. "Who is fairest of us all. How surprising can it be that women fall for these promises when we're taught from childhood it's the beautiful princess whom we love . . . the ugly stepdaughters we despise . . ."

Stacie listened, her heart in her throat, her hands shaking.

"For the first clinical trials, Clarke Cosmetics targeted women with few ties in the community," the SDA woman said. "Unmarried women. Women without children. Those whose deaths might not raise too many questions if a few months—or even years—later, they should experience severe loss of muscle coordination. It would have been difficult to trace the deaths back to the clinic. The scientists behind the program knew the symptoms would look like the results of some unknown brain disorder, something that had gone previously undiagnosed."

The tears came down Stacie's cheek. She thought about Garrett, how he'd coaxed her to sign up for the clinic, encouraging her to take those medications. And now, it turned out the Clarke Spa and Clinic was a front for some diabolical human experiments. Something that would have surely killed her.

Sobbing quietly, she grabbed the phone. She misdialed the first time, her fingers were shaking so badly. She hung up and dialed again.

"Hello, Mama? Yeah, it's Stacie." She brushed back her tears. "I want to come home."

McCall brushed Belinda's hair, watching the boar's hair bristles glide through the silver strands of hair. They were seated on McCall's bed in Barb's guest room, McCall fixing Belinda's hair, something they'd never done as children.

"So I was thinking maybe I could open a ballet school,"

Belinda said. She'd been talking to McCall about her plans. McCall thought it was a good sign, that Belinda was thinking about the future.

"That's a wonderful idea," she said. Three days had passed since the incident at the lab. She and her sister had spent a lot of time together since then, trying to heal their wounds, leaning on each other. "You would be really good at that. Will you let me help you? I have some money saved up."

Belinda nodded. "Thanks. That's really nice." And then she smiled. "It's great, you know. How I can look in your eyes, and I see you believe I can make it work. That I can succeed."

"And that's not just blind faith because you're my sister and I love you," McCall said firmly. "You have the credentials; you've danced professionally for years. I know how talented you are, Belinda. I've seen how well you can dance, how you dance from your soul."

Belinda's smile broadened. The bruise on her mouth appeared only as a faint yellow mark now. "Yes. I really do, don't I?"

"And from your heart," McCall added. "You'll be good for those girls."

Belinda turned around again, letting McCall return to brushing her hair. McCall could tell she was thinking about what she'd told her. She wanted to give Belinda something else to think about as well.

She ran the brush through her sister's hair, approaching the problem directly. "You know, after what happened four years ago, when my career fell apart and Daddy disowned me, I saw someone for a while. To help me work through it."

"A therapist?"

McCall nodded. "Barb talked me into it . . . so my heart wasn't in it. I quit too soon. But it helped. I think it really did help." She turned her sister around by the shoulders gently. "Would you go with me? I think the two of us have a lot to work out."

"Yeah. Yeah, I'd like that. Kyle said the same thing. That

I should see someone." She bit her lip. "And it would help if we went together."

She squeezed McCall's hand. She sat for the longest time in silence, just holding McCall's fingers, so tight. But McCall could see she had something she wanted to say. So she waited.

"You know." Belinda looked up at her, those clear blue eyes familiar now, not just a memory from when they were children. "The last weeks, it was strange. I was feeling so lousy about everything, but every once in a while, I would hear your voice in my head, telling me things, good things about myself—encouraging me." She shook her head. "That had never happened before. All the other voices in my head, Mama's, Daddy's, Roger's, they were always saying that I wasn't good enough. But you, you were the only one that said something nice. That's why I called Kyle after I hung up with Daddy that night. Because, I thought it had to mean something, that you would be the one to say the nice things in my head."

McCall hugged her sister. It hurt her heart to hear that soft confession, but it was a good hurt, the kind that came when the emotions inside you were just too much. They were going to make it, she and Belinda. "I want you to know I will be here for you from now on. I've changed, Belinda. This time, I want to be your big sister."

McCall could feel Belinda weeping quietly against her. She pulled back and wiped her sister's tears, asking, "What's wrong?"

"It's just that, when he shot himself. McCall, I was so happy. I felt like this big weight just fell off my shoulders." She shook her head. "I was glad he killed himself."

"Me, too," McCall said, sharing her sister's confession. "He was an evil man. He used everyone who ever loved him. We were just lucky that, in the end, he had a shred of humanity left inside him. That he chose to kill himself instead of his daughters. It was us or him, Belinda."

She saw the relief in her sister's eyes, the guilt fading. She smiled. "I love you, McCall."

She hugged her sister. "I love you, too, Lindy."

Jake knocked on the door using his cane. A few minutes later, Barb Rojas opened the door.

"So, Guru Barb," he said, leaning on the cane, "what do you think. Will our first child be a boy or a girl?"

She gave him a good looking over, shaking her head. His leg was in a brace and his arm was taped and secured in a sling. "For someone who looks so pathetic, you sound awfully cocky."

"You tell me," he said, grinning just the same. "What do the stars say my future holds?"

"A girl," she said without hesitation. "And you'll name her Barbara, after a good friend."

He followed Barb inside, shaking his head. "I like your style."

It took him a while to make it up the stairs. But he'd told Barb not to call Mac down . . . because he had something special to ask her. And it was the kind of thing you had to brave stairs or any obstacle to ask.

On the way up, he passed Belinda, who was just leaving. He thought she looked pretty good, all things considered. He knew it was great for McCall, that her sister was starting to accept her. A good thing for both women.

"I would have come down," Mac said, when he peeked inside the room. She came over and helped him limp to the bed—as if he were some damn invalid. But what the hell. He held her close, leaning into her a bit, taking every opportunity to touch her. Maybe it wasn't such a bad thing, this invalid stuff.

"Heck, I'm actually getting good at this," he said, sitting down, holding up the cane.

She cuddled next to him, careful of his arm, and pulled

the afghan over them. She stared at the complicated pattern. "Whoever made this must love you very much."

"Oh, I don't know. Mom says she tried to drown me when I was two. But I must have grown on her because she's been okay the last twenty years. You'll meet her Sunday. At the house in Slidell. Molly. My oldest sister." He reached over and brushed her hair from her face. Today it fell in slight waves to brush her shoulders. "How are you doing?"

"Better. Awful."

"You know I'm here for you, Mac. Always will be." He kissed the top of her head. "How's Belinda doing?" he asked.

McCall sighed. "I think this is somehow harder for her. But Kyle. It's amazing. I was so frightened of him, worried that he would hurt her." She looked up at Jake. "He's so good with her. I think he must love her a great deal."

"Yeah," he said, pulling Mac close to him with his left arm, his good arm. "I think she feels the same."

"She's talking about starting a ballet school."

"I could see that," Jake said. "But you're going to have to finance it somewhere other than Garrett's blackjack tables," he added, knowing Mac would want to help. "You and I are *persona non grata* at the *River Palace."* He held her face up to his. "I gave notice today. I told Gus I wanted my old job back."

She smiled. "I'm so glad."

"He's going to need help and I have volunteered my services. *Gratis,* if I have to. Curtis Clarke has hired his own dream team . . . not that it's going to do him any good."

When the FBI arrived at Clarke's home, they found Curtis stretched out on the floor, clutching his chest. A mild heart attack. At the moment, he was recovering nicely in the hospital. Fortunately for Gus, Clarke had his bags packed for the Caymans, where he had a nice little nest egg. Which meant he was a flight risk. Which meant he wasn't getting bail.

Conspiracy, kidnapping, felony-murder . . . and then there

were the federal charges. Oh, yeah. Curtis Clarke was going away for a nice long while.

"Garrett didn't take my leaving too well," he said, stroking Mac's hair. "Seems he's feeling a little abandoned. Dino and I giving notice. Stacie taking off."

"Do you think Stacie will ever forgive him?"

"Let me see." He paused, as if he were thinking about it. "Nah."

"No, I don't think she will, either."

"She's a beautiful woman, he said, knowing Garrett's motives for forcing the clinic on her. "Garrett couldn't stand the thought that her looks would fade. That he could lose that face, that body. He didn't understand . . . we all need to change." He sighed, actually feeling sorry for Garrett. It was going to kill him to lose Stacie. "The pills really scared her, though. But I had them analyzed. Garrett was actually right. Fancy vitamins, some antibiotics."

"My father thought they were going to use homeless women," McCall said. "I suppose he wanted them in the best shape possible before coming to the clinic."

McCall pulled back, then draped the afghan around their shoulders, the air conditioning actually making the room cool. She huddled closer, careful not to hurt him as he sat on the edge of the bed. "It smells like you, the afghan."

"I made sure it had my pheromones all over it. Hey." He kissed her lightly on the mouth. "I missed you."

"I missed you, too."

He glanced around the room. The last three days, she'd spent most of her time with the cops and the prosecutors on the case, making a statement—or with her sister. "How about we just throw all this stuff in a big box, and buy ourselves a little house? We could work on getting all that garbage straightened out about the data Roger fixed. My mom could nose around Tulane. I bet they would jump at a chance to get you on board. Then, when you're ready—like maybe next month—we could start on a couple of kids. Michael's getting

412 Olga Bicos

real pushy about the baby thing. Bring on more siblings, he says."

He held his breath.

"I think I'll make you say it this time," she told him. "No more 'Want to join the team?' or 'Let's buy a house.' " She looked up at him. "Jake Donovan, are you proposing?"

He smiled and said gently, "Happens that I am."

"Well, then, I say yes," she told him, looking stern. "I think I'm going to try my first legitimate experiment in a very long time," she whispered. "I'm going to disprove the Donovan Curse."

"You have my full cooperation." But then, a little more seriously, he added, "You think you can beat the curse, Mac?"

She frowned. *"Now* you're having doubts?"

"Not that we love each other. But how long do I get to keep you? I've been married and divorced twice. What if I screw this one up, too?"

She was watching him with all this love in her eyes. And it was strange, because he couldn't remember anyone ever looking at him like that. "To be successful as a scientist," she said, "you must learn to be farsighted, forgetting any short-term gratification, always looking toward the long term. You have to have an incredible belief that you can succeed at what you're doing, because it can take years to get a result. You have to know how to persevere."

She placed her hand on his chest. He remembered what she'd said that night, that she'd fallen in love with his heart.

"I'm a very good scientist, Jake," she said, smiling at him with everything she had. "I'm not worried."

"Yeah. Okay," he said, getting it. His soul mate. He kissed her then, a long deep kiss that sealed the moment, thinking that the Donovan crew was going to beat the odds after all. First his two sisters, happily married. Now him. And this time, it was just like he wanted it. The whole enchilada.

"Where's Michael?" she asked, stroking his face in that way of hers, touching him like he was special.

"He wanted to go with Hope and Dickey when they took the baby to her first doctor visit here." He reached for her hand and kissed her fingers. He shook his head, giving her a sad look. "Her name is Tiffany. They named her Tiffany."

"It's a nice name."

"What? Do I call her Tiff? Or worse, Fanny? What kind of name is that?"

"Whatever you call her," she said, smiling as she pulled him down for another kiss, "something tells me she'll get used to it."

Megan Chandler sat in front of the television, changing the channels with the remote. But every station had on the same thing. No cartoons, just some dumb reporters asking questions about some company.

Suddenly, the screen filled with the image of a dog. A golden retriever with soft floppy ears and a distinctive tail that curled, almost making a complete circle.

Megan caught her breath. She pushed up the volume, shouting, "Mom!"

The woman on the television was talking about how they had found these dogs in a lab where they did animal testing. How these horrible men stole the dogs from their homes and sold them to research labs for a lot of money.

"Oh, dear Lord," Megan's mother said from behind her. They were flashing an eight hundred number on the screen. Anybody who was missing a pet should call.

"James?" Megan's mom said to her father in the kitchen. "It's Sierra, James."

"I'm dialing now," Megan's dad said, picking up the phone.

Megan pressed her fingers to the screen, smiling as she felt the tears running down her face. "Sierra. You're coming home."

YOU WON'T WANT TO READ
JUST ONE—KATHERINE STONE

ROOMMATES   (0-8217-5206-5, $6.99/$7.99)
No one could have prepared Carrie for the monumental
changes she would face when she met her new circle of friends
at Stanford University. Once their lives intertwined and became
woven into the tapestry of the times, they would never be the
same.

TWINS   (0-8217-5207-3, $6.99/$7.99)
Brook and Melanie Chandler were so different, it was hard to
believe they were sisters. One was a dark, serious, ambitious
New York attorney; the other, a golden, glamourous, sophisticated supermodel. But they were more than sisters—they were
twins and more alike than even they knew . . .

THE CARLTON CLUB   (0-8217-5204-9, $6.99/$7.99)
It was the place to see and be seen, the only place to be. And
for those who frequented the playground of the very rich, it
was a way of life. Mark, Kathleen, Leslie and Janet—they
worked together, played together, and loved together, all behind
exclusive gates of the *Carlton Club*.

ROMANCE FROM JO BEVERLY

DANGEROUS JOY   (0-8217-5129-8, $5.99)

FORBIDDEN   (0-8217-4488-7, $4.99)

THE SHATTERED ROSE   (0-8217-5310-X, $5.99)

TEMPTING FORTUNE   (0-8217-4858-0, $4.99)